Snakes

in

Paha Sapa

BY THE SAME AUTHOR

Crossing Burning Bridges, One Woman's Amazing Journey

Snakes

in

Paha Sapa

Tale of a Lakota Nation

Cyndie M. Styles

Snakes in Paha Sapa
Tale of A Lakota Nation
by Cyndie M. Styles

Published by:
CMS Enterprises
P.O. Box 8039
Van Nuys, CA 91409-8039 U.S.A.
Orders at http://www.cyndiemstyles.com

Library of Congress Control Number: 2005908575

ISBN, print ed. 0-9768170-1-2

Printed in the United States of America

First Printing 2005

This book is a work of fiction; names, characters, places and incidents either are the product of the author's imagination or are used fictitiously. Any resemblance to events, organizations or persons, living or dead, is entirely coincidental and beyond the intent of either the author or the publisher. Although some names and places are real, as in the U.S. Constitution with Amendments and the Fort Laramie Wyoming Territory Treaty of April 29, 1868, they are used fictitiously in this novel.

Many thanks to my friends for proofreading. Many thanks to Jeri for all of her help and friendship. And many thanks to Doug for his continual support in all of the crazy things that I do.

For my beloved kids:
Killer, Foxy Lady and Sherlock

Chapter 1

Land generally north and centrally located within the boundaries of what is known as the United States had once belonged
to the Lakota people, a tribe known to the White man as Sioux.
It had a bountiful food supply from its plush vegetation. The
hunting grounds were stocked with enough deer, antelope and
buffalo to last tens of thousands of lifetimes. The land had
crystal-clear unpolluted streams which offered a plethora of
catch, where the eagle could soar above and free to enjoy a meal
unhindered from poisoned sea life. The air was fresh enough to
enable the wildlife to smell prey for miles. The coyote's howl
could be heard in village after village. Because of their beauty
alone, the wondrous mountains could be marveled over until the
end of time. These elegant mountains of Paha Sapa, translated
to the Whites as the Black Hills, got their name due to the
closely woven foliage that forms their unique rich color of
blackish-green.

The Lakota and the governmental army of Blue Coats
engaged in many bloody battles during the 1860s. One in 1867
was particularly abominable. Many men fell to the ground.
Limbs were severed, wounds gaped open, and bodies were
horribly mangled. With so much devastation to both sides, there
was no clear winner. Many attempts were made to declare peace
between the Lakota and the Blue Coats. Both sides wished to see
their sons, brothers and husbands soon return to continue future
generations, yet neither side was interested in forfeiting their ego
by being the first to suggest a compromise.

By the following year, the two sides succeeded in
communicating. In 1868, the Blue Coats employed an interpreter

and ceremoniously gathered together with the Lakota on the prairie. A temporary camp was assembled and signing tables stood inside the military tents. Outside beside the tents, many Blue Coats stiffly paced as the Natives sat on the ground smoking pipes while they discussed the terms of the agreement presented to them. Their travels through history led the Lakota Nation to the mandatory signing of the FORT LARAMIE WYOMING TERRITORY TREATY OF APRIL 29, 1868. In it was the protection of their sacred Paha Sapa, which would be deeded to the Lakota Nation for eternity. Apprehension from the Lakota people was evident, but in the end the treaty was signed. The Natives would be confined to live on specific areas of land, known to the Whites as reservations, and the boundary lines were outlined in the treaty. Various reservations were designated due to the Blue Coats wanting to divide and separate the Lakota, in line with the wish to conquer them.

Even though some Natives traveled by wagon to the reservations, others were forced to walk only to be encumbered by the long journey through the arduous Trail of Tears. A few were not compliant, many were disillusioned, but the majority submissively surrendered themselves to the reservations. The Blue Coats had fastened the Lakota with a reputation of being difficult *before* the signing of the treaty, which had already brought them a surplus of unenviable and brutal attention from the Blue Coats.

Only four short years later in 1872, the Whites broke that treaty when they allowed miners to invade Paha Sapa in search for gold. Then, in 1874, the Blue Coats ordered a reconnaissance mission, sending Son of the Morning Star, known to the Whites as Custer, to protect the treaty-breaking trespassers from the Natives. The Lakota Nation was not told of the order, and lesser, not asked for consent as outlined in the treaty.

Paha Sapa was the kind of place where one could see spirits. It was the kind of place where one *would* see spirits. It was holy land. But all of that was changing as more and more trespassers arrived equipped with Blue Coats by their side. As a result, that glorious beauty was stolen from the Lakota Nation in 1877 and held in Federal custody. To the Lakota people, the loss of Paha Sapa was the turning point in their heritage and their spiritual culture.

There were **Snakes in Paha Sapa**...the kind that slithered unscrupulously with the worst of intentions...the kind that struck without warning or provocation. The Lakota Nation endured strikes from the Whites for many more years.

The beginning of the end for Chief Clever Spirit's Lakota village was in the year 1879, which harbored **THE DAY OF DISHONOR**. Chief Clever Spirit directed his 200 villagers to strike their winter camp adjacent to the hills, and haul it across the wilderness. The villagers moved slowly over the rocky terrain to their summer village site on the prairie, firmly within the reservation's borders. Once their land had been so vast with the inclusion of Paha Sapa that one could have forgotten they were restricted to boundaries.

Chief Clever Spirit was filled with contradictions. He was an older man yet had a sense of objectivity usually seen in someone much younger; this characteristic empowered him in leading his people through the aging turmoil with the Whites. Even though he was smaller than an average-sized man, his persona was like that of Paha Sapa. The Chief was respected by many who saw fair-mindedness in him, but no one foolishly mistook that for weakness. He taught his warriors to stand their ground and fight to the death for the honor of his people.

Wasu Kage, or Hail Maker to the White man, was one of those warriors. He was a seasoned hunter of thirty-eight. Unlike Chief Clever Spirit, Hail Maker's size matched his ego; the warrior was both of above-average stature and confidence. His lengthy, straight jet-black hair was a sign that he had not felt the sorrow of death, as the ritual of hair-cutting was reserved for those of loss. Hail Maker had always been the most feared warrior of neighboring villages. The warrior ways were taught to him by the whispery spirit of his grandfather's grandfather. Hail Maker had always been the first of his peers to experience life's trophies and to be asked to seek the adventure of honoring his people. By the time his younger brother, Zuzeca Wawoyuspa, or Snake Catcher in White words, repeated those events, the spirit and excitement were missing. Still, Snake Catcher's competitive nature back when he was a child made him into a great warrior as well, maybe even more so than his brother, but the three-year age span made a great difference in the pecking order of the warriors. Hail Maker even procured his first human kill–a White trapper skinning buffalo to steal their hides. The elder brother became a warrior that day as Snake Catcher could do nothing but watch on. Snake Catcher knew he would be unmercifully hissed if he tried to begrudge Hail Maker his day.

As time passed, Hail Maker became so efficient at defending their territory that legends were being spread of how he spoke the White man's words through the spirits of his kill. There were *many* words emitted. Hail Maker taught Snake Catcher those words, but it was not permitted to utter any such thing in the Lakota population. His teachings were for bragging to his brother, and not entirely for sharing. Concurrently, Snake Catcher did gain enormous respect when he won the heart of the Chief's daughter, Matching Spirit, a Native woman substantially younger than him. That honor was saved for the most worthy. Hail Maker barely knew of Snake Catcher's accomplishments until he married into such a prominent family. One year prior, at the wedding, was the first day Hail Maker truly recognized his brother's worth—a brother that was of the same height and stature as Hail Maker, along with also being virile and having the fortitude of an accomplished hunter. He had the same lengthy, straight jet-black hair as Hail Maker, which showed the evidence of their community's good health.

Hail Maker and Snake Catcher were the only ones who whispered the White words, and they kept this hidden from the others, except from a precocious youth Kagitaka Makoce, or Earth Raven as translated to English, who would not tolerate being neglected.

Earth Raven was still a boy of seventeen but he yearned to be asked on hunting expeditions. His name signified a person of the earth and sky, as well as a trickster by way of the raven—a trickster who was a shape changer and could take many forms. He loved to strategize and cause disturbances, but in a good way for his people, which was a bad way for those with views not of his own.

Snake Catcher included Earth Raven in the telling of the warrior stories, and the learning of the White words because he knew the feelings of envy, and did not want that for Earth Raven even though they were not kin. While continuously worshiping Snake Catcher, Earth Raven discerned Snake Catcher's pain of envy as word spread among the villagers that the older brother would once more be first at a quest. Some whispered that Chief Clever Spirit would be leaving behind the best man to protect his villagers, or perhaps he was just granting his only daughter's request of keeping her husband safe. Nevertheless, Snake Catcher did not understand what held him captive.

Chief Clever Spirit sought assistance from Hail Maker, saying: "You are being sent to secure the location of this season's deer. Take your choice of men, but omit your brother."

Snake Catcher stood nearby but out of their sight of the conversation. Even at his ripe age of thirty-five, Snake Catcher deeply idolized yet was torturously jealous of his older brother's adventures...fatigued of endlessly being in his shadow. Competitiveness was clearly present between them though not as much as when they had hearts of young warriors.

Snake Catcher wore a face of torment as Hail Maker and his party disappeared into the distance. The younger brother reluctantly retreated into the tepee that he shared with his wife.

Nightfall bestowed the villagers a full bright moon that early summer's eve. Their horses were restless, sensing trouble. As the hours passed, Snake Catcher could not sleep, restless himself, had led him to pace the perimeter of the village. Soon he jumped onto his horse, and with the fullness of the moon to guide him, rode down to the river. The river had always been a source of serenity for Snake Catcher. As he stared into the tranquil stream of water, the Native huntsman reminisced of the days when he and his friends were young warriors slaying the White prospectors stealing gold from their hills. That was a time of control for him. Back then, Snake Catcher could honor his people with the peace of believing he was protecting their children's futures. Snake Catcher was brought out of his mesmerization when he heard the distant howl of a coyote, which merely left the image of an aging man staring back at him in the pool.

Simultaneously, with the moon beaming bright as daylight, Blue Coats were strategically sprinkling themselves across the ridge of a slope overlooking the village. A signal was rendered before firing commenced from the Blue Coats onto the Lakota villagers without warning with Snake Catcher situated far away from their view. When Snake Catcher heard the firing, he launched his horse toward the battle. Suddenly, the animal lost its footing, slipped on the rocky riverbed, and threw its six-foot rider to the shore where he lay unconscious and bleeding. His skittish horse meandered a short distance away. As Snake Catcher slumped at the water's edge, one could hear the gunfire for miles echoing down through the rocky river banks. The Blue Coats continued firing on the village, killing at random. Many fell to the ground. Some scattered into the foliage nearby, but it was difficult to stay hidden with the brightness of the full moon. Earth Raven successfully disappeared into the night. Chief Clever Spirit was not as fortunate. He was pelted with Blue Coats' bullets, and fell to the ground.

There was no warning...there was no mercy...the Lakota people were ambushed. The pounding of their village was relentless and it only took a short time before the Blue Coats had no more targets in their sights. When the ruthless clearance of the village subsided, so many from the tribe were dead or lay dying. The Blue Coats seized the scarce living and uninjured Lakota in view, shackling the men. They departed, stepping over the bloody dead and injured bodies. The remaining were left where they lay to rot in the wilderness, or to be picked apart by the wildlife that day, **THE DAY OF DISHONOR**, as it became known to the Lakota people from that night forward. The news that the Blue Coats were tracking a renegade warrior not of their tribe was not released to the Natives, nor the fact that they had mistakenly attacked a village not of that renegade's people.

Hail Maker and his party were unaware of the slaughter of their villagers. They found a comfortable location for their first night's campsite, unpacked their gear, and settled in. Hail Maker felt troubled, and headed out for a brief night ride. His camp soon found slumber and was unaware of Hail Maker's return a short time later.

About an hour later, with the river water babbling beside him, Snake Catcher slowly rose with his hands on his head while discovering the massive amounts of blood dripping from his wound. He slowly mounted his horse, and headed back to the village. Snake Catcher reluctantly rode through what was left of the village when he saw the devastation of bodies lying on the ground, including his wife still sheltering their unborn child, and his brother's wife and children. As far as he could see, only ghosts remained, and any unimpaired living were absent.

Remembering his brother's mission, Snake Catcher rode hard to find Hail Maker, his heart heavy with the need to warn him of the danger that Blue Coats were on the prairie. When Snake Catcher descended on the camp, he found Hail Maker barely alive while lying a short distance from the temporary tents, and everyone else there dead. He was briefly perplexed to find a civilian White man amongst the lifeless. Snake Catcher

learned that a few wandering Blue Coats took it upon themselves to gun down those at the campsite, while his party slept.

As the two brothers spoke their words in English, Snake
Catcher revealed the demise of the villagers, including their
wives and families. Hail Maker deeply felt the pain of the news.
He requested Snake Catcher to lean closer and then made his
bequeath of a blood-soaked lessons and poetry book that rested
in his hand. "Give this to Susan, daughter to Jacob Paradise who
lives in Sundance, next valley west of Paha Sapa. But first, you
must bury me alongside wife." Then Hail Maker's last words on
this earth were spoken in Lakota. "It is time to take the final
journey."

Hail Maker's last words *heard* on this earth were spoken
by his brother in Lakota. "Then it shall be."

Immediately after Hail Maker died, Snake Catcher wrapped his
brother's body in a buffalo skin, and then dragged him the long
way back to the ravaged village with his horse. When Snake
Catcher returned, he found a scared uninjured teen standing
within the ruins. Earth Raven was crying over the dead bodies
of his friends and family.

The two spaded then buried as many of their people as
their physical natures would allow, but Snake Catcher was very
weak from his blood loss, and Earth Raven was not yet a man.
They rested the remaining under buffalo hides, and then placed
large rocks around the outside shrouding them from the wildlife.
Snake Catcher's wife was among this latter group.

During the placement of the buffalo hides, the two
discovered that Chief Clever Spirit had been injured but not
mortally. It was at this juncture that the Chief approached Snake
Catcher and Earth Raven with a small following, a dozen
wounded men along with a few dozen women and their
children. Snake Catcher's first response upon seeing the Chief
alive was to declare a goal of charging into battle against the
Blue Coats.

"Where do you go?" Chief Clever Spirit inquired of Snake
Catcher in his native tongue.

"Blue Coats will be no more–the duty falls to me," Snake
Catcher answered in their language. "And it is my obligation to
complete the act of honor for my brother."

Even though Snake Catcher drastically spiraled up the
rung in village seniority that day, Chief Clever Spirit still

outranked him. "You are outnumbered like all the stars to one. There is much to do. Your first obligation is to the surviving villagers, not of the dead."

Snake Catcher and the remaining villagers gathered what they could, and Chief Clever Spirit led the survivors further east with whatever they could carry out of the burial grounds.

Chief Clever Spirit remarked wearily, "Now, with so few to track, they may let us rest."

Snake Catcher exhaustingly nodded in agreement.

The villagers traveled for two days before feeling sheltered enough to stake claim to the earth beneath them as their new summer site.

Starting over was difficult, especially for those who had lost wives and children, as witnessed in the meagerness of Snake Catcher's hair length. Many of the villagers had shortened theirs as well out of respect for the fallen villagers. As time passed, Snake Catcher would often seek solace at a nearby stream. While there, he mentally placed his psyche in Paha Sapa and asked the high spirits to help ease his heartache and guide him to peace. Twenty-six full moons passed overhead, yet Snake Catcher still could not find enough pieces of his heart to make it function again. His resolve to remain separate from affection worried his villagers.

One late summer's night in that year of 1881, Snake Catcher and Earth Raven gathered food, water, supplies and two extra ponies for their expedition.

Chief Clever Spirit was awaken and approached them in the attempt to postpone their departure. "Where do you go?" he asked.

"It is time to complete my act of honor for my brother. No family remains for me to care for," responded Snake Catcher.

"Many Blue Coats surround the area, we ought to stay united."

"Then we must be brisk." Snake Catcher turned his horse around with no further conversation with Chief Clever Spirit, and he and Earth Raven left.

Snake Catcher and Earth Raven reached the first sizable river just outside of the reservation's border before being captured by Blue Coats. Snake Catcher was shackled and treated as a hostile, but not before secretly transferring Hail Maker's book to Earth Raven. Snake Catcher was transported by wagon going east. Not seeming to be as great a threat, Earth Raven was transported by another wagon going north, back to his native land.

The Blue Coats snarled at Snake Catcher as he was being transported. They knew what they had, they knew what a great catch they had made. They captured a notoriously dangerous warrior, and would be paid handsomely in recognition for their conquest.

Snake Catcher spent his days in prison at a soldier fort with Blue Coats guarding against his escape. They did not make the expense toward prison clothes for the convicts, he wore the same clothes for the duration of his stay. Daily, for two years, Snake Catcher was mercifully granted one meal and two facility passes. Some days the Blue Coats inadvertently forgot. The conditions were despicable and filthy. Deceased Natives would not be extracted for many days, adding to the horrors there. Flies constantly swarmed the area, being Snake Catcher's only visitors. With as wretched as it became, Snake Catcher had peace knowing Hail Maker's book was safe with Earth Raven–a book Earth Raven could now read since the young man was reaping the opportunities of an education that was offered to him as outlined in the treaty. Earth Raven spent endless hours studying on the reservation, securing an education for himself.

Meanwhile, Native chiefs were negotiating for all Lakota to be released from incarceration and returned to their homeland. Even so, Snake Catcher was not transferred back to the reservation until 1883; whereupon, the Blue Coats shaved his head before allowing his release as his final punishment, and to boast of their interpretation of scalping.

Somehow Snake Catcher retained his free spirit, and was feeling increasingly distraught over being forced to stay on the endlessly shrinking reservation. The Whites knew Snake Catcher would be more imprisoned on the reservation, then continually being supported from the White man's pockets in prison. Some Blue Coats who were posted near the borderline of the reservation would egg Snake Catcher to cross the boundary. Snake Catcher tried escaping many times; one of which earned him a broken leg and a dislocated shoulder. Snake Catcher's remaining villagers feared that since he could not be tamed, he would soon die at the hands of the Blue Coats.

Earth Raven stood by powerless. He could not advocate

his friend and mentor's desire to become a fugitive. Snake Catcher finally granted a request from Earth Raven, he allowed him to help obtain the travel permission needed to fulfill Snake Catcher's act of honor for his departed brother. Snake Catcher was endlessly haunted by **THE DAY OF DISHONOR**, as he felt incredibly guilt-ridden about not being able to fight and die amongst his people as a warrior that day.

Snake Catcher and Earth Raven witnessed many atrocities. The hardest were of children dying in childbirth from unsanitary and disgraceful medical conditions. This was all that was available to the people on the reservations, even though their treaty promised them adequate provisions. Nor did they have a practicing medicine man in their village, this was not allowed. With a determined spirit, however, Earth Raven routinely wrote letters to those in Washington for medical aid with minimal recognition in return. And with that, it was not surprising that Snake Catcher's impatience had grown almost out of control from their neglect. His fellow Natives would gather with him on mail day as they waited for word from Washington that their supplies and medical assistance were in transit. But none were received. Snake Catcher was angry and he lashed out blaming those in Washington for the lack of care on the reservation, but no one was listening; not about the aid for his people, nor his permission to leave the reservation. Others, including Earth Raven, were granted permission to travel, but the Blue Coats excluded Snake Catcher from that privilege. As his frustration grew, Snake Catcher knew he could not permit anyone else to make *his* act of honor for him; Hail Maker had made the bequeath unto him.

At the end of that year, the Blue Coats insisted there be another way of communicating with the Natives, other than actually riding all the way onto their land each time they needed information from them that could not wait until mail day. That was when a small wooden one-room shack, a structure they called their telegraph office, was built to house a telegraph machine. The Blue Coats taught some of the Natives how to decipher the codes, Earth Raven being one. Even though some of the Natives were insulted that the Whites were trying to force an industrial progression onto them, Earth Raven was thrilled to see it installed, as more messages of the Lakotas' needs were sure to be dispatched due to the telegraph's expeditious delivery to Washington.

Since he was of twenty-one years, Earth Raven continued his studies by learning from the other children in the village who were still of age to receive schooling. But after the treaty-guaranteed educational provision had elapsed due to the ages of the willing participants, Earth Raven took it upon himself to continue his education by meeting with whomever was available for his teachings. Earth Raven was on another path. He would further an education that his people encouraged. A select few who could understand the English words by this time were assigned to quiz Earth Raven on his continuing studies. When accepted into a college, Earth Raven was granted his passage to leave the reservation. He forged ahead through the world of being educated by professors, earning a college degree. As the years were passing, Earth Raven was aging into a man.

In a Washington chamber room, a prominent Native aide reread his letter addressed to Snake Catcher before it was en route care of Earth Raven. "Sir, I am an assistant to a member of the House of Representatives in Washington. I am writing you today with exceptional news. I have secured permission for you to travel the 250 miles to your destination in the Wyoming Territory. You are allowed two weeks to conclude your business and return. You will be escorted to the reservation's border, where you will then ride solo southwest through the land once belonging to the Lakota people to Fort Pierre, where you will roster with them within two days of your departure. There, you will be allowed to continue into Sundance to the Paradise family homestead located at the Paradise Valley Ranch. Jacob and Elizabeth are no longer living; however, their surviving daughter is known to reside there. Truly, Nathaniel Black Deer Davis."

Outside the Washington chamber room, Mr. Davis relinquished the letter and the permission papers to a trusted special messenger. The courier was instructed to ride to Snake Catcher's reservation with it.

It was a glorious spring day in the year 1884 when Snake Catcher's day of honor had arrived. He held up his permission papers to view them again before he folded them up, and then packed for his trip–securely including Hail Maker's blood-stained lessons and poetry book as well.

The 1868 FORT LARAMIE treaty encouraged the Native

children to obtain an education, which is exactly what Earth Raven had accomplished. Earth Raven had much to do with Snake Catcher being able to fulfill his promise. He too learned the White words, and was a very powerful and dangerous warrior to many–he was a lawyer. Even though Earth Raven was forbidden to take the law bar exam among the Whites, he was knowledgeable in law to the fullest degree possible for his kind. That was where Snake Catcher's and Earth Raven's separate trails would begin, but they would meet again very soon.

Chapter 2

Snake Catcher's trek began smoothly as he traveled to the boundary of the reservation accompanied by a cavalry of Blue Coats. Only a few wished him a safe journey, on this Day One away from the reservation.

As Snake Catcher wandered through the land once belonging to his people, he was forced to recognize that life as a Lakota Native would never be the same as in years gone by. He could see what the Whites were doing to the land; the most striking was killing off most of the buffalo just for a few of their advantages while not utilizing much of their usefulness. Through incident after incident, Snake Catcher felt the violation and invasion of his world that was littered now with evidence of what the White man deemed expendable.

Snake Catcher carried his travel papers during the first stage of that thirty mile trip to Fort Pierre, where he sensed the first sign of trouble. He arrived at the fort by day's end. The Blue Coats there postponed Snake Catcher's trip, stating that the officiating of his paperwork was required. They sent a message through the telegraph lines to Washington asking for verification of his permission. There, Snake Catcher was detained in and confined to dormitory-like housing.

A flood of old scars surfaced, and Snake Catcher began to relive his days in prison. The room where he stayed was only of a minute improvement over his former cell with only the betterment of the smell. After an eternity of four days, the Blue Coats released Snake Catcher to continue his quest. Embarking on his fifth day away, he found that much of that day had deteriorated, so Snake Catcher camped for the night. The next dawn he continued on the trail, traveling 140 miles closer to his destination by Day Eight away from the reservation.

A nefarious chill swirled the air as Snake Catcher passed a wooden sign for Fort Meade. When Snake Catcher reached the outskirts of the fort, two patrolling Blue Coats assumed he was an unfriendly Native and drew their guns. Snake Catcher tried to present his travel papers when they violently pistol-whipped him to the ground for sport. Snake Catcher did the only thing he could at the moment, he fought back long enough to flee the scene. Snake Catcher found his way to a nearby creek and soaked his wounds. Within eyeshot of Fort Meade shortly thereafter, Snake Catcher sat hidden on his horse as he watched the two men from a distance. He was angry, battered and fearful to return to the fort to provide an explanation of the misunderstanding. Realizing the two Blue Coats were not interested in seeing his papers, Snake Catcher concluded that they were just having fun at his expense. With being so close to his destination, he could not chance being transported back to the reservation without completing his mission. Snake Catcher knew it would be necessary for pride to be shelved because of what was at stake. He turned his horse around, and continued onward toward the ranch. Over a week had already passed, and he felt there was no more time to waste if he was to return to the reservation within his allotted time frame, as per his orders.

While approaching a bridge on the path, by dusk, a staked fence marking the Paradise Valley Ranch boundary line was within Snake Catcher's sight. Even though he could not actually read what the sign presented to him, Snake Catcher was feeling more fulfilled the closer he came. That perception ended when the Lakota Native was berated by a rancher, spooking him so that he accelerated his horse onto the Paradise Valley Ranch property. When Snake Catcher turned to see if he was being chased, the mysteriously hostile rancher took a shot at him. Snake Catcher continued to make haste, and the rancher lost him in the night.

The Paradise Valley homestead sat on 800 acres of land eighteen miles southwest of Sundance in the Wyoming Territory, nuzzling a vein of the Belle Fourche River. By that year, Sundance had been made up of the minimum values of a town. The trading post housed a telegraph booth, bank teller with minimal funds in reserve, food goods, general supplies and various building materials. There was a jailhouse with one Sheriff directly across from the courthouse. The courthouse employed a bailiff to the part-time Judge who seconded as a Deputy to the Sheriff. The tombstone engraver also governed the mortuary and employed two gravediggers. A artillery shop was assembled, and just next door, a blacksmith ran the stables with his employees caring for horses for sale—mostly nags that no one wanted. The local doctor resided within ten miles west of town; however, he had an office in Sundance that he frequented a few days during the week. It was the wish of most towns in that area to construct a public facility for bathing and such, and this town embraced theirs, especially with all of the new Easterners prancing in from their long jaunts on those dusty trails in recent years.

The next structure on the main avenue in that stretch of buildings was *Willy's Saloon & Show Palace*. There was a sizable stage plus a backstage area with dressing rooms for Willy's starlets. The upstairs, dedicated to entertaining high-paying patrons, included a section for private poker tables. A short distance away along the street, there was an eatery with boarding rooms up top for those who could afford the lease. Plans for more housing in the near future were kept at the courthouse. The town's church and public cemetery were situated a few miles east of town, and just minutes by wagon to the local schoolhouse.

Merchant competition would be scarce, and for it, one would be required to travel into Deadwood City some twenty-nine miles away. Even though Sundance was a smaller town during the early days, it had been slightly more civilized with the hiring of a Sheriff than Deadwood City was back in 1876 when the Gold Rush began. The city of Deadwood was located in the Dakota Territory fourteen miles east of the Wyoming Territory border. In the early days of Deadwood City, the only law had been that *he who carried the smaller gun loses the right to his claim, and to his life!* Deadwood had seen many growing pains through the past eight years with the lack of decorum from many uncivilized fortune hunters sprouting roots there. Even though Deadwood had been slow in developing a judicial following, there was most certainly money in the form of gold to pay for lawfulness since that time. Many of the overpriced stores' shopkeepers hired an army of their own Sheriffs to keep the peace and to keep from getting killed due to the exorbitant cost of their wares.

There was a higher demand for housing, eateries and entertainment in Deadwood City than in surrounding towns, and the village had seen the construction of three eateries in the year of the Gold Rush. Housing was slow to follow, but log cabins were assembled for those who found their claim to be lucrative. With the many other added amenities, Deadwood City had only one saloon but with three levels. The third level was reserved for the staff's private quarters, with the second level reserved for those who could afford to be personally entertained.

The folks in Deadwood City, too, fancied the idea of a public bathing facility, which was located at the east end of town for those few who were civilized enough to use it.

While most townspeople from Sundance patronized their own town's shops, one could find more of a variety in Deadwood City. Included there was a specialized hardware and mining store, a makeshift lumber mill, a printing shop, a tin shop, two dress shops, a full-time doctor, along with a barber.

Occasionally, the gold rush brought wanderers into the area of the Paradise Valley Ranch but they were promptly pointed in the direction of Deadwood City. The ranch house that sat on the property uncommonly had *two* levels that was made of blackjack oak. Its front porch that extended the length of the house faced east toward Paha Sapa and offered the enjoyment of several rocking chairs. A trellis led to the second floor balcony which featured two French doors from the hallway that allowed fresh air into the upper level.

Off from the south side of the house was a separate constructed outdoor facility with a bathing room hosting a bathtub. Nearby was a fire pit for warming bath water.

The interior of the house was not fancy, and it largely showed a woman's point of design. The house was not wanting for anything, featuring comfort yet not boasting of wealth. The lower level included a kitchen, a diningroom, a lounge and a music parlor. Its kitchen was spacious enough to work three staff members and accommodates a door leading to the back of the house. The diningroom appeared small with the enormous diningroom table and eight companion chaired that snuggled the walls. The lounge, a splendid place to enjoy tea and dessert, displayed many portraits on its walls that invited those interested to bask in its history. The music parlor sported a small Steinway piano and a cabinet housing musical arrangements.

The upper level was configured with an apothecary room, a lady-in-waiting's bedroom, a guest bedroom, and a master bedroom. All of the bedroom designs included bathing areas; however, the only indoor bathtub was in the mistress's master bedroom. The guest bedroom and apothecary room benefitted from their own window that opened up onto the balcony toward the front of the house to further circulate the upper level's airflow, and ambiance.

The twenty-eight year old Susan Paradise was pretty but not beautiful. A White woman of average height and a fair complexion, she had soft soothing eyes and waist-length wavy medium-thick light-brown hair. Her body was fit, not athletic, slender while being somewhat busty. Susan notoriously possessed a high level of integrity, nobility and compassion. That compassion was one of the reasons she sought a high degree of knowledge in medicine. Her ambition in life was to assist those in need of accomplishing their life's desired goal; however, her first obligation was to the legacy that her father began–his dream of ranching. Social situations left her somewhat shy, which was in direct conflict with her fiercely independent side. Susan's shyness and independence teamed up to prevent her from finding someone to share her life with, and it was suggested by some townspeople to be the primary reason she was alone.

The morning after Snake Catcher's brush with the shooter, two of the five Paradise Valley ranchhands were working Susan's herd of cattle. Both men were White, with Buck Edwards being the ranch foreman. He was muscular, and somewhat dangerous and passionate about protecting Susan. The foreman was more rugged and weathered than the others, perhaps due to the six-foot man's checkered past of having a few too many secrets.

The other ranchhand there that morning was Larry, who was of average height and size; not being of a brawny build that was notorious of ranchhands in that area. Larry was a bit slow-minded and somewhat child-like, but he worked hard and was loyal to Susan. All of her ranchhands looked to be misfits, men who were not accepted anywhere else, other than working for a woman.

Larry and Buck found Snake Catcher lifelessly lying on the ground with a gunshot wound to his mid-section, and a jagged gash on his head from falling off his horse, on Day Nine away from the reservation. Several bruises were arranged around his shoulders and lower back from the pistol whipping near Fort Meade. After determining that he was still breathing, Buck and Larry suspended their herding duties to load Snake Catcher and his gear onto their wagon, then transported him to the house. Accompanying Snake Catcher was his horse who had been standing near him; the stallion was tied to the back of the wagon. Buck shot one bullet from his pistol into the air indicating that a visitor was approaching the house.

Soon thereafter, Larry and Buck carried Snake Catcher's unconscious body to the apothecary room. Larry dropped Snake Catcher's saddlebags on the floor, then tied his hands and feet to the awaiting cot which had been previously nailed to the floor for stability. Buck removed Snake Catcher's nearly foot-long Bowie-type knife in addition to its holder, and placed them on the fireplace mantle before leaving the room. Larry gave a sympathetic expression toward Snake Catcher as he made his departure.

Susan entered the apothecary room to assemble the operating area. She poured a clear liquid of a disinfectant aroma into a basin housing metal utensils. Water was then poured into another basin for rinsing. Rags were arranged around Snake Catcher's gruesome mid-section wound. With being all too familiar with the gunshot wounds of her time, Susan dug for a bullet with one of the previously soaked utensils while Snake Catcher's firey red blood oozed out. The clang of the retrieved pellet filled the air around them as Susan dropped it from the tip of her blood soaked utensil into a small metal pan. A coating of bee's wax on a strand of thread would allow a needle to glide smoothly through the skin. Susan disinfected the festering head wound with the clear liquid from the basin, and placed gauze over it as her last act before washing her hands with a large bar of khaki-colored soap.

Susan's two dogs, sisters of three-quarters husky and one-quarter coyote, entered the room and rested obediently next to her chair positioned next to the cot. Susan reclined and read from her medical book, formulating a program of medications for her patient. "Slows bleeding: witch hazel," the text stated. "Replaces blood: meats, eggs and cauliflower. Helps bruising: dark green vegetables and whites of fruit rinds. Heals skin: sap from the aloe vera plant. Heals inner wounds: organ meats, milk, eggs, shellfish and the Echinacea plant." Susan slightly tilted her head and the book to read a line written lengthwise in the margin. "Personal note: large quantities of organ meats and shellfish increases human libido." Susan looked up at Snake Catcher in thought for a moment, then continued. "Pain remedies: willow bark can be smoked or brewed, along with the Elderberry's inner bark. For severe pain: the Marijuana plant can be smoked or brewed. Flavorings to mask the harshest tasting remedies: wintergreen (also for pain), spicebush and sugar. Susan sat in thought, watching Snake Catcher for a moment, before exiting the room. Chores were next on her agenda.

The stables were approximately a hundred feet out from the east side of the house, and it was there that Sammy and Larry were well into performing their own chores for the day. Sammy was a robustly-large Black man, one of both stature and strength, a ranchhand who had never learned to read because he was not allowed by law. His worth came in the form of knowledge that embraced every aspect of ranching.

On that bright sunny day, Susan entered the stables accompanied by a notepad in her hand. "Morning boys. Where's Buck?"

Sammy returned the greeting. "Mornin', Miss Susan."

Larry echoed the greeting. "Morning, Miss Susan. He rode back out to the pasture." Larry paused, then asked, "How is the mysterious guest doing?"

"He has not yet awoke, so it is hard to say," she reported. "I will keep a close watch on him, thank you for asking. I'm making my monthly supply list. Do we need anything for the stables?"

As Sammy displayed a bridle bit, he helpfully claimed, "Yes, Miss Susan. I be afraid these bits can't be used again. They've be fixed once too often. Buck thinks he can fix 'em forever, and ain't sayin' nothin' bad about him, but he can't."

Susan secretly smirked regarding his considerate approach describing Buck's skills while she wrote on her notepad. "Thank you, Sammy. We'll get some new ones."

Sammy continued, "We be needin' horseshoes, too."

Larry blurted to Sammy, "You are going to break Miss Susan with all of your requests."

"Well, I can't make 'em."

Larry grinned, then goaded Sammy with: "Well, when I strike it rich, I'll buy new ones for all of us."

"You ain't never gonna find no gold worth haulin' down

from that mountain!"

"You don't know that, I might."

Susan smiled at their banter. "Well, thank you Larry, but I can afford to pay for what we need. I'll put it on the list."

Larry strung out the banter. "Then when you come into Sundance after I build a saloon there, I'll give you all the drinks you want for free, Miss Susan."

"That's very kind of you Larry, but I don't drink."

Susan left Larry and Sammy chattering about Larry's big dreams of owning a saloon by striking it instantly rich from gold he aspired to hit upon by mining in Paha Sapa.

At lunchtime, Susan sat alone at the eight-chair diningroom table staring off in thought while pushing the food around on her plate. The increasing feeling of emptiness filled her from a life lived alone since her parents had passed–her father for five years and her mother for a few more than that. Susan had often thought about finding a mate but with all of the struggles she had endured for women's rights, the concept scared her. The feminine rancher was not opposed to having a husband, she was opposed to forfeiting all that she had over to him just because of her gender.

Cook entered the diningroom. Cook was an older stocky Mexican woman, a bit temperamental, somewhat confrontational, but she had a good heart and was a great cook. Cook also prepared meals for the staff, and was simmering food for them on the stove in the kitchen.

"How's our patient?" Cook inquired, pulling Susan from her trance.

"He is still out. If he does not come out of it soon, he may not recover."

"I will pray for him."

"Thank you, Cook. I'm sure he would appreciate that."

Painted Pony, a pretty blend of White and Cherokee, entered the room and sat at the diningroom table. She had the normal curiosity of a thirteen-year-old. The teenager was related to another of Susan's ranchhands, Slim, a man of the same heritage, who was dubbed with the nickname from being tall and gangly-thin. Painted Pony had grandiloquently decorated her own room in the staff quarters, next to Slim's, with whatever she could find that others found discardable. The staff quarters were on the east side, approximately fifty feet out from the house.

The seven bedrooms, lounge and dining area made it more spacious than many other staff quarters in the area.

"Do you really think he will die?" asked Painted Pony, fearful but intrigued.

"Perhaps. That is all a part of life, Painted Pony."

Cook authoritatively grumbled, "Come child, out of the room."

Painted Pony continued to question Susan over being psychologically dragged from the room by Cook. "Miss Susan, you won't forget about our lesson today?"

Susan smiled and meagerly shook her head. Cook and Painted Pony left to explore the kitchen duties awaiting them, leaving Susan in solitary once more.

Mid-afternoon in the apothecary room brought Susan gratitude for the distraction of cleaning and redressing Snake Catcher's wounds. She would have preferred conversation but the wounded Lakota had not awoke. Susan diverted her loneliness by sitting with him while grinding dried plants and herbs that she had retrieved from a drying rack stand near the fireplace. She then mixed them into a tea according to her notes. Susan manufactured many different blends by chore time.

Painted Pony was eagerly awaiting her daily lesson with Susan, when the multitask woman arrived in the lounge of the staff quarters. That day unmistakably held Painted Pony's favorite type of lesson. She would learn about world events of the past month. Painted Pony could experience being with anyone she wished, whether having crumpets and tea with the Queen of England, or playing badminton with a Peruvian Princess. The teen would hypothetically sit and discuss domestic social issues acquiring ways to better educate the children of their respective nations. They audaciously discussed economic development for their countries, and speedier ways of discovering cures to live in a world free from life-threatening diseases. Painted Pony would be able to resolve all of the world's issues in one sitting. Susan thought Painted Pony had the capability of feeling compassion for helping those less fortunate. Painted Pony was headed for greatness, and was being groomed for diplomacy as one would witness in a First Lady. Even though Susan suspected Painted Pony just liked fantasizing about being a princess-for-a-day, that was acceptable because unbeknownst to Painted Pony, she was learning.

Susan had also made Painted Pony aware that when the day had arrived that she was interested in learning more about her Cherokee heritage than what Slim had taught her, the teacher would research their customs and their general geographical location for her. However, Painted Pony seemed to be lost regarding knowing what she wanted to know about her Native half due to having Susan as the primary influence in her life thus far and being quite comfortable with the White culture.

After this lesson, once again, Susan sat solo while eating supper, and later she found comfort caring for Snake Catcher in the apothecary room once more. Susan's dogs were normally where she was, and had seldom wandered far from her sight. Susan was an avid sketcher, and had a variety of sketch pads accessibly placed throughout her house. She retrieved one from the floor by her feet and began sketching Snake Catcher, categorizing every curve of his face and every characteristic of his features. Her eyes followed down his dark-skinned muscularly toned physique. While this Lakota appeared to be a decade older than her, he was scarred in various places showing the signs of a once courageous warrior in his youth. His hair was jet-black and lengthier than the men in the area, yet not as long as she remembered that of a long ago dear friend of hers with the same ethnicity.

Susan must have enjoyed her sketching of Snake Catcher so much to have lost track of time, rarely being awake during the hour of hearing the ranchhands return from their night in Sundance.

Chapter 3

The next morning just before the dew rose and dissipated, Susan sat joyfully in a rocking chair on her porch and sipped tea as she commonly had each morning, with morning being her favorite part of the day. There was something special about the world getting a fresh, clean and new start, especially those mornings which included a clear view of Paha Sapa. Susan lingered there a while suspecting Buck would soon walk up to join her. Along with the task of protecting Susan and his foreman duties, Buck was somewhat of an inventor and carpenter. He had designed then installed a plumbing system for Susan's bath water made of deeply scooped wooden planks, where the refused water traveled down the planks and out to the garden water barrel used for irrigation. Buck had also designed a waterproof trough for storage of her bedroom bath water made with wood smeared with a tar-like sap substance that hardened when dried. In addition, Buck had built a wooden coldbox for the kitchen with various shelves for keeping perishable foods cool to prolong their usefulness. He had insulated and sealed it with the same tar-like sap. He attached a wooden plank out the back of the box for drainage from a block of ice that Susan purchased from Deadwood City once per month for their refrigeration system. Cook was delighted to have it and bragged of its function to all that would listen.

Buck had arrived at the porch as anticipated. "Morning, Miss Susan."

"Morning, Buck."

"How is our visitor doing?" Buck asked.

"I'm not exactly sure; he has not awoke yet."

"Let me know if you need anything from Sundance for his recovery. I would be happy to get it."

"Thank you Buck. And speaking of Sundance, did you have a good time last night? I heard you come in."

"We weren't too loud, were we?"

"No, not at all, I was still awake." Susan paused before adding, "Did you see her? Was she singing last night?"

"Yes."

"Did you speak with her?"

"Yes, for a minute. Nothing came of it," Buck regrettably explained.

"Did you tell her?"

"No, I didn't have it in me to."

"You should," Susan coached. "It would be better if it came from you."

Buck smirked, then teasing Susan, he asked, "What am I to say? That I was in prison for two years, and oh, would you marry me?"

Smiling, Susan rebounded by saying, "Yes, I see your point. But you could tell her that it wasn't your fault, and you were falsely accused. Besides, it was a bar fight, and everyone knows how they turn out." Susan paused slightly. "You were, after all, protecting a showgirl. You might even impress the world famous Miss Angel Blue with your gallantry."

"Not a chance, she barely knows I exist."

"Then you should make yourself known to her."

Buck smiled and stared off toward Paha Sapa. Susan excused herself, and stepped into the house.

Susan soon entered the apothecary room to check in on Snake Catcher, and to change his dressings, Day Ten away from the reservation. She then entered her bedroom and closed the door. A half hour later after grooming, she checked herself in the mirror next to her dresser. Susan was wearing a pale yellow dress, white shawl and carrying a silk embroidered purse. There was a reflection in the mirror of fresh flowers in a vase on the table.

Soon thereafter, Susan stepped into her wagon for her weekly trek to church. The chapel was situated nearby the schoolhouse approximately half the distance to Sundance. Accompanying her was Buck, Slim and Painted Pony. Instructions were given to Rains Down, Susan's lady-in-waiting, to remain behind for Snake Catcher's unremitting care.

Rains Down's demeanor was even tempered, gracious and a bit shy; however, the twenty-two-year-old knew what she wanted out of life, and settling for less was unacceptable. That was because she was from two very distinctly proud nationalities—Lakota and Mexican, and she could speak both languages including English. Snake Catcher was in good hands.

Susan spent her day, as she did practically every Sunday, with the other church parishioners listening to God's words and singing in church. Afterwards, Susan unfailingly made a stop on the way home even though the others were with her. It was for the simple and congruous task of picking flowers before maneuvering the wagon back to the ranch. Accompanied only by the flowers, she predictably visited the family cemetery that was within walking distance of the house. The two erect headstones were for her deceased parents. Susan respectfully placed the flowers on their graves. She stood over them for a moment before retreating.

As Susan walked toward the house, Ferdy, who was Cook's son as well as a Paradise Valley ranchhand, was trying to appear inconspicuous while standing at the porch waiting for her. In questioning Susan, the thirty-two-year-old man tried not to exhibit the sweetness he felt toward Rains Down, nevertheless Susan had already discovered his secret.

"Miss Susan, would you know where Rains Down would be?"

"She is probably in the kitchen helping Cook with supper, Ferdy."

"Thank you, Miss Susan," Ferdy said with excitement in his voice as he stepped away. He then stopped and quickly retrieved the hat he had left on the porch railing. Looking up, he then added, "Oh, how is the injured man that was found on the property?"

"I do not know yet; I have not been in the house to check on him since returning from church, but thank you for asking." A smile came over Susan's face as she watched Ferdy trot around to the back of the house toward the kitchen door. Susan entered the front door, and headed for the apothecary room to check in on Snake Catcher. After freshening his bandages, Susan changed her church clothes, and sat on the porch gazing out at Paha Sapa. She occasionally glanced at Buck as he tended to a small garden of vegetables, and the herbs for her mojo mixtures, until she was called into supper by Rains

Down.

That supper was no different than all the others. Susan sat alone in the diningroom with the seven empty chairs as her only companions. Unbeknownst to her, she would soon receive a visitor. A Crow brave climbed up the trellis, and entered the guest bedroom that was situated across from the apothecary room and next to Susan's bedroom. No one was in the guest bedroom as he entered. The painted brave wore a face of war and had a Mohawk-style haircut. He had a tomahawk strapped to his chest.

After her supper, Susan optimistically walked up the stairs with a small tray of food, anticipating Snake Catcher's awakening. After hearing shouts from the hallway, Susan swiftly entered the apothecary room to calm him. There she found the Crow Native bearing down on Snake Catcher with his tomahawk poised to strike. Susan spoke out to him to stop, but she did not alter the brave's behavior in the least. Susan then flung the tray at the intruder with a loud clatter, immediately startling the Crow. Susan stared at him, and backed out of the room, enticing the trespasser to follow her. She inconspicuously reached into a table in the hallway, pulled out a small handgun, and then pointed it at him. The Crow was unaffected and crept closer to Susan, raising the weapon up to strike. Another verbal attempt was made to stop him, but to no avail. In knowing that the gun only fired one bullet, a lethal aim would be required. Susan surrendered her hopefulness for an amicable resolution as she made the decision to fire the pistol, making a softened but undeniably deadly sound of a firearm. Blood sprayed all around the area before the Crow fell to the floor with a loud thump.

Snake Catcher's bellowing was still echoing in the hallway as Buck and Rains Down ran up the stairs to find the scene. Buck quickly seized the brave's tomahawk, and handed it to Rains Down to secure. After Susan checked the Crow's pulse, she then gravely shook her head. Buck then threw the Native over his shoulder and dutifully carried him down the stairs. Rains Down hurriedly pranced down the stairs to fetch the cleaning supplies for the spills–from the tray, and the blood.

Snake Catcher struggled to free himself from the gripping ropes, and angrily shouted in Lakota to be released. Susan entered the apothecary room, reached for a wet towel, and dabbed Snake Catcher's forehead to cool his fever. For reasons due to his fever and the fear of being restrained in a unfamiliar place, Snake Catcher spoke Lakota, even though he knew many words in English. Snake Catcher's demands for being released fell on deaf ears, as Susan could not decipher them.

Susan frantically explained, "I do not understand. Please calm down."

As Snake Catcher shouted, the dogs barked at him, and everything was noisy and full of chatter. Susan shushed the dogs. After a moment, Snake Catcher stopped shouting. He had stopped struggling but mostly because he was too weak and faint to continue. Everything was silent. Being the first White woman Snake Catcher had ever seen, he looked deeply at her. He studied Susan's soft soothing eyes behind her flawless and unweathered fair complexion.

Susan was calm and did not fear him. The rancher was unaware but Snake Catcher had managed to free one hand from the ropes. As she stood near him, Snake Catcher covertly latched onto Susan's dress with the secured hand, forbidding her from leaving his side. He then grabbed an unlit lamp from the side table with the freed hand while smashing into a glass ramekin dish used for mixing the herbs. Snake Catcher lifted the lamp up to strike Susan, but paused. She did not scream...she did not cry...she did not fear him. Susan smiled at Snake Catcher tenderly and softly as she reached up toward the lamp, and pulled his hand toward her. Snake Catcher's hand was bleeding, cut from the broken ramekin. Susan wiped the blood from his hand with the dabbing towel to see the severity of the cut. She pulled the lamp from Snake Catcher's hand, returned it to the side table, and walked over to the potions table as his weak grip of her dress from the other hand released. While becoming calmer, Snake Catcher realized that he was able to communicate with her.

Scowling, he demanded, "Why ropes? What want? Who...?"

With surprise Susan turned and smiled as she softly spoke, interrupting his questions. "You speak English?"

Along with bandages and an ignited wooden twig, Susan fetched a pen, ink bottle and her sketch pad from the potions table. She walked over and lit the lamp before she sat in the chair next to the cot. Susan tended to Snake Catcher's new wound as the dogs settled down and sat on the floor next to her.

"I am Susan Paradise and this is my home. My men found you on the property," she said. Pointing at his wounds,

Susan added, "You were shot, and you have a head wound. Do you understand?" Susan was ready with the notepad in her lap to write down any Lakota words that Snake Catcher produced, which she planned to have translated, as she tended to the cut on his hand.

Snake Catcher shrugged, then continued. "Susan, daughter to Jacob Paradise?"

With surprise and delight, Susan asked, "You knew my father?"

Shaking his head, Snake Catcher answered, "Brother did."

"Yes, I am Susan and who are you?"

With the pain from his mid-section wound, he had to struggle to speak. "Snake Catcher, brother to Hail Maker...was Lakota...is no more."

Solemnly, Susan confirmed, "Yes, I know. I was there the night he died alongside my father. Hail Maker came here that night. He claimed he snuck off while the camp was sleeping; they were on a mission to find deer for the villager's meat. Later that evening, Father and I rode out to their campsite to give Hail Maker a lessons book he had left behind. The Blue Coats charged up on the campsite and started firing without provocation. Father whipped my horse to ride away as he stepped in front of Hail Maker. I looked back to see both of them fall to the ground. My horse ran frantically until I was almost too weak to hold on. The ranchhands and I rode back that night to bring my father's body home, and to see if Hail Maker had lived–but Hail Maker was gone. When he never visited again over the years, I assumed he was dead."

Even somewhat perplexed by the information in her story about his brother befriending Whites, Snake Catcher pointed to himself as he answered, "His brother came for him."

Susan continued, "I tried demanding answers to why my father and the rest of them were killed by the soldiers. I demanded to know who was responsible. The Blue Coats told me that the soldiers claimed Hail Maker had killed my father, and that was why the soldiers then killed his men. They tried blaming it on my father for being there, but I knew better. I tried telling the Blue Coats that I was there, and I saw what happened, but they argued that I was distraught and didn't know what I really saw. I never trusted them much after that. Don't think I ever will."

As Susan finished bandaging Snake Catcher's hand, he

looked down at his new bandage, then asked, "Why Susan not fear warrior? Is warrior inside lost?"

"I do not know about your warrior ways, I cannot answer that question. If you seek to kill me then you will kill me, I do not have a say in that. I will continue to care for you, and treat your wounds until you do so. Those are my ways."

"Susan kill Crow."

"Yes." Susan paused but Snake Catcher waited for an explanation. She rose and walked over to the bright crackling fireplace, and dipped out a small amount of hot water from a bucket to brew a tea. Susan added her mojo concoction to make a painkilling serum for Snake Catcher. She set it down on the side table to cool before continuing. "I am not proud of that, but with taking one life, I have saved two. I could see the Crow would not have trusted my generosity. Do you know about trust?"

"Does not come easy."

"Neither does mine," Susan agreed, wearing a smile. "But I can already see that you have your brother's giving nature."

Somewhat offended, Snake Catcher voiced, "Brother did not have mercy with Whites."

Calmly and cheerfully, Susan countered, "He did with us. Hail Maker was our trusted friend. I will tell you about our friendship someday."

Even though Snake Catcher was already enchanted by Susan, he felt that trusting her was naive. After a minute, she attempted to get him to drink the tea, but he unquestionably refused. Snake Catcher tipped his head at Susan to drink it first. She smiled then took a quick sip, then another. Susan soon helped Snake Catcher lift his head, and he took a sip, then agreeably drank the rest of the cup.

Snake Catcher looked down at his mid-section wound before explaining, "Near river, pass wood walk."

"That's the Belle Fourche Bridge. You made it across and onto my property before falling off your horse. You were lucky; the bullet wasn't very deep. Do you remember anything?"

Snake Catcher shrugged, not fully understanding Susan's explanation of that dreadful night.

Susan pointed to Snake Catcher's mid-section wound. "Do you know who shot you?"

Snake Catcher's medication had begun taking affect. His pain had lessened to where it was becoming easier for him to speak. "Wears hat color of night. Horse of spots."

Susan flipped her sketch pad to another page and presented him with a sketch. "Is this him?"

Snake Catcher hesitantly nodded, somewhat fearful that Susan not only knew him but had a sketch of the man.

Susan turned up her nose and stated, "Yes, that's my despicable and vile neighbor to the northwest just on the other side of the river–Carter."

The sketch of Carter showed him to be a tall and somewhat intimidating man, especially to anyone of average height. Carter owned much of the land in the county making him very powerful, but he was a greedy bully. He wanted Susan's land just to show he could simply take it from her. Carter was at peace with the idea of taking what he wanted no matter what the circumstances. Susan was not special to him; Carter was an evil man to nearly everyone he crossed paths with.

Snake Catcher struggled to lift his head, then tipped his head to his restraints as to request their removal. Susan untied and removed all except one of the ropes. She loosened but left one leg tied. "I will leave this one to remind you of where you are. I don't want you to hurt yourself if you wake and forget you are here. You might be injured again."

Snake Catcher sluggishly laid his head back down as if he understood Susan's explanation, but more to the truth was that Snake Catcher did not have the strength to argue with her. One would be foolish to mistake that for vulnerability, as he had already made a full audit of the room's exits.

Susan fetched another batch of the pain-killing tea serum, and helped Snake Catcher to lift his head as he drank an additional cup. Susan gently fed him some food from a replacement tray that Rains Down had left in the hallway. Snake Catcher took a few bites, but was too weak and uninterested in it to eat very much.

"It's been a tough day for you. You should get some rest now," Susan suggested. "Good-night."

Susan attempted to leave the room when Snake Catcher spoke out, postponing her departure. "Bring book. Buffalo pouch." Snake Catcher tipped his head to his saddlebags, and then powerlessly rested his head back down as if a huge weight had been lifted off of him.

Susan walked over to Snake Catcher's saddlebags, and

pulled out the horribly blood-stained lessons and poetry book. Sadness came to her face instantly as Susan remembered it belonging to Hail Maker from years ago. A flood of feeling engulfed her, and she thought, "How can one feel joyfulness and sadness at the exact same time?" She brought the book over to Snake Catcher and offered it to him. He refusingly shook his head, pointed at it and then to her. She was grateful beyond words for his generosity; she was not ready to let go of it. Susan had a firm grip on the book as she sat down in her chair. She then pulled a slightly tattered afghan from the foot of the cot over onto her, and opened the book. A huge smile came over Susan's bewildered face when she saw that Hail Maker had sketched her father's and her likenesses on the first page. She showed Snake Catcher these sketches and the ones she drew of him while he was dozing. Snake Catcher grunted, as if to criticize the likeness of him.

Still somewhat emotional, Susan laughed out loud. "Well, I think it looks just like you."

Susan began reading the poetry out loud from the book. Snake Catcher listened to her poetically soothing words before drifting off to sleep.

A short time later, Buck gently knocked on the door. Susan rose and stepped out into the hallway. "What did you do with the body of the Crow?" she asked him.

"Larry and I buried him down at the north end of the river where the earth is soft. No one will know to look there."

Susan sympathetically nodded. Buck left for downstairs as Susan stepped into her bedroom. Even though Susan knew she had to make the kill, she was still distraught over the death of the Crow. Lying down on the bed, she cried to release her pent-up regrets. After a while, Susan composed herself while looking in the mirror, and then returned to the apothecary room. She was eager to continue reading Hail Maker's book. Susan eventually fell asleep to the poetic rhythms of his words in the chair next to Snake Catcher's cot while still holding onto the accomplice to her drowsiness.

Chapter 4

When Susan woke the next morning, an expressionless Snake Catcher was gazing at her, Day Eleven away from the reservation. While she rose, Susan noticed that the lamp had extinguished; having no fuel remaining, before she excused herself and went downstairs to summon her ranchhands to help care for Snake Catcher. The dogs followed her out. Trust was a stranger to Snake Catcher but he was beginning to feel Susan was authentically concerned for his well-being. That was until she returned with Larry and Buck.

Snake Catcher was startled. He began struggling and yelling at them in Lakota to get away from him. As Snake Catcher struggled, he reached for the lamp again but this time he turbulently knocked it off of the table. It crashed to the floor and broke into several unmendable pieces. Susan tried to calm Snake Catcher with her soothing voice, and when that did not work, she tried a word in Lakota: "No, no, they're just here to help you. Please calm down, there's no need to be afraid. Hiya...Heee-ya!"

It surprised Snake Catcher to hear Susan speak Lakota, so much so that he paused before continuing his protest. Susan ordered Buck and Larry to remove themselves from the room, and to wait outside until she could get Snake Catcher settled down. Buck was understandably reluctant to leave, especially since Snake Catcher was no longer restrained.

"I don't feel good about leaving you alone with him. Let us handle him."

"No, I will be all right. He won't hurt me."

"Are you sure? He looks angry."

"Yes, thank you. Go now."

After Buck and Larry had left the room exhibiting assurance to Snake Catcher that he was safe, the Lakota immediately calmed down and scowled at Susan. She softly smiled at him while kneeing next to his cot. "It's okay, I won't let anyone hurt you. Look, they're gone. Do you understand?"

After a moment of pondering the question and looking toward the door, the maimed Lakota slowly nodded.

"Are you all right? Let me see your hand."

He cautiously nodded again, then showed Susan his hand. She examined Snake Catcher to find that he did not re-injure it with the breaking of the lamp. Susan paused, then motioned toward the door. "Can they come back in? They are just going to help you, not hurt you. Okay?"

Snake Catcher reluctantly nodded, but he knew deep down that they could easily hurt him if they wanted to because of the fragile state he was in. Susan walked to the door where Buck and Larry were waiting, and instructed them to be extra gentle with Snake Catcher as they untied the last restraint on his leg. The two ranchhands then helped Snake Catcher climb downstairs and walk out to the outdoor facility.

Moments later in the kitchen, Susan reached for a wooden box from the kitchen shelf that crated vegetables. She emptied the contents of the box on the counter with Cook looking strangely at her, then took it upstairs to the apothecary room. As Susan placed the lamp pieces into the wooden box for disposal, Snake Catcher returned with Larry and Buck helping him. Buck had a pile of clothes with him and placed them on the potions table. Snake Catcher wearily sat down on the cot. The ranchhands were not given instruction to restrain him again. Snake Catcher became uneasy not knowing why Larry and Buck still stood over him as they waited for further orders from Susan. She was still kneeling on the floor collecting the lamp pieces with her back to Snake Catcher, inadvertently establishing trust for him to see. Snake Catcher lightly grunted and Susan glanced back at him. "You boys can leave now."

"Yes, ma'am. I left Sammy's clothes on the table."

"Thank you, Buck."

Larry stepped out of the room instantly but Buck hesitated before leaving. Snake Catcher tipped his head toward the broken pieces of the lamp, as if to ask about its origin.

"My mother gave this lamp to me; it was the last gift I

ever received from her before Mother died." Susan finished putting the last jagged pieces into the box and stood up.

Snake Catcher drew in his fist to his chest. He was unsure of the correct word. "Cate sice, ah, sorry?"

Susan understandingly shook her head. "I know you did not mean to. That is why I had the ropes on you, so you wouldn't hurt yourself," Susan said over lifting up Snake Catcher's former restraints, to show him.

Snake Catcher regrettably nodded. "Understand."

Susan walked to the potions table to retrieve the pile of clothes and brought them over to Snake Catcher. She indicated for him to put them on to replace his bloody ones.

"I'm not sure these will fit you, although you and Sammy are generally the same size. There is fresh water in the basin, and soap and towels on the table if you want to wash. I'll be back in a few minutes to check on you. Do you need any help?"

Snake Catcher looked bewildered and tired due to his injuries, yet free-spiritedly shook his head. Susan gathered the book and her sketch pad, and carried them out of the room. Snake Catcher held up the clothes and grunted, not really knowing how they functioned, this being the first time he was to wear White man's clothes.

Susan prepared the guest bedroom for Snake Catcher, and petitioned Buck to place a rocking chair from the porch next to the bed and a log in the fireplace. She placed Hail Maker's book on the side table.

Meanwhile, Snake Catcher washed, and then dressed in the fresh change of clothes.

Susan gently knocked on the apothecary door, and slowly entered, not knowing if Snake Catcher had finished dressing. He was patiently sitting on the cot waiting for her; he wore the fresh clothes in the usual style, with the omission of buttoning the shirt.

"I'd like to look at your wounds and treat them, okay?"

Snake Catcher agreeably nodded, removed his open shirt and leaned back. Susan noticed that Snake Catcher had donned his knife from the mantle. She said nothing, and continued to treat his wounds. As Snake Catcher noticed Susan viewing the knife, he moved its holder back and out of her way while she changed his bandages, never taking his eyes off her face. Susan was not certain if it was mistrust that she was sensing from him, or if he was not comfortable being that close to a White woman;

in any case, the knife made her slightly uneasy. Susan tried pulling an aloe vera plant apart but was unsuccessful. Snake Catcher pulled his knife out of its holder to offer it to her, startling Susan. She promptly shook her head. After realizing that he was just offering it to her, Susan then instructed Snake Catcher to slice the plant in half, lengthwise. She swirled the slimy plant on his wounds, then redressed them. After Susan was finished, and while Snake Catcher redonned his shirt, she mixed another pain-killing tea concoction for him and placed it into hot water to steep. When Susan noticed his unbuttoned shirt, she then realized the knowledge of buttons escaped Snake Catcher, which she courteously buttoned it for him. Before helping her patient up, Susan placed the brewed tea and more dried tea mixture in the guest room.

"Why leave?"

Teasingly as she smiled, Susan explained, "Because that room is for sick people, and you are much better now."

Susan guided Snake Catcher out of the apothecary room. As they made their way across the hallway into the guest bedroom, she petitioned Buck to bring Snake Catcher's saddle-bags over for him. The dogs were instructed to lie down there. Susan then walked over, pulled down the covers, and motioned for Snake Catcher to get into the bed. As Snake Catcher sat down on the bed, Buck dropped the saddlebags on the floor next to him, and left. Snake Catcher was somewhat confused as to why the mattress moved, being the first time he sat on a White man's bed with springs. He made his way to a comfortable spot in front of two soft fluffy goose down pillows. The inviting tea seduced him into drinking it, not waiting for the tepidness to cool.

"That is still very hot," Susan cautioned.

Snake Catcher did not seem to hear Susan, and drank the tea down before asking for more.

"That is very strong medicine, you need to wait a while."

Snake Catcher insistently shook his head, and spoke softly still showing signs of pain. "More."

Susan accommodatingly nodded, walked to the bright crackling fireplace to fetch water from a warming kettle, and brewed more tea. She set it down and told Snake Catcher to wait for the tea to cool before drinking it, after which he compliantly nodded this time. Susan sat in the rocking chair. After reaching for her sketch pad which sat on the floor next to her, Susan began sketching him. Snake Catcher eased back into the pillows again. Susan gently rocked as he began a conversation with her while using hand gestures to help with his communication.

"Practice what to say when here. Lakota words not in same path as White words. May mistake them." He paused before continuing. Then as he pointed at her, Snake Catcher asked, "How Susan know brother?"

Susan spoke while sketching. "My father was a rancher but he taught at a nearby schoolhouse a few days a week. Hail Maker raided the school one day. Father stood in front of the children protecting them, and spoke some words in Lakota politely asking him to leave. Hail Maker was intrigued, and left them unharmed. He later returned after the children had left, and asked Father to teach him our words. Being a teacher at heart, Father was thrilled to and agreed. Hail Maker came back every week or so with a better pronunciation to each word he learned, and was ready for his next lesson. Soon Father invited him to our ranch house instead of the schoolhouse. That was when I met him and we broke bread together."

As Susan unfolded her story, Snake Catcher's world, as he knew it, was changed forever. He subsequently realized that his brother was only mortal, and no longer a legendary spiritual icon. A flood of new feelings came over him. Snake Catcher had believed he finally reached his brother's worthiness of an equal warrior by fulfilling his honor of delivering the book. That was all that Snake Catcher could think about since the day his brother asked it of him. But now he felt he was not Hail Maker's equal. He was not even one step below his saintly brother. To his way of thinking, Snake Catcher had lost all of his status by now knowing his brother benevolently forfeited his legendary fame to set Snake Catcher free. Free of envy and the torment of worshiping someone who did not exist—a legend! Hail Maker knew by sending Snake Catcher to Susan, he would learn of the method in which Hail Maker acquired the White words, and the legend would be forever dead. Even though his brother was trying to set Snake Catcher free, he imprisoned him again by being selfless in his offering.

Snake Catcher's psyche was challenged to find some sort of normalcy from his past. Only new conflicting feelings remained—ones of anger for competing against a legend knowing he would never have measured up; ones of relief now knowing he was not always inadequate; ones of righteousness that he was the honest one; ones of forced acceptance that Hail Maker unquestionably had befriended a White man, which had been inconceivable to him; and ones of guilt for now being angry with Hail Maker for lying to him. But all of that paled to the ones of envy, not being as brave as his brother who unleashed his secret to set his brother free.

Continuously, Susan added, "I once asked Hail Maker why he wanted to know the White words. He said to keep his enemies close, to understand them better."

"Understand them better, to kill them easier," added Snake Catcher. "He taught White words to us. Bragged knew many White words from each White man he kill."

"I don't doubt that. Hail Maker was a storyteller with the proof of his double life, and he had kept it hidden well."

Susan reminisced as she told Snake Catcher of a memory with Hail Maker. *One night, she spotted Hail Maker out of the front window of the ranch house at dusk. She screamed like a child and ran from the room. Someone who did not know of their friendship may have viewed her response as being full of terror. Her father then walked over to the same window to witness the outside scene and smiled as he watched his daughter run up to Hail Maker and his horse. Susan was full of joy, jumping up and down and pulling Hail Maker toward the house.*

As Susan returned to the present, she continued, "I would drag Hail Maker inside and couldn't wait for him to tell me of his stories in the great wilderness. Hail Maker also told me of the great Indian chief, Chief Clever Spirit, and how he had many wives." Susan giggled, then commented, "I know some of your customs and words. But not just from Hail Maker."

At that moment, a gentle knock came on the door. Susan rose and answered it to find Rains Down with a tray of food. Rains Down modestly walked across to the far side of the room, and set the tray down on the table.

"Can I get you anything else, Miss Susan?"

"No, Rains Down, thank you for this. You can use this time as your own."

Rains Down graciously tipped her head to Susan, and had started to cross the room to leave when Snake Catcher questioned her in Lakota. "Are you happy here? Do they treat you well?"

Rains Down stopped, looked at Snake Catcher, smiled,

and answered him in Lakota. "Yes, very well. I have much to eat
and a room in the main house across the hallway from this one.
I am treated more equal here than anywhere else."

Snake Catcher nodded with acceptance to her explanation. Rains Down proceeded, and left the room. Susan smiled at
him with an expression as to ask what they were discussing as
she made her way over to the tray of food.

"It is good living here," Snake Catcher freely offered.

Susan graspingly nodded as to then understand the
conversation, and why he questioned Rains Down. "I'm glad. We
think it is good having her here."

"That how know Lakota words."

Susan smiled and cheerfully nodded before commenting,
"You are a warrior with a heart."

Snake Catcher was not sure he fancied that description
of himself and scowled. Susan smiled at his macho reaction
while continuing to plate his food.

"How she get name?" Snake Catcher wondered out loud.

Susan explained, "Rains Down told me that she was born
during the worst rain storm her family could ever remember,
and that her mother's screams were drowned by the sound of
the storm."

Susan finished plating the healing breakfast of eggs, ham
and fruit for Snake Catcher, and brought it to him. She placed
his orange juice on the side table to the bed. Susan returned to
the food tray, and also prepared herself a plate of food. Snake
Catcher wasted no time as he began eating, being famished from
days without eating much, but then slowed due to his shrunken
stomach capacity. He had already given up by the time Susan
sat back down in her rocking chair.

Susan continued the conversation. "I think I am comfortable around you because I was comfortable around Hail Maker.
Even though the government allowed us to stake claim to this
land while never mentioning that it was land that they promised
your people, Hail Maker did not blame us and allowed us to live
here in peace. We did not steal from him or his people, that is
why he befriended us. Hail Maker told us that the Lakota did
not find grievance in sharing this land with others if they could
live by the laws of the Lakota world. The laws that one does not
own land, one cares for it and belongs to the earth rather than
the earth belonging to them. He said the Lakota did not want
their way of life taken from them; they would rather share the

land out of choice instead of being told they would have to forfeit the right to govern over the land, and have it stripped of buffalo and all that it had given them. Hail Maker was good to us, and would bring us a gift every time he came to visit. I think maybe that was his way of repaying Father for the lessons, but I just liked Hail Maker's company and, of course, his stories and that was enough for me."

"Many Whites come to our land, not try to understand our words. Your father knew how to be accepted and live among us. We did not have hate against prospectors, even stealing from us. It was Chief of White man, Grant, that we send message to by killing Whites caught on our land."

Susan was a compassionate person and was uncomfortable with the talk of killing, so she went on but changed the subject. "Tell me about your brother in the eyes of his brother."

"Lakota believe not polite to speak of dead. He was your friend, will tell about him. Good trade-*er*. Good fight-*er*. Good broth-*er*. Brave. Good husband." Snake Catcher then discouragingly shook his head before adding, "Bad gamble-*er*."

Susan had a tiny tear running down her cheek from desperately missing her friend, but let out a soft chuckle over "bad gamble-*er*" as Snake Catcher wore his first smile for her. Snake Catcher continued, "Learn White words well. Learn fast."

"He never spoke of his wife. Who was he husband to?"

"Shadow Talker. Good Lakota wife."

"Are you married? Do you have a good Lakota wife, or several wives?" Susan asked somewhat teasingly, as she tried to pull herself out of her sadness.

Snake Catcher's face became stoic. He briefly nodded. "Lakota man have several wives. Matching Spirit was enough wife for me. Daughter to Chief. Was with child. Both have left for final journey as one."

Susan sympathetically tilted her head slightly, reached out and consolingly touched Snake Catcher's hand before offering "Sorry."

Snake Catcher was somewhat startled by Susan's gesture of touching him, not as a nurse but something different. After a brief pause, and after Susan pulled her hand back, Snake Catcher requested the same information from her. "Good husband for Susan?"

Shaking her head from side to side, Susan answered, "No, not yet. I usually chase them off because they aren't used to an independent woman. Doesn't matter anyway; if they don't fall out of trees around here, I have no time to meet anyone." Susan chuckled. Snake Catcher did not understand the joke but slightly smiled when he saw Susan amused by it.

"Tell about Susan. How come to have all this? Where come from?"

"Before I tell you that, I will first give you a lesson for the White words. The Whites do not say the person's name each time when we are speaking to them directly. We say 'you' instead."

"You?"

"Yes."

"Tell about *you*?"

"Yes, that's it. Well...I was living with my parents in Chicago. Father didn't really like it there, so we came here. It was always Mother's wish to live close to her parents when they were alive. Father always wanted the adventures of living in the great West. Mother died from tuberculosis, ah...the coughing sickness, a few months after we moved here. After Father died, I inherited this place, and since the '62 Homestead Act allowed women to be landowners, I got to keep it. After I was older, I learned about medicines because I was curious from mother's illness. That's how I came to have an apothecary room."

Snake Catcher remarked, "Do not know that word."

Susan pointed toward the door. "That other room we were in is used to heal people." She gestured mixing plants together. "It means what the plants make when you add them together."

"Medicine man makes?"

Susan nodded and proudly pointed to herself. "Medicine *woman*." She then proceeded with her story about herself and her family. "Father hired several workers when they needed jobs badly to feed their families. That is why they are loyal to me today. My neighbor Carter wouldn't have given them the time of day, much less a job. Father purchased 400 head of cattle and now we have 800. Not a large ranch but it pays the bills. Not that I need it; Father left me well off, mostly from Mother's inheritance from her wealthy parents. I continued the ranch because it was what Father loved, and because I don't have anything else in my life right now. I do enjoy fighting for the rights of people, being an advocate. Women passed a great milestone in '68 when the ratification was completed of the

Fourteenth Amendment guaranteeing that women would be considered equal in this country. Women jumped over another great hurdle in '69, passing the first woman's suffrage law, or the right to vote, in the country right here in the Territory of Wyoming. And that is pretty much my life, except my dogs." As Susan introduced her dogs, she pointed at each of them. "My dogs are one-quarter coyote which makes them feisty. Her name is Coyote, and her name is Killer."

Snake Catcher said, "Heal sick, fight for weak. Who cares for Susan, ah...you?"

Susan self-consciously sipped her beverage, lightly shrugged, and camouflaged her expression as she glanced away avoiding the question. She had no one special to care for her. Susan knew, all too well, that living life alone was one of the burdens of being an independent woman in her time. Most men did not know how to be with such a woman, one they could not control.

From experience, Susan also knew how to smoothly change the subject off of her. "Now tell me about Snake Catcher. I'm guessing you are fast enough to catch snakes, and that is how you got your name."

Snake Catcher cryptically smirked, briskly nodded, and used hand gestures to tell his story. "Am warrior, warriors move fast. Ride hard. As boy, looked to older warriors in tribe and Hail Maker to learn warrior ways. To be asked to hunt with warriors, had to be fast. Would practice catching snakes to prove worthy of being asked. We hunt buffalo for meat and hides. We fight those who take, not ask. Blue Coats fear me, sent to prison."

"You were in prison? How did you get out?"

"A Lakota, Earth Raven, man with law help free me. Hail Maker taught him White words. Wrote letters and men listen. Was sent to reservation partly from treaty. Was push east when Whites broke treaty. Sent many places when Whites want our land. Not have same laws as other Lakota. Am still warrior to Whites. Reservation prison now."

Susan sympathetically responded, "You have lived many lives."

Snake Catcher stared off beyond Susan's image as he withdrew into his tormented past. His only response was: "All Lakota lived many lives."

"What laws are you not granted?"

"Take many moons to gain papers to come here after prison. Not take many days for rest of Lakota." Snake Catcher paused. "Look for you when capture, sent to prison."

Horrified, Susan responded with surprise, "You were sent to prison while looking for me? Why were you looking for me?"

"Hail Maker last spoke of you." Snake Catcher pointed to the lesson book. "Hail Maker want you to have."

Susan instantly realized Snake Catcher's sacrifice for his brother and for her. She mournfully picked up the book, and held it close to her. She spoke softly and somewhat distractedly, thinking of the past. "You could have lived a free life if it weren't for this book, if it weren't for me."

"Hiya. Hail Maker want you to have–*all* Lakota want you to have. Not have Lakota word for I, for good reason. You did not ask us, that was to be our decision. It was not about loss to one but honor to many. Have sacrifice *more* than freedom to complete honor." Proudly, Snake Catcher pulled his fist from his heart, then waved it away. "Have no worries, choice was made." He went on to explain how the children of his people were all taught to respect the four cardinal virtues in life: bravery, fortitude, wisdom and generosity.

Susan softly smiled before asking, "How did you know to find me here?"

"Hail Maker, before final journey. And Earth Raven write letters, hear from Washington man of your home, of Jacob and Elizabeth leaving."

"Then you already knew my story, and yet you asked?"

"Want to hear *your* truth."

Susan humbly smiled, paused, then inquired, "How do you say your name in Lakota?"

"Zuzeca Wawoyuspa."

"Zuze..."

"Zuzeca Wawoyuspa." Snake Catcher helped Susan with the pronunciation of his name while Susan repeated it over and over. He then proceeded to explain the specifics of his travel conditions. "Return home next morning. Must ride hard," explained Snake Catcher as he pointed toward his saddlebags, and then toward Susan; indicating her retrieval of his travel papers. As Susan reached down and freed the documents from their harborage, four arrowhead tips fell out of his saddlebag. Susan scooped them up and returned the weapons inside of his pouch.

Snake Catcher explained, "Return soon or trouble be here."

"I will contact the authorities and tell them that you have been wounded and cannot yet ride."

Snake Catcher seemed meaningfully frightened for Susan, and asked, "No trouble for you?"

"No, no, there won't be trouble for me," Susan reassured him.

Snake Catcher nodded in agreement.

Susan stood while saying, "I must tend to my chores now. Try to get some sleep. There is no more danger, you will be safe here in my home."

Susan stepped out into the hallway where she found Rains Down awaiting instructions. "Check in on him throughout the day. Please tell Cook that I want organ meats and green vegetables for his lunch."

Susan, feeling good about her morning, contentedly left to perform her daily chores.

Meanwhile in the stables, Sammy and Ferdy were devotedly performing their duties. They were engrossed in the type of conversation that is shared between those who have felt the sting of oppression. Ferdy bared his soul with stories of his mother and him banding together with many other Mexican fugitives while crossing the Texas border into this country. Ferdy spoke of how the Mexican General, Santa Anna, was perpetrating a fraud of bettering their territory by seizing Texas, when he actually wanted only the betterment of his political power. "I was only a baby when we left, strapped to my mother's back, but she told me of how Santa Anna had been exiled many times then allowed to return and die on his home soil. That favor to him was injustice to us."

Sammy shared his story with Ferdy of how he, too, wanted to flee his captives. "You be lucky to be able to leave that place. You be well-to-do bein' a baby, and not to be a man livin' in such a bad place. I—not so lucky. I be a Georgia slave. There be many different standin's of slaves. Some be indoor slaves, who have it good, and some be workin' in the fields. I be a stable slave for our master on the plantation. I be needin' for nothin' and content when I worked for my first master. He be kind and fair to us. But then his neighbor run him out of biz'ness and we became his prop-tee. He not be so kind. He not see the value of how we be trained. I worked in the fields pickin' his cotton when I had more skill workin' with horses. I would displease him often 'cuz of me not knowin' about what is good cotton. I hide afraid of him most of the time. I be plottin' to run away when the war ended and we all scatt'd to parts unknown." Sammy begrudgingly shrugged, as to pretend it did not matter about missing his kin. He continued, "He took over the other plantation much like Carter is tryin' to take this place from Miss Susan. You know we would not be treated as kind if we worked for Carter."

Ferdy empathized, then added, "Mother said Father was not paid enough to support one person, much less a family, that it too was like being enslaved. We were free to go *nowhere*. We did not have the money to clothe or feed ourselves, much less travel to where we wanted to be. We were not given shelter when it rained, or medicine when we were sick. Nevertheless, we were not given a cell to live in, either. I am not sure which was worse. We were both enslaved."

Sammy agreeably nodded then concluded, "I can work three times as hard here and it be the easiest work I ever done 'cuz my work is 'preciated, not demanded."

They both whole-heartedly agreed.

A few times during the day, Snake Catcher gingerly wandered the house, mostly to the outdoor facility, and then he returned to bed. Rains Down timed his departures from the room so she could brew his tea to leave in his room while he was absent, as to not disturb him. She brought him lunch of healing foods, and he ate alone. After dining, he was fidgety and bored, and flipped through Susan's sketch pad. The faces of people at the ranch, and some townspeople, lifelessly stared back at him, including those he had not yet been acquainted with.

Snake Catcher was noticeably, however unexpectedly, looking forward to Susan's return. Partly because he was bored, and partly because he was anxious to practice his English words, but mostly because he was wanting companionship from her. A long time had passed since Snake Catcher had someone other than Earth Raven to converse with as a confidant. Snake Catcher was not yet fully aware that he was feeling good from Susan's attention–attention that was given because she was feeling the loss of Hail Maker, and also that she was utterly alone in her life. Susan was not yet fully aware that she was feeling good from Snake Catcher's company, largely because of resurrecting Hail Maker's memory and the friendship they had shared. But these factors were enough for both of them to begin fancying friendship from the other.

Susan joined Snake Catcher in his room where they shared supper.

Snake Catcher inquisitively inquired about her day. "What you do today?"

"I have chores just like everyone else. Granted, I don't shovel out horse stalls, but I have other chores. I teach some studies. I make sure everyone is comfortable, and they have plenty to eat. I pay them. I make the list of supplies...and chores like that. Much needs to be done to run a ranch, and we all pitch in. Once a month we go into Deadwood City to pick up supplies, and once a quarter we go up to Montana or over to Deadwood to auction our cattle off or to buy new ones."

"Why not man do for you?"

"I like staying connected to my staff, and because we are all in this together like a family. They can't live without a job and I can't run the ranch without help."

Snake Catcher understandingly nodded and subconsciously yawned.

Susan and Snake Catcher casually chatted a while longer before saying good-night.

"I have had a nice supper but I have to rise early tomorrow to send your message. Let me change your bandages first before I leave you tonight."

After Susan changed Snake Catcher's dressings, the dogs were instructed to depart with her, and she retreated into her bedroom. After dressing in her nightclothes, Susan nestled into her bed before double-checking the contents under her pillow; a revolver was hidden underneath.

Chapter 5

In the morning, Susan anxiously dressed in her riding attire for her errands in Sundance. After retrieving a tray of medical supplies from the apothecary room, she placed a gentle knock on Snake Catcher's door, Day Twelve away from the reservation. Susan apprised Snake Catcher, "I need to change your bandages before I leave for town."

"Send message?" Snake Catcher inquired.

"Yes, all will be taken care of. I need you to rest. I will be back in time for lunch, so save me some food. Okay?" Susan smiled over her razz while she finished replacing Snake Catcher's dressings. He courteously made a request before Susan left.

Pointing toward the door, Snake Catcher asked, "Have pipe smoke plants in room?" He then asked, "Stick to make pipe?"

"Yes. I will instruct Rains Down to bring you a mixture." Susan quickly walked through the doorway. Requests were written down, and Susan handed the notes to Rains Down before explaining them. "Here is the new tea mixture for Snake Catcher, please see that he gets three cups this morning. This next one is a recipe for smoking tobacco that he would like. And this last one is the menu I'd like us to have for lunch today. Please inform Cook. Check on him a few times to make sure he is resting comfortably. I'll be home by lunchtime, thank you."

Rains Down compliantly nodded before returning to her chores.

Susan gave Snake Catcher a quick reassurance that all would be taken care of, closed his door behind her, and left for downstairs.

Snake Catcher rose out of bed, stepped close to the balcony window in his bedroom and watched as Susan gracefully galloped away on her horse with great speed. Buck and Slim followed her on their trotters; the horses' hooves were thumping loudly. Susan's ability to ride competently impressed Snake Catcher.

On that slightly misty day, Susan made the two-hour ride to the Sundance trading post with her two ranchhands, and once there, the men separated from her. The post's telegraph booth was the first of Susan's stops, to send Snake Catcher's message to Fort Meade, and another to Fort Pierre. The clothing merchandise counter was Susan's focus for her next mission, where she made several purchases, which included clothing items for Snake Catcher, along with replacements for Sammy's borrowed set.

In the meantime, Buck and Slim made a purchase of a bottle of spirits at the saloon. Buck's attentions were not fully on his patronage; he was scouting any signs of his obsession–Angel. Sadly, Buck did not detect her whereabouts.

By lunchtime, the three of them had returned home.

Susan believed that it would be beneficial for Snake Catcher's healing process if he were more mobile. She charitably assisted him down the stairs and into the diningroom. Ferdy was there, and he tried to be secretive by whispering to Susan.

"Hello, Miss Susan. Would you know where Rains Down would be?"

"She is in the kitchen, Ferdy."

"Thank you, ma'am."

Ferdy hurriedly headed toward the kitchen. Susan helped Snake Catcher to a diningroom chair as he inquired, "His wife?"

Susan smiled over her answer. "He wishes. Ferdy has a liking for her. He doesn't think anyone else knows, but he asks me where she is nearly every day."

Snake Catcher was starved for companionship and conversation which brought him to comment, "Watch you leave today, good rider."

"No, I think my horse, Sparks, is just a good carrier."

Susan and Snake Catcher began their meal. Large quantities of organ meats and fish garnished his plate. Snake Catcher looked down at his plate perplexed, then back up at Susan. She smiled but did not offer the knowledge of the food increasing human libido. In observing her plate, Snake Catcher discovered that someone had carved all of Susan's food items into bite-size pieces.

Without missing a beat, Rains Down entered the room with a tray of drinks. Speaking in Lakota, a smiling Rains Down clarified the status of Susan's plated food. "She is afraid of knives."

Rains Down set the drinks in front of them, and then left the room. Assuming that Rains Down was commenting on Snake Catcher's full plate of food, Susan's only response on the subject was: "They are healing foods," then she quickly went on to a different topic. "So, how was your day so far? Have you been able to move around much?"

"It is slow. Body not want to work."

"It will work again soon; it will only take some time to heal," Susan said. "I sent your message. I also purchased some clothes for you while I was at the trading post. After Rains Down has prepared them, she'll put them in your room. I also bought you a smoking pipe, but I'm sure it's not as nice as those you have made for yourself."

Snake Catcher seemed confused as to the meaning of the offerings. "Will trade or work for them once able."

"No, that isn't necessary; they are a gift. It's the least I could do after you risked your life, twice, to bring me my gift from Hail Maker."

"Pilamayaye is word do not use often."

Rains Down, demonstrating impeccable timing, and appearing because she had overheard Snake Catcher struggling with his words, unobtrusively entered the diningroom. She offered, *"Thank you*, he says thank you."

Susan graciously tipped her head to him. "You're welcome."

"May I get you anything else, Miss Susan?"

"No, not right now, thank you." As Rains Down quietly exited the room, Susan continued, "You have begun healing; your appetite is back."

"Rains Down good feeder."

Susan smiled, but not entirely for innocent reasons knowing how the food may affect him. Painted Pony's small face shyly appeared around the corner from the kitchen, and when Snake Catcher spotted her, a smile covered her face. The teen was abruptly pulled back into the kitchen by Rains Down.

After the two had finished their desserts, Susan escorted Snake Catcher upstairs. As she redressed his wounds, he drank another batch of healing tea. A nap was next on Snake Catcher's agenda, and Susan turned to her afternoon chores.

Susan's first stop was at the stables where she found Slim, Sammy and Larry performing their assigned duties. "Hello, Sammy, how is the mare doing?" Susan asked. "Is she ready to drop her foal yet?"

"Hello, Miss Susan," answered Sammy as all of the ranchhands stepped over to speak to her. Sammy continued, "Not so far, but I not be a horse doctor. I be told that when she loses her muscles in her tail to where you k'in fold it flat on her back, then she be ready."

Slim added, "Pete over at the Triple R Ranch says she will drop after two days without eating."

Larry blurted out to Slim, "What does he know? He's not a horse doctor either." Susan merrily smirked at their disagreement. Larry had yet another suggestion, "No, you are both wrong. She will drop when the moon is bright, that's when horses are ready. It has to do with gravity pull."

Laughter filled the stables with Larry's suggestion.

Susan remarked pleasantly, "Larry, I think that one is an old wives' tale. Well boys, all I know is that she is coming up on 340 days, and that is her due date. So we wait."

They all nodded in agreement. The ranchhands parted ways from their cluster, and continued their respective duties. Susan hurried out of the stables to tend to her remaining chores.

In the diningroom that evening, Rains Down routinely brought in supper. Snake Catcher practiced his English while Susan patiently helped him with his words.

It was a good day for Snake Catcher. His vocabulary was increasing, his body was healing, and his appearance was improving, and not just from wearing some of his new clothes from the trading post.

Susan commented, "You look better."

"Feel better. Tired of being tired."

"Sleep is good for you now, but you will be stronger soon. You look very nice in your new clothes. Did they all fit you?"

Snake Catcher concurrently nodded while trying his new

words. "Yes. Thank. You."

Susan angelically smiled.

"What you do today?" Snake Catcher inquired.

"The usual," Susan replied quietly, but then perked up to the announcement of anticipating a new arrival. "We have a mare that is going to foal soon. I'm not sure when, she's on her own time schedule. It's the offspring to my horse, Sparks."

"Horses all on own time."

Susan agreeably nodded as they stood in completion of all except the last course of their feast. Susan instructed Rains Down to serve dessert in the lounge while she and Snake Catcher meandered into the room. The dogs collectively and unwaveringly, sat on the floor next to her. Susan sat on a blue velvet-covered sofa, and after pulling out a sketch pad from the side desk, she began sketching one of the dogs. Snake Catcher moved conservatively around the room looking at photographs on the walls. Out of the many that were displayed there, some photographs were of her staff and their families.

Snake Catcher pointed at the images. "You know all people?"

"No, some are of the families who live here."

"Why do you have, when not your family?"

"In a way, they are. This is home to all who live here, and this is a fine place to display them with all of the others my father and I have commissioned."

Snake Catcher admiringly pointed at a photograph of his brother with Susan and her father. Jacob and Hail Maker were standing, while Susan was sitting in a chair. She was several years younger at the time. Snake Catcher looked bedazzled at the photograph while saying, "Wasu Kage, ah...Hail Maker and Susan family." Snake Catcher couldn't help but feel somewhat envious of their union.

Thinking back to happier times when the two men were still living, Susan slipped deep into memories of the life that she had with her father, and of having Hail Maker in it. "Yes, but that was taken long ago and getting further away." Susan was uncommonly silent, and she continued sketching as Snake Catcher continued looking at the documented proof of his brother's friendship with Susan. Snake Catcher spotted another more recent photograph of Susan. He obscurely grinned at her angelic smile in it.

Susan and Snake Catcher soon stepped out onto the

porch for some fresh spring night air, and also to admire Paha Sapa. Susan sipped her tea. Snake Catcher looked at his new smoking pipe as if he'd never seen a White man's pipe before this one. He seemed to be trying to decode it. Finally, he did, and spent some time smoking. Susan smiled at Snake Catcher's innocence of her White world.

Chapter 6

The day began early, and Snake Catcher retreated to his room to rest after breakfast, Day Thirteen away from the reservation. Shortly thereafter, two echoey gunshots sounded from the pasture. A gunfire signaling system had been prearranged for the ranchhand communication. One gunshot was a warning that someone, not immediately threatening, was approaching the house. Two rifle shots meant a warning that someone of an immediate threatening nature was on the property. Two shots from a handgun meant there was trouble of any variety in nature in the pasture, and Susan was requested for advisement. And if at any point they could actually get three shots off from their rifle *or* handgun, it would bring all of the reinforcements possible to the area in which the shots were made.

After hearing the gunshots, Snake Catcher rose and walked to the balcony. Once again, he witnessed Susan's impressive ability to ride with great speed on Sparks. He did not know of the signaling system, nor why Susan was in a fury to leave. Unbeknownst to her, he continued to watch until she had traveled over a hill in the pasture and out of his sight.

As Susan made her way around the herd of cattle and over the sloped terrain, she arrived at the scene of trouble in the pasture and dismounted her horse. "What's the trouble, boys?"

Slim responded, "Carter's men were on the property branding over your brand on some of the cattle."

"We scared the cattle thieves off, Miss Susan," Larry excitedly added.

Slim continued, "They rebranded three of them."

"Let's bring the cattle closer to the center of the ranch,

so they don't try to claim them as theirs," directed Susan.

They all mounted their horses. Susan and Larry rustled the abused cattle, and steered them toward the house; Slim stayed behind to tend to the remaining herd.

Back at the house, curiosity brought Snake Catcher into Susan's bedroom to meander around. He noticed the bathtub and looked perplexed as to what it was. Snake Catcher ran his sight around it, then followed the makeshift plumbing of wooden planks that were layered and woven together before funneling out of the wall. When he figured out its purpose, he inquiringly looked around for water. He then filled the tub, and slipped down beneath the surface of the water for a spell. Snake Catcher decrypted pulling the stopper and the water drained while he redressed. As the water lowered, he scowled and mildly grunted at it. Snake Catcher inquisitively roamed Susan's bedroom, smelling the fresh flowers in the vase, and swirling her dainty frilly clothes on his cheek feeling their texture. He was startled at his reflection peering back at him in her mirror, then watched with wonder, as if seeing it through the eyes of a child. He then examined his mid-section wound in the mirror. Snake Catcher went on to smell the scented candle on the fireplace mantle. He strummed the bristles of her hairbrush with his thumb. He looked out the window, wanting to see the view Susan saw. As Snake Catcher sat on her bed and bounced to test the firmness, the gun from under her pillow slid toward him. He examined the weapon before sliding it back to its hiding place. Snake Catcher took one last glance around the room, then left.

Susan returned to the ranch house yard on Sparks with just as much force and speed as she departed, all the while with Snake Catcher observing her from his window. She entered the stables with Sparks, and spotted Sammy tirelessly performing his chores. Sammy was shirtless, and with not expecting passerbys, he was startled. Sammy turned sharply to his front side but it was too late, the graphic whipping scars all over his back were visible to Susan.

"Hello, Sammy."

"Hello, Miss Susan," Sammy responded nervously. "K'in I care for Sparks for you?"

"Sammy, it's all right. I already know."

As he took control of her horse, and without making eye contact, Sammy responded, "How so, Miss Susan?"

"Just before you arrived here to inquire about a job, two

bounty hunters came to the ranch and claimed you were a runaway slave. They said you were wanted by your owner. I promptly reminded them that the war was over and there weren't any slave owners anymore."

A quick grin came to Sammy's face. "I be sure they didn't like that, Miss Susan."

"No, and I told them that you weren't here but I would be on the lookout for you. I'm sure they were thinking that I would report you, not hire you. I knew who you were before you arrived."

"And you still hired me?"

"Yes, why not? You didn't do anything wrong. The war was over and you left, that was your right. You were hired because you are very knowledgeable in ranching, and are an asset here."

Sammy, no longer guarded about concealing his back, guided Sparks to his stall and began brushing him. He had an undeniable smile on his face.

Susan left the stables in good humor. Moments later, Rains Down greeted her in the foyer as Susan entered the house.

"Hello, Rains Down. How is our guest doing?"

As Rains Down took possession of Susan's gloves and riding paraphernalia, she responded, "He came down once, and he took a bath in your bedroom, but I haven't seen him since." Then Rains Down gave Susan an expression as to say that Snake Catcher had lost his mind. "There was no fire in the fireplace; the water was *cold*."

Susan giggled a bit as she headed for the stairway. While starting the climb, she smilingly commented, "He must be quite frisky then."

She gently knocked on Snake Catcher's bedroom door. Having gained his strength back, Snake Catcher walked over to greet her.

"Is this a good time? Can I tend to your wounds?"

Snake Catcher approvingly nodded, and answered, "Yes." He was looking at Susan differently. He stood mildly closer to her, the gap between them was lessening. An indisputable mutual trust was developing as they were becoming friends. Snake Catcher never thought that to be possible, a friendly compassionate White was an oxymoron to him. He was now realizing what Hail Maker had seen in Susan's family: generosity and integrity. Why had he never known there were these kinds of Whites in the world? Why were they never the kind who came to the reservation, or were sent as Blue Coats? Had they been, the encounters between the Lakota and Blue Coats may have been quite different.

Susan assessed the condition of his bandages that had gotten damp with his bath, and determined a change could wait until after supper since they were mostly dry. She brewed Snake Catcher's healing tea, and as he drank that batch, he fished for information from her. "Not see you much."

Susan had befitting hesitation in her voice. "I had chores to do" was all she offered. Susan could not justify telling Snake Catcher about the trouble with Carter, it was not his fight. Moreover, Snake Catcher was not strong enough to enter into a battle with the man who nearly killed him.

"Are chores over? Will you be in diningroom?"

"Yes."

Susan stepped out and headed for her bedroom. She quickly washed and slipped into a powder-blue dress embroidered with tiny flowers. She removed a flower from the vase and smeared the petals on her hair for scent before styling it.

Susan came down the stairs to find Snake Catcher already waiting for her at the diningroom table. Painted Pony stuck her head out the kitchen doorway, and gasped when she discovered that Susan was wearing a pretty dress. Without letting Snake Catcher see her, Susan nervously motioned for Painted Pony to pull her head back into the kitchen. Susan and Snake Catcher sat for supper.

Snake Catcher eagerly began their conversation. "Different clothes."

"Yes."

"Trading post clothes?"

"Yes. I haven't bought any in a while, so I thought I would treat myself. I purchased them the same day you received yours."

"Good clothes," Snake Catcher complimented. The ritual of flattering a woman did not escape him.

"Thank you," Susan said shyly.

Tonight seemed different. There was an uncomfortable pause in the conversation. They were both feeling it, a distinct tension of attraction that neither was ready to own.

Susan told him, "I am glad you could stay longer. It's peculiar, but I feel as if I've already known you for a long time."

"That is good?"

"That is very good."

The enchanted mood was extended throughout supper. There was an atmosphere of awkwardness like one would feel on a first date. They were both experiencing the nervousness of expectations. During their concentration on Snake Catcher learning more English words, the pair enjoyed the only entirely unawkward moments of the meal. After dessert in the lounge, their stroll upstairs took them to Snake Catcher's bedroom. While walking in there with her, he glanced over at Susan and saw not the nurse she had been, but a woman now. As he perched on the bed and she redressed his wounds, Susan did not notice him looking at different areas of her body which were adorned by her new dress. She brewed Snake Catcher another batch of healing tea and set it on the table. Susan began to finish the day with "good-night," but he cut her off.

"Will see you early?"

"Sure, I'll be in to change your bandages before I start my chores."

"Hiya, early to watch sun wake."

Susan accepted Snake Catcher's invitation, smiling softly. "Okay."

Susan quietly left and walked to her bedroom to turn in for the night. She stopped to smell the intoxicating aroma of the flowers on the night stand. After dressing for bed, Susan ran her fingers around the tub, and blushed as if Snake Catcher were still soaking in it. Susan finished her day with a wide smile that brightened her face, then she dropped off to sleep.

Chapter 7

Susan and Snake Catcher were feeling less sheepish about spending time together, and they comfortably sat on the porch enjoying the sunrise, Day Fourteen away from the reservation. The brisk morning air lightly swirled the area as Susan draped her pashmina off her shoulders and across her torso freeing her hands to sketch the spectacular sunrise of a cloudless sky. Snake Catcher was drinking his healing tea and he occasionally puffed on his pipe. The dogs were lying down close by with perked ears scouting signs of any new exciting episodes to the day. As was their usual custom, the ranchhands rose early, as well. Buck was in the distance making repairs on the fence. The dogs jumped up and pranced around Larry as he ascended onto the scene riding his horse with a mule packed for a trip. He gave a quick and friendly wave and then he rode away from Susan and Snake Catcher.

"He is leaving?" probed Snake Catcher, as he looked at Susan.

Susan called the dogs back before commenting, "Larry has some time off, and he enjoys panning for gold in the hills. He doesn't ever find much, but he likes it anyway," Susan added, somewhat making fun of the prospector.

Snake Catcher quickly peered back at Larry as he was leaving, and continued, "Our hills, Paha Sapa?"

"Yes, I guess. Is that where your reservation is?"

"It was. Whites demand to buy what was not for sale. When we refused, they were stolen. They are sacred to us, center of our nation. They shelter us in winter with caves. They are the place we bury our dead. They were the beginning of life for us."

"I think they are mighty special, too. I sit here nearly every morning gazing at them because of their beauty. They are so inspirational that it makes each day productive. I finish up nearly every night with them in my view because of their tranquilness."

Snake Catcher gave an instinctual look of mistrust toward Larry. As Snake Catcher continued to explain the Lakota's accounts of the theft of Paha Sapa, Susan turned her focus from the eastern sunrise to Paha Sapa in their southeastern view. The moment was sadly turned from cheery to sorrowful. While Snake Catcher spoke his words in broken English, Susan inherently yet voicelessly filled the gaps between his manner of speech hearing an unmuddled interpretation from his recollection of events...

"The 1868 Treaty with our Lakota people was signed, promising Paha Sapa to our nation. Congress passed the 1872 Mining Act that stated an unlimited number of claims may be filed by prospectors on land in Paha Sapa that already belonged to the Lakota. When patents were granted, that land would be transferred to the miners.

"Son of the Morning Star invaded Paha Sapa in 1874. By the next year, President Grant offered purchase for the hills, which was rejected. Grant retaliated the refusal by forbidding the Lakota people from entering Paha Sapa. By 1876, Congress stated that the 1868 treaty-guaranteed allotments would *not* be provided until the Lakota agreed to sell the hills. That was known to the Lakota Nation as the 'Sell or Starve' option.

"In June, the Lakota and our allies defeated Son of the Morning Star at Little Bighorn. Since we received no provisions promised to us, we set out to hunt. When half of our Nation was away for the hunt to feed our families, another commission came to our villages. With less than ten percent of the Lakota Nation represented, an agreement was signed, understood to be a *lease* on the land. Article 12 of the treaty was violated stating that there must be *at least* three-fourths of all the adult male Natives to sign any agreement.

"Congress passed the Black Hills Act in 1877, unilaterally transferring Paha Sapa to the government, which completed the theft of our sacred land; the most grossly misused form of eminent domain in United States history only to gold-line the pockets of the White man. We predict that this will be known as a national disgrace and this unjust transaction will, in all likelihood, never be repeated to this degree. Generosity is in our nature. And because of it, that allowed these vigilante mercenaries to hold us at gunpoint to take our land.

"Paha Sapa was the beginning of time and place for the Lakota people when Inyan, a name meaning stone, was the creator of all we know and see. Inyan was our first God and our religion to whom we offer gratitude. But in his time, he was so lonesome that he detached a piece of himself to form Maka, who is the Goddess of the ground below, what you call your earth. Most of Inyan's powers had flowed away from him during this process that he fused and turned to rock. Streams and rivers were derived from his blood of greenish-blue. Skan, the sky God was then formed as our third God and to the highest degree of holiness in our world. When Maka tells Inyan that it is too dark and cold for her, he then created Anp, which is a form of daylight. Not being sufficient for Maka, he then created the sun above, giving us the God, Wi. Hanwi was formed the exact moment Skan was to form the night sun or what you call your moon and the one of fertility. Wohpe, or what you would call White Buffalo Calf Woman, is the daughter of Wi and Hanwi. I would like to tell you about White Buffalo Calf Woman a later day. This harmonious rock formation of Paha Sapa is the only place which deems suitable for us to etch the faces of our great chiefs someday, not to be marred and defaced by the White man."

Susan and Snake Catcher, now both in somber moods, strolled into the diningroom and sat. Rains Down brought in their breakfast while Snake Catcher continued fuming over the theft of the hills.

"No justice when thieving White men free to cross prairie, Lakota cannot go into our own Paha Sapa. Whites speak of freedom as something good." He pushed his plate to the side, feeling no appetite as he added, "There is no freedom in this country for Natives."

Susan felt compelled to offer, "Maybe we can find a solution to that. Maybe I can start by granting you freedom here. It would be somewhere to start."

Snake Catcher's mood turned from anger to sadness when reminded that he would not be staying. He did not want to leave his new friend. "We not permitted to live other than reservation."

"By whom? There must be a legal way you can stay. Would your lawyer friend know of a way? I'm sure he is an expert in Indian affairs."

"Only he would know."

"Would you want to stay? It would be trading one prison for another. You would probably still be bound by my boundary lines most of the time, a much smaller area of land than you have now."

Snake Catcher poetically commented, "With leg in trap, would one want barren land that could see for miles, or fruit of land at one's reach? Blue Coats kill most our Lakota villagers. Few of us left. No family remains to care for."

"Then I will send for your friend to help us?"

Snake Catcher graciously nodded as he made his way toward the front door for a view of the glorious hills. Susan had Rains Down summon Slim to send a telegram to the reservation to petition Earth Raven's presence to assist them with this legal issue. Susan did not feel much like eating either, and went on to begin her morning chores. Snake Catcher remained at the front door as Susan left, but he soon retreated upstairs to rest.

Susan was in the stables when a single gunshot was heard, and she recognized it coming from Sammy in the pasture. Susan, Buck and Ferdy inquisitively hurried out of the stables to see who was approaching the house. The trio then walked toward the house and strategically positioned themselves on the porch to greet their guests. As two Blue Coats rode up to them, the others could see that they were wearing their usual blue uniform decorated with metal pins and both wore hats garnished with a tassel dangling off one side. Each had saddlebags on their horses with various camping items along with a bedroll. Neither removed their hat during the exchange with Susan.

"Good afternoon. We are here to speak with the owner of this ranch," stated the private.

Susan promptly replied, "You are addressing her."

"Ma'am? *You* own this ranch?" the private asked with extreme disbelief, somewhat challenging her.

With her mistrust of Blue Coats at the surface, Susan curtly fired back, "Sir, state your business."

"Ma'am, we are from Fort Meade," stated the other soldier, a lieutenant. "We are here for the surrender of an Indian we believe you are harboring."

Susan responded with sarcasm, and meaningfully taunted: "You jocose? I harbor many Indians, which were you referring to?"

With a grimace, the private answered, "The Sioux Indian known as Snake Catcher. He had a scuffle near Fort Meade, and is in violation of his agreement. We believe he is here, and we have orders to take him back as our prisoner."

Both soldiers uninvitedly dismounted their horses. The lieutenant began retrieving shackles from his saddlebags. Just at that moment, Snake Catcher quietly made his way down the stairs and, unnoticed by the Blue Coats, appeared by the curtains in the window off the parlor. Only Susan, who glanced back at that window noticing the movement of the curtains, observed his arrival. Snake Catcher tipped his head toward the private as to indicate that the man who was on the right was the same one who beat him.

The conversation continued with Susan speaking firmly to them, and the Blue Coats halted. "Then I suggest you be on your way to obtain those *written* orders," she countered. "I assume you have none or you would have produced them by now. And while you are *flawlessly* upholding the law, find out who the soldiers were who illegally bludgeoned him within an inch of his life."

The private challenged Susan again. "Ma'am, do you have proof of this?"

"I surely do, Sir. I'm the one who treated his wounds, so I know they exist. And he says *you* were the one who did it."

The lieutenant was quick to confront Susan's accusations

regarding his comrade. "Ma'am, with all due respect, you weren't there. You don't know what went on."

"Well Sir, apparently neither were you, or you would have seen that his papers were in order." Susan assertively posed a question to the private. "Sir, can you read?"

"I don't know why that would make a difference; he charged us," the private blistered loudly.

"Sir, can you read?" Susan repeated, not allowing him to distract her with another allegation.

The private shrugged.

Susan abruptly continued, "I thought not because if you could, you would have known the same information that he knew; and that was he didn't have to charge anyone. This Lakota had legal passage to be there. And with not being able to read, how would you know whether he was or wasn't in violation of his agreement which brought you here today? Do you have any proof that he did anything wrong?"

The private looked to the lieutenant to lie for him. However, not having been there that day, the lieutenant shamefully shook his head. The private deflatedly shrugged again.

"No, I didn't think so. Get off my land and stay away unless you have proper authority to be here," Susan demanded.

"He is a fugitive, and we have the right to apprehend him," the private said as he took a step toward the house. Buck and Ferdy relocated themselves, blocking the steps and cocking their rifles. The dogs snarled at the Blue Coats baring their teeth.

Susan was quick to retaliate. "Oh Sir, I'm sure you didn't just threaten my men; that wouldn't be a prudent thing to do. Especially since you are on my land illegally. My men are very well paid, which makes them very loyal, and very deadly. Sirs, the next time you step foot on my land without proper authority, I'll instruct them to shoot off a piece of you where it won't grow back."

"At the least, you must give us a time when he will be returning to his reservation, which all Indians are required to do."

"I am knowledgeable in medicine, and I will decide that. Everyone from here to Deadwood City will vouch for my capabilities in this field. All I can tell you at this point, *gentlemen*, is that he will be able to travel when he has healed to *my* satisfaction. And that is all. Good day to you both."

Snake Catcher was seen smirking at the porch confrontation by Rains Down, now standing to the side of him also inquisitive about the encounter knowing Ferdy was out there. Snake Catcher had a look of retribution toward the soldiers. Both soldiers reluctantly mounted their horses and rode away while vowing to return for Snake Catcher with written orders.

Snake Catcher anxiously stepped into the foyer and met Susan at the door as she walked in. He eagerly responded, "You found trouble, maybe should return now."

"No matter, I'm always in trouble for helping people. You don't have to go if you don't want to; I won't let them hurt you. They are only here because they made a mistake and are covering it up. You will be safe here until you are healed."

"You are brave."

Susan smiled, and appeared invigorated from the fight with the soldiers. After so long, she now had a campaign in which to repay the Blue Coats for unwarrantedly killing her father and Hail Maker while lying to conceal their real reason for the massacre.

Susan's act of defiance to the Blue Coats on Snake Catcher's behalf was a major turning point for the Lakota warrior. In Snake Catcher's subconscious, he now felt he would be able to take the leap of faith necessary to believe that a White could be trusted to aid him with recapturing the holiness of his people's land.

Susan and her staff returned to their duties while Snake Catcher rested before supper. Her first chore would be to station Buck as a lookout in the pasture in case the Blue Coats returned.

That evening, Painted Pony brought out supper for Susan and Snake Catcher.

Knowing she was trying to be unassuming, Snake Catcher teased Painted Pony. "Are you woman of the house now?"

Susan smiled at Snake Catcher's sense of humor.

Painted Pony answered, "No, it is Rains Down's night off. It is my turn tonight."

Susan asked Painted Pony, "Have you done your studies for tomorrow?"

"Soon."

Susan countered, "*Now*. We can serve ourselves. Go. Learn. Be brilliant."

Painted Pony flirtingly smiled, and trotted off. Susan and

Snake Catcher finished their supper, and cheerfully cleared the table themselves.

Susan and Snake Catcher strolled out onto the porch, and sat with Paha Sapa in their view. They sipped their beverages, and discussed Paha Sapa's wildlife and beauty. Snake Catcher smoked. After a while, Susan and Snake Catcher said good-night. And as she left, he secretly watched her feminine movements walking away from him.

Chapter 8

Susan began her day at sunrise, sitting in her favorite rocking chair on the porch while sipping tea. This morning, as with many of her others, was spent attempting to capture the magnificent view of Paha Sapa on her sketch pad. The morning precipitation ricocheting off the hills formed the most spectacular rainbow of the season. Susan made several efforts to convey her perspective onto the paper, yet never completed an acceptable simile. Her staff and Snake Catcher were sleeping in, Day Fifteen away from the reservation.

Meanwhile on the reservation that morning, there was much chitchat perpetuating in their small wooden one-room telegraph office. The Natives were pleased to receive word that Snake Catcher had arrived at his destination alive. They were equally chatty that an invitation to the ranch had been extended to Earth Raven, and how he would soon be off on a new adventure. Earth Raven wasted no time in requesting permission from the upper echelon of Blue Coats to leave the reservation to join the fellowship at the Paradise Valley Ranch.

Later that morning after Susan had dressed for her daily chores, she headed out to retrieve her horse from the stables. It was at this time that Carter's men initiated a stampede of Susan's cattle out in the pasture.

Susan and Buck were unaware of the oncoming disaster. From the window of the balcony off his bedroom, Snake Catcher secretly watched the two mount their horses, then head out. He was observing the relationship between them. Noting their ease with each other, Snake Catcher was unsure if he had misread Susan's intentions of wanting to become closer friends with him, or if she was promised to Buck. White culture still perplexed him.

Susan and Buck were thirty feet out from the stables on their horses before they discovered an approaching herd traveling directly toward them and the house. They found it difficult to believe that the billowing cloud of dust they were seeing was from the herd because they neither heard nor felt the rumbling of the stampede. Simultaneously, Snake Catcher's keen senses felt the thunder of their hooves before the others in the house. Even with the pain of his injuries, he zealously ran down the stairs to warn the household to be prepared. Snake Catcher's yelling brought Cook, Painted Pony and Rains Down in to gather, and they huddled together in the center of the down-stairs.

Snake Catcher stepped out onto the porch to judge where the herd would head. He stood stoic–the perfect courageous warrior in the face of danger. He watched as Buck pushed Susan's horse back into the stables, and out of the way of the fast-approaching stampede. The cattle headed straight for the house, passing through the house's barrier fence and tearing down the gate with great force. An attempt was made by Ferdy to make his way around the herd in order to direct them away from the house area. He was dreadfully unsuccessful, and fell off his horse, immediately being unmercifully trampled by some of the cattle. Three cows managed to jump up onto the porch, and as Snake Catcher stepped back inside the house, they maneu-vered their way around the rocking chairs and two small tables, never spilling a drop of tea in a cup left behind by Susan. Another four cows were cut off and darted behind the house before meeting up with the herd on the other side. The destruc-tion of the area lasted several minutes before the painfully loud thundering forces finally faded into a muffled rumble.

The ground was hideously torn up all around the house. The wagon was tipped over and sported a damaged wheel. The stench from the mostly demolished outdoor facility could already be smelled from a great distance.

Buck finally released the reins on Susan's horse, which allowed her to emerge from the stables. As a guardian-figure, Susan was feeling a responsibility to help her people. As the dust was clearing, Snake Catcher stepped back onto the porch and discovered Ferdy sprawled on the ground and raced to him. Susan sped over to them on Sparks, and dauntlessly slid down off of her horse to analyze Ferdy's gruesome disfigurements. Her evaluation was that, although Ferdy was lacerated in various places, he showed no signs of broken bones. After Susan determined that Ferdy was not injured badly enough to summon the county doctor, Doc Brown, she instructed Buck, Slim and Sammy to ride out to get the herd under control. She told them to move quickly before the cattle hurt themselves further or would break through the perimeter fence. If Susan's cattle were to wander onto Carter's property, retrieving them would be an insurmountable task.

Buck, Slim and Sammy rode off as Susan and Snake Catcher helped Ferdy up to the apothecary room. Ferdy sat down on the cot as Snake Catcher backed out of the room, giving Susan space to treat Ferdy's injuries. Susan brewed a tea for her ranchhand to help with the bruising and the pain. Cook, Painted Pony and Rains Down joined Snake Catcher outside the room to wait for news about Ferdy's condition. Rains Down appeared especially worried.

Susan determined that Ferdy's wounds would not improve any faster with sutures than bandages, so she cleaned his bloody cuts and covered them. She then opened the partially closed door to speak with those gathered. "He'll be fine. He has some healing to do, though."

Rains Down did not wait for consent for her admittance and hurried into the room to Ferdy's side. She worriedly empathized, "Ferdy, you were so brave. Are you all right?"

The gatherers looked in from the hallway on the scene and smiled as they witnessed Ferdy milking the incident to get Rains Down's sympathy, pretending he was worse than he was.

Susan turned her attention to the others and asked, "Is everyone here all right?" They all confirmingly nodded. Cook and Painted Pony went downstairs, and Rains Down helped Ferdy to the staff quarters. Susan then turned to Snake Catcher. "You did good protecting my staff. Thank you."

Snake Catcher, seemingly somewhat possessive, stood close to Susan while commenting, "Buck did good protecting you."

Susan smiled and demurringly nodded, not knowing how else to respond to Snake Catcher's concern for her. She recognized it to be concern from a friend, and not just from someone whose job it was to protect her.

Buck *was paid* to keep his boss safe. Of course, Buck was also overprotective toward Susan because of his propensity for protecting any woman in trouble. In her life, it was often Susan though, who was the nurturing caregiver to the people around her. Not since being under her parents' umbrella of safety had she felt exclusively sheltered. As fiercely independent as Susan was, she found herself unexpectedly attracted to the thought of someone with a personal connection caring for her.

Susan withdrew herself, and trotted downstairs to check on the state of the house. She found Painted Pony sweeping the porch and dusting the chairs. Sammy returned with Slim, while Buck remained in the pasture to tend to the herd. Sammy then helped with the cleanup with the lifting of the heavy items. Soon Snake Catcher ascended on the scene to help Sammy. At the yard's perimeter, Slim was gathering the broken pieces of the fence. After a while, Cook brought drinks out to the workers, then assisted Painted Pony in cleaning the porch area, stretching the entire width of the house. Moments later, Ferdy and Rains Down emerged to do effortless straightening. They were all working in silence yet in total concert.

By midmorning, Buck had returned to the house from the pasture and made his report to Susan. "The herd is under control. From what I could see, most of the cattle look to be uninjured despite their trying day."

Susan was understandably relieved.

Buck and Susan joined the clean-up procession outside. Buck, in a gesture appreciative by all, began reassembling the outdoor facility. Cook tirelessly brought food and drinks to everyone. By mid-afternoon, the group took a break. Susan assessed the damages, and added needed items to her monthly supply list. She also determined that the stampede put her back three days worth of chores from her ranchhands.

During the late afternoon, Susan informed Snake Catcher that his stitches would need to be removed. Snake Catcher amicably agreed, not entirely knowing what it entailed, never having stitches before.

In the apothecary room, Susan instructed Snake Catcher to remove his shirt, and lie down on the cot. She offered him a stick to bite on over her question: "This will probably hurt. Would you like a stick?"

Snake Catcher slightly scowled and grunted it away as if his manhood was in question. *"Hiya."*

Susan tossed the stick aside and began. She cut the first stitch and expeditiously yanked it out. Snake Catcher lightly gasped but did not speak. Susan methodically continued until all the stitches were extracted. She cleaned and redressed the wound. Snake Catcher had been expressionless during the procedure, keeping the face of a fearless warrior. Afterwards, he sat up and donned his shirt before making a joke. "That is all?"

Susan laughed out loud at Snake Catcher's sense of humor. "Yes, that is all."

Without missing a beat, Snake Catcher led into the next topic. "Buck be good husband to you?"

Susan looked up at Snake Catcher dumbfoundedly. "Where did that come from?" she asked.

"You spend time with him. Guard you with his life. Good husband."

Susan shyly lowered her eyes toward her medical equipment while disassembling her procedural area over refuting the idea. "He works for me, and we have to spend time together. He guards me because that is his job. Perhaps he will make a good husband someday, but not for me." Susan nonabrasively ended the subject. "You need to rest now. You don't want to reopen your wound."

Susan finished cleaning the area and began to excuse herself. Looking up from the fresh bandage, Snake Catcher spoke to delay her departure. "Will we eat supper together?"

Wearing a soft demure smile, Susan answered, "Yes, I look forward to it."

Susan pirouetted and left to return to her chores.

Just before supper, Susan enthusiastically placed the final touches onto her ensemble in her bedroom, and then left for downstairs. Snake Catcher was waiting chivalrously for her in the diningroom. They greeted each other and sat down. Rains Down and Painted Pony spied in on them from the kitchen.

Painted Pony gossiped to Rains Down, "Do you think they fancy each other?"

With a hidden cheerful glint in her eye, and a dishtowel camouflaging the fluorescent smile on her face, Rains Down abruptly retorted, "That is none of our business."

During their supper date together, Susan and Snake

Catcher were much more relaxed with one another than in past meetings; less obstruction was between them. Their friendship was moving forward, though somewhat slowly, and they knew they wanted to spend time together. Susan and Snake Catcher spoke of the unfortunate trouble with the cattle. The two spoke of how well Snake Catcher was healing. There was also talk of what the future may hold for them when Earth Raven arrived to discuss Snake Catcher's options of living at the ranch.

After supper, Susan stood out on the porch sipping her beverage and frowning at the mess from the stampede. She then looked toward Paha Sapa with an endearing grin.

With a beaming smile on his face, Earth Raven stood in the telegraph office on the reservation. He was reading a message granting him permission to leave the region. He sent a telegraph message to the trading post in Sundance notifying Susan of his arrival date.

Chapter 9

That morning, Day Sixteen away from the reservation, Snake Catcher believed he felt well enough to mount his horse for a ride. He donned his bow and grabbed his saddlebags before meandering over to the stables. There, he found Buck and Sammy fixing the wheel from the broken wagon. Painted Pony was loitering nearby petting the horses. A smile came over her face when she saw Snake Catcher, and the dogs pranced around him. Snake Catcher spoke to Painted Pony as if to practice his much improving English.

"How are you?"

Snake Catcher grinned at her as Painted Pony shyly parroted back at him. "Good, how are you?"

"Do you work *here* now?"

"Yes, with my dad. Do you?"

Without answering, Snake Catcher bantered, "Why are you called 'Painted Pony'?"

Painted Pony showed Snake Catcher a small birth mark on her shoulder that resembled a Pony, then echoed, "Why do they call you 'Snake Catcher'?" Painted Pony did not wait for a counter-response and ran off, flirting and laughing.

Snake Catcher turned his attention to his horse, which Buck was brushing, and commented, "He is fat."

"We feed the horses well here. I hope you don't mind that I was caring for him."

"Hiya, ah, no. That is good."

Snake Catcher mounted his horse, and the horse appeared frisky. Buck concluded, "I think he missed you. Do you need me to go with you?"

"No. Thank. You."

"Have a good ride."

Snake Catcher headed out toward the pasture for a short excursion. To his surprise, the dogs trailed behind him. The Lakota found his way down toward the south end of the river, as he had always felt harmonized from a rippling waterway. The current there was swift, and the water, crystal blue. He removed his clothes, and went for a swim. Killer and Coyote wrestled together, and tried getting close to the water, but were shy about getting in. Snake Catcher spent a few hours away from the ranch reconnecting with nature.

Meanwhile, Susan remembered a nostalgia treasure from her past. Hail Maker had given it to Jacob in exchange for his English lessons. After he and her father were killed, Susan had placed the item in the music parlor cabinet because its presence was just too painful to be a daily reminder. Hail Maker had dedicated many hours to the making of the decorative smoking pipe, including carving designs all around the handle. Since her father had never taken up smoking, the pipe had not been used; she nearly forgot its existence.

While Susan was dusting off the pipe, Sammy fired a warning shot from the pasture to alert them that someone was approaching the house. Snake Catcher heard the gunshot from his position by the river and quickly maneuvered himself back toward the house on his horse. He returned to find Susan standing on the porch in a dispute with the man who shot him a week ago. Snake Catcher was startled to see that she was alone, and looked around for Buck and the others. He slipped off of his horse and headed toward the kitchen entrance in the back of the house to avoid a confrontation. The dogs stayed close to him. Snake Catcher dropped his saddlebags just before entering the back kitchen door.

The front porch scene continued with Carter sitting on his horse and two of his ranchhands hovering beside him on theirs. His ranchhands were of Carter's stature, and they had a reputation of being ominous in order to please their boss.

Susan confidently said, "Get off my land, Carter."

Carter was smirking while countering, "I'm just being neighborly, and making a right fine offer for this tumbleweed barren deformity that's been infected by you running some sort of dormitory for wayward Ingins and such."

Sarcastically, Susan snapped, "And I suppose you had nothing to do with this deformity yesterday? You own half the county; why would you be interested in this place? It wouldn't even complement your land, Carter."

"I'm not *that* interested. I just thought I would do you a favor, you being a woman and all, having to work the land all by yourself. It can be very *dangerous* out here, and I wouldn't want anything to happen to you. Shouldn't you be off having babies somewhere?"

"I'm not all by myself. Where did you get an idea like that?"

Snake Catcher was the first to appear. He was upstairs on the balcony in plain sight. The Native had his knife extracted from its holder and behind his back–ready for battle. His bow, accompanied by arrowhead-tipped branches, stood at the ready just inside of the French doors. At that moment, Snake Catcher would have liked nothing better than to cut through the man who shot him unwarrantedly.

Buck and Slim were the next to come into view, stepping out from around the sides of the house holding scatter guns. Ferdy emerged on his horse from the stables accompanying a shotgun.

Carter looked around to each of them before glancing back at Susan when making his offer. "I'll double whatever she is paying you if you come work for me, boys."

The ranchhands chuckled while shaking their heads in dissent, out of loyalty to Susan. The men also knew Carter was evil enough to just fire them as soon as they showed up for work the next day.

"You got your answer all the way around. Now leave," she told him.

"Does *he* speak English? I haven't heard from him yet." Carter smirked at Snake Catcher while his adversary did not take his cold deadly stare off of Carter or make a sound.

"I hardly think you'll get the loyalty of a man you shot," said Susan, speaking for Snake Catcher.

"Shot? I didn't shoot anyone, no *man* that is."

Snake Catcher began to feel invigorated. After so long, Carter had rekindled the warrior in him.

Susan reiterated, "Get off my land and stay off. If you ever come back without an invitation, I will take that as a direct threat and I'll shoot you on sight."

Carter snickered at them as he turned his horse to leave, initiating his men's departure as well.

After Carter's cabal was escorted off of the property by Slim and Ferdy, Susan's two ranchhands returned to inform her of his repetitive threats. She thanked them all for their steadfastness. Susan walked upstairs where she found Snake Catcher. "Are you all right?"

"That is question for you."

"I'm fine. Up until he shot you, he had just been a bag of hot air." When Snake Catcher looked puzzled at Susan's statement, she clarified, "He wants my land but I won't sell. Much like your Paha Sapa. He could probably make it very difficult for me since he owns most of the businesses in Deadwood City, including a partnership in the feed store, but he hasn't yet. I have provisions to last me four to six months if he does. That will be enough time to get my supplies elsewhere. I have some pull in this area as well. I own the telegraph office that also employs a banker in Deadwood City, and I can cut off future bankrolls to many of the people in several surrounding counties if they side against me. I figure that's why he hasn't made his move yet."

"You are thinker. You are also powerful woman?"

"Powerful enough for now."

Snake Catcher turned his attentions to his prior whereabouts from his day away. "Am hunter, brought supper." He motioned downstairs.

Snake Catcher and Susan walked to the back kitchen door while encountering Cook in their path. The hunter pulled a dead rabbit from his saddlebags.

Somewhat startled, Susan asked, "You killed a rabbit?"

"Am hunter, will provide when can."

"We have plenty to eat, and we get our meat from town."

With a brief nod, Snake Catcher concluded, "Am hunter."

Susan forced a smile as Cook was salivating over the catch. Since none of the ranchhands were hunters, her usual preparations only included meats delivered from the trading post that had been cured beyond toxic.

At suppertime, Snake Catcher and Susan were prepared the rabbit for supper. Cook was beaming while standing in the doorway of the kitchen waiting for the two of them to comment on the meal.

Faking her joy with somewhat of a crooked smile, Susan complimented, "Very nice, Cook."

Cook appreciatively nodded for the comment and retreated into the kitchen. Snake Catcher unnoticeably grinned at Susan's squeamishness.

After supper, Snake Catcher and Painted Pony strolled out onto the porch while Susan made a stop in the music room. After Susan joined them on the porch, she pulled out Hail Maker's pipe from under her shawl, and then presented it to Snake Catcher.

"I forgot I had this. It was given to my father from your brother. I want you to have it. Hail Maker put many hours into the making of it, and it would be a shame if it were not used."

Snake Catcher's face abruptly showed a flood of feeling welling up inside of him. He was without words for quite some time. Susan smiled at Snake Catcher's tender feelings for his brother and sipped her tea. Snake Catcher proudly lit the pipe and smoked. Painted Pony filled the night air with questions for Susan about why the stars were so bright.

Snake Catcher was intrigued by Painted Pony's questions and offered, "They are bright to guide us. That was what a sister and her seven brothers do for us."

"Who? *Tell* me."

Painted Pony sat by Snake Catcher's feet, and listened as he began his story. "Quill Work Girl and her Seven Star Brothers. Star Woman, as she was known after reaching sky, was brightest star in sky. It was their destiny to burn bright for us, to find our way when we are lost."

Susan and Painted Pony had listened diligently to Snake Catcher's ancestral tale. Bonding was inevitable as both of the ladies were enchanted by Snake Catcher and his story, a story that had been passed down through generations of the Lakota people, including from a long ago friend of hers. After the story, the trio regrettably said good-night and went their separate ways.

Later that night in his bedroom, Snake Catcher heard the ranchhands coming back from a Saturday night in Sundance. He walked over to the window, and disgustingly shook his head at the drunken men. "Foolish juice" was all he uttered.

Buck had brought back a message from the trading post's telegraph office and set it on the diningroom table for Susan to view the next morning. It was word from Earth Raven.

Chapter 10

After receiving the telegram retrieved from the table that was sent from Earth Raven, Susan stepped into the newly repaired wagon for her weekly trek to attend Sunday church services. Painted Pony, Rains Down, Ferdy and Buck escorted her. The group rode past the stables where Slim and Snake Catcher were, only the two men were too distracted with the horses to see them leave, Day Seventeen away from the reservation.

Susan spent another inspirational Sunday with the other church parishioners singing in church. After arriving back at the Paradise Valley Ranch in mid-afternoon, Rains Down and Ferdy went about their daily routines as Buck walked Susan toward the cemetery with Painted Pony trailing behind. Snake Catcher was poised at the parlor window downstairs cautiously keeping his feelings discreet in watching Buck and Susan walk away together toward the graveyard. The Lakota curiously watched as Susan stood over the tombstones, putting flowers on them. Buck removed his hat while he and Painted Pony stood close by but they did not intrude on her time there. After paying their respects to the dead, they all walked back to the house together.

Susan and Painted Pony joined Larry on the porch, who had just returned from his time off. Nearby, Buck began tending to the reconstruction of the garden. Larry excitedly blurted out the news that he had brought some gold back with him.

"Did you strike it rich, Larry?" teased Susan.

"Not this time, Miss Susan, but I did find some. See here?"

As Susan and Painted Pony looked at his haul of only a few nuggets, Snake Catcher stepped out onto the porch. Larry

gave a quick show to Snake Catcher, and then took his belongings to the staff quarters before he planned to put in a few hours
of work. Painted Pony saw the sorrow on Snake Catcher's face,
and walked into the house, giving way to the inevitable adult
conversation.

Susan looked at Snake Catcher with concern as he
reacted to the scene. *"That* was why we lost our land," he
declared.

"I am sincerely sorry," Susan replied. She offered a
compassionate look to Snake Catcher before exiting from the
porch area and entering the house. Snake Catcher stood there
awhile and watched Larry ride out toward the pasture, then
gazed out at Paha Sapa with ongoing despair.

At supper in the diningroom, Susan and Snake Catcher's faces
were sober and the mood was somber.

Susan tried what she could to bring him out of his
depression over the mammoth loss to his people, but Snake
Catcher had retreated deep inside of himself. The silence
between them was agonizingly deafening. The only break in the
muteness was the sound of Ferdy's voice surfacing on the scene.

Ferdy whispered, "Miss Susan, would you know where
Rains Down would be?"

"She is in the kitchen, Ferdy."

"Thank you, ma'am."

After supper, Susan stood alone on the porch sipping her
beverage, looking out at Paha Sapa. Simultaneously, Snake
Catcher stood alone looking out of his bedroom window at the
same view. He did not know how to explain his sadness and
anger surrounding the raping and pillaging of his homeland; she
was void of knowing how to help with such a large issue that
was so close to his heart. Even though the communication gap
between them was widening, they had a common goal.

Before turning in for the evening, Susan constructed a
letter:

"Dear President Arthur, I want to first thank you
for taking the time to read my letter. I am Susan
Paradise, a landowner and rancher near Sundance in the Wyoming Territory. I am writing
you today to discuss the treaty between the
United States and the different tribes of the
Sioux Indians orchestrated in 1868. There is still

a Civil War raging in this country, Sir. The war over land and of freedom. I am aware that you were associated with President Grant, and he appointed you to be Collector of the Port of New York. I am also aware that you were a lawyer and a teacher, giving continual efforts of service to help those of a lesser education.

"I am sure you were apprised that the Lakota land under this treaty was taken from them in a process beginning in 1875 by President Grant when he forbade the Sioux from entering into their Black Hills. You Sir, as a lawyer, would know that this was blatant thievery of their land that they hold sacred.

"Clearly you know the importance of an education in this country, having graduated from college *and* by being a teacher. I am sure that your former students have benefitted from all that this country's educational institutions had to offer. Can we say the same for those locked up on a continually shrinking reservation?

"Please consider the educational welfare, promised land rights, and religious freedoms of these people as well with returning what does not belong to the United States government, the Black Hills–the Sioux's *house of worship*. If just the land that is being held in Federal position would be returned at this time, it would be of great consideration to them. Thank you very much. Respectfully, Susan E. Paradise, Sundance, Wyoming Territory."

Susan was not feeling confident concerning President Arthur's willingness to listen to her plea, especially considering his reputation of not being a fan of reform as with the former president, Hayes. Susan put pen to paper once again while writing a similar letter to them who would be more responsive to continue their cause. She went on to thank President Hayes for reading her letter, then wrote of her plea to help the Lakota with their monumental task of reclaiming Paha Sapa for their future generations.

"I do not hold much hope for our success in President Arthur because of his adversity to reform in this country, that is why I am writing to you. I am aware that you were an officer, one of high regard. I am also aware that you offered this country new reform with the changing times. You had done much for the dignity of your House in such a short time, proven with the abolishment of alcohol from the White House. I am asking that you consider helping with the reform of the Sioux people as well.

"Clearly, you know the importance of an education in this country, having graduated from Harvard Law School *and* being married to the first President's wife to graduate from college. I am sure that your children have benefitted from all that this country's educational institutions had to offer. Can we say the same for those confined to a consistently diminishing reservation?

"Please consider taking your passion of reform a step further with assistance for the return of the Black Hills to their lawful owners."

Susan signed it, folded the letters, and then inserted them into their respective envelopes addressed to Washington and Ohio before retiring for the evening.

Chapter 11

The mood was tensely heavy. Because of his ongoing sorrow and anger about the theft of the hills, Snake Catcher did not emerge much during daylight hours, on Day Eighteen away from the reservation. Unavoidable reminders seemed to be all around him. Snake Catcher was profoundly grateful for all of his new friendships, yet found it difficult to shake the loner in him acquired during his years of solitude on the reservation after his wife died. He stood wearily looking out his bedroom window at Paha Sapa–metaphorically within his reach. Susan sat on the porch consuming her tea and sketching how the morning dew would slowly rise off of the hills. Painted Pony sat attentively watching her. The morning was chilly; however, the sun was rising to rapidly warm the day.

Just before midday, Buck and Rains Down were in the staff lounge separately eating their lunch. The room was bright with flowers in a vase on the table. This dining table was large with several chairs situated around, and it was positioned in the middle of the room. The table was not like that of the main house; however, it was adequate for their needs.

Rains Down seemed dispirited, which brought Buck to kindly ask, "Are you not feeling well?"

Buck was taken back when she asked, "Where do you find the courage to step in and help women in distress?"

A slow steam of anger began bubbling up inside of Buck thinking that perhaps Rains Down was being abused by someone. "It is not courage, it is more about guilt. I cannot stand to see any man beat up or abuse a woman, and it's because I wasn't old enough to help my mother when my father beat her."

Looking off in the distance through the opened door, Rains Down remarked, "As did my father."

Buck looked up from his meal with surprise. The air was heavy for a moment, then Rains Down added, "That was why I left my family because I could not save my mother, and she could not save herself. I wanted something different for myself, something better."

"And is the life of a single woman better for you?"

"Yes. I sought out this job here so that I would not have to marry to survive as my mother did."

"Where are your parents now?"

"He finally succeeded" was all she would offer about the topic. Rains Down then made a declaration. "I will probably never marry."

"Not all men hit. How do you know that would happen to you?" he asked, gently defending the softer side of his gender, and from knowing his friend, Ferdy, was sweet on her.

"How do I know it wouldn't? My father was a kind person before they were married, as told by my grandparents."

"All I can tell you is that not all men abuse women," Buck assured her. "All you have to do is tell me if anyone *ever* hurts you, and they will have to answer to me," Buck added firmly.

Rains Down smiled appreciatively. She was still not entirely convinced that she would never marry. Rains Down needed so desperately to feel safe by having a single life away from what took her mother's life, but she could not help how her beliefs were detouring because of Ferdy. She liked him, and all of the wishing in the world was not going to change that.

Buck and Rains Down made pleasantries before parting to continue their chores.

Later that afternoon, while Buck was rebuilding the barrier-fence gate that the stampede had brought down, Susan went to speak with him. "Hello, Buck. What will it take to get the gate working again?"

"Hello. It will have to be entirely rebuilt. Even the nails are bent beyond use. The cattle did a perfect job of destroying it."

"Do we have the supplies to complete the project?"

"Yes, I have what I need. It's just going to take a while

to get things back the way they were."

"Yes, thank you Buck."

Susan had far more on her mind than just the gate, and was saying yes to much more than the rebuilding of it. The return of Paha Sapa to its rightful owners would also take time. What Susan did not possess, was the time she needed to pursue its return before Snake Catcher's presence would be demanded back at the reservation. She did not know if his friend, Earth Raven, would be able to help them and time was running out for her. Susan briskly walked over to the stables where she found Slim. She instructed him to take her presidential letters into Sundance to mail.

Simultaneously, Snake Catcher, who had seated himself on the back steps, was glumly sharpening his knife. Painted Pony sat in silence watching him.

Shortly thereafter, Cook called Painted Pony into the kitchen. "Come child. It is time to do your chores."

Once in the kitchen, Painted Pony asked Cook, "Why aren't they speaking?"

Cook replied, "Sometimes people need to be silent to hear others."

"But no one is talking for anyone to hear anything."

"Yes child, but there is still communication."

Painted Pony looked undeniably puzzled.

After a somewhat silent supper that evening, Snake Catcher once again stood looking out his bedroom window at Paha Sapa while Susan sat on the porch sipping her tea insightfully studying that same view. Cook came out to the porch, greeted Susan, then parked herself in a nearby rocking chair. "Nice evening."

"Yes," Susan responded.

"Not too many bugs out tonight."

"No."

"You have a heavy heart tonight?"

"No, not really. Some things are just out of my control, and all I want to do is help."

"Some things are our choices, and some things are forced upon us. I see only choices here."

"So why does it feel like sadness is being forced upon me?"

"Sadness should be used sparingly. One never knows

when they will need their strength to escape life's hardships. What's forced is sadness from a loved one's death, like when I lost my husband."

"What *did* happen to your husband, Cook?"

"My husband fought in the Mexican War, under protest. We wanted to flee to Texas but he was coerced into fighting by the Mexican government. They threatened to kill him if he didn't, and he died in the war anyway."

"I'm sorry. Do you miss him?"

"Yes."

"Don't you want to find someone again to be in your life?"

"All I want in life now is for my only son to get married and give me a hundred grandchildren running about."

Imagining that Rains Down might be Ferdy's wife someday, Susan slightly smiled. "I'm sure his wife would have something else to say about that."

Cook grunted, "Not likely." She paused before adding, "You are young. You will need to live a life first before you can stop having one." Cook stood up without any more conversation and stepped into the house. Susan sat alone for a spell as she pondered the profoundness of what Cook had said to her, before turning in that night.

Chapter 12

Snake Catcher began his day by standing a while gazing out his bedroom window at Paha Sapa, Day Nineteen away from the reservation. Sadness still so haunted him that he could hardly be seen in the company of others. The only motivating factor that would bring him out of his room was the hope of his old friend helping him to remain on the ranch in order to make a better fight to regain Paha Sapa for his people. Susan was also in his thoughts for wanting his peace of mind about the subject.

Susan was daintily pacing the porch as she sipped her tea. Merely looking out at the blackish-green hills of Paha Sapa brought empowerment to her, igniting enthusiasm within her spirit while conjuring optimistic aspirations of what the day would bring. If she were to be a Lakota advocate, she would have to fight hard for the impetuous stability of her new friend; showing her worthiness of Snake Catcher's people.

Susan's first chore of the day would take her to the kitchen. "Hello Cook. The guest that we will be having for lunch today will be staying into tomorrow."

"Very good, Miss Susan. What would you like for the menu?"

"I will leave that up to you. You are always much better at that. Thank you, Cook."

Susan left to carry out her second chore. She met up with Buck on the porch. "Hello Buck. I have a job for you today. Please go into Sundance and wait for Snake Catcher's friend, Earth Raven. He will be arriving today and needs someone to guide him back to the ranch."

"I'll leave right away. Anything else I can get for you

while I'm there?"

"No Buck, that will be all, thank you."

Susan continued her chores with the completion of last minute tasks before their guest's arrival.

Around noon, Earth Raven had arrived at the ranch. Susan, Snake Catcher and Earth Raven made friendly greetings as they walked into the lounge. Susan was elated when she observed Snake Catcher wearing his first smile in days. Earth Raven presented Susan with a gift wrapped inside of a canvas cloth. Also with Earth Raven was a brown-paper wrapped package for Snake Catcher. This package was filled with some of Snake Catcher's belongings from the reservation that Earth Raven anticipated he would want. Earth Raven told Susan that the women in his village began working on her gift when they heard Snake Catcher would be allowed to visit the ranch. Even without the benefit of an introduction, Susan had become somewhat of a celebrity to them, being the first White person they had befriended. She received a beautiful Native dress with brightly colored beads dangling from it. Susan felt honored.

Painted Pony did not waste any time familiarizing herself with the new arrival as she stuck her head out of the kitchen to see the trio in the diningroom. She was smitten with Earth Raven the moment she first laid eyes on him. Earth Raven's deep dark twenty-two-year-old eyes dazzled Painted Pony. He was nearly as tall to that of Snake Catcher; however, he had a slimmer frame. Painted Pony had not seen anyone with his nationality of that age and stature before, living in a mostly White world. Painted Pony knew of what he spoke, being an educated person herself, and Earth Raven's intellect fascinated her. Nevertheless, she was, in fact, a teenager, and much younger than Earth Raven in maturity and in life's experiences.

Rains Down pulled Painted Pony back into the kitchen and told her to stop pestering them; but when Rains Down was in the diningroom performing her duties, Painted Pony popped her head back out to gawk at Earth Raven.

In the diningroom, Susan spoke to Earth Raven of how Snake Catcher was shot by her neighbor and accosted by the Blue Coats, and she wasted no time discussing the matter at hand. Susan grilled Earth Raven about what Snake Catcher's legal stance was for the scuffle at Fort Meade, along with being able to stay at the Paradise Valley Ranch indefinitely. "I fear he will not make it back to the reservation alive with these two soldiers gunning for him. They were humiliated by not being able to apprehend him, which makes them very dangerous."

Earth Raven empathized with Snake Catcher's situation and gave them counsel. "I trust I can make the legal standing that he believed his life was in danger. Therefore, Snake Catcher would not be charged with a crime. Unquestionably, he did comply with the order fully."

"Yes, and he has me, along with my staff, as witnesses to his injuries."

Earth Raven continued, "Snake Catcher did arrive at his scheduled destination, and you did notify the authorities of his whereabouts through the telegraph system. Consequently, he cannot be considered a fugitive." Earth Raven paused, then thoughtfully added: "You are right, those men will be after him. We have much experience with men like them. Also, Snake Catcher has been in prison, and they will be harder on him even without giving him legal punishment. The Blue Coats are biased toward Snake Catcher where anyone else would be blameless. However, I have seen a similar situation before, and believe there *is* a way that he can stay here at the ranch and be safe." Earth Raven looked at Snake Catcher while continuing to address Susan's concerns. "He can be married to a property owner."

Snake Catcher did not waste any time vehemently opposing the suggestion, and stood during his protest, yelling, "Hiya! Hiya! That cannot be asked of Susan!"

Earth Raven motioned for Snake Catcher to be reseated as the Counselor made his rebuttal in the Lakota language for only Snake Catcher's comprehension. Snake Catcher complied and sat but was hesitantly uneasy about the topic. "There is no other way that I know of that would be this immediate. You know what the White man's government thinks of you. It would take years to gain freedom like this. You are my friend, and you deserve some peace and freedom."

Not knowing what Earth Raven had explained to Snake Catcher, Susan responded to Snake Catcher's last statement. "You did not ask me, that is to be my decision; I have no worries with it. It is not about loss to me but honor to our families; I would have sacrificed *more* than my freedom to complete this honor. Is that not what you said to me about the book? Was there a word for *I* when we suffered tragedy here with the stampede, or finding you wounded? No, everyone pitched in. I have made my choice. I, too, am stubborn."

Earth Raven sheepishly smiled at Susan's tenacity in standing up to the great warrior so early in their acquaintance. Earth Raven only would have approached the stance conservatively toward Snake Catcher. An ambush of conspiracy was afoot to make Snake Catcher realize that the marriage plan was in his best interest.

Snake Catcher worriedly responded to Susan's statement. "This is more trouble than you need." He then turned his attention to Earth Raven, somewhat scolding him for the trickery advice. "We do not wish trouble on Wasu Kage friend."

Susan woundedly reacted, "Is that how you see me? Just as your brother's friend? I thought I was friend to Zuzeca Wawoyuspa as well. And I was raised to defend and protect my friends when they are in need of my help."

"Am friend to you," Snake Catcher clarified, regretting his negligent remark. But before he could protest further, Susan ended the disharmony.

"Then it is settled."

Earth Raven noted, "There is danger for Snake Catcher. We must move quickly."

Susan soon instructed Rains Down to sound the bell summoning Slim and Larry. When they arrived, Susan instructed Slim to go for a Lakota Holyman who Earth Raven knew lived nearby, and sent Larry for the local preacher from her church. Susan seemed calmly in control of the events, but Snake Catcher still appeared uneasy surrounding the decision. He knew all too well the trouble the Blue Coats could cause Susan. Snake Catcher could not stay in one place for very long, being restless, and he impulsively paced the perimeter of the room. Earth Raven looked on with budding apprehension, as he knew that trait in Snake Catcher.

After lunch, Snake Catcher and Earth Raven retired to the porch outside and out of the way of those preparing for the ceremony inside. They spoke their words in Lakota, assumingly to passerbys to catch up on all the news back at the reservation; however, it was to mask their conversation from those within earshot of them. They spoke mainly about the asset of Susan's strength of fighting for worthy causes.

Rains Down and Painted Pony were upstairs excitedly

dressing Susan for the ceremony. Cook was in the kitchen preparing refreshments to serve after the ceremony and a feast for their celebratory supper. Ferdy was in the pasture tending to the cattle. Buck was gathering chairs and setting up the wedding area. Sammy was finishing the stable chores as Slim and Larry returned with the Lakota Holyman and the Preacher.

Snake Catcher wore his traditional clothes that Earth Raven had brought for him. Susan wore a plain white dress with a lace shawl from her mother's wedding dress material that had been made years earlier for such an occasion. She held a bundle of sensuously intoxicating flowers. As the ceremony began in the lounge, Earth Raven and Buck stood behind the couple as their witnesses. Everyone from the ranch, except Ferdy still overseeing the herd, gathered in the foyer and watched as Susan and Snake Catcher were married.

The Lakota Holyman recited a prayer in his language, as did the Preacher. They then performed their respective ceremonies simultaneously. Neither Holyman spoke much to anyone, other than just doing their jobs, as if they did not condone the interracial marriage. The others in attendance did not give the wedding pair's differences consideration because of the equality that had always been shown by Susan to her staff regardless of their heritage; and so the gatherers gave thought only to the joyous union. Earth Raven signed the marital document as a witness along with Buck.

Afterwards, the officiaries were eager to leave, and were escorted out by Slim. Snake Catcher surveyed Buck for signs of disgruntlement but the foreman seemed pleased and enthusiastically congratulated the couple. Snake Catcher thought that perhaps Buck's easiness and congratulatory offerings were only because the entire household knew that it was a marriage of convenience for the sake of helping someone in need.

Cook had garnished the table with refreshments. Earth Raven lifted a glass to toast the newlyweds. The entire company of people noshed on hors d'oeuvres and visited together for a while. Buck offered Earth Raven a walking tour of the structures on the grounds. He accepted but stopped to speak to Susan alone before leaving. "You have sacrificed your freedom and risked your future to help another. I am grateful that it is my friend. You already know that he is a good man, and he will be a good husband."

"It does not seem like a sacrifice," she replied with a new

joy lighting her eyes. "I am helping a friend, plus his brother was a friend to me, and a friend to my father. It is I who am grateful to have such good friends come into my life."

Buck and Earth Raven departed for the tour with Painted Pony secretly tagging along from a reasonable distance, mooning over Earth Raven. The partygoers dispersed. Moving outside, Susan and Snake Catcher sat alone together for a while soaking up the coolness of the afternoon. While Susan sat in her favorite rocking chair, Snake Catcher sat on the top step of the porch. Rains Down, consistently anticipating their necessities, brought them cool drinks. Snake Catcher withdrew his knife from its holder, and began whittling on a piece of wood from a stack of branches piled off from the foot of the steps while he and his new wife conversed. The dogs were lying down on the porch next to Susan. Killer got up, walked over to Snake Catcher, and snuggled next to him. Ferdy was in the distance riding in from the pasture heading toward the stables.

Susan clearly had a distaste for Snake Catcher's knife, and secretively made fearsome faces as she stared at it, somewhat in a trance. "That is very sharp, isn't it?"

"Yes, one cannot whittle with a dull knife," Snake Catcher teased wearing a straight-face.

Susan was amused from Snake Catcher's humor, then drifted back into her fear of the knife. "Doesn't it ever scare you? Don't you ever slip and cut yourself?"

"Hiya. Spent many years with knife. Here, will teach you."

"No, no, that's okay. I can't," Susan shuttered with a nervous laugh.

"Yes. Do not know this Susan, fear from someone who is so brave. Brave to ride horse the way you do. Brave to help others in face of danger the way you do." Snake Catcher sat looking at Susan, patiently waiting until she reluctantly agreed. He then spread a napkin that Rains Down had given them for their drinks in front of him, and motioned for Susan to sit on it. Snake Catcher curved his arms around Susan while holding onto the knife over her hands as he taught her how to cut the stick by moving the blade away from herself. She was demure with Snake Catcher sitting so close but he did not show to be affected by Susan's closeness. Gradually, she gained confidence with the knife.

When Earth Raven returned with Buck from the tour a

few hours later, Snake Catcher, Earth Raven and Susan collectively sat down to supper. Painted Pony's shy face was sneaking glances from the kitchen as Rains Down would periodically have to pull her back in. The trio celebrated their united alliance toward the fight for freedom and land rights. They continued light banter through supper, then stepped into the lounge to enjoy dessert and tea while seated in the overstuffed high-back chairs. Earth Raven rose before stepping over to the wall of memories and was nostalgically haunted, yet smiled while viewing the photograph of Hail Maker with Susan and her father. Earth Raven had never seen a photograph close up before and definitely not of someone he knew; nevertheless, he was enamored by the possibility of someone's image on a piece of paper. Earth Raven was also utterly amazed at the likeness of his old friend, especially knowing he was no longer living. On some level, Earth Raven was not ready to believe that Hail Maker, the great White exterminator, could have befriended White folks. He now had irrefutable proof staring back at him.

Susan inquired of Earth Raven, "Have you ever had your photograph taken?"

"No. For some, they think it takes away their spirit."

"Is that what you believe?" Susan probed.

"No, not really. Not now. I see Hail Maker in these photographs, and he had much spirit in him."

Snake Catcher interjected while pointing at the blanketed wall, "Next visit, *we* will be in one."

Susan smiled as to approve. Their hostess went on to mention that she would soon be required to prepare for her teaching studies scheduled for the following day, and would have to excuse herself.

Earth Raven asked Susan, "You teach? How many students do you have?"

"I only have one at the moment, Painted Pony."

"Her father must be of a higher seniority here to afford to pay private-schooling for his daughter."

"They do not pay me, I offer her studies for free."

"Why would you offer studies for free; is that not rare for private tutoring?"

"Because I believe an education should be free, and it is not Painted Pony's fault that the community will not allow a Native to be educated with the White children here in this county. If my father were living and still teaching at the school, there would certainly be an inflamed controversy over him allowing her to attend. And he would have fought the good fight. I honorably stand in his shoes."

Painted Pony giggled, now knowing that since Earth Raven was discussing her, she existed in his eyes. It was, to her interpretation, the next best thing to being formally introduced by a matchmaker.

The three of them chatted a while longer, until Earth Raven and Snake Catcher walked out onto the porch to smoke. Susan sat in the lounge reading to prepare the studies, and also to give the men male-bonding time. Snake Catcher and Earth Raven went on to privately discuss the political aspects of their matrimonial union, including what it might mean for their people.

At bedtime, Earth Raven entered the guest bedroom as Susan and Snake Catcher stood alone in the hallway together. Being their wedding night, it was awkward for a moment before they said good-night. They retreated into their respective bedrooms. Instinctually, the dogs promptly followed her.

Earth Raven had been supplied with a temporary cot which was previously assembled and placed in Snake Catcher's bedroom by Buck. After settling in, Earth Raven attempted to be nonchalant, and respectfully interrogated Snake Catcher regarding his relationship with Susan. Snake Catcher conveniently dodged Earth Raven's questions by pretending to drift off to sleep. Amusingly, Earth Raven suspected that he was faking. Earth Raven could not find a comfortable position, and moved from the cot to the floor where he soon drifted into sleep.

Chapter 13

As Earth Raven was preparing to leave, he was telling Snake Catcher that he would orchestrate the publishing of the notice of marriage, Day Twenty away from the reservation. Earth Raven added that, Snake Catcher should contact him if there were any further problems with the Blue Coats. Soon Earth Raven mounted his horse, and he spoke to Snake Catcher in Lakota as being his parting words. "Be happy, my friend. It is time."

Earth Raven departed with Buck, and Susan and Snake Catcher stood on the porch watching them ride away. Buck had been instructed to escort Earth Raven to the main trail back toward Sundance.

The saddened face of Painted Pony was looking out the front window from the parlor. Sammy and Slim were working in the garden. Sammy sensitively felt the gloomy mood of the house, one matching what occurs with most good-byes among dear friends. Slim neglectfully avoided witnessing how Earth Raven amorously influenced his daughter. Snake Catcher looked the perfect warrior seeing his friend leave as Susan waited for him to translate Earth Raven's message, but he did not.

As Earth Raven neared the horizon, Painted Pony, not wanting others to witness signs of her attraction, ran through the rooms, out the kitchen door, and around the house just to get one last glimpse of him.

After Earth Raven rode out of view, Susan inquired, "Do you want to tell me what he said?"

Still looking at the horizon, Snake Catcher responded, "Hiya." The comment seemed rude, prompting him to add, "Someday." Snake Catcher did not want to verbally acknowledge that Earth Raven wished them to be an authentically married couple. He did not wish to scare Susan away from him as he was beginning to feel more than friendship toward her.

Snake Catcher sat on the top step of the porch and started whittling arrows retrieved from the stack of branches at the foot of the steps. Susan took a seat in her favored rocking chair and began sketching him with the chips from his carvings flying outwardly. Killer and Coyote danced about sniffing the discarded shavings as they hit the ground. The cherished view, as always, was that of Paha Sapa.

About an hour had passed before Larry barreled up to Susan and Snake Catcher, who were still sitting on the porch. He was screaming excitedly, something about the stables, a colt and some horses. They could not understand his rantings.

Susan inquired vigorously, "Larry, Larry, slow down. What's the matter?"

"It's here, it's here! The colt! It's about to be born! We have to send for the horse doctor–now!"

Susan appeared shaken yet delightedly excited, while Snake Catcher plainly remarked, "No reason. We will deliver."

Snake Catcher calmly rose, grabbed his bow and the whittled arrows, and walked toward the stables. Everyone else from the ranch was an ungovernable frenzied mess, with many of them wandering aimlessly.

In the stables, Sammy was tossing hay in the delivery area as fast as he could. Larry was filling buckets of water, and placing them close to the delivery stall. Buck had returned from escorting Earth Raven out, and was steadying the mare. Slim was scolding Painted Pony for her inappropriate curiosity of wanting to witness the maturely sophisticated event. Ferdy was gathering supplies. Susan began pacing. Snake Catcher placed his bow and arrows near his horse before he began feeling the mare's stomach for an estimation before the time of birth. "Soon" was all he would offer.

Susan nervously questioned Snake Catcher, unsuccessfully avoiding a show of doubt in his capabilities. She was also excited about the new addition. "Are you sure she be all right without the horse doctor?"

Snake Catcher raised an eyebrow toward Susan in response to her doubtfulness, searching for confirmation of trust from her in his reliability. Susan gave a nervous laugh, raised her hands to surrender to Snake Catcher's self-assuredness of his adeptness to deliver the colt. Snake Catcher then instructed the ranchhands with their duties; however, they were reluctant to follow his order, and looked to Susan for her approval. She nodded at her men for compliance.

"Buck, keep horse feet from kicking colt. Sammy, find cloth to wipe. Ferdy, need rope."

Then Snake Catcher worked effortlessly to deliver the colt. Blood and placenta splattered indiscriminately, but he was unaffected. Larry was too squeamish and could not handle the scene, whereupon he left. Painted Pony, who had not completely adhered to Slim's orders, peeked around the corner, but did not enter the delivery area. She was extremely curious about the birthing process, yet too afraid to actually look in at it.

When the colt was out, Snake Catcher took out his knife and cut the colt free from the sack.

Buck remarked, "Man, that is one sharp knife."

"Yes, better to cut with," Snake Catcher whimsically replied. Before Snake Catcher stepped over to the bucket to wash his hands, Susan and the others laughed with emotion at Snake Catcher's sense of humor.

Susan was in awe of Snake Catcher's talents, and she was full of excitement, being caught up in the moment. When Snake Catcher was drying his hands, Susan hugged him for successfully delivering the colt. While dispassionate and guarded, Snake Catcher looked down at her hugging him. He did not know how to respond to it, though he wanted to do something. After Susan realized he would not be responsive, she stepped back and composed herself. Snake Catcher continued to stare amorously at her while she was focused on being congratulated by the ranchhands. Not knowing in what fashion to react, Snake Catcher slowly began to remove himself from the scene, he picked up his hunting gear and then led his horse out of the stables. Snake Catcher jumped on his horse, and rode in the direction of his favorite site at the south end of the river. Ferdy and Larry were cleaning up the stables as Susan joyously walked toward the house with Painted Pony skipping alongside.

Shortly thereafter, while Snake Catcher was at the river swimming, Sammy and Slim went to the pasture to safeguard the cattle as Buck tended to the garden. Susan and Painted Pony sat on the porch chatting about the birth of the colt when Cook walked up and joined them. Rains Down brought out some refreshments, then retreated into the house to continue her chores.

"What will you name the colt?" Cook wondered out loud.

Still joyous over the colts arrival, Susan responded, "That's a good question! What will we name him?"

Painted Pony blurted out! "We should name him *Sparky*, after the father. Isn't that what people do?"

"That's a great suggestion, Painted Pony. The colt's name will be Sparky after Sparks."

Painted Pony blissfully smiled and clapped her hands. They all smiled, and agreed that it was a fine name.

Later that day and nearly into the evening, Snake Catcher had returned. To Cook's profound amazement, Snake Catcher was transporting a small dead elk draped around his shoulders. Snake Catcher brought the animal through the back door of the kitchen and flopped the trophy down onto the butcher block like a cat who had caught a mouse offering it to the master first. Rains Down laughed at Snake Catcher's contribution. Snake Catcher grunted, pointed at the catch, and while looking at Cook, he offered, "For you." Cook smiled nefariously as if she had acquired the best gift she'd ever received.

Continuously in the diningroom, Susan began to eat her supper alone. She speculated about what must have mysteriously pulled Snake Catcher from the stables without any word after delivering the colt. Susan admired his free spirit, yet felt lonely from it as well. Tension filled the air when Snake Catcher walked out of the kitchen and Susan saw him. She greeted him before adding, "I did not know when you were returning. Rains Down has your supper. Would you like me to call her?"

"Hiya. Good-night," Snake Catcher responded abruptly as he quickly turned to walk away.

When he had lowered his saddlebags, Susan spotted the fresh blood from the elk on Snake Catcher's shirt, and she gasped, "Are you all right?"

Snake Catcher, seemingly unconcerned for her deep interest, did not explain, but complacently nodded as he entered the stairwell.

Susan whispered, "Good-night." She sat deflatedly as she watched Snake Catcher disappear. Rains Down came into the diningroom and told Susan of the banquet they would soon enjoy. She asked about bringing out Snake Catcher's supper, but

Susan regretfully shook her head and softly contended that she was finished with hers. As she removed Susan's undisturbed plate, Rains Down's expression went from joyfulness to concern, suspecting there was a disturbing conflict between the two of them so soon after their nuptials. After Rains Down took the plate back to the kitchen, Cook entered the diningroom to investigate Susan's lack of appetite. Cook was rubbing two butcher knives together, getting ready to dismember the elk.

Cook asked, "Did you not like your meal?"

"It was delicious as always, Cook. I'm just not very hungry."

Smiling widely, Cook offered, "Tomorrow will be *much* better!" Cook excitedly headed back into the kitchen with the knives clicking together.

Susan smiled for Cook's happiness before heading off to her bedroom to read.

Snake Catcher sat alone on the balcony off his bedroom thinking about the day. He was unclear as to what had happened in the stables with Susan. The unfamiliar physical public-display of gratitude from her startled him. White culture still befuddled Snake Catcher, as he did not know what the event meant. He did not know if Susan was ready for a marriage outside of the agreement that they struck–of helping Snake Catcher with reclaiming Paha Sapa, or if that was the way all Whites reacted. Snake Catcher regretted his ignorance on the subject, and vowed to learn more information regarding White rituals in the upcoming days.

Before retiring for the night, Susan sat on the bench in her room and brushed her hair while venting her confusion to the dogs. "I really messed up today, didn't I, Killer? I've made him feel uncomfortable here, and that's not what I wanted to do. Now he feels he has to avoid me, and I fear I've lost his attention. It only took me less than two weeks to alienate a possible suitor this time, ay Coyote? I think that's a record, don't you?" Coyote looked up at Susan with her head tilted as if to show she knew less than her owner did on the subject. Susan cheerlessly looked at both huskies as she tossed the brush on the table and slipped into bed.

Chapter 14

Susan was laggardly rocking on the porch somberly sipping her tea while staring out at Paha Sapa in a daze. Painted Pony sat and watched her in silence. Simultaneously, Snake Catcher stood lifelessly looking out his bedroom window at Paha Sapa, Day Twenty-One away from the reservation.

Both Susan and Snake Catcher found it difficult to *accidently* happen upon each other for a conversation on this day. Unbeknownst to the other, that would have been their perfect scenario.

That afternoon, Susan made time to check in on the new colt in the stables while Slim and Sammy were there doing chores. Snake Catcher sat on the back kitchen steps whittling with his knife, distractively pondering his situation. Painted Pony now sat with him and observed the whittling quietly. After a while, she asked Snake Catcher, "Don't you like her anymore?" Painted Pony startled him so intensely with her question, that he stopped whittling.

Snake Catcher was not prepared for anyone to suspect there was something between he and Susan, much less that there was something that had gone wrong between them. Snake Catcher had not thought through his approach on what to do about the relationship yet, never mind explaining it to someone else. He did not offer Painted Pony an explanation, and returned to his meaningless whittling. Silence loomed over them again until Cook called Painted Pony inside the house. After she left, Snake Catcher stopped whittling and motionlessly stared at the ground.

A short time thereafter, Snake Catcher was distracted by helping Sammy with a few minor two-person repairs on the storage shed. Soon it was late, and he realized that supper had passed, as well as, another opportunity of a casual meeting with Susan.

At sunset, Susan was alone again on the porch cupping her tea while staring out at Paha Sapa. Snake Catcher stood alone looking out his bedroom window at the same view–yet again.

Chapter 15

Susan approached her day in better spirits than in past days. As she sat comfortably in her rocker on the porch enjoying the morning, she sketched a smoldering stream of condensation coming off of Paha Sapa. Soon thereafter, while finishing the last dribbles of her tea, came a warning shot from the pasture indicating that they would have visitors at the house shortly. Already close by, Snake Catcher stepped out onto the porch; to some degree to see who was anticipated, but mostly to safeguard Susan from any unwanted intruders, Day Twenty-Two away from the reservation.

Soon, two soldiers were, again, riding toward the house from a distance. Susan protectively motioned for Snake Catcher to return back into the house until she unveiled their reasons for being there. Snake Catcher promptly stepped into the parlor and discreetly watched through the window. Larry and Buck moved up onto the porch with Susan. Her stance was that of the matriarch, being positioned in front of her men, symbolizing her authority.

When the Blue Coats reached the house, the corporal was the first to speak. "Morning ma'am. We're going around to the ranchers in the area to find out if they have seen an Indian man with a young girl. They are both half breeds. Have you seen anyone matching that description?"

Without missing a beat, Slim immediately pulled Painted Pony out of their sight, and into the stables. Susan witnessed Slim's actions out of the corner of her sight yet did not decipher his motivation for doing this. Always cautious when answering questions to any Blue Coat, Susan paused before responding. Her mind was on Snake Catcher's ongoing disputes with them, and it took her a moment to realize they were not concerned with him. "No. I suppose I should know what they are accused of, not wanting trouble here."

The private was quick to answer. "Kidnapping, ma'am. Some say he took the girl and is working her to pay his way."

Susan was quick to dispel that thought. "Well I assure you, I wouldn't allow anything like that to happen here. If I see anyone of their descriptions, I'll send for you."

The corporal answered, "Thank you, ma'am."

Susan watched them ride out of sight before she meandered over to the stables. Snake Catcher secretly followed her, being curious in part, and also to protect her if she came upon the man that the Blue Coats described.

Slim was busily cleaning out a horse stall when Susan entered the stables.

"Slim?" called Susan.

Without stepping out or even looking at her, Slim distractively answered, "Yes, ma'am?"

"You know we have to talk about this."

"Yes, ma'am."

Susan gently persisted. "Slim, step out here for a moment please."

As Slim stepped out of the stall, he answered, "Yes, ma'am." He gruffly and authoritatively instructed Painted Pony to go into the house to help Cook with her chores.

Amusing herself with Sparky, Painted Pony protested," No, I want to stay."

"Now!"

"Oookay." Painted Pony skipped toward the house.

"Where did she come from Slim? Did you steal her?"

"Yes, ma'am," he said shamefully, then defendingly added, "but there is more to it. You wouldn't understand."

Susan spoke softly, not wanting to alienate Slim. "How do you know that? You haven't told me your story yet. I understand many things. The first thing I understand is that you love Painted Pony like she's your daughter, and you care for her like you are her father, that is what I understand so far." While shaking her head, Susan added, "And Painted Pony doesn't pay *your way*; everyone here knows that. Who is she, really?"

Slim slowly began his explanation. "When I was a young man, my mother was, well..." He paused searching for the right word, then continued, "*taken* by a White soldier. Mother did not want Painted Pony when she was born. She would have been thrown around from family to family. I did not want that for her, so I took her, and now I am a thief."

"You are no thief. You are a good man. Your secret is safe here. But why did you not just say that she was your sister?"

"After we moved away from there, I told everyone she was my daughter and my wife died in childbirth to make it more believable because of the age difference between us. That way, I would not have to explain anything to others."

Susan acceptingly nodded as to acknowledge his explanation. "Carter is the only one we may have to worry about. He knows what you look like, and that you have a daughter."

"Yes, ma'am. Thank you."

Susan compassionately smiled at Slim before starting back to the house. Snake Catcher covertly slipped behind the stables and watched her pass.

Lunch was a hearty one of elk meat. Susan found herself alone in the diningroom but she ate that of a child's portion. Her appetite was poor partly from being alone and partly from the disturbing subject matter from her conversation with Slim. Susan decided to lift her spirits and begin her afternoon chores, which took her into the stables. Susan also went there with the intention of coercing the new colt to follow her, but he was still clinging to his mother.

In a high-pitched soothing voice, Susan solicited, "Come on out here, Sparky. Come here." Susan was determined to get a better view of Sparky, and began to climb the ladder to the loft when she unexpectedly slipped and fell backwards. Disaster would have struck again, if not for the quick reflexes of Snake Catcher, who had walked in a moment earlier. He swiftly caught Susan; then he helplessly stumbled up against a wall of hay and was nose to nose with her–close enough to feel her breath and the outline of her body next to his. Susan surprised him as much as Snake Catcher surprised her, but she was thankful to see him, and not entirely just for the catch. They both took a breath, and then sweetly and bashfully smile at each other. They were close enough to kiss, but after a brief pause, Buck called to Susan to come see who had returned, and the trance was broken. She and Buck walked out of the stables to discover that the soldiers from that morning had returned. There was an absence of a warning shot.

Cautiously, Susan walked toward the porch to speak with the soldiers. Painted Pony had not adhered to Slim's request of doing chores indoors, and was sweeping the porch in plain sight. It was too late to shield her.

Cook was in the kitchen. Snake Catcher exited the stables and darted toward the back kitchen steps just as the soldiers reached the front of the house. Cook left the kitchen for outside, and she peaked around the corner of the house at the porch scene. Snake Catcher also moved into position nearby Cook to secretly eavesdrop on the conversation.

"Sirs, I thought we concluded our business?" Susan formally affirmed.

While pointing at Painted Pony, the private accusingly remarked, "We were told by one of your neighbors that you *do* have ones of that description here, and there is one of them now."

Susan circumvented the situation calmly. "No, you inquired about a *man* and a girl." Susan turned to Painted Pony and gave her instructions. "Go into the house now, dear."

Painted Pony began to turn to follow Susan's request but she stopped at the soldier's command.

The corporal demanded, "No. Ma'am, we'll have to take her with us."

Surprising everyone, just then Cook stepped out from around the house, and spoke gruffly while snapping a kitchen dishtowel at the soldiers. "She is *my* daughter. What do you want with her?!"

The private studdered, "Ah, ah, ah, well, we were told that she is half Indian, not Mexican, ma'am."

Cook, still snapping her towel at them and now spooking their horses, continued, "Well, they were wrong! She is *my* daughter so leave her be!"

The corporal apologized. "Ah, sorry, ma'am. We must have gotten the wrong information."

Susan brashly shook her head at the soldiers, pretending to be sympathetic. "I tried to spare you from having to tangle with her, but you wouldn't listen." While crinkling up her nose, Susan sarcastically added, "Perhaps you should leave now."

The cowardly soldiers quickly tipped their hats, and

eagerly departed before commencing into a gallop to get away from Cook and her snapping dishtowel. Susan smirked at their naivete, that they did not even have the sense to challenge the differences between Cook and Painted Pony. Snake Catcher emerged from around the house, and Slim walked up from the stables.

Painted Pony looked irritatingly confused. "Why is everyone lying about me? What won't you tell me?"

Slim parentally commanded Painted Pony: "Go to your room."

Painted Pony indignantly resisted by stomping her foot. "No! Tell me!"

Susan heedfully stepped forward and spoke delicately to Slim. "Don't you think she has the right to know what's going on? Painted Pony is practically a woman now. She has a right to know, Slim. It will protect her to know the truth about all of what happened."

As if he were not entirely convinced that he himself was correct while postponing the inevitable, Slim quietly stated, "No, I am her father, and I think she is too young."

Painted Pony was still pleading to her closed-lipped kin to be told of the cryptic history. "Why won't you tell me?"

Susan, still talking to Slim, added, "You are always going to think she is too young. She knows something is wrong now, Slim; please tell her. Tell Painted Pony that you loved her so much, that you were willing to be jailed to save her. Tell her that she is so special, that everyone here wants to protect her." Painted Pony began to sob from her frustration. Susan lightly put her hand on Slim's shoulder, before adding, "Tell her she has all of us to help protect her."

Slim shielded Painted Pony with his arm, and they retreated to the staff quarters. As the others were watching Slim and Painted Pony depart, Susan was the first to swiftly vanish, stepping softly into the house undetected. Susan expeditiously trotted up to her bedroom and closed the door. Cook somberly entered the house and walked toward the kitchen. The remaining staff echoed them, going their different ways. Snake Catcher found himself all alone on the porch. Not just alone, but despondently lonely.

Moments later, Snake Catcher curiously entered the house and stood in the middle of the downstairs with a view to every room there to discover that he was just as alone; Susan had disappeared.

Susan was profoundly absent at supper that evening. Snake Catcher stood in the diningroom, waiting as he yearned to share a meal with her after their pleasurable encounter in the stables earlier in the day. A steaming stack of aromatic elk meat sat in the middle of the table soliciting the allure of those with an appetite. Cook hesitantly stepped out of the kitchen to catch a glimpse of the diningroom table as she waited for comments on the feast, but then retreated back into the kitchen when she discovered it undisturbed. It was after the steam from the elk's meat had dissipated when Snake Catcher decidedly sat and began plating his food. He primarily stared at his plate, not actually eating much. Snake Catcher courteously spread the elk's meat thinner on the serving platter, as to give Cook the impression that he enjoyed more of it than he had. Snake Catcher stepped outside to smoke his pipe.

Moments later in the kitchen, Cook, who had retrieved the stack of elk, gave the platter of meat to Ferdy, who was at the back door retrieving the staff suppers for the night. "Ferdinand, you may as well have it; no one around here is eating," she barked, almost offended by the lack of interest in her masterful achievement.

Upstairs at bedtime, Snake Catcher stopped by Susan's door, but decided not to disturb her.

Susan was lying in bed awake while staring off in thought. It was an emotional day for her in discovering the inconceivably despicable violation of Painted Pony's mother, especially due to Susan's still maidenly way.

Chapter 16

Susan's mood had improved when her next morning began. She was standing in the foyer putting on her riding gloves when Painted Pony entered and cheerfully greeted her. Snake Catcher was descending down the staircase, but halted when he heard voices, Day Twenty-Three away from the reservation. Snake Catcher remained motionless on the stairs as he overheard their conversation.

Painted Pony modestly requested, "Susan, will you please buy me something special while you are in Deadwood City?"

"I surely will; you have had a tough week."

"So has Snake Catcher. Don't you like him anymore?"

Though surprised at the bluntness of the question, Susan kept her composure as she cordially explained, "Yes, I like him very much, but there are many kinds of marriages and not all have a closeness." Susan tried to keep the topic frolicsome as she jiggled Painted Pony's nose. "And you shouldn't be worrying yourself with other people's concerns." Susan then quickly changed the uncomfortable subject. "Have you done your studies?"

"No, but then afterwards I'm going out to see my horse Sparky."

Susan, fascinatingly grinning, responded, "*Your* horse?"

Painted Pony briskly nodded, nefariously smiled and affirmed over skipping off, "Yep, he is just my size."

Susan swiftly exited the house, mounted the horse which Buck had ready for her out front, and left with the foreman and Larry for the auction in Deadwood City. Snake Catcher stepped closer to the door to woefully watch her leave.

Meanwhile, Painted Pony hopped toward the staff quarters where she hurried through her studies. She then cheerfully trotted over to the stables where she met up with Slim and Sammy doing their chores. "Can I brush him?" she asked, eager to help.

Slim answered, "No, he does not need brushing at his age."

Persistently, she offered, "Then what else can I do for him?"

"Did you finish your studies?" Slim asked.

"Yes. Now I want to help with Sparky," she answered, not being deterred.

"You can give him and his mother some fresh water and hay," Slim answered with a cryptic smile, relieved at how well she bounced back from her trying episode the previous day.

Painted Pony filled the trough with water, then replenished the bucket of food, as she had witnessed the ranchhands do in the past. "Come here, Sparky. You will like this," she said as she offered the hay to him and warmingly petted the colt as if he were her own.

As the two ranchhands went back to their chores, Sammy spoke to Larry as if to continue a casual conversation they were having before Painted Pony entered the stables. "How many new ca'fs do you think Miss Susan will buy?"

"She said she was looking to buy a dozen or so. We should have enough food and medicine for all of them into the fall, even with the new arrivals."

"I sure be likin' the branding part of gittin' new ca'fs."

"Yes, me too, Sammy," Slim agreed as he was secretly surveying Painted Pony, still distracted with concern for her mental well-being. He pondered that Painted Pony seemed to be bearing the burden well, or perhaps she did not fully understand the very adult subject matter; especially since she insisted on still referring to him as her father.

Snake Catcher was afflicted. He was missing Susan, yet did not know how to connect with her. The Lakota entered the lounge to reminisce about their pleasant nightly chats. An unexplainable warm spritz of air maniacally drew Snake Catcher over to Susan's photograph. The bronze-faced Native was finding himself staring at every curve of the fair-faced beauty in the photograph when Rains Down caught him in that clairvoyant way about her. Rains Down felt a bit saddened for Snake Catcher as she asked, "Can I get you anything?"

Snake Catcher was moderately startled from the interruption, but remained focused on Susan's photograph while he answered, "Hiya. When will Susan return?"

"She did not say."

During Snake Catcher's immediate silence, Rains Down exited. Snake Catcher needed some fresh air to clear his head. He decided to go for a ride. On his way to his favorite site at the south end of the river, Snake Catcher passed Ferdy who was in the pasture watching over the herd.

By lunchtime, Sammy had positioned himself at the pasture post so Ferdy could return to the ranch for a meal. Only Cook and Rains Down were in the kitchen. Ferdy walked up to the back door to the kitchen to retrieve his lunch, but stopped short of stepping inside while he looked in at Cook as to ask for privacy. Cook understood and left without letting Rains Down see her.

"Hola, Rains Down," greeted Ferdy.

"Hola, Ferdy," she answered aloofly, continuing her duties.

"Would you like to join me for lunch?"

"No gracias, Ferdy. I have work to do."

"Maybe later we can talk in the lounge?"

"Maybe" was all Rains Down offered before departing the kitchen with a stack of dishes on her way to set the diningroom table for Susan's supper. Cook now stood nearby and she watched Rains Down's expression as the younger woman vacated the kitchen. Cook was concerned for the welfare of her son's heart. Ferdy exited the kitchen with a plateful of food and headed for the staff lounge.

After his lunch, Ferdy trotted back out to the pasture on his horse to work. With Sammy nearby, he headed for the staff quarters. Resting atop his bed covers before his shift would begin again, Sammy drifted off to sleep, and he began to dream. Sammy's dreams were often haunting. His dreadful dreams were mostly filled with his time on a Georgia plantation picking cotton for his abusive owner, Master Briggs. This master was a large pasty balding White man, one of a width that matched his height. Gluttonous would be how most people chose to describe him; however, that honest depiction would never be presented directly to him. Sammy's dreams also included the infatuation he once had for one of the indoor slaves, Annabella. She was the product of her mother's slave owner, who, as was common in those times, had a family of his own. Even though Annabella was treated better than most of that family's slaves, they would not let her mistake that for being a part of their household. Surely, they would remind Annabella if she had forgotten. Nevertheless, Annabella was sold to Master Briggs after her owner father was caught, and later lynched, for embezzling funds from his partner at the local bank. The partner retaliated by selling Annabella to the most foul man he knew in the county.

After she joined his community of slaves, Sammy wanted nothing more than to marry Annabella and begin a life with her. Occasionally, marriage was permitted between slaves, but only if they had a "fair owner." After all, a "fair owner" would see the bottom line of profitability because if more slaves were birthed, then more money could be made by their sale.

Sammy faced a much higher hurdle than not having a reasonably fair owner, especially since Master Briggs knew of Sammy's infatuation with Annabella. Master Briggs was also somewhat sweet on her, but of course he would never be known as someone who would be seen in public with one of his slaves no matter how bright her beauty illuminated. After the Civil War ended slavery, Master Briggs offered Annabella to stay with him as his secret mistress. When she declined his proposition, and knowing that she would rather be with Sammy than to live a life of wealth with him, Master Briggs whipped Annabella's face beyond recognition.

Nevertheless, tragically, Annabella would jump from the top floor of the estate and be forever lost to both of them. Still Sammy knew Master Briggs would hunt endlessly for him only to appease his bruised ego. Sammy would always awaken from his dreams in a cold sweat as he realized that Annabella was no longer his reality.

Just before suppertime, Snake Catcher anticipated Susan's return home and he looked to be genuinely excited to see her. That was until he discovered that Susan was not alone. She was with a man. Accompanying Susan was a friend from a neighboring ranch she had come across along the way home; Jeremy Jones was an old school friend a few years older than Susan. Jeremy was tall, slender and of a fair complexion. He owned a ranch on the west side of the county and had much in common with Susan. With being a rancher, he was also well educated and exhaustedly tried helping those less fortunate. Unlike Susan, he was unmarried.

When Jeremy was introduced to Snake Catcher, it was an awkward moment. Jeremy did not know how he felt about his longtime friend helping someone in such an intimate manner. Snake Catcher felt jealous, as Jeremy was more of Susan's similitude.

Snake Catcher was calculatingly quiet during supper with their guest even though this would normally be his time to practice his English words. Snake Catcher agonized through the meal; however, he felt that the only thing worse than being there seeing Susan with Jeremy, was leaving them alone together. Jeremy seemed unaffected by Snake Catcher's presence, even to the point of Snake Catcher believing the guest was ignoring him.

Jeremy seemingly continued his conversation only toward Susan. "I heard you had some trouble here the other day. I can see what the stampede did to your fence."

Susan agreed, "Yes, another of Carter's ploys in getting me to sell my land to him."

"Well, don't give in to him. If you need me, I will intervene for you."

Snake Catcher peered over at Jeremy, and curtly retorted, "She has a husband."

Before Jeremy could respond, Susan quickly defused her husband's ill-mannered comment to their visitor. "No, we will be all right, but thank you anyway. Carter is just more of a nuisance than anything else. I doubt he will persist. Carter knows I won't sell."

Susan instinctively sensed that the table's occupants needed a change of scenery, and the lounge had always been a source of fondness for Snake Catcher; however, it was not to be this particular evening. The tension in the air was heavy, and after dessert and a social drink, Jeremy said good-night and left.

Susan was concerned about Snake Catcher's mood. Once alone with him, she asked, "Are you not feeling well? You didn't say much."

"Did not say much, not much to say."

While the two of them were conversing in the lounge, Ferdy stepped in, and whispered his usual inquiry about Rains

Down's presence. A moment later, he was headed for the kitchen from Susan's directive.

Susan could see Snake Catcher was not wanting to discuss the evening and effortlessly changed the subject taking advantage of Ferdy's interruption. "The boys will be branding the new cattle tomorrow. Maybe you'd like to go to see how they do it."

"Maybe. Good-night." Abruptly, Snake Catcher began to leave the room, but Susan blurted out: "Are you angry with me? Have I done something wrong?"

Seemingly unconcerned, Snake Catcher answered non-abrasively. "Hiya." Snake Catcher did not know what to do with his feelings, never having to fight for the affections of a woman before. Reminiscing to his early days, he had always had the girls in the village competing for *his* affections because Snake Catcher was that of a great warrior. Even though Matching Spirit was the catch of the village, she was one of those girls who had always had a crush on Snake Catcher, and possessed no threat of leaving him. Snake Catcher did not know if he had even won Susan's heart yet. What he did know was that he was jealous and perplexed about the situation just the same.

Snake Catcher left for upstairs. Susan sat in the lounge a while in thought before stepping out onto the porch. As she gazed out at Paha Sapa, she was reminded of this one tranquil constant in her life. Snake Catcher stood looking out his bedroom window at Paha Sapa, mirroring Susan's thoughts.

Later that evening, many people, mostly men, were gathered in Sundance at Willy's Saloon for card playing, drinking and fraternizing with the saloon girls, as they did most every Saturday night. The room was large with many card-playing tables in the center, and there was a bar that ran along one side of the room with many liquor bottles on a back shelf, all of the same vintage. The stage was situated on the far wall away from the front door. The backstage area was hidden; however, there was a door shrouded with a velvet curtain leading backstage on the far side of the piano on the opposite wall from the bar. Not everyone knew of its existence; Buck was one who did.

Carter was leaning on the bar with his arm wrapped intimately around a saloon girl. Some of his ranchhands were sitting at a nearby table playing cards. These men peered toward the front door when Larry and Ferdy walked in and sat at an adjacent table of card players. Carter's men did not act on their hostility for Susan's ranchhands, but they constantly watched them to track their movements. Buck walked in moments later, and leaned against the bar at the opposite end to Carter. The bartender made friendly conversation as he poured Buck a drink.

The jesterish piano player began tapping the ivory keys and immediately introduced the main event for the evening. "Now, here all the way from San Francisco, California, the world famous Miss Angel Blue!"

Angel slowly slinked to the center of the stage, teasingly taunting the audience. As she began to sing, Buck could not take his eyes off of her, and neither could many of the other male patrons. Angel had hair the color of fire and a velvety voice that Buck felt was singing straight to him; he was mesmerized by her femininity. She was dressed in a tightly-fit black corset and a high-riding red skirt that showed off her long vivacious legs; legs that were covered only by sheer black stockings. As she strutted from table to table enticing and teasing the men, the feathers from Angel's boa danced around her.

After Angel's number, dancing girls exchanged the stage with the saloon's star performer. Buck slammed back his drink, and headed toward the backstage door. Carter's men gave him malicious looks as he passed them, but Buck was unaffected, being on a mission. While the frilly dancing girls were on stage, one in particular was watching Buck slip backstage–Lily. Buck did not notice Lily looking at him, nor noticed her in general, even though they had spoke many times. Lily believed she was in love with Buck, but was always too afraid to tell him because she knew of his infatuation with Angel. Lily could only hope that Angel would soon leave Sundance to move onto another unsuspecting group of naive men she could dazzle, leaving Buck to her. Lily was a twenty-year-old slender and petite dishwater-blonde.

After reaching the backstage area, Buck pulled his hat down off his head, and bravely knocked on Angel's dressing room door. Buck became sheepish when she answered the door in only a sheer satin robe.

"Hello, Miss Blue. You were...fabulous tonight."

As Angel was waving her hands to dry her hand creme, she responded, "Why thank you, Billy. I appreciate you coming to see me perform."

"Um...that's Buck, ma'am. I was wondering if you would

accompany me out for supper on Tuesday?"

Angel, somewhat dizzy and distracted, replied, "That is very sweet of you, Hank, but I don't eat supper, and I have to rehearse; my job is never done. Maybe some other time." She turned and floated back into her dressing nook.

"Okay, well, how about the next night then? We can..." Buck's conversation was cut off as an enormous blundering stagehand rudely stepped in front of Angel's door while explosively pulling it closed. Buck instinctively took a step back to swing a punch at him, but decided that he may not successfully come out of the brawl a winner due to the stagehand's massive size. Buck retreated to the bar where he preceded to drink himself helpless. Lily joined him a while to try and cheer him up, but Buck was inconsolable. It broke Lily's heart that he was so torn up over someone she knew would never make him happy.

After Larry briefly spoke to another rancher regarding some part-time work, he and Ferdy assisted Buck to his horse and began to escort him back to the ranch. Carter's men thought they were being inconspicuous about a plan to follow a drunken Buck back to the ranch, but Ferdy and Larry were on to them. Seeing Susan's men exit together, Carter's thugs just shrugged, laughed and continued their drinking and card-playing.

When the Paradise Valley ranchhands returned from their night in Sundance, Snake Catcher was smoking his pipe on the balcony off his bedroom. Buck was clearly more intoxicated than the others. Snake Catcher disgustingly shook his head at the drunken men uttering, "Foolish juice."

Chapter 17

At sunrise, the new calves awaited their day to unite with the Paradise Valley Ranch cattle herd population. Snake Catcher and the dogs rode out to the "White branding ritual" arena on the outskirts of the ranch property with Slim, Larry, and Sammy, on Day Twenty-Four away from the reservation. The ranchhands volunteered for the branding duty on a Sunday, usually their day off, to straighten the ranch's schedule after the routine was disheveled from the stampede.

Meanwhile, Cook and Rains Down were in the kitchen preparing their meals along with meals that Ferdy would take to the branders later that morning. With hopes of spending some wooing time with Rains Down, Ferdy arrived early at the back door of the kitchen. He stopped just shy of entering when he heard his mother's voice; Ferdy stayed and listened when he heard his name in a conversation between his mother and the woman of his dreams. The women were discussing the future, and how Ferdy might fit into Rains Down's life.

After some meaningless conversation, Cook had bluntly asked out of nowhere, "Do you think that there will ever be a place in your heart for my son?"

Rains Down demurely answered, "I care deeply for Ferdy, you know that. I am wary of getting him in the middle of my family issues. He is a good man, but my father will make it quite difficult for Ferdy if he ever catches up with me. I do not want that for the man that I cherish; I will save that for someone of a lesser value."

Cook responded, "My son is a wise man; he will know what to do if that happens. He has put much time into his heart for you, but be warned, he will certainly run out of that time someday."

"I am afraid that Ferdy will be blinded by love and not see the danger he is in."

"That is to be his choice, once you have *told* him of these issues." And with that, Cook departed the kitchen for the dining-room for possible comments related to Susan's breakfast.

The tone Ferdy heard from Rains Down gave him reason to go forth with his pursuit of her. Ferdy turned and vacated the area, not wanting Rains Down to know he had overheard their private conversation.

Later that morning after breakfast, Susan relaxed at the porch sipping tea and gazing out at Paha Sapa with Painted Pony accompanying her. Buck rode in from the ranch's boundary carrying a telegram. He dismounted and delivered it to Susan. She quickly read the notice before translating the contents. "It's news from Earth Raven."

Painted Pony immediately perked up. "What does he say? Anything about me?"

"He writes that all is well with the authorities and they harbor no ill-will toward Snake Catcher with the soldier incident. And not only do the Blue Coats acknowledge his place here at the ranch, they also congratulate him on his nuptials," Susan relayed. As she folded the telegram, she happily added: "It is great that he no longer has a deadline hanging over him to return to the reservation, and he can stay as long as he would like."

Buck added, "That's great news; he will be pleased."

Painted Pony slouched and pouted, "Nothing about me?"

Susan and Buck both smiled at Painted Pony's secret infatuation with Earth Raven, yet secret only to her. Susan tried giving her some hope: "Maybe next time. We have to go get ready for church now."

Frowning, Painted Pony left for her room, leaving Buck and Susan alone on the porch together.

"Did you have a good time last night?" teased Susan.

"Too good. I don't remember riding home."

Susan smiled at him.

Buck continued, "But she turned me down for supper. I'm not sure what else to do."

"You could be persistent. Angel must get hundreds of

offers, and probably doesn't know which men are sincere and which just want to be seen with her. You just need to let her get used to you being around. That will show her that you are genuine."

Buck nodded agreeably prior to Susan entering the house.

About a half hour later, Susan stepped into the wagon for their Sunday jaunt to church. Painted Pony and Rains Down accompanied Susan as Ferdy was asked to remain at the ranch due to their recent trouble with Carter. Waves were exchanged as they parted, mostly between Ferdy and Rains Down.

Later that afternoon at the cemetery, Susan stood over the graves of her parents as she placed flowers on their headstones. After a respectful visit, she hurriedly returned to the house. Susan was enthusiastically anxious about giving Snake Catcher the wonderful news from Earth Raven, which meant they could now devote their time toward Paha Sapa's return. Susan encountered Ferdy on her path to the house. "Ferdy, when Snake Catcher returns his horse to the stables, please ask him to find me. I would like to speak with him."

"Yes, ma'am."

Meanwhile, Snake Catcher and the ranchhands were branding the new calves. Having fun and bonding was the last experience Snake Catcher expected from the day. It was his first experience at the White man's technique of claiming their property. He enjoyed the sizzling sound the iron made when it touched the calf's skin. As the hide turned bright red and smoked, it released a pungent ghastly scent of burnt flesh; that aroma just before a steak releases its deep-seared barbecue bouquet.

By mid-afternoon, enough time had passed to make Larry feel confident in discussing his gold-mining in Paha Sapa with Snake Catcher. Any longer than with someone other than a slow-minded person as in Larry, and the sincerity would seem to be absent. "Miss Susan explained to me how your people regrettably lost your land, including the place where I mine for gold. I'm not going back there because it is the right thing to do. Are we friends?"

Snake Catcher graciously nodded, instantly accepting Larry's apology. "We are good." That truce was a huge step for Snake Catcher; excepting forgiveness for the ravishment of his land. Snake Catcher had killed many who dared to do what

Larry had. Snake Catcher felt Larry's sincerity, and eagerly shook his hand with pride. They both felt cleansed about the exchange. Snake Catcher wanted peace on the ranch with all of his new friends. Likewise for Larry, as he was not a complicated man to have such worries hanging over him.

Snake Catcher was having such a good time branding the cattle and bonding with the men, that nightfall was hovering overhead when they all returned to the ranch.

There were a collection of empty wooden buckets kept in the corner of Susan's bedroom to be available for scooping out her bath water from the waterproof trough. There were four filled waterproof wooden buckets, two on each side of the fireplace, warming. There were fresh roses in a vase on the table for her enjoyment. No lights were lit in the bedroom, only the waning fire in the fireplace. Sleepily, Susan had earlier abandoned waiting for Snake Catcher to return. She had entered her bedroom, assumingly closing the door behind her; however, the dogs ajarred it before the door could be latched, then they departed after hearing Snake Catcher enter the front door. They scampered down the stairs to greet him, and Killer and Coyote ran out the front door as Snake Catcher closed the door behind him.

After receiving Susan's message from Ferdy, which was hours old, Snake Catcher stepped into Susan's open bedroom, and walked in on her washing herself with a cloth from the basin in her room. Tonight, she had decided a quick wash would satisfy her until bathing in the morning. Her back was to the door and she did not see him. Snake Catcher did not leave, instead, stood watching Susan and her busty silhouette-shadow which danced on the wall as she moved. Susan slipped on a robe and walked into the bedroom area where she discovered Snake Catcher had been standing. She was not angry, but he had surprised her bringing her to blush.

"You sent for me?"

"Yes, I asked Ferdy but that was..."

Snake Catcher interrupted, not wanting Susan to evade him again. He took advantage of the misunderstanding, and decided that since he was there to move slowly but persistently. Snake Catcher touched his shirt, as to show its filthiness. "Will want to bathe."

Susan instantly offered, "I can make you a bath."

"How does one *make* a bath?" he inquired.

"I mean I will pour some water into the bathing tub for you if you'd like."

Snake Catcher acceptingly nodded. He had not moved from his original stance, and observed as Susan selected one of the four warmed buckets of water from the side of the fireplace. When she attempt to pour it into the tub, he walked over and took the handle of the heavy bucket from her, lifting it for her. When Snake Catcher touched Susan's hand in grasping the handle, she pulled away, but only because she feared he would leave again if he felt her touching him as before. After pouring another warmed bucket in and then two room-temperature buckets of water from the trough in the tub to midway, Snake Catcher swirled his hand in the pool of water to check the temperature. "Warm."

"Too warm?" Susan asked softly.

Snake Catcher briefly shook his head. "Not had warm bath since water bubbling up in Paha Sapa."

"I'll be across the hall in the apothecary room if you need me." Susan began to slowly walk toward the door.

Without looking directly at her, Snake Catcher made his plea. "Lakota wives bathe husbands."

Susan stopped with her back to Snake Catcher, and without speaking looked down and sheepishly smiled. With her eyes diverted away from him, she mutely walked over, pulled a towel down from the shelf and began setting up the area for him, along with a washcloth and a khaki-colored bar of soap.

Snake Catcher was not a modest man, and undressed before stepping into the tub to sit down. Susan dunked the washcloth and began stroking his back with it, then his chest. After the completion of his bath, Susan held out a towel for Snake Catcher with her head slightly turned and her eyes diverted. After he donned the towel, Snake Catcher touched her face to look at him and pointed to the water. Susan mildly shook her head.

Snake Catcher insisted, "Yes. I will make new." With only the towel around him, Snake Catcher stepped out of the room for a moment only to return wearing fresh clothes. He then placed another log on the fire while Susan gathered more towels and her hair brush. Snake Catcher pulled the stopper to drain the tub, then replenished it with fresh water from the remaining two warmed buckets of water and room-temperature water from the trough.

Susan apprehensively removed her robe and stepped in, all the while he had no problem watching her. Snake Catcher washed her as she gained the courage to look into his eyes. He looked back unaffected, and continued his job. Unencumbered now, Susan stepped out to receive the towel that Snake Catcher was holding for her.

Susan dried off and donned her nightgown. He pulled the blanket off of the bed and spread it on the bench. Snake Catcher motioned for her to sit on the bench in front of the fireplace where a crackling fire was burning brighter. He brushed out Susan's damp hair, alternating with towel-drying and drying it against the warmth of the fire.

At that moment, the dogs made a noise from the yard behind the house, and Susan stood to look out the window. After seeing the dogs, she disregarded the noise. Susan returned to face the fireplace. Standing in back of her, Snake Catcher stepped closer until he was standing just inches from her back. When he brushed her shoulder with his cheek, Susan turned to face him. Snake Catcher brushed his cheek with hers until a kiss entwined them. Without leaving the kiss, Snake Catcher pulled the blanket to the floor with them. Flickering shadows of them making love illuminated from the firelight.

At midnight, after Susan and Snake Catcher had moved from the floor to the bed, she whispered, "Ake." Susan and Snake Catcher made love once again before the sun rose the next morning.

Chapter 18

Susan and Snake Catcher woke lying in bed together in each other's arms. Snake Catcher commented, somewhat scowling, "Bed moves, not firm like ground."

Susan laughed, knowing Snake Catcher was talking about the lovemaking in bed. "Should we move back to the floor?" she teased.

Snake Catcher, hiding his smile, rejected the idea. "Hiya." After a brief pause he continued, "You are Lakota wife now. You will need a name."

Susan giggled, then asked him teasingly, "You mean, something like *Snuggles-A-Lot* or *Pretty-Cold-Feet*?"

Grunting, Snake Catcher light-heartedly shook his head, fighting back his smile. "Hiya. Wicahpi Kute, Shooting Star." Snake Catcher demonstrated with hand gestures by putting his hand on her heart, then up to the sky to show Susan that she felt love deep from the heart. "No other rides off on horse as you do. No other shoots for stars in all you do."

Susan nestled with Snake Catcher for payment of his flattery.

"Will move my room here today," Snake Catcher announced, as a matter of a statement instead of a question.

Susan blushingly smiled and nodded in agreement. Face to face, Susan studied Snake Catcher's eyes. He tilted his head as to ask why. Susan clarified, "You are beautiful. I am in awe of your courage, your bravery, and not just because you are a warrior and hunter...but because you have lost so much. Another man would have given up, but not you."

"Do what needs," Snake Catcher said, waving off the

compliment.

"That's what I mean; I've never known anyone like you before. You move forward when most men would have given up."

Snake Catcher vulnerably looked down at Susan's angelic face while asking, "Move forward with you?"

Appreciative for his love, Susan replied, "Yes."

Snake Catcher offered to clarify Earth Raven's statement, "When he leave, Earth Raven said it was time to be happy."

"And are you?"

"Yes."

"That reminds me. I received a telegram from Earth Raven. He reports that all is good, and the Blue Coats even wish you well."

Snake Catcher jumped out of bed with joy at the announcement. "We will go to the river, bring food. No chores. Much to praise."

After dressing, Susan and Snake Catcher ate breakfast in the diningroom. Appetites were huge from not eating of late. Cook packed them a picnic lunch and set the basket on the table for them. Smirking, she commented, "I see everyone has their appetite back."

Cook walked into the kitchen wearing a look of contentment. Susan playfully reached out her foot, and secretly coiled it around Snake Catcher's leg under the table. Ferdy stepped to the door and whispered, "Miss Susan, would you know where Rains Down would be?"

"She is in the kitchen, Ferdy."

"Thank you, ma'am."

Ferdy trotted toward the kitchen.

Snake Catcher dumbfoundedly shook his head before interjecting, "When will he not look there first?"

Susan's gigglish laugh filled the room.

Ferdy stepped around the corner to the kitchen, and he caught his mother's eyes before Rains Down could spot him lurking about. Cook received Ferdy's message, and stepped out of the back kitchen door. Approaching Rains Down, Ferdy said, "Hola, Rains Down."

"Hola, Ferdy."

"Can I help you with those?" Ferdy asked generously.

"No gracias."

"Then maybe you will let me take you into Sundance tonight."

"No, I cannot. I have chores to do."

"No, you will be done. I know you do not work tonight."

"I won't be able to."

"Why not?"

"Because after you court me, you will want to marry me."

"I already want to marry you; it is you who won't unless you are courted."

"I am to be single if I want to keep my position here."

"No you don't. Miss Susan won't mind."

"Si. She wants me across the hall, and she wouldn't want your skinny behind up there."

"We could ask her."

"No! I do not want to lose my job," Rains Down protested. Then, panicking, she announced, "You do not make enough money for the both of us."

"What do we need money for? We have a place to stay and food to eat."

"What if I would want to have a family someday? And a nice hacienda I could decorate?"

"What's wrong with here?"

"It is not mine. I am not the lady of this hacienda. I work here. I know Miss Susan makes us all feel like this is our home, but it is not."

"Don't you like me?" Ferdy appealed.

"Si, Ferdy, I do like you, but I have to think about my future."

"I can be your future."

"I must go" and with that, Rains Down left the room.

The kitchen was engulfed by the sounds of Ferdy's sighs as Rains Down quickly moved toward the stairs.

Susan and Snake Catcher had relocated to the porch rockers and finished their tea while having a conversation about how Paha Sapa appear to be thickening its branches, as it seemed to also be enjoying the bright sunny day that was bestowed upon them. The dogs curiously sniffed at the contents of the unopened picnic basket sitting beside them. After a while, Snake Catcher commandeered the basket, then the couple and the dogs walked toward the stables where Susan and Snake Catcher mounted their horses. Susan teased Snake Catcher by challenging him to a race. Then she commanded, "Let's go Sparks, live up to your name!"

The chase was afoot, and after Snake Catcher allowed Susan the first starting position by pretending to be repositioning the basket, he began pursuing her. The dogs devotedly chased after them.

Meanwhile, back in Susan's bedroom, Rains Down began replenishing the trough and buckets of water at the fireplace. She looked perplexed as to the quantity missing. After deciphering the mystery of the missing water, a soft smile came to her face.

Snake Catcher braggingly escorted Susan to his favorite tranquil location under a tree near the river. After setting up a picnic site, Snake Catcher coerced Susan into skinny-dipping with him. Playfulness brought them to make love in the river.

In the staff lounge, Painted Pony sat quietly without the sounds or presence of anyone else. With the window open and the door ajar creating a cross-breeze, the air flowed steadier than in her private quarters. She readily had her study material and Bible beside her, just in case anyone would happen by to inquire about what was occupying her time–especially her father. Painted Pony knew it was misleading, but she did not want others to know of her intimate writings. Excerpts were being recorded in her private journal with respect to Earth Raven. Painted Pony had secretly retrieved Susan's telegram received from Earth Raven the day before, from her bedroom's wastebasket. The high-spirited teenager had been analyzing every word of the message to embrace his unique writing mannerisms. Painted Pony would imagine Earth Raven at the reservation tapping out each letter. Except, in her imagination, the room in which he sent his message would be that of gold statues, long-tabled buffets and lace draperies. It was just as she had imagined what the Queen of England would environ herself with in her everyday life, instead of the small wooden one-room shack where Earth Raven's message was actually sent.

Painted Pony thought of Earth Raven's next visit to the ranch, and about how she might wear her hair to entice him, and about which clothes she would wear to impress him. Painted Pony knew she would have to be clever to escape Slim's overbearing parental guardianship, forever watching her around Earth Raven.

Painted Pony wrote out three topics of conversation and took them to their logical conclusions, just as Susan had taught Painted Pony within her teachings. The discussions, of course, would be articulated at an exquisite gala held in Earth Raven's honor for successfully orchestrating a truce between Natives and Whites for all time, as medals were given to such men. She would be the one he would invite to premier on his arm during the event as they flawlessly mingled with the country's most elite society. Painted Pony would wear a canary-colored gown made of European lace decorated with spun gold embroidery. A golden diadem, made of the most precious jewels from around the world and designed exclusively for Painted Pony, would be set in her magnificent hairstyle. Earth Raven and Painted Pony would dance together into the night, floating as light as a feather while twirling effortlessly. Earth Raven would end their evening with one breathy lightly-placed kiss on her cheek. Then Painted Pony would be swept away by a horse-drawn carriage; all the while, Earth Raven watching her leave until the carriage was well out of sight.

As Painted Pony sat in her dreamy state writing his name over and over in her journal, the minutes turned into hours. The shadows in the room shifted, showing the passage of time.

A few majestic hours later, Susan and Snake Catcher were dressed again and talking while lying in the tall willowy grass.

"Is this the way you saw your future?" teased Susan.

Almost convincingly, Snake Catcher replied, "Yes."

Susan spontaneously laughed as she challenged his truthfulness. "Wowicakesni."

Chuckling, Snake Catcher responded, "Maybe not but am happy with this future."

As the softly blowing breeze danced with her hair, Susan softly smiled and lovingly asked, "What do you want for your future, besides me?" She paused, then continued with a change of tone, "Would you like to stand and make a fight for what you have lost? Without saddening or angering you again, maybe we can try to bring about the reinstatement of the '68 treaty. We can fight to have it upheld, and have Paha Sapa returned to the Lakota people. I have already written a letter to the President, and then to another former President that might be better suited to help us. That is somewhere to start."

A soft smile of contentment came upon Snake Catcher's

face for the generosity of his wife. "We will make a stand. It will be our children's heritage."

Susan was greatly surprised, and impressed with Snake Catcher's improving vocabulary. "Heritage? That's a big word..." She was then abruptly struck with what Snake Catcher had snuck into his statement. "Children?! No one said anything about children," Susan teased, as Snake Catcher insisted that she bear him many to fill the ranch house. They playfully rolled around on the ground together.

A rabbit frantically jumped out of the grass and hopped away from them. As it caught Snake Catcher's attention, he announced, "It is time to provide supper."

Snake Catcher was about to commence the chase, when Susan distressfully grabbed outwardly to stop him. "What? No, don't kill it; I can't eat a rabbit if I've seen how cute and fluffy it was."

Snake Catcher grunted, disregarding the pleas to save the animal, and took out his knife.

Susan demanded, "Hiya."

Susan's compassion for all things cute and fluffy brought Snake Catcher to shake his head, and he returned the knife to its holder. He mumbled to himself sarcastically, somewhat mocking her: "Fluffy, humph. Tasty, *yes!*" While wobbling his head back and forth as he walked over to his gear, Snake Catcher added rhetorically, "Is fish fluffy?"

Snake Catcher and Susan passed their day as she sketched him masterfully spearing fish for supper. After gathering up their belongings, they leisurely rode through the pasture and past their herd. In the near distance, Paha Sapa was so radiant a site, that it brought them to a halt.

Snake Catcher commented with pride, "Land is most sacred to people. It will be here long after our grandchildren's grandchildren leave. We are only borrowing it from them, and we have let it slip away."

"Then it is time to get it back. I did not see the importance of land, that was my father's dream. I am so glad that I continued his quest. This will be our children's someday."

Snake Catcher wittily affirmed, "Yes, all ten of them."

Distressed, Susan objected, "Pardon me?!"

Snake Catcher lightheartedly smiled and gleefully trotted off, leaving Susan there in her astonishment. She soon began trotting after him to get a clarification on his understanding of their numbering system.

When the couple arrived back home, Snake Catcher quickly relinquished the fish he had caught to Cook. The mistress of the kitchen was joyous; that was until Snake Catcher informed her that he and Susan had decided to skip supper. Cook appeared confused. "Are you two not feeling well?"

Not returning an answer, Snake Catcher headed straight for the stairs, and up to the bedroom where his wife was waiting for him.

Chapter 19

Susan and Snake Catcher were sitting on the porch drinking tea together and gazing at each other, taking breaks only to gaze out at the brilliance of Paha Sapa. The pair had risen before any of the staff to view the dew, drifting within the hills, slowly descended into the earth. As he smoked, Susan sketched on her sketch pad, amused at the ringlets of smoke swirling around Snake Catcher's head.

When called into breakfast by Rains Down some time later, they discovered that Cook had plentifully prepared them poached fish with their eggs for breakfast. Grins came over the faces of Susan and Snake Catcher, knowing Cook must have been faintly annoyed at their skipping supper of the previous evening. Susan and Snake Catcher uttered nothing and happily ate their unorthodox breakfasts. Cook stood anonymously in the vicinity of the kitchen door while smirking at the repercussions they reaped for crossing her. She then began smiling at the betrothed couple, knowing they were just that now–a couple.

After their copious breakfast, Susan and Snake Catcher rode out to the pasture together to begin the daily chores. This was the first time he had joined her in these efforts.

Larry was enjoying the crisp brisk morning during his time off forenoon while sitting out on a bench just outside of the staff quarters. He was pondering the conversation that he'd had with Snake Catcher two days earlier during their cattle branding session. Larry felt a mixture of sadness and contentment over abandoning his hopes of striking it rich. Saddened thinking sprang from how his *golden* dreams would no longer be a reality.

And contented thinking rose from knowing that any riches that would come his way would not be at the expense of another. Even with his mental slowness, Larry indubitably knew that he would need another avenue for creating additional income in order to complete his dreams of owning a saloon in Sundance. This was precisely why Larry was acutely proud of himself that morning, for he was moving forward with another plan.

When Larry had been in Sundance at the saloon that past Saturday night playing cards, he was approached by a neighboring rancher about a job opening for breaking horses. Larry had accepted the job right on the spot with the condition that it would not interfere with his current ranching hours or duties for Susan.

The good part of his new job was that the pay would be equal to what he made from the Paradise Valley Ranch by only working part-time; however, the bad news was that it was backbreaking work so it could only be done sparingly. Another negative was that if he hurt himself breaking horses, he would not get any pay from either job.

Larry chose to be optimistic about his new adventures, and he mounted his horse before heading off to begin his new part-time job.

After his first morning of horse taming, Larry returned to the Paradise Valley Ranch just before his afternoon shift for Susan was to start. He undoubtably felt sore, but had returned unhurt.

After a long unquestionably rewarding day out doing chores together, Susan and Snake Catcher were prompt when coming to supper, as to not upset Cook again. They greeted her with blaringly cryptic smiles. Cook grinned skeptically at their behavior, grunted and stepped back into the kitchen. Susan and Snake Catcher chatted, smiled and looked into each other's eyes like newlyweds during their supper, oblivious to any sense of cares of troubles.

In their bedroom that evening, Susan and Snake Catcher were drifting off in slumber when an unfamiliar creek sounded out from the floor. Knowing the dogs had wandered outside that night, Susan quickly looked up in a panic for other signs of an intruder before picking up the revolver hidden under her pillow. She aimed it at their shadowy visitant, and paused for a moment, not registering friend or foe. "Stop where you are or I'll shoot!"

Snake Catcher awoke as the ominous murky figure continued creeping toward them. Susan caught a glimpse of their assailant from the flickering light off the weakening fireplace glow. She recognized him as being one of Carter's ranchhands, and now a prowler who was quickly bearing down on them with a gun in his hand. Susan unflinchingly squeezed the trigger, firing into him. Snake Catcher watched the event and was readily prepared for the blast, but the loud eruption startled him, nonetheless. Susan and Snake Catcher witnessed a protruding puff of smoke at the end of the barrel, and a simultaneous red spraying of droplets outward from the ranch-hand's chest. After a moment, the smoke dissipated, and the man fell backwards with a loud thump. Susan and Snake Catcher sprang out of bed and donned wraps before others appeared just outside their bedroom door. Snake Catcher instinctively kicked the weapon from the invader's hand while Susan checked the man's pulse. He was deceased. Right away, Susan regimentally instructed Larry to ride into Sundance for the Sheriff. While they waited for the lawman to arrive, the couple dressed and moved themselves into the guest bedroom until the blood could be cleaned up.

It was an hour and a half later when Susan spotted Larry from a distance returning with the Sheriff. Walking Snake Catcher to the staff quarters, she cautiously suggested, "It would be best if you wait here until he leaves, then we can return to the guest bedroom."

Snake Catcher, clearly reluctant, agreed to the seclusion as Susan gently nudged him with counsel to stay there; soon after, she left.

The Sheriff was not a large man, but he had the presence and ego of one. He often smelled of tobacco and spirits, being a frequent visitor of Willy's Saloon. He did not have the time nor patience for a wife and family, which also gave him reason to frequent the second floor of Willy's. Susan was always apprehensive about him, being in the same good-ole-boy's club as Carter.

The Sheriff came up to inspect the area of dissension. "What in the blazes of hell happened here?"

"I was sleeping when I heard a creek, and he was standing over me with his gun drawn. I told him to stop where he was but he didn't, so I shot him."

"Well, Susan, you *did* do that."

After the Sheriff grumbled and muttered around the area, including in the surrounding rooms, he continued, "He's one of Carter's men. It looks as though he came in through your front medicine room window. I'm guessing he used his pocket knife to lift the latch. I accept that your story is accurate. I'll have Carter come by tomorrow with a wagon to pick up the body. Will that be agreeable to you?"

A placid nod came from Susan as she unmaliciously requested, "Can I get him out of my bedroom?"

"Sure. Roll 'em up and set him outside."

As the Sheriff left, Buck and Larry retrieved a tarp from the storage shed located beyond the stables. Then the two men wrapped the intruder, and stored him in the stables. Rains Down and Susan earnestly cleaned up the blood with somberness.

Susan exhaustedly retreated for the night in the guest bedroom with her husband. When they nestled into bed, he felt her shivering and lovingly comforted her. He had a stoic expression. Snake Catcher was a warrior, and knew what death felt like. It was not the first life's end at Susan's hands but she was not comfortable with the deed. Snake Catcher displayed pride for her that she made the kill, like a trophy wife; like a Lakota warrior's wife.

Chapter 20

The morning was tense. Susan was sitting on the porch very early warming herself from her hot tea while waiting for Carter to show. All five Paradise Valley ranchhands were armed and positioned strategically around the area, Sammy and Larry on horseback. Supportingly, Snake Catcher had stationed himself alongside Susan's rocking chair, and in back of him stood several arrowhead-tipped arrows beside his bow. The body of Carter's ranchhand was now on the ground in front of the house, still wrapped.

Soon a trail of dust in the distance indicated that Carter was approaching. He arrived on horseback with two of his men manning a horse-drawn cart.

Carter wasted no time as he squawked out, "What the hell did you do to my man?"

Susan agitatedly responded, "Do to your man? Were you recently dragged by a horse, Carter? *Your man* was shot standing in my house in the middle of the night with a drawn weapon."

Carter blistered back, "I have better things to do then to come here and tidy up for you."

Susan did not show to be intimidated. Carter's ranchhands busily loaded the body onto their wagon as Carter and Susan continued bickering. Susan sarcastically sassed back at Carter. "Really? Well, there is a large puddle of blood in my upstairs bedroom that needs tidying up now. How about you tidy that up? What the hell was he doing in my house, Carter? Did you send him?"

Carter leisurely leaned back on his horse, somewhat smirking. "I don't know what you are talking about."

"Suppose that's what you'll be telling his family?"

Carter ignored Susan's comment and added, "I imagine with all of the trouble you've been having here lately, you'll be looking to sell this heap. I could take it off your hands for five dollars an acre and fifty cents a head."

Susan did not justify the mockery with a response. "The Sheriff was out here last night looking over the area. I'm sure he'll have some questions for you."

Carter continued smirking, and when he turned his horse around to leave, Susan, while rocking in her chair, casually and coolly stated with abundant confidence, "I'll be expecting reimbursement for my tarp, Carter."

The comment was not acknowledged by Carter as he and his men left. Sammy and Larry rode a fair distance behind them, making sure they did not start trouble with the herd again. Rains Down, Painted Pony and Cook all stepped out onto the porch while watching them leave.

Susan gave a warning to her staff about their future at the ranch: "It will probably get worse around here before it gets better. If any of you want to leave, I will harbor no ill will."

As their heads confidently shook from side to side, they all returned to their chores.

Pridefulness surrounded Snake Catcher as he grinned at Susan's courage and tenacity. "Today is day we change the future," he said.

Satisfaction filled Susan as she smiled, gently mocking him while bantering back, "The future of our grandchildren's grandchildren?"

In the lounge a few moments later, Susan graciously extended to Snake Catcher, "I will write what you want." She put pen to paper, and about a half hour later, Susan read the outcome of the letter aloud for Snake Catcher.

"Dear Mr. Nathaniel Black Deer Davis, I am writing you today to thank you for all that you have done for me. I am here at the Paradise Valley Ranch and am very pleased with the outcome of my mission.

"There is still something that weighs heavy on our minds, though. My wife, Susan Paradise, also known as Wicahpi Kute, wrote a letter to your President several days ago. We also would like for others to know of our intentions.

We are seeking the return of Paha Sapa to the
Lakota people as initially outlined in the 1868
Fort Laramie Treaty. Perhaps you may know of
any answers that impedes the return of our
sacred land. Very truly yours, Snake Catcher,
Zuzeca Wawoyuspa, Lakota, Paradise Valley
Ranch, Sundance, Wyoming Territory."

Snake Catcher agreeingly nodded. Susan contently smiled
as she addressed the envelope. Rains Down was asked to
summons Slim to deliver the letter to the postmaster; however,
Sammy offered since he planned a ride into Sundance later that
evening. Susan and Snake Catcher were famished after their
scuffle with Carter, and went in to eat an early lunch in the
diningroom.

As Sammy's departure time arrived late that afternoon, Buck
decided to accompany him for the ride into Sundance. Sammy
was on his way to have an enjoyable time visiting with others.
He was not meeting anyone specific that evening, but was
hopeful for some polite conversation. Although, due to Sammy's
ethnicity, he was not permitted to fraternize with any of Willy's
patrons; he *was* welcome at the town eatery and that was
agreeable to him inasmuch as Sammy did not drink what Willy
was serving.

Once in Sundance, Buck and Sammy went their separate
ways. Buck set off on a mission to entice Miss Angel Blue to join
him in sharing a meal or a walk. He entered the saloon and
ordered a drink for encouragement. In the meantime, Sammy
entered the town eatery and was greeted by the hostess. She
informed him that the wait for a table would be greater than
forty-five minutes; not giving mind to the fact that the estimation was somewhat exaggerated. After hearing his sighs, she
offered a solution to his delayed seating predicament; she said,
"If the patron at Table Nine would be agreeable, you can be
seated there right away."

Nkechi, a housekeeper from a neighboring ranch in
Sundance, occupied Table Nine. Sammy was in luck that
evening, because Nkechi had seen Sammy there before and
actually had an eye for him. After making the introduction, the
hostess went about her duties.

Sammy was immediately taken with Nkechi's beauty and
proper etiquette. They had instant chemistry and embarked on

a lengthy conversation during which Sammy learned that Nke-chi's family was from Igbo in Central Africa just north of the equator in the Congo. Her name meant *God gave me a blessing.* Sammy expressed to Nkechi that she was lucky to have known where she came from, especially living in this country, as he had no idea about his heritage other than being born in a southern state. Sammy did not tell her he was from Georgia for fear someone would overhear him, which could spark a message to the retaliating Master Briggs of Sammy's whereabouts.

Nkechi had never been a slave, and was of a Black family that was educated. Sammy was a proud man, and did not offer an apology for not having better grammar; nonetheless, she was not seeking one. Nkechi had already been somewhat smitten with him since the day she spotted him at the eatery six months prior. Sammy, however, was still reserved about any paring, only because of his uncertainty about being ready to find love again after Annabella's tragic end. It was a demise for which he blamed himself. Nkechi would be fortunate to have developed a patient way about her that appealed to Sammy. They made polite conversation that night, and agreed to meet in Sundance once a week to share a meal together. That was all the commit-ment Sammy could muster.

Meanwhile, Buck sought Angel at the saloon; however, she was nowhere to be found. The relief bartender suggested that Angel might be out for the evening in the company of another gentleman caller. After realizing his misfortune, Buck strolled over to the eatery hoping to salvage some of his pride by having supper with his friend before riding back to the ranch together. When Buck spotted Sammy having supper with the African beauty, he backed out of the room, only to have stepped on Lily's delicate foot in the process. After apologies were offered from Buck, the hostess suggested that he might buy Lily supper to make up for his clumsiness. Buck was astonished at the employee's forwardness, yet delighted to have the company. After the hostess sat the two at an "unexpected" open table, she returned to other duties.

Since Lily worked with Angel, Buck assumed that she would know of Angel's activities. The first half of their evening's conversation was spent with Buck asking what Lily knew about Angel, and the performer's new gentleman caller. As Lily sidestepped the topic, she began telling Buck about herself. Buck was surprised to learn that Lily had also lived all the way across the country in the smaller town of Los Angeles. Even though it pained her to speak of Angel while she was trying to get Buck to notice her, Lily's impeccable ability at rerouting the subject would bring them to spend a good amount of time talking about their daily lives. Buck was also surprised to discover that Lily had a nightingale singing voice; however, Willy would not allow her to perform due to being an unknown.

Lily had actually followed Buck over to the eatery that evening after spotting him in the saloon talking to the bartender; nevertheless, she did not offer that information. As the four of them timed their departures perfectly and left the eatery, the hostess winked at the girls and gave herself a smile for match-making jobs well-done.

As the men were riding home that evening, Sammy was surprised that Buck was very chatty about his evening with Lily and never once mentioned Angel. Of course, he did not point that out to him. Sammy was also beaming from the *accidental* encounter of his own.

Snake Catcher and Susan walked out of the diningroom after sharing their supper together and sat on the porch a while. Painted Pony soon joined them. Snake Catcher routinely lit his pipe and smoked. Painted Pony filled the night air with questions for Snake Catcher about why Paha Sapa was so important to him.

Snake Catcher was honored by Painted Pony's curiosity and offered, "They are the beginning of all time for the Lakota people." He went on to tell of how they were developed, then added, "Do you know why the two-legged animals are superior to the four-legged?"

"No? *Tell* me." Painted Pony sat by Snake Catcher's feet, and listened as he began to paraphrase his story.

"There was controversy over who would flourish and who would be the submissive. So all of the different breeds of creatures in the world gathered at Paha Sapa, the center of the universe, to conclude the matter once and for all. They decided that the winners of a race around the hills were the way to domination for all time, giving the winners the right to be the hunters and the losers would be the prey. They would divide into the two-legged group and the four-legged group. Even though the birds could fly, they had two legs, so they would be paired with the two-legged racers.

"As the race seemed to go on forever, the magpie decided to rest itself on the buffalo's ear to regain its strength. After a while, the magpie determined that it was comfortable there and concluded that it would stay. The weather conditions would hinder both sides at times, yet even after some had perished, the others pressed on. Nearing the end of the race, the buffalo looked to be in the lead, but then the magpie simply flew off with much energy and over the finish line, consequently winning the race. The magpie was cheered and given a rainbow of colors to sport on its tail for eternity. That was also when the humans, being of two legs, were presented with arrows and a bow in order to authoritatively hunt the buffalo."

Susan and Painted Pony had listened intensively to Snake Catcher's tale, and as always, both of the ladies were enchanted by him and his story; another that had been passed down through the generations. After the storytelling, Painted Pony dreamily wandered off toward the staff quarters. Susan and Snake Catcher were still on the porch to greet Buck and Sammy back from their night away, and they turned in shortly afterwards. The married couple were delighted to be back in their own bed and in a room free of ejected blood.

Chapter 21

A few days had passed with calmness on the ranch. The Paradise Valley Ranch dwellers were counting their blessings, especially since it was a Sunday. Susan rose early, leaving her husband in bed to sleep. She, with her church clothes over one arm, entered the apothecary room to dress. Soon thereafter, Susan stepped into the wagon for her trek to attend church. Slim, Painted Pony and Rains Down joined her with the ranchhand driving.

Ceremoniously, after church, Susan stood over the graves of her parents with the anticipated flowers for them. Simultaneously in the stables, Snake Catcher looked out at Susan and asked Sammy, "Why does she stand there?"

Sammy explained, "That's where her parents be."

Snake Catcher looked strangely at Sammy. "That's where she buries the dead?" he asked, thinking that was where the Crow brave was buried as well.

"Yea, she visits there every Sunday afta' church. Have you never seen her leave?"

Snake Catcher looked back out at Susan. "Hiya. Do not know that word. Church."

"That be a place to pray. Pa'haps next week she will take you."

Snake Catcher, still looking out at Susan, answered, "Perhaps." Snake Catcher watched as Susan walked back to the house. Susan was so immersed in her thoughts, she did not see him standing by the stables. Even when he followed her into the house, Susan did not awaken from her thoughts, and she still did not notice Snake Catcher as she walked upstairs.

A half hour later when Susan reappeared, her clothes were that of common-day. Susan joined Snake Catcher, now sitting on the porch. She sat but did not speak, only watched as the smoke from Snake Catcher's pipe swirled around his head.

There was no awkward silence between them, yet Snake Catcher felt compassionately compelled to ask, "Wicahpi Kute have a bad heart?"

Susan lightly rocked in her chair, as she looked outward toward Paha Sapa. She leisurely answered, "No, why? Does it look as though my heart is bad?"

Snake Catcher, turning away from Susan, disclosed, "Yes."

Snake Catcher and Susan sat in silence briefly before Susan continued, "When you were there when your brother died..."

Snake Catcher turned to look at Susan. After she paused, he again said, "Yes."

Susan was still looking out toward the hills while adding, "Was he at peace?"

Snake Catcher looked away again toward Paha Sapa before answering the difficultly painful question. "Blood flowed from him. He wait for his brother to be there with him, and to make known about you through his book. Then he left peacefully."

Susan soberly nodded. She and Snake Catcher sat in silence for some time that late afternoon. Susan began sketching Paha Sapa with the ranch graveyard in the foreground.

Chapter 22

Susan began her day alone on the porch, smiling as she appeared amused with thoughts of her husband tirelessly chopping wood out back so soon in the day. She sipped her steaming tea, and watched the yellowy-orange aura of the sun rising above the horizon of the earth.

Another of Carter's men had previously ridden onto the Paradise Valley Ranch property while the hour was still in darkness and snuck over near the house. He hid behind the stables until he deemed it an appropriate time to aim and then shoot at Susan. Afterwards, he wildly rode off on his horse, just as Buck and Sammy ran out of the stables after breaking away from immersion in early chores. Susan fell to the floor of the porch in the remnants of her own blood. Blood splatter had danced while decorating the front of the house and the nearby chairs. Snake Catcher flew through the house and was the first one by her side. He scooped Susan up into his arms and held her as he cursed the shooter in Lakota and watched the blood ooze from her head.

Snake Catcher urgently raced up the stairs and then carried Susan to the apothecary room, her body being as limp as a rag doll. Rains Down followed the blood that was marking their trail winding up the stairs. He tried to enlist help from Rains Down, but she was at a loss as to what to do. Then Rains Down decided to mimic what she had seen Susan do with those who were hurt. She placed a clean towel to Susan's head with a fair amount of pressure. This seemed to stop the bleeding.

Immediately, Buck rocketed off on his horse to call on Doc Brown, twelve miles away. A snippet over an hour and a half later, Doc Brown was tending to Susan's head wound. The doctor was a round man who always carried a black leather bag. His lined face had seen more than his share of tragedies, but none as bad as with women and children. His words were simple: "The good news is that the bullet only grazed her head. The bad news is that it is my opinion Susan should be awake by now. I want you to watch her for the next twenty-four hours. If she wakes, keep her awake for at least four hours. Do you understand?"

"Yes, doctor," Rains Down confirmed.

After the doctor completed his examination of her, Snake Catcher did not speak but knelt at Susan's side and reached for her hand. Doc Brown observed Snake Catcher's behavior as he acknowledged, "I guess many people in the county were wrong about you. You really do care for her, don't you? You are a misunderstood creature, my friend. I hope she recovers."

Snake Catcher did not respond but stayed focused on Susan. Sometime later, when her dogs were scratching and whimpering at the door, he realized Doc had departed.

By midmorning, Cook was infuriatedly throwing buckets of water, which had been supplied by the ranchhands, on the front of the house to wash away the coagulated blood. A sniffling Painted Pony swiftly swept the bloody-water from the porch as if it were made of fire.

After conferring with the other ranchhands, Buck headed back into Sundance–this time to fetch the Sheriff. Snake Catcher and the dogs continued to sit with Susan as daylight passed into night.

Sammy sat on the porch for hours waiting for word from Snake Catcher concerning Susan, or Buck regarding the Sheriff. Then Buck deflatedly returned without the Sheriff and informed the anxiously awaiting Sammy, "The Sheriff wasn't there, but I left word for him to come out here right away."

"Buck, what we gonna do without Miss Susan? This can't be happenin'."

Buck was eager to put Sammy's fears to rest. "Don't write her off just yet, Sammy. Miss Susan is a fighter. We'll keep the ranch going for her until she recovers."

Sammy nodded somberly in agreement.

The Paradise Valley Ranch folks held a vigil for Susan. They lit candles and prayed for her recovery. They sang hymns to bring a merciful God closer to her and into the house.

Chapter 23

When the sun rose over the homestead, Snake Catcher was right beside his wounded wife. However, he was feeling weary when Rains Down entered the room to begin watch over Susan. Snake Catcher collapsed on the bed that he had shared with his wife, passing out from exhaustion.

When the Sheriff finally arrived mid-afternoon, Snake Catcher rose to the sounds of him shuffling about outside. While listening to the Sheriff interview Buck now in the house, Snake Catcher moved quietly down the stairs.

"Did anyone see anything? Did you see who did it?"

"No, Sheriff, but we know it was one of Carter's men," Buck offered.

"But did you see him do it?"

Buck sarcastically fired back, "No, but I don't have to see my horse *mess* to know he was the one who dunnit."

Snake Catcher unchallengingly emerged from the stairs and spun his flippant accusation toward the Sheriff. "Is this White man justice?"

"Without a witness, there's nothing I can do. Sorry."

"As are we," retorted Snake Catcher, wearing an ominous expression.

After the Sheriff left, Snake Catcher assessed Susan's condition with the help of Rains Down, but no change was apparent. He wearily returned to bed. The mood at the ranch was grim while Susan remained unconscious.

An hour later, Snake Catcher rose from bed and sat in the chair at Susan's bedside tending to her as she did for him. As he laid his head on top of her body outside of the blankets with his arms out around her, a lone tear trickled down his hardened face emitting a thousand words of worry. Snake Catcher stared motionless into the thirty-sixth hour of Susan's unconsciousness. The apothecary fireplace dimmed through the passing of time.

By midnight, Snake Catcher had dressed in the original Native clothes that were on his back the day he arrived at the ranch. They were still blood-stained by the malicious bullet from Carter's gun. The Lakota warrior utilized paints and mixtures from Susan's apothecary supplies to don his tribal face–ready for battle.

One last task was necessary before making his journey toward retribution. Snake Catcher began burning a bundle of sage. A feather was used to disperse the smoke from the *smudging* bundle. It was offered to the north, south, east, then to the west. The smoke was offered up to the heavens and down to the earth. Snake Catcher drew the smoke upwards to his heart, inhaling small amounts of the cleansing aromatic smoke before he drew the smoke over his head, and then over his entire body to spiritually cleanse himself while driving out the negative and unwanted spirits. Snake Catcher spoke toward Susan in Lakota as the energy and aroma were released with the smoke, he chanted, "Today is the day of honor, standing before you with my fist to the heart, your death will be avenged."

As Snake Catcher brought himself to leave the room, a weakened but strong-willed voice came back to him. "Do not write me off just yet, my husband."

Snake Catcher hurried to Susan's side. "Wicahpi Kute, you are a timeless star. Do not leave me."

Seeing his painted face of war, Susan replied, "You are my shining star, do not leave me. If you go to seek your revenge, you will surely leave me."

Snake Catcher compliantly nodded and called for Rains Down. To keep Susan awake, a mojo formula of strong caffeine was made from tree bark, as per Doc Brown's orders.

Chapter 24

The next morning brought Snake Catcher to fuss naggingly over his wife, despite his true intentions of making her comfortable. Susan sat in bed while fending off her husband's bothersome mothering. Fresh roses replaced wilted ones in a vase on the table that had resulted from days without Snake Catcher leaving her side. As Susan appeared somewhat annoyed, she recapitulated, "I am feeling much better. Stop doting on me!"

"You will be better when *I* am ready."

Susan snickered at Snake Catcher's nervousness and lightheartedly teased, "I thought you didn't know *how* to say I?"

Snake Catcher affectionately poked fun at Susan. "*I* am learning."

Susan watched as Snake Catcher tidied the room before leaving, having volunteered to complete his wife's neglected chores.

With thoughts of Susan's recent brush with death, her staff secretly and privately took stock in what they all had in their lives, besides the obvious fortune of knowing Susan. Buck was thankful to have been qualified for the premium job of foreman, especially with such a checkered past as his. Rains Down knew deep-down that Ferdy would be someone who would protect her from any upheaval from her family, and she felt fortunate that she was the one Ferdy loved. Painted Pony was appreciative for the opportunity to have had an education, along with being Sparky's caregiver, and she could not help but to include thoughts of her fondness for Earth Raven who happened upon her life. Larry, even with his slowness, was a wise man in knowing the importance of being taught not to profit from someone else's loss, while not allowing that discouragement to extinguish his ultimate dream of owning a saloon. Slim was thankful for the courage to have taken Painted Pony out of her situation as an infant, and even more thankful for the courage to have told her about it. Sammy had gratitude for gaining his freedom, and having the strength to consider a life with someone after losing Annabella. Ferdy could think about few things in life other that Rains Down and, of course, his doting mother. Cook was grateful for having been a wife to the bravest man she had ever known, and for his giving her a wonderfully devoted son. Susan, too, added to the litany of gratitude and thought to herself, "I'm grateful for not having just one thing to be grateful for."

That afternoon, Susan wobbled out onto the porch where she found Snake Catcher and Buck whispering in an alliance. Startled to see her, the two men sprang to their feet to help Susan to a porch chair.

Snake Catcher squawked, "I did not say you were ready to be well."

"I'm feeling much better, stop fussing. I needed some fresh air."

After assessing the temperament around her, Susan directed her question toward Buck while knowing that Snake Catcher would not understand the meaning. "What are you two conspiring?"

Without recognition to Susan's interrogation, Buck did not return to his seat, but excused himself. Susan poked fun at Buck's unwillingness to fess up and spill the topic: "Coward."

After a pause, Snake Catcher questioned, "What did you see that morning?"

"Unfortunately I do not remember what happened. The last thing I remember before waking up last night was enjoying the morning sunrise."

"He will come again."

"Yes." Susan paused. "And we will need to be more careful from now on."

"Yes."

Susan instantly recognized that something was amiss with her husband. She was becoming acute at reading Snake Catcher's body language, which was saying *yes* to something other than her cautionary statement–something nefarious. Susan and Snake Catcher sat silently on the porch observing the beauty of Paha Sapa and further counting their blessings until Rains Down called them in to supper.

Painted Pony's sorrowing face appeared around the corner of the kitchen, as the teen's mind was full of thoughts of Susan's horrific ordeal. The girl was also still feeling the effects of her matriarchly paragon and mentor's clash with disaster. Both Snake Catcher and Susan could sense the worry in her small face. After supper, they invited Painted Pony to spend the night in the front guest bedroom in order for her to feel closer to Susan. Reassurance was their intent for Painted Pony, and the two offered words about how everything was going to be fine while tucking her in that night.

Chapter 25

Even though Susan's ranchhands were anticipating another attack from Carter, they were finding it difficult to effectively police the five miles of boundary fencing. As a result, Carter and four of his men managed to sneak onto the Paradise Valley Ranch property from the furthest entry point from Carter's ranch, one very early morning before daybreak. Bandanas were worn over half of their faces for camouflage. While Carter sat on his horse out front with his men doing the dirty deeds, two of his men snuck into the staff quarters and subdued the four ranchhands they found there. The kitchen matron, Cook, was not considered a threat and oblivious to their rampage. Those two men immobilized Larry, Slim, Ferdy and Sammy by wacking them over the head with pistols while the other two invaders snuck into the main house and up the stairs. These two did not spend their time examining the layout of the house, nor the condition of their captive. Carter's men quickly hooded their catch, and flew down the stairs before she could stir the rest of the household. Out the front door they dashed to their awaiting horses and to Carter and the other two men waiting for the deed to be done before riding off. Their bound hostage violently struggled to free herself but they had managed to affix her to a horse.

Buck was in the stables when he heard something strange, and this sparked him to step out as the posse rode by him. When the intruders were leaving, he witnessed Carter's face as a bandana slipped from it. Slim staggered out of the staff quarters just in time to witness that the prisoner was wearing Painted Pony's nightclothes. By the time Buck got his horse saddled, the trespassers had disappeared into the night. The other men from Susan's ranch were not lucid enough to make the chase. The abductors had taken the contents of the front guest bedroom instead of the back master bedroom, contrary to their intended plan. Slim staggered over to the porch and wildly rang the alarm bell. There was a note stabbed into the porch post with a dagger.

The missive read: "It is time for you to leave."

Since Buck was the only ranchhand who was unhurt, Susan sent him to fetch the Sheriff. She then tended to her wounded men, even still somewhat weak herself.

A panicked look was cemented onto Slim's face. He began pacing while asking questions, yet did not pause for the answers. "Miss Susan, do you think Carter will hurt her? Do you think he will turn her loose now that he knows he got the wrong person?" With a lump in his throat, he went on to ask, "Do you think he will turn her over to the soldiers who came for her?"

"I don't know Slim, but I'm thinking that he just wants a showdown with us. He would lose his leverage of banishing us off of this land if he gave Painted Pony away or hurt her in any way."

"Thank you, Miss Susan. I will hold onto that thought."

A slowly ticking clock on the lounge wall showed about an hour had passed before the Sheriff arrived at the ranch.

"Sheriff, they took Painted Pony," stated Susan.

"Who took her?"

"Carter and his men."

"Did you see him do it?"

"*I* did as I already told you, it was Carter–for sure," Buck declared.

The Sheriff nodded with the confirmation. "Okay, I'll be back later. You all stay here and don't interfere." The Sheriff rapidly rode off in the direction of Carter's ranch.

Everyone from the Paradise Valley Ranch was present in the lounge with Slim, who was wringing his hands. They were all anxiously awaiting any news about Painted Pony. The Sheriff returned in the morning while the darkness of the hour still loomed about. When he entered the lounge, everyone gathered around him.

"Well Slim, I rode out to Carter's ranch, and everyone

there was in bed asleep. I woke Carter and spoke with him. He claimed they had been there all night and had witnesses. He said he doesn't know where the girl is. I even went into his stables and checked their horses to see if any of them were hot or sweaty. Buck, you must have made a mistake. Susan, can you think of anyone else who would do this?"

Buck reiterated, "Sheriff, it was Carter. I saw him when his bandana slipped down off his face."

"I'm sorry; without any proof, I can't do anything."

Slim belted out, "They left a note." He showed the note to the Sheriff and added, "They took her. Believe me, Carter has been wanting this land for a long time, and he was the only one who wants us to leave."

The Sheriff disagreeingly shook his head. "Well, this might not have anything to do with the land. They may just want everyone except the White folks here to leave. This doesn't mean anything."

Snake Catcher, who was standing back behind the others, while speaking straight-faced about the Sheriff's responses, sarcastically remarked, "More White man justice?"

The Sheriff tossed the note down on the table ignoring Snake Catcher's insinuation of his favoritism toward Carter. "Slim, I still don't have any proof. From what I saw there, they were all sleeping and never went out tonight. If you come up with anything else, I will intervene for you." The Sheriff headed for the door as Susan escorted him out.

"Thank you for coming out in the middle of the night, Sheriff." The Sheriff tipped his hat in acceptance of Susan's esteem and left.

As soon as the Sheriff was out of earshot, Susan bellowed, "Carter has gone too far this time. Perhaps it *is* time for that showdown that Carter has been wanting. An eye for an eye. Is everyone with me?" The group nodded with a confirmation before Susan added, "Since Carter has not asked for a ransom, we have to assume that he only wants to rattle us to leave. The town dance is tonight. Some of us will attend to show them that everything is normal here; that will disorient Carter and throw him off balance. He is expecting us to be distraught and agreeable to anything he proposes. Plus, the more we are out there, the more we will learn. So, in addition, Buck and Sammy will go out to the Carter ranch and snoop around. Even if they don't find Painted Pony tonight, they can study our neighbor's

movements and routines so we can get closer to finding her."
Susan and her ranchhands huddled while continuing to plot for
the return of their beloved Painted Pony.

Slim retreated to the staff quarters, as he was too
distraught to work that morning. He entered Painted Pony's
room and began tidying up, anticipating her return. The
ranchhand was too nervous to hope for her return and too mad
to weep. There would be a great self-restraint to prevent him
from just trotting over to Carter's ranch and strangling the
crooked rancher with his bare hands. Slim was not a violent
man and had never so much as punched anyone before, but he
now knew what murderous instincts he had within himself.

Buck volunteered to fill in for Slim with watching over
the cattle as Painted Pony's father confined himself to the staff
quarters; Sammy was alone to tend to the stable chores. Snake
Catcher tended to Susan's chores while she rested, still weak
from Carter's attack. She knew the exertion of the town dance
that evening would be stressful; especially if any of Carter's
associates attended.

Early that evening, the townspeople were gathered for the
annual festivities in the town's newly-built pavilion to celebrate
the anniversary of the town's birth. The air was cool, yet clear.
Music was playing from a six-piece band, and candles, which
had been strategically positioned earlier around the area for the
best illumination, were now all afire. Some of the people
attending the celebration were dancing and some were playing
games of horseshoes, but most were just enjoying visiting with
one another about their fortunes or failures of the past year.
Because of smoke from some fire pits around the pavilion, the
bugs were not biting on that night as Susan, Snake Catcher,
Ferdy and Rains Down arrived to attend the event and be decoys
covering for Buck and Sammy's reconnaissance at Carter's ranch.
Being the first time Snake Catcher had joined Susan in public,
she cordially introduced him around to the townspeople and her
friends from church. A story surrounding Susan's bandaged head
was concocted as to not alert any of Carter's acquaintances to
any retaliation of him. The fabricated story entailed that
someone at the ranch was in the process of cleaning their
handgun when it accidently discharged, and that the bullet did
not come from an intruder as originally thought.

Carter uncharacteristically appeared at the function with

his wife and his ten-year-old son, along with several of his men. At first, Carter was confused at Susan's lack of concern toward Painted Pony's absence from her nest, but then he soon found it gratifying to be verbally antagonistic toward her and her clan. This included disrespectfully speaking about Susan to his mob of male friends and ranchhands that many could hear, but not directly to her. Snake Catcher stood close by Susan and watched every diabolical move Carter made. Susan ignored Carter, and began speaking with Mrs. Gaines, who was an elder at their church.

"Mrs. Gaines, have you met my husband? He is known as the Lakota, Zuzeca Wawoyuspa; a name which translates to Snake Catcher."

Mrs. Gaines was pleasant and tipped her head to him. Snake Catcher acknowledged her in return, but only long enough as it took to be polite, and then he returned his focus toward Carter's actions.

Carter huddled with his group, but spoke in a loud whisper to his entourage. "Now there is the biggest band of misfits I've ever seen. I wonder who is left watching the flock?" As the rancher belittled Susan and her conspirators, his cohorts were laughing loudly.

Ignoring Carter, Susan continued, "Did you know one could be hung for cattle rustling?"

Mrs. Gaines was aghast; she replied, "You don't say?"

"Yes. Can you believe that someone actually tried branding over my brand on a few of my cattle not long ago?"

Mrs. Gaines gave a look of surprise at Susan, unaware of her intentional goading of Carter. In retaliation, Carter, seemingly trying to sound jovial, rhetorically blasted back, "Who's to say you didn't brand over theirs?"

Without looking directly at him, Susan refuted, "Witnesses."

"You mean that band of convicts of yours? This gathering is for decent folks and they shouldn't be here," Carter jeered. He then looked directly at Ferdy before spewing, "Especially those who flaunt their concubine in public."

Rains Down's face turned flush, bringing Ferdy to take an aggressive step toward Carter. Susan intervened calmly and collectively as she responded for all to hear, especially Carter's wife: "Perhaps you should be more concerned about yours, particularly those who pace the halls of Willy's Saloon."

Mrs. Gaines dumbfoundedly huffed at Carter. Ferdy victoriously grinned. Carter tipped his hat with civility to Mrs. Gaines, gave Susan a loathsome scowl, then took his wife's arm and left with her and their son. Mrs. Gaines would not acknowledge Carter's pleasantries. Susan and her group stood there a moment longer in order to procure their alibis before leaving.

Hours later at nearly midnight on Carter's ranch, Snake Catcher inconspicuously snuck into Carter's ten-year-old son's bedroom as quietly as a whisper. Aided with a rag soaked with one of Susan's mojo concoctions, Snake Catcher quickly subdued the boy by placing the cloth to his nose. That left the child temporarily incapacitated for an easy transport. Snake Catcher left a note, then blindfolded the boy, and transported him out of the house. As with a ghost in the night, Snake Catcher unobstructedly rode off with Carter's son.

Larry collected the groggy blindfolded boy from Snake Catcher and confined their detainee to the ranchhand's shanty located at the boundary of the Paradise Valley Ranch property. The boy soon drifted back into sleep on a cot there, under Larry's keeping.

Chapter 26

Susan and Snake Catcher were standing on the porch apprehensively anticipating Carter's presence that morning. The coolness from the prior night spilled over onto the morning. Carter and two of his ranchhands furiously rode up to them while expelling a massive dust cloud that spread out over the entire length of Susan's homestead lot showing signs of a rainless week. Before Carter could speak, Susan remorselessly baited him. "Lose something, Carter?"

Carter disrespectfully threw down the note that Snake Catcher had left at his ranch the previous night. As it floated to the ground in front of Susan, he barked, "What is this? *It is time for a showdown.* What does that mean? And where the hell is my son?!"

Calmly, with an act of innocence, Susan responded, "How should I know? I've been here all night, and everyone here is my witness." Concurrently, *all* of Susan's staff that were present at the ranch promptly appeared from around the sides of the house, or out the front door to show an unwavering alliance against Carter.

"Where is my son?! I know he is here," shouted Carter as he turned to those gathering. He then announced, "One hundred dollars to the first person who speaks up about my boy's whereabouts." There were plenty of smirks to be had, but no location information on the boy.

Susan countered, "Carter, if I were to have him, do you think that I would be so foolish as to harbor him here at my house? There is so much you have underestimated about me."

Carter calculatingly looked around to size up the fire

power, then retreated when he realized the imbalance. "I will be back with the Sheriff!" Carter threatened.

Susan was quick to respond. "It won't do you any good. He won't find anything more here than he found on your property looking for the girl."

"I don't have the girl, I told you that."

"Then I don't have your son." Susan turned to conclude the conversation. Looking back at Carter while stepping toward the front door of her home, she added, "Let me know if you find her. Perhaps then we'll look around here for your son."

"You won't hurt him. I know you don't have it in you. You're too much of a *do-gooder*," Carter stated, challenging Susan. He said it more out of anger for her getting the upper hand on him than from any fear of them hurting his son.

To make her point as she turned back to Carter, Susan resonated a sinister malice-toned laugh. "I am a woman in a man's world out here. I do as I please, and you don't think that I'm strong enough to kill if I have to? I've already done that. Don't you have one less man in your employ? How narrow-minded of you, Carter. Besides, I won't be the one who slits the boy's throat." With turning to look up at Snake Catcher, Susan was clearly allocating the vicious deed onto him for Carter to witness. Snake Catcher leisurely dragged his hand over to his knife's handle, clutching it without taking his cold, deadly, unrelenting and unnerving stare off of Carter. Susan pulled her pashmina tighter around her and strolled into the house, leaving Carter with a feeling for just how cold and ruthless she could be. Her armed ranchhands aggressively pushed their weapons toward Carter and his men, as if to tell them it was time for their departure. Carter's posse rode off, leaving a billowing cloud of dust behind them.

That afternoon, a warning shot rang out from the ranch boundary. Susan and Snake Catcher stepped out onto the porch to investigate. When the Sheriff rode up, he addressed them by condescendingly reprimanding, "Well, Susan, don't you think it's time to end this?"

Susan snapped back, "I wanted to end this the other night Sheriff, but no one was listening to me." Sarcastically, she added, "Think some are listening now?"

"Turn over the boy or I will have to arrest you."

Mockingly, Susan extended, "Arrest me for what, Sheriff?

You will need proof, remember? My horses are neither hot nor sweaty."

"Come on now, Susan. We all know you have the boy."

"Then feel free to search my ranch, Sheriff." Susan tightened her pashmina and walked into the house with the same show of ruthlessness she had given Carter. The Sheriff briefly snooped around the stables and staff quarters before leaving.

By late afternoon, Cook was straining to get Slim to eat something. Neither pleading, demanding nor guilting him seemed to work. Slim was feeling weary, yet he could not bring himself to eat while worrying about Painted Pony. Meanwhile, Ferdy had rode out to the ranchhand shanty to give Larry and the boy food. Assuredly, that child was not being neglected, as Larry was playing a memory game with him to keep the youngster amused.

All and all, Painted Pony was being treated humanely as well–for a hostage. She was so charming and angelic that Carter's domestic staff was sneaking food to her in the stables. Nonetheless, Painted Pony was still moderately frightened, especially being tied to a horse's trough in the stables with the stallion stomping all around her. Painted Pony was fortunate to have had training with horses or she would not have been so self-collected. She also felt better hearing screaming sounds of desperation coming from the woman of the manor toward her husband.

After the staff had held a prayer meeting for Painted Pony that evening, Susan and Snake Catcher decidedly retired with hopes that they would receive word about her the following day. Susan was eminently confident that Painted Pony would be returned unharmed soon due to Carter believing that Susan had the boy. So confident, in fact, that she decided to use the waiting time to regain another of their losses. In their bedroom that evening, and with her husband peacefully asleep in bed, Susan constructed another letter to the President centering on the return of Paha Sapa as she sat at her desk. The timing of the function was primarily to ease her mind of Painted Pony's dangerous state of affairs. Susan wrote:

"Dear President Arthur, I know of your very busy
schedule and taxing issues; however, it has been
one month since I have written you concerning

the treaty between the United States and different tribes of the Sioux Indians, and I have yet to received a response from you or your office. I am asking that you take a moment to explore the issues of the Sioux people, particularly the theft of their land, specifically the Black Hills.

"I have reviewed the treaty and find it deplorable that the government has taken this area of land only to fill their pockets with the grand resources from these Americans native to this country–Americans that were here long before Whites set foot on this land. Not only did the government agree to this treaty, they wrote it, and yet they are now reneging on their word. Is that what this country has become? One which cannot be trusted to barter with? Perhaps you will not give merit to my opinion; however, may I remind you that even though I am a woman, I am allowed to legally vote in the Territory of Wyoming. Thank you for taking the time to read my letter. I will expect that you will give worth to this issue. Respectfully, Susan E. Paradise, Sundance, Wyoming Territory, Wife, Rancher, Landowner and Voter."

Susan slipped the letter into her desk and then turned in for the night.

Sometime before midnight, and unbeknownst to anyone there, a note was stabbed onto the Paradise Valley Ranch porch post with a dagger. It read: "Come get her. She is in the stables."

Chapter 27

Susan was the first to discover the note as she stepped out onto the porch with her morning tea. She rang the bell to summon everyone. All, except Larry who was still with the boy, emerged to read the cryptic message. Slim instinctively ran to the stables, but deflatedly returned to tell the gathered group that she was not there. "Now what?" Slim asked, desperate for a suggestion.

Susan assumingly concluded, "Carter must mean *his* stables. We'll have to go there, but must be very careful. I'm sure he will have a plan to ambush us. Sammy will stay behind to watch the ranch and to make sure there is no trouble here for Rains Down and Cook. With Larry watching the boy, the rest of us will ride out to Carter's ranch. This is what we'll do..."

Being somewhat early in the day still, Cook groggily returned to the staff quarters as Rains Down walked into the house to return to her bedroom. Susan, Snake Catcher, Buck, Slim, Sammy and Ferdy huddled around to make their plan for Painted Pony's rescue.

By midmorning, Susan, Slim and Ferdy leisurely rode up, as to not be challenging to Carter as he casually sat on his porch. Carter smirked at the ease in which it took him to entice them onto his turf. Susan sensed a flickered hint of suspicious behavior when she realized that not many of Carter's ranch-hands were present. In the meantime, Snake Catcher and Buck were covertly riding onto Carter's property. The duo maneuvered around a few of Carter's men for a short time, then Snake Catcher positioned himself to cover the others at the porch for their safety. Buck sneaked over toward the stables to locate Painted Pony.

At Carter's porch area, Susan was the first to speak. "Where is she, Carter?"

Carter cryptically responded, "I thought you already got word as to where she was?"

Slim was paternally antsy, and he rode over to the stables to locate Painted Pony while leaving Ferdy and Susan to deal with Carter's arrogance. The bully antagonized the two for his entertainment. Riddles were ejected by Carter of where Painted Pony might be hidden only to gain meaningless points, and never asking the condition of his son or even suggesting an exchange. That gave Susan reason to think they would not be leaving without the threat of being harmed.

Meanwhile, Slim found Painted Pony crying mildly, but unharmed in one of Carter's horse stalls. Suddenly, one of Carter's ranchhands leapt out and aggressively attacked Slim with a knife, startling him. Slim was sliced on the hand, but not to the point of rendering it dysfunctional; giving him the opportunity to draw and fire his gun. The undeniable blast of gunfire was heard by all, and Carter's man was down. Two of Carter's other men who had been stationed around their boss began zealously running toward the stables. Ferdy and Susan turned their horses toward the stables and began galloping after the running men. In reaction, Carter leapt to his feet and began shooting toward Susan and Ferdy as they bolted away, bullets buzzing by their heads. Escaping unscathed, the pair also managed to maniacally knock the darting men to the ground while speeding past them on their horses.

After Susan and Ferdy met up with Slim, who had a distraught but indebted Painted Pony with him, they rode off the property and toward the Paradise Valley Ranch.

During that interim of time, Carter made his way to the stables and swung around the corner of the stable door to find Buck. He randomly fired at him. The bullet pierced Buck's shoulder indubitably dropping him to the cold, unyielding ground. Snake Catcher soundlessly stepped close behind Carter, close enough that Carter could feel the Lakota's breath on the nape of his neck. When Carter turned to the faint breeze surrounding him while bringing his gun around with him, Snake Catcher ungloatingly sunk his knife into Carter's mid-section—as did the perfect warrior, face to face. Thereupon, Snake Catcher expressionlessly pulled the knife upward. Carter grabbed Snake Catcher's shoulder, and gasped his last tempestuous breath. With Snake Catcher firmly gripping the knife, the blade slid out of the rancher's body as Carter fell to the ground in a heap. Snake Catcher wiped the bloody blade on Carter's clothes, then helped the wounded Buck to his horse. They successfully rode away without further incidences at Carter's ranch.

After returning to the Paradise Valley Ranch, Snake Catcher gingerly helped Buck down from his horse and inside to the apothecary room as Buck did for him when he first happened upon the ranch.

Susan expeditiously tended to Buck's wound. "It's not bad, but we have to clean it up. Rains Down, please set up my equipment and supplies."

Susan quickly and efficiently determined that the bullet had traveled clean through his shoulder and surgery was unnecessary. She stitched and cleaned Buck's shoulder before placing his arm into a sling suspending movement to his damaged shoulder. After brewing him a tea, Susan contentedly stepped out into the hallway to inform the others of Buck's non-life-threatening condition. It was then that she noticed blood draped on Snake Catcher's shirt. "Oh no, are you hurt too?" she nervously asked.

"Hiya."

"Is all of that Buck's blood?" Susan asked with skepticism.

As Snake Catcher looked at Susan to judge her tone, he answered, "Some."

"What happened?"

"Had trouble with Carter."

Susan asked with caution, "Is he dead?" After Snake Catcher undoubtably gave the confirmation, Susan replied, "That wasn't a part of the plan."

"Am still warrior," Snake Catcher commented, as to announce that he would assuredly defend a person or land when protection was necessary for an ally. Then after a slight pause, he added, "Are we good?"

Susan rebutted mockingly at Snake Catcher with: "*Hiya*, a whole lot of trouble has found us now." Without missing a beat, she routinely instructed her staff as to their next tactical maneuver. "Sammy, go tell Larry to take the boy to the bridge,

and then release him. Rains Down, get the letter out of my
bedroom desk and bring it here to Slim. Slim, I want you to go
to the telegraph office and send a message to Earth Raven like
before. Tell him to come quick; Snake Catcher needs his help
desperately. Afterwards, I want you to mail a letter that Rains
Down will give to you before you go." Susan then looked at
Snake Catcher and replied, "I want you to change your clothes
and give those to Rains Down to wash."

Susan's staff obediently complied with her instructions.
After the immediate issues were addressed, Susan prepared a
warm bath for Painted Pony. After the disheveled teen completed her washing, Susan made sure that Painted Pony was fed
and then left her settling back in her room. Slim was grateful for
Susan's help.

As the afternoon came up to them, the Sheriff rode onto the
Paradise Valley Ranch property. Susan, Sammy and Snake
Catcher were standing on the porch after receiving a warning
shot from the pasture. The Sheriff greeted with: "I tried to warn
you, Susan, not to take matters into your own hands. Now I
have to arrest him."

"He didn't do anything wrong."

"I have witnesses, Susan."

"It was self-defense, Sheriff. We went to get Painted
Pony, and it turned ugly. They summoned us to collect her, and
then they attacked us. We have witnesses."

"Well, I have witnesses at the Carter ranch that say
otherwise. They claim you already had the girl and came for
revenge of some sort. Who am I supposed to believe? I'll need to
take him in and have the Judge decide the matter."

Abruptly, Susan lashed back, "Sheriff, you know that's
not true. They all lie over there. Why would we take a girl to a
shootout?"

"To make it believable, I suppose. His widow is the one
who told me; is *she* lying?"

"She must be distraught over losing her husband."

"Is that what you are now? Distraught over losing your
husband, Susan?" the Sheriff asked as he hopped down from his
horse. "One could make the same argument about what you are
assuming of them."

Susan paused before asking, "When will the Judge hear
this case?"

"You know he only comes into Sundance once a month to hear cases."

"When, Sheriff?" Susan reiterated.

"I suppose when he gets back from his fishing trip."

Sarcastically, Susan added, "Is that the same fishing trip he went on with Carter's brother?"

"Now don't be putting the cart before the horse, Susan."

Slim emerged from the staff quarters and inquisitively walked over to the porch while Susan tenderly turned to Snake Catcher. "You have to go with him now. We will get you out. Please, do what they say, and it will be easier on you. You are in my heart." Susan turned back to the Sheriff, then demanded, "They had better treat him right. If I find out they haven't, I will have such fury, the bloodshed at the Alamo will seem like a tea party with the girls."

"He will be," the Sheriff insisted.

The Sheriff tied Snake Catcher's hands together as the warrior stood expressionlessly looking at Susan, the face of a man being falsely accused once again. Slim removed Snake Catcher's knife before he and Sammy helped Snake Catcher onto his horse. Snake Catcher and the Sheriff uneventfully rode off. Fear and emptiness filled Susan. That night, she would be utterly alone without the protective sounds of her husband sleeping beside her.

Throughout the night, Painted Pony's eyes were equally as wide as a full bright moon as she clutched the sheets covering her. She would not give into the unconscious thoughts within the darkness, for fear she would not see life in the morning or ever again.

Chapter 28

During the early morning hours, Susan and Painted Pony sat together on the porch and gazed out at the rich blackish-green of Paha Sapa's foliage. Painted Pony was happy to be alive and chatting about living somewhere genuinely beautiful. The most brilliant days were those which began with such an unclouded view of Paha Sapa, leaving all the other murky issues in life more manageable.

They discussed Painted Pony's past few days, and how life could be precariously fragile. Susan advised Painted Pony that while self-assurance was a positive trait, it is wise to heed the warning of those with hubris of an excessive degree, as with Carter. Susan encouraged Painted Pony's young mind to steer clear of gluttony or greed and reap the knowledge that good fortune will be rewarded to those with a charitable direction in life and a divine loving treatment of others. Susan also prepared Painted Pony for the gossip that could occur surrounding her ordeal. Many people in Sundance now knew of her abduction and of Carter's death, and while some might be doubtful of her guiltless participation, most had good hearts and would wish her well. Susan undoubtably knew she would catch Painted Pony's undivided attention with comparing this lesson with her favorite subject. "Earth Raven seems very at peace with himself, and he has chosen the path of helping his people."

Hearing Earth Raven's name seemed to make Painted Pony a bit less frightened of those with a nefarious nature, and actually brought a soft smile to her blanched face.

After their conversation, Susan rode toward the church with Rains Down, Painted Pony, Ferdy and Slim. With Ferdy to escort her, Susan chose to visit her husband at the jailhouse in Sundance after dropping off the others at the church. However, her first stop was that of a grim nature. She would leave a note at the mortuary to commission the engraving of a tombstone.

Susan's brightest moment in her day was seeing her beloved husband and touching his hand. With her she manipulatively brought the delicious preparations of Cook's beef stew and freshly baked herb-bread for dipping. This was accompanied by a fresh-out-of-the-oven apple pie. Of course, Susan was not foolish enough to bring less than a sufficient amount to feed the Sheriff and the Deputy as well.

When Snake Catcher looked perplexed as to why Susan was being nice to them, she replied, "Did you not know that the way to a man's heart is through his stomach? And the bigger the heart, the nicer one would become."

That made Snake Catcher smile, knowing his wife was full of wisdom at such a youthful age.

Meanwhile, the church parishioners gave Rains Down prayers for Susan and Snake Catcher. Halfway through the service, the Preacher smiled as he looked out onto his flock, specifically one in particular. Painted Pony had fallen asleep in church. The congregation looked back with sympathy and concern for Painted Pony, who was slumped over in the last row of the pews.

Rains Down vindicatedly explained, "She hasn't been able to sleep since, well, in days. I am glad she feels safe enough here, and so at peace in church, that she is able to finally get some much needed rest."

The Preacher tipped his head to Susan's staff and inadvertently added to his sermon: "May God bless his children and keep the innocence of a child surrounded by his love."

"Amen" came from the congregation before the Preacher continued, then finished his prepared sermon.

At the service's end, Slim buoyantly carried Painted Pony back to the wagon as others offered their promises of prayers to him for her recuperation from her stressful ordeal. As the group met up again with Susan, they made sure Painted Pony was comfortable during her ride back to the ranch.

At sunset, Susan ended her day as it began, sitting on the porch taking in the presence of Paha Sapa's glorious beauty accompanied by a chalky Painted Pony.

Chapter 29

After another reflective and quiet morning on the porch raising her tea cup and watching the sunrise and Paha Sapa, Susan rode into Sundance with Ferdy for the purpose of visiting her husband in jail. Before she would have the pleasure of his company, she visited Doc Brown first. She consulted with him on a medical matter.

As before, she brought to the jail another of Cook's culinary specialities; this time, pot roast with savory roasted potatoes and a fresh vegetable medley. The menu also included the crowning event for the meal–a cherry pie. Cook had provided a small pitcher of sweet cream to drizzle over the top of the pie, as well. The Deputy was salivating at the sight of it all.

During the time that the Sheriff and Deputy unfailingly devoured their share of Cook's magnum opus, Snake Catcher was extraordinarily surprised to see his wife eating a slice of the pie, which was never her favorite.

After three hours of chin-wagging with her husband, Susan left for an appointment with the town photographer in the area, at his house. As Susan sat for her photograph, he could not remember anyone having a more bewitching smile as the one she wore that day. Thereafter, as Susan and Ferdy returned to the ranch, only she knew of her reasons for the euphoria that she was feeling.

Meanwhile, Slim was feeling overly protective of Painted Pony to a point of distraction on her part. Painted Pony noticed this less than she might have, being busy trying to prepare for Earth Raven's arrival. She was planning what the topic's of conversation could be when he wasn't preparing for trial. Slim had other plans for his daughter's time; he wanted her within his sight always. Even though Painted Pony was still not sleeping well, she was anxious about seeing Earth Raven again.

Additionally, Buck would need minimal attention to his arm; however, he would only be able to function at the ranch in a limited capacity for some time, and was unable to serve Susan as a protector right now. Ferdy would occasionally fill-in for him.

At sunset, it was a bittersweet moment for Susan as she sat on the porch with her tea and looked out toward the hills. She wore a face of intense joy which was in direct conflict with her feelings of paralyzing aloneness.

Chapter 30

Only two others knew of Susan's morning routine better than she did. Killer and Coyote traditionally and obediently sat on the porch while watching Susan drink her morning blend of tea. The duo watched as Susan had thoughts of how Earth Raven could help her husband stay out of prison for the remainder of his life. As Killer and Coyote only had eyes for Susan, she occasionally tossed a slice of bacon to each of them. After polishing off their governess's breakfast snack that particular morning, they followed Susan to her first chore of the day, visiting the staff quarters to check Buck's shoulder wound. They looked up at her as she redressed the wound before reattaching the shoulder harness sling.

By late morning, Earth Raven had expectantly arrived at the Paradise Valley Ranch. After receiving the message belatedly from the reservation's telegraph office, his path had taken him to ride all but a few hours during the night in order to be there to help his friend. When the aspiring attorney arrived, Painted Pony was in the staff lounge. She was drawn to the window by the sound of Earth Raven's voice outside speaking to Buck regarding the care of his horse. Susan then met Earth Raven at the front door and invited him in for lunch. After a short visit and a relocation of his belongings to the guest bedroom, he, Susan and Buck headed into Sundance in the wagon. Rains Down watched as Painted Pony stared out of the front window of the staff quarters at their departure, and the young woman's expression spoke of her worry about whether she would see Earth Raven again. The teen clutched her wrap tighter around her, seemingly not sensing it tightly enough to feel safe and secure as she once had.

While chatting on the ride into Sundance, Susan learned that Earth Raven did not waste time asking for permission to leave the reservation this particular time. Earth Raven also told her that he did not offer the necessary paperwork and the Blue Coats did not ask for any, as they must have assumed he had his papers in order because of his many trips off the reservation.

Once in Sundance, Earth Raven stepped inside of the courthouse for a moment, then returned out in front of it to inform Susan and Buck of his plans. "I was just told that the Judge has recently returned from his fishing trip but will need some time to clean up before hearing the case. With this spare time, I want to do some investigating before court begins. I'll meet you back here later."

Susan and Buck agreeably nodded.

Buck headed over to the saloon, unarguably to get a glimpse of Miss Angel Blue or to even speak with her a moment; however, it was still very early in the day for the likes of her. Once he arrived, Buck was told that she would be asleep for many hours to come. He sat down on the only unoccupied barstool and ordered a drink. Lily spotted him and watched from a distance to see if he would ask for her.

Several others had gathered in Sundance to witness the trial. It would not be the trial of the century, but many viewed it as a historic moment in time. Many wondered if Snake Catcher would be able to escape the punishment of killing a well-known businessman and member of their community, even one of an infamously vile standing as Carter. Even thoroughly exonerated, Snake Catcher would still find it difficult to be found completely innocent in the eyes of those not of his skin. But that was the way of the world, certainly the way *his* world operated within the other. Snake Catcher's only trump card, as the townspeople would see it, was Susan.

Meanwhile, Susan walked over to the jail to see her husband, arriving with lunch for him and, of course, for the Sheriff and Deputy. After giving Snake Catcher the meal of fried chicken, mashed potatoes topped with giblet gravy and cornmeal dressing, and a large slice of sweet potato pie, she commented, "You look good but tired."

"Cannot sleep without wife."

Susan affectionately smiled at him.

Snake Catcher continued, "Why is wife without color?"

Susan was quick to continue the banter. "Wife can't sleep without husband. I have good news; Earth Raven is here. He'll be talking to the Judge. Are you ready to do this?"

Snake Catcher eagerly nodded, imagining that the trial was just a formality, and he would be going home soon with his wife once it was over.

While Snake Catcher ate his meal, Susan continued, "You have to let Earth Raven talk to the Judge for you. You won't be permitted to talk during the court session unless the Judge asks you a direct question, no matter what. Earth Raven will let you know when you need to speak. Do you understand?"

Snake Catcher nodded enthusiastically just as the Deputy received word that his orders were to take Snake Catcher to the courthouse.

Back at Willy's Saloon, Buck could see others starting to leave, so he departed the bar to be available for Susan's support or Snake Catcher's defense. He would leave the saloon without asking for Lily. As Buck stepped out of the saloon, he encountered Earth Raven, and the two men had a brief conversation.

In the courtroom, the Deputy untied Snake Catcher's hands and domineeringly instructed him to be seated at the defendant's table. Susan supportively sat in a chair directly behind her husband. Others from town filled the courtroom, leaving standing-room-only in the rear of the room. When Earth Raven entered, Snake Catcher showed his relief and happily greeted him. The two were whispering together in Lakota as the Judge arrived through the back door. Barely a moment later, Barney, the prosecuting attorney, rushed in. The Deputy, now acting as the bailiff, announced the Judge's arrival as the officiate entered and then sat behind a desk in the front middle of the room assuming his authority over the proceedings. The large White man was somewhat intimidating just with his size, much less the realization of how judicially powerful he was. With one slam of his gavel, he could change a life's direction forever. While he spoke in a deep voice, the magister organizingly shuffled his papers on the desk before belting out, "Where are we? Barney, what do you have?"

Barney was of medium height, very slender, wore wire-rimmed glasses, and spoke with a pitch higher than an average man. Somewhat bumbling, he dramatically jumped to his feet and began his statement. "A case of murder, your Honor. The defendant is accused of killing Ben Carter in cold blood at his ranch."

The Judge, without pause, directed his question at Earth Raven. "Sir, are you representing the defendant?"

Earth Raven acknowledged, "Yes, your Honor. I am Earth Raven, counsel for the defense."

The Judge scrutinizingly surveyed Earth Raven, knowing Native attorneys did not exist. Without predetermining that he was not qualified or showing blatant prejudication, he asked, "And you are a lawyer, Sir?"

Earth Raven was quick to respond, "No, your Honor, but a legal one is not required. My client is aware that I am not licensed."

"So noted Counselor. Do you have anything to add concerning the accusation made against your client?"

Earth Raven confirmed, "Yes, your Honor. My client is not guilty. There has been no crime here. He was acting out of self-defense after Ben Carter shot Buck Edwards..."

The Judge abruptly interrupted Earth Raven. "What the hell were they all doing at Carter's ranch in the first place?"

Earth Raven held his ground while showing no signs of being intimidated from the Judge's outburst. He continued to inform the Judge of the situation according to Snake Catcher's story. "They were securing the safe return of a kidnapped girl who was stolen in the middle of the night from the Paradise Valley Ranch. They were told to come for her from a note left hanging by the front porch post at the Paradise Valley Ranch, your Honor."

The Judge grumbled, "Well, we seem to have a conflict of stories here. Barney, call your first witness."

Barney feebly fumbled about his papers as he announced, "I call Mrs. Ben Carter to the stand, your Honor."

Mrs. Carter timidly rose out of her seat in the courtroom, then walked over and sat in the chair next to the Judge's desk. Still acting as the bailiff, the Deputy dutifully held up a Bible to swear her in. Mrs. Carter was an attractive woman even though she showed signs of aging. An outfit of black, suitable for a mourning widow, was purposefully draped over her.

Barney briskly began his official examination. "Mrs. Carter, did you see who killed your husband?"

"Yes," she replied in a mousey tone.

"Is that person here in the courtroom today?" asked Barney.

As Mrs. Carter pointed at Snake Catcher, she disclosed, "Yes, that is the man."

Barney loudly and dramatically announced to the courtroom, "Let everyone know that Mrs. Carter is pointing at the accused." He then turned back to Mrs. Carter and asked, "Did your husband have a weapon on him?"

"No, he didn't," she answered while shaking her head.

Grumbling gasps arose from the courtroom. The Judge slammed his gavel down on the desk. "Settle down people. Barney?"

"I have no further questions for this witness, your Honor," Barney said yielding his examination of her.

The Judge instinctively turned to Earth Raven and candidly asked, "Sir, do you have any question for this witness?"

Earth Raven promptly rose out of his chair and stepped out from behind the defendant's table while self-assuredly answering, "Yes, your Honor." He earnestly walked over to Mrs. Carter. She seemed somewhat frightened by his authoritative stand over her, and the fact that he was someone of the same ethnicity as the man who killed her husband.

Earth Raven calmly and sympathetically began with: "Mrs. Carter, let me first say that I am sorry for your loss." She seemed somewhat thrown off-balance by his polite show of charitableness toward her, but moreover, from his clear dialect and remarkable understanding of the English language. Charming her was most certainly his technique for dislodging her defensiveness before commencing his cross-examination. "You say you saw that man there kill your husband?" Earth Raven clarified while pointing at Snake Catcher.

"Yes."

Earth Raven unconvincedly nodded while adding, "I see. Then perhaps you can tell me why three people claimed they saw you at the trading post at the precise moment that your husband was killed. Can you see all the way from the town of Sundance to your ranch, Mrs. Carter?"

Mrs. Carter began wringing her hands together, and flusteringly answered, "Why no, one cannot see that far. I was at the trading post the day *before*," she snapped back, sounding as if the claim was fabricated.

Without missing a beat in the exchange, Earth Raven continued, "Yes, Mrs. Carter you were. But you were also there *that* day as Mr. Smith, the trading post owner, will testify. You are there most everyday, aren't you? Is there something or *someone* of interest for you there that you are in the store every day, Mrs. Carter?"

Mrs. Carter ashamingly blurted, "I don't see what that's got to do with anything."

Barney boisterously interrupted, "Objection, your Honor. No grounds for asking these questions."

Surprising to everyone, the Judge concluded, "Overruled, but make a point here soon, Counselor."

Earth Raven, in control of his interrogation direction, continued, "Yes, your Honor. Mrs. Carter, were you not told of your husband's death while you were in Sundance? Remember, you are under oath and can be sent to jail if you lie."

Mrs. Carter alarmingly peered up at the Judge while he nodded back to her as if to indicate it was okay to answer the question and that Earth Raven's warning was correct. "Well, yes, but they told me he murdered my husband."

Gasps hailed from the courtroom as Earth Raven persisted in his questioning. "So, you didn't actually *see* the defendant kill your husband like you told everyone, correct?"

"Well, no, I didn't."

Gasps came from the courtroom once again. The Judge was not amused, and he slammed his gavel down on the desk with such uncompromising force that most of the people appeared startled. "Settle down, people, or I'll clear the court-room!"

Completing his interrogation of the witness, Earth Raven said crisply, "Thank you, Mrs. Carter." He then appeasingly turned to the Judge while stating, "I have no more questions for this witness, your Honor."

The Judge monotonously informed her, "You can step down now, Mrs. Carter." With the same show of pensiveness, he turned to the prosecuting attorney. "Barney, call your next witness."

Barney flamboyantly trumpeted, "I call Mr. Murphy to the stand, your Honor."

Murphy shuffled his way to the witness chair and plopped down. A few indiscreet giggles resonated from around the courtroom due to the lackadaisical clumsiness of the middle-aged man. The bailiff systematically held up a Bible to swear him in. Murphy was an unusual choice as one of Carter's ranch-hands as Susan's neighbor commonly employed the most virile of men. Murphy was quite possibly someone of lower rank in Carter's employ, according to his physical stature and age.

Barney, antagonistic to the defense, began his examination. "Mr. Murphy, what did you see the day your boss was murdered?"

Earth Raven sprung out of his chair protesting, "Objection, your Honor. Bias to my client. No verdict has been rendered here."

The Judge sternly reprimanded Barney. "Sustained. Barney, you know better than that. We will have a fair fight in my courtroom. Don't do that again. Proceed."

"Yes, your Honor." Barney turned to Murphy and in an unwavering tone repeated, "Mr. Murphy?"

"Well, I saw Carter go to the stables to see what all the ruckus and fuss was about. Someone was shootin' in there. Mr. Carter was standin' at the doorway and that guy there stabbed him for just standin' there." The swing of Mr. Murphy's hand was toward the direction of the defendant's table but not actually directly at Snake Catcher.

Barney was quick to add, "Let the courtroom know that Mr. Murphy, *too*, is pointing at the defendant."

Earth Raven vaulted up. "Objection, your Honor. I think we have established that Mrs. Carter did not witness the event; therefore, she could not identify my client, eliminated her as a viable witness."

The Judge ruled on Earth Raven's complaint. "Sustained." He then exasperatingly fired back at Barney. "Careful, Barney!"

"I have no more questions for this witness, your Honor."

The Judge ceremoniously motioned to Earth Raven, "Sir?"

Earth Raven unhesitatingly began his cross-examination. "Good afternoon, Mr. Murphy. Can you tell me how far away you were from Mr. Carter and my client when you saw the alleged incident?"

A perplexed look came across Murphy's face as he turned to the Judge while shrugging. "Wha'd he say?"

Whispery snickers echoed indiscriminately from various places in the courtroom.

The Judge clarified, "Murphy, how far away were they from you when the deed was done?"

"Oh...well, why didn't he just say so? They were about twenty-five feet away."

Earth Raven continued, "So, twenty-five feet to you

would make it further than, say, the front doorway there?"

"Oh, yes."

"Further than the horse trough out front?" Earth Raven questioned while pointing toward the open door.

"Yes, I suppose," stammered Murphy somewhat suspicious as to where Earth Raven was leading him.

Buck unnoticeably entered the courtroom with a woman, stood her at the door then left by himself in the same manner.

Earth Raven then unremittingly asked, "Then you would be able to tell me who is standing at the door of the courtroom right now?"

Shuffles were produced from the courtroom as heads spun around to look toward the door.

Murphy looked confused by Earth Raven's question. "Sir?"

"The door, just tell me who it is over there standing in the doorway. Take your time."

Murphy squinted before admitting, "No, I don't know his name."

An outburst of gasps and giggles rang out from the onlookers in the courtroom. Earth Raven promptly walked over to her, rested his hand on her shoulder, and reiterated, "This person here. You don't know this person's name?"

"Oh, that person. I think the boy's name is Frank."

Cackling vibrated the air in the courtroom. Earth Raven guided her closer to Murphy while continually interrogating him. "Isn't this, in fact, your dear sweet mother, Mr. Murphy? Isn't it true that you can't see ten feet in front of you, Sir? And if you can't see ten feet in front of you, you want us to believe you saw what a man had or didn't have in his hand twenty-five feet away?"

Begrudgingly grumbling, Murphy sputtered out, "Well, I know what Mr. Carter looks like, and ah..."

Earth Raven masterfully interrupted and ended his cross-examination with: "Thank you, Mr. Murphy. One would think that you would know what your mother looked like as well." Snickering sounds were made from the spectators as he contently turned to the Judge to convey, "I have no more questions for this witness, your Honor."

Barney leaped up out of his chair. "Objection, your Honor. Objection."

The Judge interrogated, "On what grounds, Barney?"

"He was leading the witness and didn't let him answer."

All eyes from the courtroom, except Murphy's, observed and fixated on the gun that the Judge lifted high above Mr. Murphy's head and about ten feet away. "Murphy, can you see what I have in my hand?"

Murphy turned his sights to the Judge and squinted. "Ah, your gavel?"

The Judge annoyingly turned to Barney. "Does that answer your question now, Barney?" His next statement was directed at the witness. "You can step down now, Murphy." He turned back to Barney. "Barney, call your next witness."

"Well Judge, that's all we have. They killed all the rest of them."

Earth Raven immediately sprang to his feet and argued, "Objection, your Honor. There were two deaths at the ranch, and both were in self-defense. Your Honor, I would like to move that my client be found not guilty. It is clear that these people are trying to railroad my client with no clear evidence and the only true eyewitnesses collaborate my client's accounts of that day."

The Judge countered to Earth Raven, "Well, that doesn't mean that he didn't murder him, Sir." As the Judge paused, Earth Raven held his breath until the official announced, "But since they don't seem to have a case...case dismissed."

The Judge then procedurally banged his gavel on the desk and stood to leave.

Earth Raven instantaneously smiled at him before the Judge's exit and appreciatively responded, "Thank you, your Honor."

After realizing that the Carter clan was attempting to frame Snake Catcher for murder, the observers in the courtroom joyously erupted with congratulations for him and Susan. Susan, teary-eyed, smiled and reached for Snake Catcher. Once understanding just how close he came to never being with Susan again, Snake Catcher could not take his eyes off of her. That thought had been unfathomable to him. He noticed that a new glow resonated about her.

Barney deflatedly scurried out the back door of the courtroom. Arm and arm, Susan and Snake Catcher left through the main entrance to the courthouse, with a widely smiling Earth Raven trailing behind. Awaiting the trio, Buck was stationed at the reins of the wagon out front. Snake Catcher's horse had been retrieved from the town's stables by Buck, and it was now tied to the wagon. The stables had released the horse due to Snake Catcher's two pending options, either being set free or being sentenced to jail; either way, they would not need possession of it any longer after the trial.

Standing on the courthouse steps as a photographer snapped a photograph of the aftermath, Susan looked up at Snake Catcher and made her appeal to him. "Home, let's go home."

Susan was unable to release her grip of Snake Catcher's arm the whole ride home. As they reached the wondrous sight of their house, they could see the ranch community members waiting out front to either lend sympathy to Susan or to enthusiastically congratulate them and welcome Snake Catcher back home, depending on the verdict. The sentiment over-whelmed Snake Catcher as he had not felt so much communistic devotion in such a long time; and certainly never from those not of his skin. The porch was full of chatter with everyone talking at once and the dogs barking their greetings correspondingly. Susan and Snake Catcher said few words to anyone as they only communicated with each other through their eyes.

As a matter of politeness, Earth Raven pulled a despon-dent Painted Pony aside and generously added his thankfulness that she survived her trying ordeal. She demurely thanked him, to the point of actually wearing a modest smile for him while loosening the tight rein of her wrap. Rains Down interrupted the exchange to assist Earth Raven upstairs where he then retreated into the guest bedroom to rest before supper.

Susan and Snake Catcher excused themselves as they settled back into their home. Susan drew a relaxing bath for her husband and pampered him as they became matrimonially reacquainted again.

As the day wound down by suppertime, Earth Raven, Snake Catcher and Susan joined one another for supper at the dining-room table. While noshing, they talked and celebrated their victory in court. Susan blissfully and graciously questioned Earth Raven about his amazingly masterful defense. "How did you know all of that?–where Mrs. Carter was, about Mr. Murphy's eyesight, who his mother was?"

"Well, that was what I was doing before the trial began. I started by asking around about Mrs. Carter, and someone pointed her out as the person talking to the young female sales clerk at the trading post. So I waited until Mrs. Carter left, and then moseyed on over to have a conversation with the clerk. Fortunately for me, she liked to gossip about her boss, and told me how Mr. Smith and Mrs. Carter were getting along splendidly and were together *frequently*."

Susan snickered. "You blackmailed her into telling the truth, threatening to expose their tryst."

Earth Raven continued, "Then when I walked up to the courthouse, Mr. Murphy thought I was someone else and was about to greet me, but when he got about six feet away, he stopped and retreated. I just asked around if he had any kin there. Figured if he couldn't pick them out from a distance, we were safe."

Susan sincerely thanked Earth Raven for his adeptness. "That was amazing. You are our lifesaver. We will never forget this."

"Thank you. I am pleased that Snake Catcher is safe. That was my first trial and it was exhilarating."

Snake Catcher added, "You will do good in this law business. Thank you for being my friend."

Earth Raven nodded to him.

Susan added, "With the stories from Hail Maker, I always thought how hard it would be to live out in the wilderness like the two of you have done. However, civilization isn't so easy either, is it?"

They all wholeheartedly agreed.

Susan made a covertly manipulative request of Earth Raven. "You don't have to go back right away, do you? Can you stay a few days?"

"I would need to explain my absence with the authorities and secure permission for staying on, but sure, I would like to stay, thank you."

Just then, a faint giggle came from the direction of the kitchen. They all smiled. Painted Pony was gently pulled back into the cookery by Rains Down, who brought out dessert a moment later and placed it in the lounge for the trio. Such routine and normalcy were a welcomed sight at the ranch.

"I guess we are not the only ones who enjoy your company," teased Susan. But Susan was more than just pleased that Earth Raven could stay to share his company with them; she was also happy that Painted Pony was feeling more like herself and Earth Raven was clearly the reason for that.

The three of them transferred themselves into the lounge to have tea and dessert. While there, Susan made another request of Earth Raven. "I would like you to go into Sundance with me tomorrow. I have some errands to run while sending your message to the authorities, and would like your help on something."

Earth Raven replied accommodatingly, "That would be fine."

Snake Catcher sarcastically interjected, "Back to town so soon?" He shudderingly shook his head grumbling, "Too soon."

Susan teasingly retorted, "That's fine, you're not invited. I have a surprise for you, and I don't want you to spoil it."

Snake Catcher skeptically grinned at her. Susan excused herself, leaving Snake Catcher and Earth Raven to chat a while.

Susan floated out onto the porch and stood inhaling the fresh summer's night air. She relaxed into a rocking chair, sipped from the tea cup she had carried from the lounge, and took in the silhouette of Paha Sapa against a backdrop of stars. After a while, she entered the house, passing Earth Raven and her husband who were exiting the house to enjoy a smoke with a pipe furnished by Earth Raven. They said their good-nights to Susan.

At bedtime, Earth Raven felt elated as he was entering the guest bedroom alone. He beamed knowing that Snake Catcher was happily living together with Susan and filling their house with loving memories of being husband and wife.

Chapter 31

The next morning, Susan and Snake Catcher contently sat on the porch enjoying the simple pleasures of tea and their spectacular view of Paha Sapa. They were exceedingly grateful for the small rewards of their daily rituals. Their gratitude extended to having friends inclined to visit them, and they let Earth Raven sleep in as reward for their big triumph in court the day before.

Later that morning, Susan, Earth Raven, Larry and Sammy congregated at the wagon for their trek into Sundance. As Snake Catcher stoically stood on the porch to watch them ride out of his sight, he felt uneasy about being away from his wife so soon after their threat of being apart forever. Painted Pony stood secretly behind the drapes in the parlor during their departure. Her face was saddened again watching Earth Raven leave, even though she realistically knew it was only for a few hours. She only wanted the swings of emotion to cease. Painted Pony then retreated to complete her chores so, optimistically, she would have a plethora of time later on if Earth Raven wished for a conversation with her.

The team arrived at the undertakers, where Larry and Sammy loaded a headstone into the wagon. Earth Raven stood heavy-heartedly staring at it. He was no longer smiling as he had been the previous evening. Susan smiled and stepped over to Earth Raven while putting her hand on his shoulder before asking, "You think my husband will like it?"

Earth Raven managed to choke out the words, "Very much."

"He was your friend, too. Do you like it?"

Earth Raven was unable to speak, but did spiritedly nod at her question.

When they arrived back at the ranch, Susan and Earth Raven stepped into the house while Larry and Sammy continued over to the ranch cemetery with the headstone in the wagon.

Later that afternoon, everyone at the ranch meandered over to the cemetery; Susan with her Bible, a book of prayers and Hail Maker's lessons and poetry book. The slow walk over was as much a part of the ritual as the headstone ceremony itself. The entire proceeding was overlooked by Paha Sapa, as if it were blessing the moment with all of its glorious spirituality.

Larry and Sammy had dug out an area of earth before delicately erecting the headstone in that location next to Susan's parents. Meanwhile, Susan had instructed Ferdy to discreetly dig a small but somewhat deep hole in front of the headstone. Now, standing by the stone, Susan carefully removed Hail Maker's poetry book's contents and sympathetically placed the book's blood-stained cover in the hole. Next, she instructed Ferdy to cover this with the unearthed dirt. The headstone read:

Wasu Kage

A Lakota Man

≫ ≻ ∞ ≺ ≪

Hail Maker

A White Man's Friend

≫ ≻ ∞ ≺ ≪

Beloved Husband, Father, Brother

Neighbor to All

1879

Susan turned to a page of readings in her prayer book. All, with the exception of Snake Catcher and Earth Raven, bowed their heads in prayer. Since Snake Catcher and Earth Raven did not know of the White tradition of bowing in prayer, they respectfully stood in silence as Susan recited her benediction. At the ceremony's end, most everyone who had gathered turned gracefully and began walking back toward the house. Earth Raven understood to follow suit; however, Snake Catcher stood frozen, and it seemed as if he could not move. As Susan began to saunter past him, Snake Catcher reached out for her hand, and stopped her. Together they stood there in silence for a moment.

Susan looked up at her husband to offer some peace of

mind to him. "His spirit will always be home here with us now; now that his blood is buried here."

Snake Catcher, unwarriorly, said, "I miss talk with brother. What do you miss?"

Susan softly smiled, commenting, "I miss his stories. I miss how excited I would get when he came to visit."

"Why do Whites talk about the dead? Is it not disrespect-ful?"

Susan pondered the question for a moment before answering, "I guess it is because our love is selfish, and we do not want to let go of them."

Snake Catcher solemnly nodded as if to understand, then asked, "What does the stone say about him?"

Susan read the inscription to her husband as she pointed out each word, then finished with, "He left us in the year of 1879."

It was at this moment that Snake Catcher finally knew Hail Maker had sent him there for a reason other than delivering a book. The special reason of being with Susan. Who knew them both better; that they would be a perfectly compatible match?

Susan and Snake Catcher slowly walked back toward the house, fused together. The staff had ventured off to rest or to complete chores. Earth Raven emotionally retreated to the guest bedroom, and he was not seen until supper.

Chapter 32

Susan woke to the sounds of her husband sleeping deeply beside her. She smiled at her fortune, yet felt poorly with fatigue and nausea. She tiptoed downstairs for some bread to settle her stomach. The apothecary room harbored her savory camomile tea, and there she ground a mixture before returning with it to the bedroom. Susan then dipped out some warm water from the dimly-lit bedroom fireplace and brewed her tea. There were fresh roses in a vase on a nearby table, to which Susan turned up her nose as she quietly stepped past, and she promptly moved the blossoms out into the hallway. She returned to bed next to her husband as he awoke and inquired about his wife.

"Are you good?"

"Not completely."

Lifting his head with concern, he asked, "Wicahpi Kute, do we send for medicine man?"

"No. I've already seen Doc Brown when I was in town visiting you the other day."

Snake Catcher spiritedly sat up in bed with concern. "What did he say?"

Susan began to relentlessly tease him by avoiding his questions, knowing it was time to tell him of her special news. "What would you say to asking Earth Raven to stay a while?"

"That is good. What did medicine man say?"

"I thought we could build him a room at the east side of the house."

"Why not stay in guest bedroom? Did medicine man say you are ill?"

"Because we will need it–it won't be spare much longer."

"Why's that?...who will live there? What did medicine man say?

"The doctor tells me that you made me feel this way."

"That it was me? What is that?"

"Yes. He said I am with child and it is because of you."

Snake Catcher's smile was exceedingly wider than Susan had ever seen on him before, and with a genuine giddiness in his voice, he asked, "You are good?"

Smiling widely herself before she tenderly kissed him, she answered, "Yes, I am good."

Snake Catcher naturally began yipping so loudly and at such a high pitch, that Rains Down and Earth Raven emerged from their respective bedrooms. They stood in the hallway with acclamations for the couple as they were reminded from their upbringing what that distinctive pitch-level meant. Snake Catcher leaped up from the bed and began to lovingly pamper Susan. She watched him in amazement and playfully giggled at his genuine excitement. Her husband was wandering aimlessly and did not know what to do with himself, then realized he should step out into the hallway to make the official announcement. The four all smiled as Earth Raven and Rains Down looked in at Susan sitting in bed. Earth Raven knew it was deserved and a long time in coming that Snake Catcher felt as he did at that moment; deeply blissful to be a part of a family again. The news spread through the ranch like a prairie fire.

Later, after the excitement of the news and the congratulations had faded, Earth Raven and Snake Catcher came down for breakfast; however, Susan was not up for smelling any pungent food as yet. Snake Catcher made plans to ride to the pasture to show Earth Raven the astoundingly wonderful ranch property and the herd that Susan had carried on from her father. It was a time for male bonding with a man of his traditions, something Snake Catcher had not realized he was longing for.

After a short ride that brilliantly clear and mirthful day, Earth Raven and Snake Catcher sat on their horses speaking in their native tongue and looking out onto the pasture toward Paha Sapa. Earth Raven commented, "This is beautiful country, especially with the views of our hills."

"How will we make them ours again?"

"I do not know. We will need to fight hard, I suppose."

"*You* will fight for them?" asked Snake Catcher.

Earth Raven answered, "Perhaps. I would greatly enjoy making that my life's work, to fight the White man's establishment in his own house of Washington's oppressives. I'm just not sure it will do any good."

"We will smoke to find the answers as did Chief Clever Spirit when he was searching the spirits for wisdom," suggested Snake Catcher.

Earth Raven and Snake Catcher dismounted their horses and found a comfortable place in the shade to smoke with an unobstructed view of Paha Sapa. They lit the pipe that Hail Maker had made for Jacob and smoked a while. Snake Catcher told Earth Raven the story of how he came to have Hail Maker's pipe, and his adventures since he came to stay at the ranch. The two friends spoke of how they wanted to help their people back at the reservation who had been so supportive of them both in their life's pilgrimages.

Back at the house, Mrs. Gaines and some church parishioners arrived to inquire about Susan after her burdensome week. Even though everyone in town knew of the trial ordeal, they were still immensely worried for her when she did not attend church the past Sunday, as she would rarely miss. Rains Down put their minds at ease when she informed them that, even though Susan was not feeling well enough to receive them that day, she would be fine in a few days. The parishioners thoughtfully gave Rains Down a basket of food, wished Susan well, and then left. Moments later, Rains Down deposited the basket in the kitchen, after stopping by Susan's bedside and finding her asleep.

Susan, Snake Catcher and Earth Raven met for supper in the diningroom that evening. Susan could barely contain her focus on the topic due to her incredibly famished state. Ferdy stepped to the door and had just begun to whisper to Susan when Snake Catcher interrupted loudly for all to hear. "Have you not looked in the kitchen, Ferdy?"

Ferdy sheepishly grinned. "Thank you," he whispered before enthusiastically scampering toward the kitchen as if he'd never been told of her location before. Snake Catcher and Susan smiled at each other knowing the circumstances of Ferdy's actions. Susan, who was feeling abundantly better, decidedly began having some fun by making digs at Snake Catcher. She playfully teased him about the recent news surrounding their bundle of joy.

"The baby will need a name; what will we call *her*?"

Without missing a beat nor a bite, Snake Catcher was poised to respond, now aware of his wife's teasing technics. "We will not know until after *he* is born. We need to see *his* ways."

Susan smiled at Snake Catcher's keenness. "Yes, we will see. I am guessing that the reason I was unconscious for so long was to protect this child, whatever the gender might be. That is a true testament to how strong *she* is." She turned to Earth Raven and asked, "What are the chances we can get you to stay here with us longer than just a few days?"

"I don't see why not. For how long?" their friend replied.

"Long enough to live a full life in a room that we will build for you on the east side of the house."

Earth Raven stopped his eating in mid-chew as he looked up from his supper plate with much surprise. Just then, one could hear sporadic scampering in the kitchen. Snake Catcher glanced up at Susan, knowing what she was about to pitch and the resistance she would meet, but said nothing.

Hesitantly, Earth Raven gently began with well-chosen words for Susan, to avoid seeming ungrateful for her generosity. "Do not think for a moment that I do not appreciate the offer. However, I am not of the White man's population; I do not think that I can live in his world as he does. I would, in some ways, feel as though I am abandoning my people. It was their dream to see me succeed with the White words and with a White education so that I could help them. There is a path that I need to take and I do not know if I can help my people from here."

Susan warmly explained, "This is not just a White person's house. We have people from many different cultural backgrounds living here in the place they call home, as the photographs in the lounge will attest. This is Zuzeca Wawoyu-spa's home now. He has sacrificed his world to be here with me, and I will not soon forget that. Did you ever think that a Lakota warrior could live amongst the Whites as he does, much less be married to one? What will be your sacrifice?" Susan provokingly smiled at Earth Raven for his commitment.

"No, but he was in immediate danger from the Blue Coats, as I am not–he has found safety. And he is in love. I do not see that for myself."

"It is my desire to help your people–they are my people now, too. I am set on finding a way to have Paha Sapa returned to them. There is no greater loss than one's holyland. I cannot help my husband with this mission from the reservation. I have fought with my life and my blood to keep this ranch because it comes from family blood, and not because it was *my* dream. I know about dreams now. What better place to fight the White man's power, than from a White world? 'Keep your friends close and your enemies closer' is what Hail Maker once told me. You will have funds here to aid you. You will have access to people who can help us, and most importantly, who will listen to you about making a better life for the Lakota people. They can shun you easier from the reservation than in political circles. I only have one request in your quest for a better life for your people; that you devote part of your time toward recapturing Paha Sapa for our Lakota people. Zuzeca Wawoyuspa speaks of honor for his people. Would it not be a bigger honor to sacrifice yourself for your people's holyland?"

Snake Catcher smirked at his wife's tenacity. Earth Raven found a familiarity in her persuasion, as on the day Snake Catcher married her. Earth Raven yieldingly smiled, realizing that he was outnumbered. "I see that you *two* have given this much thought. I am grateful for what you have offered. I will take this opportunity to at least try to make a difference from within. I will be *close* to them. Thank you."

Not beyond a breath later, a muffled squeal came from the direction of the kitchen as Rains Down already anticipated the event, and had her hand over Painted Pony's mouth. Snake Catcher and Susan spontaneously laughed while Earth Raven sheepishly grinned.

Susan summated, "Then it is done. And always know that this is your home as well, not just somewhere you room. It is not the destination in one's life, but the explorations you will experience that will build your future."

Snake Catcher had not seen the need to interject into the conversation, as his wife was maneuvering it in the direction of his wishes. He had, however, smile frequently at her persistence.

Earth Raven came to realize something about Susan and he spoke it to her. "We come from different worlds but we are the same; we want to help others."

Susan smiled at his gracious compliment, cordially nodded, then continued, "How will you get permission to stay?"

"I am an educated man; I will find a way. I'm not sure the Blue Coats would waste their time on one lone Lakota."

Earth Raven looked toward his old friend and mentor. "Snake Catcher is different; he was a warrior that they feared. They track those men among us. I am not that type of man. I am a different kind of warrior."

Susan remarked, "They are foolish not to fear the kind of warrior you are, as well."

Earth Raven appreciatively smiled, then continued, "I am not sure how much I can do with regaining possession of our land, as I am not a lawyer in the eyes of the Whites. But I will make sure that they hear my word and feel my sting wherever and whenever possible."

Susan glowingly interjected, "We have to get going on building your new room. I thought we might also include a second new room for you."

"What would I need with another room?"

"Your future. I would think you would like to get married someday and start a family."

The giggling sounds of Painted Pony came from the kitchen's vicinity. While shrugging, Earth Raven again smiled sheepishly but did not respond to Susan's subtle suggestion. She added, "I would also like to include a diningroom for everyone."

Earth Raven was secretly grateful to hear Susan change the uncomfortable subject.

"Do we not have one?" Snake Catcher inquired as he spread his arms out to indicate their surroundings.

Susan replied, "Yes, but this one would be in the space under Earth Raven's room, and it would be big enough so everyone would be a part of the meals. Wouldn't that be lively?"

Earth Raven acknowledged, "It would indeed."

After supper, as Earth Raven and Snake Catcher sat in the lounge discussing plans for Earth Raven's relocation to the ranch, Susan stood on the porch taking small sips of her faithful stomach-calming camomile tea while gazing out at Paha Sapa. She lifted, then tipped her cup to the hills as she winked and smiled at them. Susan whispered, "It was truly a good day...a good day indeed."

Before turning in, Susan asked Cook to include a pie of her choosing and some clippings from the ranch's rose bushes with the return of the parishioner's basket in exchange for the food that they had left for her. She believed it would be an unfortunate fate, not to mention unneighborly, to return an empty basket.

Chapter 33

Three months had passed into history while they were able to manufacture an abundance of pleasant memories. With Carter's death, the continuity of threats and destruction at the ranch had ceased. Also abolished were the harassments from the Blue Coats, which would no longer be warranted.

That summer was filled with special moments: from Snake Catcher and Susan visiting their favorite tranquil location under the tree and skinny-dipping in the river at their leisure to Susan observing Snake Catcher's nonverbal expression of happiness in gaining a male confidant with Earth Raven now on the ranch. Earth Raven had begun writing his speeches about the return of Paha Sapa, and reciting them in preparation for trips to Washington. Painted Pony would find any reason, notwithstanding the obscurity, to visit the main house when Earth Raven was around. In the meantime, she was caring for and training Sparky so efficiently, he would only adhere to the sounds of her voice. She learned early on what the power of an apple and an occasional sugar cube would do to benefit the training process. Larry was continuing to supplement his wages by breaking horses for the neighboring ranchers during his duty-free time. Cook was still holding on to hopes of a fruitful merging for her son. Buck was still pining after Miss Angel with Lily painfully looking on. Slim was challenged with keeping Painted Pony focused on her studies rather than on the newest member of the household. Sammy found himself ready to marry, and Nkechi accepted, resigning her position as a housekeeper, and they planned to live together in Sammy's room in the staff quarters. Even though Susan did not need any new help, she agreed to pay Nkechi for doing small sewing and cleaning chores around the ranch. After seeing Sammy's whipping scars for the first time, Nkechi was brought to tears; she could only imagine the depths of his pain. Ferdy was chasing Rains Down and she was letting him.

All was not favorable, though. Coyote's paw had been caught in a trap illegally set by poachers just outside the boundary of the ranch, necessitating its removal to save her leg and her life. No other dog would have been so brave, for Coyote was a trooper and she did not seem to be the worst for wear while keeping up with Killer. She was Susan's treasure, and the rancher tended to this companion's wound as she would for any injured soul. Coyote regarded the pampering as more of a nuisance, though, not humane nurturing care.

With all of the ominous distractions behind her, it was time for Susan to diligently focus on Paha Sapa and her growing family. That would move Susan to meet weekly with many of the parishioners from her church, members who had charitably joined her letter-writing campaign to President Arthur for the return of Paha Sapa to the Lakota people. The parishioners would discuss the contents of the letters and construct them with as much power as they could launch without seeming unpatriotic.

Snake Catcher, concerned for the safety of their unborn child, only made one request; that the letter writers meet at the ranch, which would limit the amount of times Susan would spend turbulently bouncing around in the wagon. Snake Catcher would proudly smile from a distance watching the congregants debate, cackle and formulate their sentences. He was eternally grateful not to be on the receiving end of the venomous words, and actually felt a bit sorry for President Arthur.

Earth Raven soon began giving speeches in Washington to whomever would listen. His first was offered on the street in front of the Capitol building. About twenty people stopped to listen to a portion of his speech...

> "The treaty between the United States and different tribes of the Sioux Indians, concluded April 29, 1868; Article 16 reads: The United States hereby agrees and stipulates that the country north of the North Platte River and east of the summits of the Big Horn Mountains shall be held

and considered to be unceded Indian territory, and also stipulates and agrees that no White person or persons shall be permitted to settle upon or occupy any portion of the same; or without the consent of the Indians first had and obtained, to pass through the same..."

Nearly one month later, Earth Raven trilled another speech in Washington as he stood on the steps of the Capitol building with about a hundred people absorbing his words...

"The Lakota Nation signed the mandatory treaty with the government to protect their sacred Paha Sapa, which was deeded to the Lakota Nation for eternity. The Fifth Amendment to the Constitution of the United States guaranteed that no state will deprive *any* person of life, liberty, *or* property, without due process of the law; nor shall private property be taken for public use without just compensation. This was clearly violated and good faith was not given. It is, however, irrelevant to our mission as we seek its return, not compensation. Since we were not considered citizens of this country, even though we are native to this land, would it not be interpreted as a hostile conquering of our land? Would that not be considered a dictatorship; one where a people who had left their homeland in order to escape from such monarchy turned around only to bestow that onto our people? Now they tell us that we must abide by the confines of this Constitution, and they have the right to take our land as outlined in the Fifth and Fourteenth Amendments. The Fourteenth Amendment states that all persons born in the United States are citizens and it was ratified in 1868; however, to this day, we are not considered United States citizens solely because of our skin, yet they hold us to their law of eminent domain."

Nearly one month later, Earth Raven lilted a similar speech in Washington as he stood in Lafayette Park with about 200 people intensely immersed in his message...

"The creation of the 1868 treaty, which was understood to 'civilize' us Natives, permitted us

to govern and regulate ourselves and our own
domestic affairs. If the United States government
did not include us in their Constitution and laws,
and willingly allowed us to have our own legal
system, then how can they force us to abide by
the their law of eminent domain? If we are
included in their laws, then we are included in
their Constitution. Where was our First Amendment rights for *respecting an establishment of
religion*? It is historically documented that the
hills of Paha Sapa are an essential part of our
religion, yet we are not permitted to exercise it.
Only four short years into our agreement in 1872,
the government broke their treaty *and* the constitutional amendments when they allowed miners
to invade and stake claims in Paha Sapa in
search for gold. In 1874, the Blue Coats ordered
a reconnaissance mission, sending Custer to
protect the treaty-breaking trespassers. The Lakota
people were not told of the order, and lesser, not
asked for treaty-binding consent..."

Earth Raven was quickly making a name for himself in
Washington. He orated a powerful speech just one month later
inside the Capitol building with approximately 300 people
standing gathered around as witnesses to his impassioned
words...

"Paha Sapa is perhaps among the Western hemi-
sphere's oldest geological formations. The hills
are considered the center of our nation where
there is fresh water, vegetation and abundant
beauty. The Lakota Nation had considered Paha
Sapa sacred since the creation of time. It is a
hunter's paradise. We once had our land and we
provided for ourselves. The government took our
land and now we have to rely on their support
because we have no more hunting grounds to
feed our families. When we tried to take back
what was ours, we were characterized as *hostiles*.
If someone stole your cattle, would you not try to
reclaim them? Do you not hang cattle rustlers in
this country? They tell us that we have to abide
and live by the ways of the Whites. Is the ways

of our country to live off of others? We do not
want that for our children. We want to provide
for ourselves but we cannot do that without the
resources from *our* land..."

Some time later, Earth Raven was invited to speak
honorably in Washington at the Brentwood Mayor's Mansion.
That night in the Mayor's diningroom, every chair of the 200
provided was occupied by influential people and many other
guests were standing...

"This government *chose* a life for my people by
dictating their language and forbidding ours to be
spoken, and by dictating White education and
abolishing our cultural ways. Does that not
violate our right to be free? How could *our*
government sell land to others that was never
sold by us? Is it not against the law to sell stolen
property? Since the land was never sold by us,
then there would be a question as to whether it
was leased. The lease was approved by only ten
percent of the adult male Lakota population
when seventy-five percent was required in order
for the transaction to be legal. We have a signed
document stating we own the land. The government has many documents stating they have
taken the land from us. The land was never sold.
That would only leave eminent domain. For what
purpose? Greater good of the people in times of
depression and hunger? Whose people? Our
people are hungry, too. They want to keep us
locked up on reservations while we are not
among these greater people. Nor did President
Grant allow us to even enter into our Paha Sapa
to flourish with these greater people according to
the 'Sell or Starve option.' They initially only
allowed us to have the land that they thought
was a mountain of stone; barren and worthless,
but then when it turned out to be fruitful, they
took that from us, too. Perhaps the disfavoring
tale of an *Indian-giver* was misappropriated.
Would the Lakota people have known about its
resources if the Whites had not publicized it?
Yes, we already knew there was gold in the hills.

That is not what makes them sacred. This is our holyland where we bury our dead. Would you allow another to buy a graveyard and let them build a trading post over it? Even with us knowing about the gold, what they have taken thus far is more than payment for any discovery fees. Paha Sapa is not for sale, our hills were never for sale and they were never sold, legally. So why do they not belong to us?"

After Earth Raven's speech, a rumble of applause erupted for him. As passionate as most seemed to be about his cause, Earth Raven knew that it would still be an uphill battle to persuade these Native sympathizers to vote in their favor on such an issue. He was skeptical yet hopeful for the help of his new allies. Meanwhile, his emotionally charged cause gave him much useful notoriety. After Earth Raven had secured himself a part-time position with a Washington delegate, he would take great consideration in running for a seat in the House of Representatives himself someday.

Most days at the ranch were that of tranquility, for their part. Rains Down had finally agreed to allow Ferdy to court her, officially, on the condition that he would not pressure her for an announcement of something permanent. While the two were enjoying each other's company openly, Cook was *silently* delighted.

Larry took a bad spill while breaking horses during his part-time job; however, with Susan's mojo medicine, he was back to work soon thereafter.

Buck was frequenting Willy's Saloon; every time there, he was put off by Angel, which brought him to see more of Lily. After around the fifth disappointment, he was known to start asking for Lily instead. Lily was *silently* delighted.

Slim was still at a loss on how to handle his daughter, challenged by keeping Painted Pony focused on her studies and not Earth Raven.

Sammy and Nkechi were divinely happy in their wedded state and rarely socialized without one another. Of course, their first few months together would not permit the desire to socialize with anyone except one another.

Earth Raven would return every month or so to help with the construction of his new abode. While there, he would also heed the advice and knowledge of Susan, respecting and appreciating her education. Susan was more suitable at constructing written sentences than Earth Raven; however, he was more knowledgeable at affixing a legal stance to them. Susan made it appear as though she was educating Painted Pony on different matters of government by having her sit in on her conversations with Earth Raven, but they all knew better. Painted Pony was *silently* delighted by this development. In many ways, she reaped the rewards of the time she could spend with Earth Raven, however limited, before he would again depart for Washington.

Meanwhile, Nathaniel Black Deer Davis was sitting in his private home constructing the last touches to his letter addressed to Snake Catcher...

> "Sir, I have received your letter forwarded from Washington and am pleased you are doing well in your new life. I, too, am concerned about the ever-shrinking reservations. Our people have endured much at the hands of a few greedy White men. Unfortunately, I am no longer in a position to help you with your quest, as I am no longer involved in Washington. I have resigned my position there for another life myself. I commend you in fighting for your homeland and wish you much success in your endeavors. Truly, Nathaniel Black Deer Davis."

Moments later, Davis was strolling down the streets of Philadelphia to post the letter with a mail carrier.

Soon, Susan was sitting on the porch reciting Davis's letter to Snake Catcher. When she had reached the end, Susan relinquished the letter, which floated down to the floor of the porch where Killer sniffed at the paper as it rested at her feet. Both Susan and Snake Catcher sat in silence for a while absorbing their defeat. Finally, Susan took a cleansing breath and contended, "This is only one setback. We will still persevere in our pursuit for justice. Earth Raven should be home soon to tell of his success."

In the meantime, it was never challenged that Master Briggs was the wiser man who sold his worthless soil to a Yankee carpetbagger with dreams of working the land in Atlanta. Briggs packed what was left from his plantation, which was nearly bankrupt, and left the majority of his belongings at the general store for sales on consignment.

Master Briggs had been told by his hired bounty hunters that his prey was nowhere to be found; however, they had felt a hint of deception looming from a territory to the northwest of Atlanta. The men hinted at how many former slaves were settling in those areas.

From there, Briggs set out to follow a cold, but indelible, trail which would take him closer to finding his adversary. He would require two horses for his trip, as one could not carry such a mammoth man for very long.

Chapter 34

Susan was in her sixth month and beginning to show her pregnancy. Autumn had already begun and a brisk chill was in the air. Loosely wrapped in a shawl while sipping her tea, Susan looked out admiringly upon the leaves of Paha Sapa. A sign of change was within their color as some of them were turning from forest-green into egg-yolk-yellow, marigold-orange and cardinal-red. With powders from dried and ground flower petals, Susan serenely stroked her sketch pad of what was in her view, while oscillating her view of those from the house working on Earth Raven's addition.

Cook stepped out onto the porch with a tray of food and a warm-up for the tea. "How are you feeling today, Miss Susan?"

As Susan longingly glanced at the workers, she commented, "Much better, but I wish I could go over and help the rest of them."

"No, no. Snake Catcher has left me strict orders not to let you do anything except sit here, eat and drink tea."

Susan concluded, "I know, I know—he's being a mother hen."

Cook laughed at the thought of Snake Catcher clucking around the yard. "I'm going to bring out food and drinks for the others now. Do you need anything else?"

As Susan stared over toward the work site, she answered, "No, Cook. Thank you. I may take a walk over there." Susan instantly held up her hand to prevent any scolding from Cook, before adding, "Just a walk—that's all."

"Fine, then I'll leave you to deal with him," Cook countered, then snorted and hoofed herself back into the house.

Susan imperceptibly strolled over to the site. In noticing a better angle from the eastern view of the house, she discovered that the construction of the frame and the roof had been completed. Susan stood unnoticed watching her staff of "carpenters" for a moment before she directed a question toward Buck, who was hammering a few boards into place on one of the walls. "Everyone is pitching in just fine. As far as a part-time project, it is shaping up quite nicely. So...what can *I* do?"

Snake Catcher caught the sounds of Susan's voice before he understood what she was articulating. He hysterically stormed over to her as quickly as he would shriek "Hiya!" then gently guided her to a sitting position on the porch steps of the new addition.

Susan pouted, "I'm not completely helpless."

Snake Catcher tenderly scolded Susan while placing his hand on her stomach. "You have job, you provide a safe place for our son."

Susan genially smiled at Snake Catcher's devotion to his family, yet she was bored and yearned to help. She treaded back to the house and plopped into a chair on the porch, yet again.

Painted Pony hiked over after Susan and sat with her. "Why is he being mean to you?"

"No, dear, he's not being mean. He's actually being protective of the baby and me."

"Why so much? He won't let you do anything."

"I'm sure it is because he lost his Lakota wife while she was carrying their first child."

Painted Pony distressingly glanced over at Snake Catcher. "That must have been terrible. When did that happen?"

Susan briefly sat motionless in thought before she solemnly reminisced about the past. "It was the same day that Hail Maker and Father died, back in '79, as engraved on their tombstones."

Painted Pony interjected, "I was only eight."

"Yes," Susan said as she floated back to that day. "The Lakota named that horrible day **THE DAY OF DISHONOR**. They were on their own land, a reservation, as outlined in their treaty when the Blue Coats grimly gunned them down without provocation. It is still unknown as to why the Blue Coats targeted them. Snake Catcher's wife was killed at their village, then Hail Maker and Father were killed on the prairie. I could not believe my eyes when they fell to the ground."

Painted Pony's eyes widened at learning that Susan was present at their deaths and actually witnessed the horrific event. She sat frozen in silence as she listened to Susan's recollection.

"I felt as though I cheated the Angel of Death that day, who must have been working for the Blue Coats. Perhaps it was so that I could reveal what truly happened to them. Hail Maker was gunned down not from fighting with the White settlers nor from the Whites passing through their land, but fighting by rebelling against the establishment of 'civilization' as the government dictated it to them. The gold rush in California was another big part of the Lakota being ousted from their land. Those who were seeking gold in California were the trespassers that the Natives would have allowed to pass through their land peacefully on their way out west if it weren't for the Blue Coats pushing their people further and further to obscurity." Susan took a breath to refocus on THE DAY OF DISHONOR. "By all rights, I should have become a part of history that day. Perhaps that was why I was spared, to help change the future history of these people. That event was the defining moment up to that point in both my life, and Snake Catcher's life, because it touched the two of us very deeply. It is surprising that we had not been acquainted until this year."

Painted Pony painfully asked, "Why did they do that to all of those people?"

"I can only speculate, dear, but I think that the Lakota people were caught in the middle of the growth of civilization, no matter how well their way of life had worked for them. They also had what others wanted–land, gold and hunting rights. The Blue Coats were employed by the government with nothing to do for years. With the Civil War behind them and the growing fear of being unemployed in front of them, they needed another cause to go to battle over."

Silence loomed over the two of them before Painted Pony, wanting to cheer the mood and bring Susan out of her blueness, added, "He is very happy now. I can see that."

Susan sweetly smiled knowing it was true.

Moments later, Slim, Larry and Buck walked over and exhaustedly sat on the main porch steps for a rest, along with consuming some food and refreshments. Painted Pony was preoccupied with drawing out a design of a bedroom on Susan's sketch pad.

"Painted Pony, don't do that," reprimanded Slim. "You

know that pad doesn't belong to you."

Instantly, Painted Pony inquisitively looked up at Susan with her big doe-eyes as if asking permission after the fact. Susan smiled, then said, "That's okay. What are you sketching?"

"I am helping, too, by designing the bedroom for Earth Raven."

"Painted Pony, why would you want to waste your time with such nonsense?" Slim pesteringly interrogated. "It is just a square room.

Painted Pony gave Slim a pouty face and then teasingly fired back at him. "Because I will live in that room someday."

Everyone laughed, except Slim, who was radically taken back by Painted Pony's bluntness. The rest of the others from the building site meandered over to join the clan on the porch for lunch.

Earth Raven inquired, "What is everyone laughing at?"

Susan gave a cryptic commentary to Earth Raven but directed it toward Painted Pony. "We were just planning the future."

Painted Pony snickered.

Slim grunted.

Susan changed the subject by asking Earth Raven, "When are you expected back in Washington?"

"Next week."

Susan commented, "Well, hopefully we will be finished with the addition by the time you return. I will take the liberty of placing a few decorative items in the room for a more homey feel for you. We can move the bed from the guest room into your new room."

They all continued to have their meal while laughing and conversing. When the break was over, everyone headed back over to the building site except for Sammy and Susan.

"Miss Susan, I know of a job you can do to he'p," Sammy nervously began.

"What is that, Sammy?"

"I would love learnin' to read and writin'."

Susan's face glowed as she nodded in acceptance. Sammy smiled gratefully at her and then trotted back to the building project.

As she watched Snake Catcher give instructions to Sammy on his next task, Susan thought about how her husband was fitting in at the Paradise Valley Ranch better than anyone ever expected he would, as his surprising knowledge at carpentry would attest. Still, Susan had no intention of changing Snake Catcher to conform to her "White" traditions and way of life. While he was intrigued with much of the White technology and many of their tools and weapons, these did not largely replace his methods of using a knife, bow and arrowheads.

Near the end of December, Susan swayed back and forth on the porch in a rocking chair early one morning and began to recall her year in a sort of review. She thought of how the year ended compared to the way it began. Life for Susan had been empty before the summer started. She hadn't realized that she was just letting life move her along rather than actually living it for herself. Susan's medical knowledge had allowed her to save a man's life that year. She believed she saved Snake Catcher's spiritual life as well when she agreed to help fight for his cause with him.

Susan now knew what it was like to love a man and to be loved by a man. With her woman's rights movement, she already knew what it was like to be personally inspired to help others, but she did not know how deeply satisfying it would be to do it for someone so intimate with her. Her gratitude extended to the experience of teaching her good friend Larry to respect the Lakota's sacred native land and not benefit from the losses of others.

A soft breezy wave of sadness came over Susan when she recalled taking a life as well that year. A life of a man who was angry and lost, who was still in a battle over losing his homeland. Sure, the Crow had wandered onto her property with the intent of harming her people; nonetheless, the death saddened her.

Susan's world was saved from another man who threatened her way of life and tried to kill her on several occasions. Susan was saddened that Carter had to die for his sins, but not as sad as she was about the demise of the Crow brave or even the man Carter sent to kill her. The stampede Carter had started was devastating, but fortunately it did not kill anyone.

Susan brought herself to reminisce about the more cheery and educational memories of the year. She got her first look at a court trial, and was blessed with adding a new friend to her life in meeting Earth Raven. She also received a preview of what it would be like to worry the fears of a mother during

Painted Pony's abduction. It had been a satisfying feeling when she fought the Blue Coats on her own turf and won. The year had also given Susan her first taste of rabbit and elk's meat, and however distasteful these were to her, she was grateful for that as well because it brought her a future memory with the man she loved. She felt honored to be able to teach him about her culture and that not all Whites were bad as Snake Catcher had once been taught or shown. Moreover, she was able to learn about someone else's culture, too. Susan also found time to recall the smaller joys of life when Snake Catcher had surprised her with a floral decorated incandescent lamp to replace the one from her mother that he had broken at the time of their introduction.

Susan was greatly appreciative that after being shot in the head, she lived to tell about it. Again, she was grateful for the ability to finally bury a remembrance of her friend Hail Maker and say good-bye to him. And there was a calm in their lives at the ranch now that they were focusing on the future.

Snake Catcher walked up and joined Susan on the porch as she was completing these thoughts. Sitting in the next rocking chair, he looked over at her amusingly while dragging his hand across her swelled stomach. Snake Catcher liked to feel the liveliness of their baby's kick within her, which the squiggler would only do at the onset of feeling his touch. With that, Susan instinctively knew that this child would be exceedingly infatuated with its father until the end of time. With her hand placed firmly on his hand that was on her abdomen, Susan thought about the very best gifts of all that year; the *two* she was rocking with on the porch that day.

Around this time, Master Briggs was tracking near Omaha. He was beginning to discover that he could extract more information from the townspeople if he were somewhat established in their town. Briggs would earn himself a job, and began discreetly socializing nightly with the saloon patrons. There, he would ply these loose-lipped customers with spirits. From this, they would become so inebriated that the buffoons would pour forth all that they knew. When Briggs was satisfied that they were not harboring his quarry, he would move to the next town heading in a northwesterly direction.

Chapter 35

February fifteenth burst onto the scene at the Paradise Valley Ranch with the first snowfall in weeks in 1885. Due to the frosty white wind swirling in circles, the only visible evidence of Paha Sapa that day was in one's memory.

As Susan's newborn was being held in the arms of its loving mother for the first time, Susan's doting husband was by her side. Even though Snake Catcher had delivered Sparky and assisted with many childbirths on the reservation, he had not been able to bring himself to actually witness the birth of his firstborn child; yet he could not bear to be far away either.

Shortly after the birth, most of Susan's clan had gathered together. There was a roaring sparking fire in the fireplace. The child was very energetic, and seemed unable to wait for the ability to move around without support–a trait unmistakably noticed by all. Susan became overly anxious when Snake Catcher lifted his son high up over his head, proudly balancing the newcomer on his hand for all to see. Still holding the child up, the proud father announced his son's name during the Lakota child-naming ceremony, "Wicahpi Wawoyuspa, *Star Catcher*–that is his name."

Prompting profound relief in his wife, Snake Catcher returned their son to her and then sat down on the bed next to Susan. Others gathered around to coo at Star Catcher. Snake Catcher added, "My son shall hear Lakota stories about bravery and honor. He will learn the Lakota ways."

Susan, seemingly feeling somewhat excluded, inquired poutingly, "*Your* son? Don't forget he is *my* son as well. He is half White. We will need to teach him the ways of the Whites as well."

"He already knows how to fall off a horse."

Susan laughed and softly slapped his arm for the dig as everyone spontaneously chuckled. Snake Catcher continued, "He already knows how to scream for what he wants. He already knows the meaning of 'hiya.' He already knows how to take what is not his."

Susan sarcastically grinned. "Okay, I get the point, but we do have some good traits." She looked at Snake Catcher and motioned for him to make his appeal.

"Lakota people have traditions and Whites have traditions. A White tradition is someone to watch over Wicahpi Wawoyuspa when we cannot–Godfather." Snake Catcher looked at Earth Raven. "Kagitaka Makoce is who we choose. That is good with you?"

Earth Raven smiled. "Yes, I would be honored." He turned to Susan before asking, "How do you do it? He has adapted so well here."

Susan replied, "I have no illusions. He is illusive and lives in my world temporarily to please me. He is still the warrior and hunter that I gave my heart to, that will never change. I am not wanting to change him, and I know I have his heart."

Snake Catcher smiled and slightly blushed at such public intimacy about his feelings.

Susan continued the teasing of her husband, this time, with a face of sourness. "*I* am the one who pleases him, by living in his world *temporarily*; proven by eating rabbits and elk." The admirers that had gathered laughed heartily. Susan then added with a smile, "We still have a lot of work here to do for the future of this child."

Without missing a beat, Snake Catcher cryptically smirked, then corrected her by remarking, "Children."

Everyone chuckled at Snake Catcher's relentless teasing toward his wife.

"And with Earth Raven's room completed before the first snowfall last year, we can now fill our guest bedroom with *children*," Susan surrendered.

Earth Raven added, "*I*, too, have a lot of work to carry out here, for the future of all Lakota people."

The following week, and just before Earth Raven was to return to Washington, Star Catcher was scheduled to be baptized by the town's Preacher. Susan dressed Star, as she would go on to call him, in his beautifully handsome christening gown before relinquishing him to Earth Raven. Susan and Snake Catcher stood close by as the Preacher christened the infant while others adoringly watched from the pews. After the ceremony, the town's photographer who normally worked out of his home, hurriedly gathered everyone outside, including the Preacher, for documentation of the event. The air was nippy which did not seem to be a burden to anyone, as they were all delightfully joyous. The photographer witnessed from his viewfinder that the occupants of the photograph were going to appear crystal clear in the picture, except for the energetic limbs of Star.

During the christening celebration later that day at the ranch, Susan affectionately snuck glances of Snake Catcher pridefully doting on their son while holding him as the Lakota Holyman gave prayer over the infant.

Star's Godfather had not yet received any repercussions about permanently leaving the reservation without permission, thus far; but the ranch folk were still concerned for Earth Raven's safety, none more than Painted Pony. Securing his stay would be an immediate task of his.

Susan's days had been spent mostly following in her father's footsteps with the chores of ranching and teaching those who desired to learn. That had also included her love of helping those less fortunate. Her ranching duties were now pared down to a part-time position due to her busy life as a mother. Nkechi was also hired full-time to help with the care of Star, and the burdensome portion of the ranching chores were surrendered to Susan's husband. Snake Catcher secretly wished for that responsibility, not wanting his wife to perform any strenuous chores; particularly if he and Susan would be blessed with their next bundle of joy someday soon.

Sammy was excelling at his studies, so much so that Susan wondered if he knew more about reading than he admitted. Of course, Nkechi would coach him without being too flauntingly assertive with her education which could weaken his ego.

In alignment with Susan's joy of helping others, she continued to make a statement with her letter writing-campaign. This was despite the fact that she had yet to hear from President

Arthur concerning the welfare of the Lakota people back on the reservation or any change to the status of Paha Sapa. Earth Raven had continued to fight hard for the attention of Washington's powerful lawmakers to recognize the Lakota's needs, but it had only returned a fleeting interest.

Spring was eagerly anticipated, especially since it had been a long winter; spreading well into March. But with all the happiness on the ranch, spring than seemed to be passing quickly, and as summer neared, Susan and Snake Catcher occasionally snuck off to skinny-dip in the river by their favorite picnic site while their son napped on a blanket nearby.

    Painted Pony was maturing and still trailing Earth Raven whenever he was in town; however, she began to acquire suitors of her own. By midsummer, Painted Pony would attract many male admirers at the town's annual festival. Slim was busily occupied by swatting them away like mosquitoes. Painted Pony only smiled at their attempts and her father's vigilant preservation of her virtue, as she knew the real object of her affections was in Washington that week. The infatuated teenager was very clever to throw the focus off of her continual preoccupation with Earth Raven by flirting and communing with other potential fanciers.

    Cook was delighted to hear that Rains Down was getting closer to accepting Ferdy's plans for the future. Ferdy and Rains Down began attending church together regularly, beginning with that week. Rains Down allowed Ferdy to sit closer to her, which was perceived as an announcement of their anticipated matrimonial union. That Sunday, the two of them prearranged to make a day of socializing with Susan and Snake Catcher, and the four planned for a nice meal at the eatery in town late afternoon when church had concluded.

    As the day was upon them, Susan heard from the Preacher at her church the startling news of how Miss Angel Blue had abruptly married one of the richest men in the state, and then suddenly left Sundance with him without explaining or even saying good-bye to Buck. Just prior to their meal at the eatery, Susan would excuse herself to carry out an errand at Willy's Saloon while the others headed over to be seated for supper. It would be the first time that Susan had called on Lily. She stepped into the saloon and was confronted by many aghast gentlemen fraternizing the establishment, including the owner.

"Hello, Willy. If you would be so kind as to have Miss Lily step outside whenever she has a moment, I would be greatly appreciative."

The overbearingly scruffy Willy was so stunned to be in Susan's presence inside of his establishment that the only thing he could think to mutter was "Yes, ma'am."

Susan would only wait minutes, for Lily was profoundly curious as to what she could want with the likes of an inconsequential showgirl.

"Hello, Lily," Susan said as a genuine smile graced her face. Lily exchanged the greeting, but was eagerly awaiting Susan to state her business, not knowing if her intentions were ominous or sociable. "Some of us from the church know of Miss Angel leaving. Did you know of the news?"

"Yes, we were all told of it last night," answered Lily demurely. "Willy was quite upset to see his star attraction leave."

Susan continued, "Would you know if anyone has told Buck about it yet?"

"I'm not aware of anyone telling Buck. He has not been here since the night before her last performance."

"I know the two of you have been spending time together and I thought that the news should come from someone close to him, instead of one of these buffoons at the bar who would only tease him unmercifully."

"Yes, I agree," confided Lily, now knowing officially that Susan knew of Buck's crush on Angel. Lily was somewhat saddened with realizing that so many people knew of "Angel and Buck," but no one knew about *her* deep feelings for him.

Susan went on to ask, "Would you like to be the one to tell him, or do you think that the news would be better coming from one of us? From what I understand, you are just as close to him as we are and we all just want what's best for Buck."

That statement said volumes for Lily. On her part, she was happy that the benevolent Miss Susan, who Buck spoke of highly and revered, knew Buck spoke of her, too. Yet she was still a bit tormented that Susan did not know her as being closer than just *one of them*. Lily responded, "As do I. You will see him before I will and maybe he should be told right away. Thank you for asking me. I did not know you knew who I was."

"Yes, of course, I make a special attempt to know the people who make my friends smile. And you do know that you make him smile? He speaks of you more than he realizes."

Lily glowingly smiled before saying, "Thank you for that. You have no idea how it makes me feel that you noticed this about him. To be honest, I was thrilled to see Miss Angel go, but I'm concerned for Buck's feelings and don't want him to be hurt."

"As am I–on both counts," Susan agreeably responded, gently smiling. After a pause and a quick glance at the saloon, she added, "I must add that I am not here to judge your lifestyle, it is not my place. I am only here because my friend could be hurt by this, and I am concerned for him. And who knows, maybe he is smarter than us women give him credit for." Susan tipped her head to Lily before stepping away toward her late afternoon with her husband and friends.

The ranch members tried hiding the news from Buck for fear he would be crushed, but Susan thought it best that he know. After she told him the following day, Buck did not appear to give it a second thought. That made Susan smile, knowing that would make Lily smile.

In response to an invitation she received from Buck, Lily appeared in church that next Sunday with many of the parishioners frowning at her presence. She arrived before Buck, and was not budging from her pew in the church even though it was clear those frowning faces were for her. It had always been her passion to attend church; however, she was too afraid of what they would do or say to her to ever step foot inside one in a town that knew of her chosen profession. After Buck arrived and greeted Lily, the busybodies in the church settled down and began to accept her presence. Susan graciously greeted Lily, and felt so comfortable with her as Buck's new lady friend that she relinquished Star to her for the entire length of the service. Lily was stunned to have such a responsibility, not having any children of her own, yet delighted to have Susan's trust for the others to see.

Still, Susan had an ulterior motive–to discover just what Lily was made of. Along with the pressures of facing the highfalutin' members of the congregation, Susan wanted to see Lily with the pressures of caring for an infant while the highfalutin' members of the congregation looked on. After the service, but before socially visiting with the fold of the church, Susan's husband would reclaim Star from Lily.

Snake Catcher greeted Mrs. Gaines and the other parishioners as he held his son while being perfectly charming. Still, when the sun would rise the next morning, he would certainly revert back into the Native lifestyle that the Lakota knew before arriving into their town–hunting in the wilderness and returning to a natural order that those people were unfamiliar with. Sure enough, Snake Catcher would leave early the next day with his sharpened arrowheads and his flawless knife for his hunting trek. He longed for the day that his son would accompany him for the teachings and traditions of his people.

Later that summer, Earth Raven returned home to find that Painted Pony had many suitors who sometimes loitered around the ranch in attempts to acquire her attention. He was curious as to why these boys were making complete fools of themselves by challenging each other to competitions of whatever they thought would get Painted Pony's focus for more than a fleeting moment. It was at that instant that he was forced to take notice of the beauty who was illusively adrift about the ranch. He also acutely noticed that Painted Pony was not freely tailing him, as she once had. To his dismay, Earth Raven would only get a glimpse of her now and then, and he oddly found it not to his satisfaction.

During that year's summation, Susan would once again rock on the porch sipping her tea in the brisk month of December, drawing on the memories of the past year. Her reflections would first bring her back to the birth of her child with how extraordinary it felt to give someone life, and how powerful that was. Susan was happy to have found such a lovely person in Nkechi to care for her new child. Meanwhile, Sammy had begun two new lives, one of marriage and the other to the dedication of his education.

However, that year had brought a dear friend sadness over the deceptions of a woman, the worst kind of duplicity in her view. Because of all the hard work she had put into woman's rights, Susan hated to have one of her own be the betrayer and user. The best side of that situation was that Angel was no longer controlling Buck's heart, for another had claimed it–Lily.

Meanwhile, Briggs was making chase toward the next possible location of his enemy as the hefty man approached Deadwood

City. Beggars, thieves and opportunists that had once plentifully graced the town in the hundreds had been scarce during the past few years. Even with being so close to his destination, he might be too far away now with the trail growing colder. That wasn't to say that some snitches couldn't be found, especially with the motivational incentive of a few golden nuggets.

Chapter 36

The year was 1886, and nearly two years seemed to have flown by since Snake Catcher had entered Susan's life. One day in early spring, she peacefully and contently sat on the porch watching her husband with their fifteen-month-old son. Even though the sun was shining brightly that day, the air was crisp enough to chill the surface of their skin. Susan was clearly with child again.

Susan's growing family was not deterring her from devoting some of her time to Paha Sapa's cause. The government was disallowing the Natives from filing any claims against their lost hills, and until they could find grounds for a lawsuit, they could only rely on a public following to apply pressure to those stagnating them in their crusade.

Meanwhile, technology seemed to be blossoming everywhere. Susan was curious to see something that was being marketed as a "cash register." That was also the year Susan would invest in a four-year-old invention, the carpet sweeper. Susan had yet to conform to the new generation's ways and she was content to do things in the old manner; however, since she was not the one who swept the carpets, she decided to concede. Truly, the neighboring towns were more advanced than Sundance, as it was also four years ago that the telephone had been presented without the benefits of her opinion—or her purchase.

Painted Pony had turned from a ungainly kid into an attractive young lady. She indisputably had been noticed by even more of the male suitors in the area. That summer, a month before the town's annual festival, Painted Pony would have her much anticipated coming-out gala at the ranch. Slim had unequivocally found the event objectionable because of what his opinion was of her young age. His only comforting aspect was knowing of Earth Raven's absence during the event.

Painted Pony had planned the function for an entire year and executed all of the details precisely how she envisioned them. She made sure, for example, that Susan arrange for a local photographer to document the occasion with a photograph of the celebrant in a pretty party dress, wearing her most bewitchingly demur smile. Painted Pony also made sure that she planned the event when Earth Raven would not be in town. She wanted him to be aware that he had missed an important occasion in her life, and then long to know the details. That was also a way for her to shine while reliving the experience every time it was told to someone not of the gala's participants. But most of all, Painted Pony wanted the feeling of knowing that Earth Raven would be yearning for her while standing in the lounge, as Snake Catcher had once yearned from viewing Susan's photograph.

At the same interim of time, Ferdy had officially proposed, and Rains Down consciously made him wait three agonizing days before he would hear her answer. When she finally came back with a yes, Rains Down also informed him that she would be waiting until she could plan a proper wedding, and not have a rushed event like what Miss Susan had assembled for herself. Despite all this, there was a sense of peace to Ferdy's ongoing frustration now. As they formally announced their engagement, Cook stood nearby with a huge smile on her face.

Susan commented to Cook, "Perhaps, it is the promise of her that he finds serene."

Cook nodded in agreement.

The town festival in August would be grander than ever that year. Sundance was doing so well financially that they would hire an orchestra of four all the way from Cheyenne. Jack-a-lanterns lit the main road from one end to the other. They were placed shoulder-high on wooden stilts as to not catch the women's dresses aflame.

Since Susan had not felt much like socializing, much less bouncing about in a wagon being nine months pregnant, she and Snake Catcher remained at the ranch.

That was the first event that Rains Down and Ferdy had

attended as an engaged couple outside of church without the benefit of chaperones. Ferdy was beaming with pride to show off his new fiancée.

Painted Pony had been looking forward to seeing all of her friends from her coming-out gala, but what she really wanted was to invite them all back to the ranch to see her portrait. Of course, she would only mention the new photograph within earshot of Earth Raven.

Rains Down, Ferdy, Earth Raven and Painted Pony would uniformly stand together as if too timid to go their own ways. It was then that Painted Pony would have her first intelligently in-depth political conversation with Earth Raven. Her views were unambiguous, perceptive to the topic, arduously thought out and void of emotional passion or prejudice. The only problem was–they weren't the same as his views. Painted Pony would charge the Natives in the United States for not fighting harder for what they wanted, which was their land and hunting rights to be returned. She viewed that they should have educated themselves better as to the ways of the White man as the both of them had. Earth Raven was churned to the point of being drawn in closer to Painted Pony with every misspoken word he heard.

Ferdy was somewhat distraught while listening to their discussion, but Rains Down only smiled at Painted Pony's tenacity, standing up to a male's point-of-view regarding politics. Painted Pony felt empowered that she was informed enough to perpetuate an intelligent conversation.

Earth Raven stood with Painted Pony a while longer discussing the recent opening of the Carlisle Indian School in Pennsylvania, an ambitious governmental crusade to *civilize* the Native children in the country. During this exchange, he would find frustration from being continually interrupted by many of the young men at the festival greeting his bewitching debater. She was undistracted and argued with him that an education was more important, and that rituals and a forgotten culture could be curbed until such time they had reaped all they could from the schools.

Painted Pony went on to add, "So what, if they make you cut your hair and burn your Native clothes for new *White* ones? You can grow your hair back and sew another outfit, but how many chances does a Native have to cultivate the mind? I would have thought that you of all people would realize that."

"I am not for a world where one would have to choose. I am for a world that allows a person to be who they are without a lot of rules forced upon them in order to be free. I am perfectly *civilized* even though I wear my hair longer than the Whites in this country."

Painted Pony countered with: "We do not live in a perfect world. Anyone who believes that an education is worth the time can reform long enough to profit from it by a few inconvenient necessities."

"Even by means of being forbidden to speak one's own native language, and punishment for any violations?"

"All that I know is that since I have had the supreme opportunity to acquire an education, I believe it will be the most important thing that I will ever do in my life. Because without it, I would truly be enslaved. I am wise enough now to know that I would have done anything under my power to assume one. Education is irreplaceable."

Earth Raven had become somewhat of a celebrity in town with the locals knowing of his dealings in Washington. That made it all the more difficult to remain polite to well-wishers when he was frequently interrupted and asked to comment on his advancements, while attempting to explain his point-of-view to Painted Pony. It did not help his position, or his mood, when one of Painted Pony's beaus uninvitedly joined in their discussion and wholeheartedly agreed with her opposing opinions; clearly only to win points with her.

Sammy and Nkechi left the festivities early due to not wanting to leave Miss Susan alone for very long so close to her due date.

A stranger rode into Sundance on the night of the festival. The festivities were so distractingly mirthful that he was not noticed by many as he settled into his boarding room above the town eatery. Soon that stranger would patron the establishment of spirits and braggers.

When the Paradise Valley Ranch group returned home from the festival, Susan was stretched out on a swinging chair on the porch, that Buck had designed and built, while resting her hand on her swelling stomach and getting some fresh summer's night air. Each party member went off into their separate paths except Earth Raven, who would sit with Susan a while. "How are you feeling? Any indication that the birth will happen soon?"

"Not that I can tell. I just feel big and I'm ready to tell the child to move out. I look forward to being the only one in this body again."

Earth Raven smiled at Susan's humor, but he looked tired and bewildered. She assumed it was due to his tremendous workload at the nation's Capitol. "Do you think you are making any headway in Washington?"

"There are times when I do not know the answer to that question. I have many supporters; however, without the government's approval to file a claim for Paha Sapa's return, we cannot proceed. It seems like it is a bit of a conflict of interest in my book; giving permission to sue one's self. How does that work? Who in their right mind would ever *give* someone the go-ahead to sue themselves and take the risk that they would be held liable? They only see this case as closed. They took the land through eminent domain, which the government was legally within their rights to do, but never mind that it was wrong or that it was excessive. What they did not have a legal right to do is take it for any other reason than public use, which they have violated when they sold it to a private mining company."

"We will keep trying," offered Susan. "We are not done yet." They sat for a moment in silence from their ongoing frustrating defeat. Susan flawlessly changed the subject by asking, "Did you have a good time in town tonight?"

"Yes, it was pleasant."

"I'll bet the parties back east are not like those."

"No," he said while smirking. "I do not really like those Washington functions. They are just for business connections."

"And tonight was not business? You look to be stressed as if it were."

Earth Raven heavily sighed before continuing. "I just don't know what to think about Painted Pony's belief about some of our people's issues. Sometimes I feel that she is the most exasperating woman that I have ever met."

In being her unfalteringly democratic self, Susan did not respond but only smiled demurely now knowing the true reason for his looks of anguish that night. She also gave a secret smile to his interpretation of Painted Pony–as a *woman*. Susan and Earth Raven would sit in silence before he shuffled off to his room.

Later that week, the birth of Snake Catcher and Susan's second child was medically uneventful. Susan was strong and could suitably withstand the labors of childbirth, even giving birth to another boy. That time it would be Susan's choice of names to be given at the child-naming ceremony. *Chasing Running Fire* was just as vigorous as his brother the day of his birth. Susan also announced that *Chase* would be his nickname, as she exercised her choice of a shorter name while appeasing her husband's wishes, as well. Snake Catcher and Susan decided on Painted Pony as his Godmother. Susan secretly recognized that this would bond Earth Raven and Painted Pony together forever. The concept did not go unnoticed by Painted Pony.

A few days had passed before Earth Raven departed for Washington once more. This time he seemed restless and unwilling to be enthusiastic about the trip as he formerly had. His last glance of the area before riding off would be toward Painted Pony's direction. While Earth Raven rode through the town of Sundance toward the trail east, he sensed an ominous wind blowing past him.

The new stranger soon discovered that these townspeople did not have the loose lips as he had witnessed from prior towns; that alone was be enough to intrigue and challenge him to remain in order to proceed with his sinister quest.

One night as Susan rested in the master bedroom from an exhausting week, Nkechi brought the children out onto the porch for some fresh night air. A moderate summer breeze was flowing throughout the second floor of the home and out through the French doors as it also swirled around the outside corners of the house. Nkechi placed Chase in a swinging bassinet, one that Buck had built a few months earlier and permanently bolted to the porch to prevent accidental tumbles.

Star Catcher was growing into an zealous child. Confining him to one area had turned quite challenging even at his youthful age. While Nkechi galloped after Star, which took the caretaker back into the house, another gentle wind would circle the house's perimeter. The scent of a newborn was alluring to all that crossed its path. No one could resist the intoxicating aroma; it was also not absent from those not of the immediate household. A magnificent specimen was found in a golden black-striped puma that would inch ever so closer to the cradle which housed his next conquest.

Concurrently, Chase was content to wish upon the

sparkling stars above as his spectacular entertainment. The creature's nostrils flared as he paced tight to the porch steps. The brightness of the house's interior glow prevented him from possessing the confidence needed to immediately seize his meal. He was stepping forward with conviction as the screams of the toddler echoed the foyer approaching the porch, being hunted by his governess, spooked the puma from his latest acquisition. Moments later, with hearing comparable to Peruvian fruitbats, Killer and Coyote charged out the front door and into the blackness of the night trailing after their intruder; however, the puma had the advantage of an early lead and would scamper off quickly–also due to the lightness of his empty stomach.

"Get back here, you two. What are you excited about?" Nkechi asked as she hooked Star and then looked in on Chase. The dogs eventually wandered back to the porch and plopped down, assertively watching out into the darkness.

The next day, Buck would inventory the herd to find that two were not in attendance. He only really noticed the change because one of the missing, an oddly shaped heifer with a deformed foot, was not in the lineup.

One day soon after Susan was feeling somewhat healed from the delivery, she and Snake Catcher began to take a brief trot down to the river headed for their favorite site. Their path was marred with the depleted remains of Buck's heifer chum. After they had retreated to the ranch, Susan petitioned the ranchhands to make an assessment within the perimeter for any others that had disappeared. They could not account for the other missing calf.

In the midst of midsummer, the golden beauty's growling stomach was on the prowl and ventured out close to civilization once again. This time his appetite would take him to a neighbor of the Paradise Valley Ranch. In the wee morning hours, one acutely placed pounce would bring the stalker his much awaited provisions. Many of that cat's relations would gather around Pete at the Triple R Ranch to feast on their reward.

During the socializing that Sunday at church, the parishioners would learn why Pete had not attended. They would hear the grueling details of how the Sheriff discovered Pete's shredded body parts in the rancher's pasture of cattle after getting word from his wife that the man was missing. His saddle was still attached to the horse's carcass. After diagnosing that the aggressor was a very large nasty feline, the Sheriff had sent out a posse to lynch the assassin; however, the bandit was nowhere to be found. While the vigilantes passed below a cliffed rock formation, the puma lounged motionless as he knew he would be better suited for a one-on-one event.

Earth Raven had returned in late summer to discover that the beaus in the county were as enchanted with Painted Pony now as before his departure. Even so, during his absence, Painted Pony had found the time to become an accomplished rider. Earth Raven was not consciously aware that he was mesmerized by watching her while training Sparky to jump. When she was not riding Sparky, her studies were occupying her thoughts these days, even though she inadvertently convinced Earth Raven that the young admirers in the county were her focus.

With the smells of autumn in the air one day soon after his return, Earth Raven discovered that Painted Pony had invited one specific male suitor, Albert, to visit with her on the property. As the wooer stood at the corral cheering her on while she maneuvered a jumping Sparky, Painted Pony flirtingly conversed with him, Earth Raven stepped closer. Her aloofness toward Earth Raven would make him feel like an outsider. By that time, Painted Pony appeared more as a young adult, and not the giggly teenager that he once knew. Albert was the fellow who would take his plea to Slim for Painted Pony's hand in marriage. Albert was also the fellow who was admonished by Slim, insisting that she was too young for any such nonsense.

Knowing how well her plot had flourished, Painted Pony would smile every time she spotted Earth Raven in the lounge viewing her portrait. After catching him for the umpteenth time, she stepped in and innocently began a political debate with him in order to imprint herself deep within his soul. Earth Raven, unbeknownst to himself, was falling for her.

The ranch members found much to celebrate that year: Painted Pony's coming into womanhood, the birth of a child, and the publication of an engagement. Each ranch member had their own way of observing the generosity that was bestowed upon them.

One night in early autumn, Buck, Larry and Ferdy would trek into Sundance for some merriment and card playing. Larry and Ferdy entered the front door of the saloon, and sat at one of the tables of card players. Meanwhile, Buck's first stop would be to have a private moment with Lily at the back door to the saloon before her performance on stage. Hours later after entertaining himself with Lily's performance, Buck joined the table where the other ranchhands were sitting to try his hand at luck. By that time, Ferdy had tapped out the funds that were allotted him by Rains Down, and was forced to sit out to watch the others play.

As the night wore on, a new player was introduced at their table. He was a lousy poker player, but a seasonable bluffer. He spoke of his travels while intoxicating the men with stories of an enchanting far-off land–Georgia. The stranger spoke of the Georgia pines, and that their trees were so tall, they didn't seem to have tops. He claimed the Georgia peach was the sweetest fruit ever to be grown. This gargantuan man said the Georgia soil was fertile and profitable for harvesting anything; that the countryside also had mountains of beauty there known as the Blue Ridge Mountains. He told them that much of the war was fought there, and many men had died in Georgia for their country.

"Have you ever been there?" he asked the table of men. Most shook their heads while he continued, "Have you ever known anyone from there?" Most, again, shook their heads. Then the stranger added, "No, you probably wouldn't; because it has such beauty, there aren't many who have ventured far from there."

Buck was skeptically compelled to ask, "Then why are you so far from home, stranger?"

"I am on a mission looking for my nephew. His mother is sick, and needs him back home. He is a young angry boy who did not know any better than to wander far from home." The outlander would then listen to the way the foreigners would respond to his stories to find out who would be more apt and able to release the information which he sought. After hearing much of the conversation around the table, the new visitor could see that befriending Buck was futile, so he directed his attentions toward the gullible soul to his left. Larry had an ample supply of liquor in front of him and was in good temper from consistently winning his hands. The newcomer thought it was time they had a private chat.

After successfully luring Larry to the bar with the promise of buying him his own bottle of booze, the stranger began telling Larry about how he knew his nephew was traveling with a friend who was a Black man. The friend's name was Sammy. Fortunately for Sammy, before Larry could unleash the knowledge of his friend's whereabouts, Buck seized him and they were off, back toward the ranch. However, not all was favorable; that man had spoken to enough loose-lippers to know that he saw a certain look of familiarity in Larry's eyes when the name *Sammy* was spoken. Moreover, he could see what was in Buck's eyes, enough to give him pause from leaving that town.

Notwithstanding, not all was unfavorable with Sammy. Just before the end of the year, Sammy and Nkechi would blessedly announce the anticipation of their first child, due in late summer of the next year.

To bring forth the events of the year gone by, Susan brought her steaming cup of tea to the parlor due to the record snow that was falling in the county that year. The snowfall began in November with no merciful surrender in sight. That worried Susan a bit, but the good part of it was the added moisture brought with the snow, as it had been a considerably dry rainfall season that summer for them as well.

Susan began her summation with thoughts of Painted Pony and what a radiant debutante she had been that year at her party. She had planned and executed the perfect event, one that would make even a First Lady proud. The young adult had definitely entered into womanhood with a bright mind and very beautiful soul. Susan knew that Painted Pony had her own determined mind and opinions, and no one was going to sway her without a compelling argument to the contrary.

Her review depicted that, once again, fear had come to their town from the vicious intruder when other livestock was terminated. However, that fear had been balanced with the delightfulness of a new child being brought into the ranch community when Susan's second child was born.

That was also the year that Susan got her first taste of a new drink on the market, sent all the way from the East, something they called a *cola*. She was not impressed.

Another ominous tide that had rolled into the area that year was the railroads–reaching Paha Sapa by way of Rapid City and bringing more carpetbaggers into the area.

Chapter 37

Earth Raven's frustrations with the White establishment were growing, early in the year of 1887, from a world without justice or compassion for his people. He was still without a law license to enable him to be taken more seriously, and quite without a consequential following for his cause to wrench those stone hearts in Washington. His efforts were not as lucrative as he had hoped. He tried playing the games of the powerful lawmakers, and unyieldingly jumped through their hoops, but he realized they were just amusing themselves with their parlor games involving him. It was then that Earth Raven decided that he would return to Sundance and remain there until he could choose a path for perhaps a future in politics.

For eleven years, since 1876, many people had felt the yellow fever of the gold rush deep within Paha Sapa with no signs of slowing. It was most difficult for Larry while he patronized the saloon, where he continually heard stories of how others were striking it rich. He stood by watching the celebrations of those who were fortunate enough to fulfill their dreams. His emotions were conflicted; however, as he knew spiritually that he had made the right decision. Larry tried explaining the Lakota's situation to these thieves, but many of the prospectors did not have an ear for such rhetoric. It was difficult to feel compassion when gold nuggets lined their palms. Willy had tossed Larry out of the saloon on more than one occasion for attempting to squash the celebratory generous moods of his paying customers.

After the wretched winter had subsided in April in the Wyoming Territory, Earth Raven was able to return to the

Paradise Valley Ranch. He and Painted Pony would find time to debate the issues of the world, which was an activity secretly planned by both of them. It was a way to be together without each other acknowledging an attempt, and without anyone else knowing they were trying. They would only have a few precious moments of an intimate touch on the hand before Slim would mysteriously appear from nowhere to dampen the mood.

By May, Rains Down and Ferdy were ready to marry. She would receive her special ceremony at the church and then they would forward the festivities into Sundance to the eatery. They spent months planning the event to complete the wedding just as Rains Down had dreamed. It was fit for a princess. Ferdy had assured her that he would be up for anything she wished, even wearing the bow tie that she made reference to.

Susan had invited Ferdy and Rains Down to stay in the main house after they were married until their own house was built as a shell of it stood at a distance from the house. Susan had pulled them aside just after the announcement of their engagement and offered to lease an acre of land to Ferdy with an option to buy if he and Rains Down decided to remain at the ranch as a working couple. Susan assured Rains Down that she now had Snake Catcher with her, and it would no longer be necessary for someone to be in the house to assist with her personal needs. Snake Catcher just smirked from Susan's assumption of his husbandly duties to fulfill her needs as with a houseboy, and secretly plotted to unmercifully tease her about it in the later weeks to come.

When the day of the event was upon them, the people from the ranch glided into the church to witness their nuptials. Only Larry remained at the Paradise Valley Ranch, for security purposes. Many townspeople were included as guests–these were mostly parishioners from their church. Cook sat in the pew in the front row smiling brightly as Ferdy and Rains Down were married. It was a longtime coming dream for Cook.

Their wedding day was turning out to be the event of the year in the town of Sundance. Inasmuch, Cook insisted that there be a traditional pinata swinging from the rafters at the eatery to be walloped by the bride during their reception. Cook included party favors of candies and embroidered handkerchiefs that she had been stocking for quite some time. Rains Down wore a beautiful white Native beaded dress representing her

Lakota heritage, while Ferdy wore a traditional Mexican gaucho representing his culture as well as her other half.

A mariachi band would bring the upstairs boarders to wonder about the festive mood below. That would include drawing the attention of a man whose presence brought in an ominous ambience to the festivities. He crept down the stairs and peered in on the event. As the eatery staff reminded him that the room was closed to the public, he told them of his invitation before making his grand entrance, all the while glaring at Sammy. Briggs had given up his plantation, however worthless, to plot revenge on Sammy; it was all that he could think about for years and his time had come for his revenge against him–Master Briggs had finally caught up with Sammy.

Aghast, Sammy sourly announced, "Briggs!"

Master Briggs was outwardly amicable, yet inwardly steamed that he was not being properly addressed as respectfully as a master should be from the likes of Sammy's kind. "Hello, Sammy. This is a fine town you have chosen to hide, I mean *live* in."

The crowd instantly looked back at Sammy. He was clearly shaken by Briggs' presence there. Susan could see what the tension was doing to Rains Down on her special day and was plotting on how to divert the tension.

Briggs offered, "What do you say to stepping outside where we can talk?"

Sammy flashed a look of contentment toward Briggs, not wanting his wife to see a coward within him.

Susan stepped forward between Briggs and Sammy while announcing, "I'm terribly sorry, but we are in the middle of a celebration and we will need Sammy to help with the preparations."

Briggs' contempt for a woman who was allowed out of the house was only surpassed by his contempt of a freed slave. As he nudged Susan out of his path, clearly not knowing who he was dealing with, his arrogance brought him to comment, "May I suggest that you back off of me, lady! This does not concern *you*."

Most of the guests gasped. The men shielded the women. Snake Catcher immediately took a step toward Briggs, making a clear announcement of his own. Before anyone could have seen him, he had his knife to Briggs' throat as others watched on. Battleground lines were being drawn. At that moment in history,

Susan had stepped into the middle of their dispute, which brought her a formidable enemy not to be taken lightly. Even so, Susan persuaded Snake Catcher to back down and step away from any bloodshed that day of all days, one of celebration. Briggs made no moves, only to smirk at them. However unintentional, an animosity had begun between Snake Catcher and Briggs. No one placed a knife to that master's throat and lived to be the boaster, especially someone of a minority and a proletariat status; notwithstanding, no one threatened Susan without answering to Snake Catcher.

After the scuffling of heels, the eatery proprietor promptly escorted Briggs from the room. Cook made fast work of getting the festive atmosphere back. She was not going to have that man ruin her son's chances at happiness by jinxing their wedding night mood. With the help of Cook and Susan, Rains Down was soon joyous again as Ferdy guaranteed that nothing more would disturb their gathering that day.

Later that evening, Susan and Snake Catcher would give the newlyweds some privacy upstairs by opting to sit on the porch basking in the cool night's breeze. They discussed the events of the day. Susan pleaded, "I want you to promise that you won't get into a battle with Briggs. We do not need a repeat of going to court as with Carter."

Snake Catcher sat in silence.

"He is only here to start trouble with Sammy. We will protect ourselves, but I want you to promise you won't seek out trouble."

Snake Catcher nodded, still silently fuming inside.

That was the time when Briggs sent for the remainder of his money back in Georgia, assuredly to pay for reinforcement during his plan of revenge.

As June approached, more ominous news would come their way surrounding the deadly puma making a name for himself in the neighborhood. He had butchered several more livestock and injured a small boy by slicing open his arm with one carelessly misdirected swipe of his paw; aiming for more than just an arm. That young lad and his parents were the only humans who had actually seen the predator and lived to describe him. Up until this time, the puma had been identified only by scattered paw prints, scat and the gruesome remains of his victims.

After receiving a series of news stories from Washington,

Earth Raven told the household about tragic developments at the Carlisle school where the Native children had been sent to become "educated." He was now getting reports that this institution was disease-ridden and that many of the children were apparently dying there. That undoubtedly angered Painted Pony; not from making her beliefs about educating their children erroneous, but because the school authorities, who were responsible for the safety of these children, were neglectfully letting them die. "How do they ever expect to have our trust and cooperation if they let our children die?" she rhetorically asked everyone at the diningroom table that evening, already knowing how pointless the question was. The household unanimously agreed with her. Painted Pony secretly vowed to someday help bring an end to the mistreatment of the Native children in this country.

Summertime arrived with only a few minor annoyances from Briggs. He was busily planting himself into the Sundance community, beginning with finding his way to owning a small homestead just south of the Paradise Valley Ranch. It was after moving there that Briggs began insinuating himself into every aspect of their lives. He would join their church, and also solicit their business acquaintances in Sundance, mostly for information about the ranch goings-on. Briggs even befriended the banker in Deadwood City that Susan employed at the telegraph office.

Snake Catcher and Susan were spending much of their time with the children on the ranch. Star was a smidgen over two and not nearly old enough to accompany his father on the hunting explorations. Their second son was nearly one; however, many had felt he was trying to keep up with his brother. Snake Catcher saw much similarity between his sons to what he had in his relationship with his own older brother. He was determined to not let Chase Running Fire feel he was the weaker son, being second, as his father had with him while they were aging into manhood.

Times had most definitely changed for Susan. She was no longer alone; in fact, she was forever trying to find an enjoyable quiet moment to herself to bask in her tea. Her world was now full of children's play, a husband who savored her companionship, barking dogs, and festive household supper discussions; and there was most definitely not a solitary moment to her day–a world in which she cherished.

During one joyous sparkling-fresh day during early summer, Painted Pony glided up to the porch in good spirits. Susan and Snake Catcher exchanged good-mornings with her as she walked into the house. Painted Pony was both a stunning and proper lady at this point. She laughed a woman's laugh now, one gaining notoriety among her male suitors who naively thought they had a chance of gaining her affections.

From the parlor, Earth Raven grabbed Painted Pony's arm and pulled her into the room for a private moment alone together. In his excitement, he nearly tipped over the floral incandescent lamp that Snake Catcher had given to Susan. He could not push Painted Pony away anymore as he once had years ago. He was drawn to her now. Earth Raven lightly kissed her on the cheek, then stepped back and announced to her that he was off to speak to her father. She demurely smiled, giving him her approval. Earth Raven hurriedly ran off to find Slim.

In the stables moments later, Earth Raven nervously pleaded to Slim, "I am here as a man who cares for your daughter, I mean sister, I mean Painted Pony...and I want to marry her."

Without looking directly at Earth Raven or giving seriousness to his request, Slim brushed him off as he had with the last seven proposal attempts by suitors. "She is too young," Slim remarked unconcernedly while he continued with his chores.

Earth Raven nervously blurted, "She is a woman with a woman's heart."

Looking up at Earth Raven, Slim reiterated his disapproval in a stronger tone. "She is *too* young."

Earth Raven was anxiously persistent. "Sir, may I at least make my plea?" While Slim was silent, Earth Raven seized an opportunity to continue. "She has chased me for three years and I have not seen her. *These* days I have seen her. She is a woman. She has a woman's heart."

Slim interjected, "You have said that."

"And...and I have grown to have a heart for her, and can no longer push her away."

Slim looked at Earth Raven with a scowl.

Earth Raven yielded cautiously before continuing. "You have known me since I have come here to live. I am a good man. I will be a good husband. We want to be together. May I please have her hand, Sir?" Earth Raven pushed his chin out waiting to be devastated by Slim's refusal.

Slim was still scowling as he editorialized, "She is my only blood. She is my life and I have given all that I had for her happiness. She will make a good wife, and you had better appreciate that."

Earth Raven exhaled a full breath, and then smiled widely. He reached out and shook Slim's hand, almost pulling his arm out of the socket. As Earth Raven began trotting back to Painted Pony to tell her of the glorious news, Slim was secretly smirking at him. Earth Raven buzzed past Snake Catcher and Susan on the porch, not even noticing or acknowledging them. They looked at one another perplexed as to the urgency of his quest. They soon heard the vaguely familiar Painted Pony squeals of the past.

Susan had secretly begun a "wedding chest" for Painted Pony some years back. The chest was brimming with linens and household goods, and included was a veil that Susan had made from her mother's wedding dress. Susan had hoped to wear the veil at her wedding, along with the shawl made of the same material; however, somehow it just didn't seem fitting to wear both during the informal ceremony. That was when she placed it inside of Painted Pony's chest. Slim had saved an endowment for just an occasion; though, he preferred she would have used it to attend college. With some of the money, Painted Pony set out, with Rains Down and Ferdy escorting her in the wagon, toward the Sundance trading post that mid-afternoon to purchase a wedding dress that she'd had fancied.

Later that evening, Slim pulled Painted Pony aside to school her about men and marriage and what was expected of her during their marriage–and the wedding night. It was clearly not a conversation that he was comfortable with; nonetheless, he told Painted Pony that she could wait a while longer if she wasn't ready for the *duty* of marriage. Painted Pony smiled and assured him that she was prepared to be married to Earth Raven.

The next morning, Susan sat on the porch with her tea, smiling and gazing out at Paha Sapa; however, by midmorning, she had arranged a fine celebration for Earth Raven and Painted Pony. She enlisted the help of Snake Catcher to provide them with a traditional Native ceremony. Earth Raven's Lakota Holyman acquaintance was better tempered for that ceremony.

Prayers were recited and Earth Raven taught his new bride some of their traditions that day. Painted Pony was a radiant bride, accumulating many congratulations, and gifts, from those gathered.

Painted Pony and Earth Raven would have two weeks together at the ranch after the ceremony before he was expected back in Washington. Painted Pony would accompany him there for the first time.

Within days of the newlywed's nuptials, odd things began happening at the ranch. Larry found himself on his backside after mounting his horse, only to find that someone had put a matted strand of jagged wire beneath his saddle. That also rendered his horse useless for a week of healing time. Then, one morning, Buck had traveled out to the ranchhand's shanty only to find that somehow it had been dismantled into hundreds of pieces.

As the days moved forward, the ranchhands would need more relaxing time in Sundance because of the added repair duties they encountered. Briggs took advantage of this good fortune to become Larry's friend as he would supply him with a plethora of spirits only to extract useful information of Sammy's activities and routine. Buck strenuously warned Larry of Briggs' malicious intentions, but Larry's good heart wanted to give him the benefit of the doubt. Especially with not seeing the scuffle between Sammy and Briggs the day of Ferdy and Rains Down's wedding; he did not understand the magnitude of the disagreement between them.

Poison began seeping into their town by way of prejudgment. Briggs decided to do more than just appear at their church, he began taunting Snake Catcher and Susan during Sunday socializing time by deliberately planting seeds of distrust through spreading clues of Snake Catcher's secretive past. Briggs' informants were thorough enough for him to tell of Snake Catcher's stint in prison and spread how he needlessly killed many Whites in his youth. Briggs covertly suggested that maybe there was no place for this Native within the decent White community. Snake Catcher caught wind of Briggs' antics from a faithful supporter in Mrs. Gaines. Snake Catcher would consistently keep one eye toward Briggs as he did with Carter, while the slow simmering eruption within him began to gain momentum.

Tension flowed through the ranch and the town about

the rumors, but there wasn't much that could be done to stop the torment from the former Atlanta plantation owner. Knowing he was Briggs' real target of pain, Sammy made an offering to Susan of how he and Nkechi would faithfully leave the ranch for the sake of their safety. Susan reminded Sammy of his loyalty when Carter was raining his venom onto them. However, it would not be long before Briggs would direct his hostility toward his true target by stalking Nkechi while she was performing Susan's errands in Sundance. His appearance alone would bring Nkechi to fear him, which was not suitable for a woman in her delicate condition.

A week after returning to the nation's capitol, Earth Raven hired on with a Washington man who was running for Governor of Virginia. He would be required to research material relating to a platform for his political campaign.

That was about the time when Painted Pony's teenage fantasy would nearly come true. Earth Raven accompanied his wife to a charity gala where she would premier on his arm during the event as they would flawlessly mingle with the country's most elite society. Painted Pony would wear an ivory gown made of material from the trading post in Sundance and decorated with gold-colored stitchery. A white orchid would be buoyant within her elegant hairstyle. Her beauty was what drew the partygoers to her; however, it was her brilliantly masterful articulated conversations that compelled them to remain. It was all that Susan had taught her. Painted Pony and Earth Raven would dance together into the night floating as light as a feather. Earth Raven would end their evening with one lightly placed kiss on her cheek before they were swept away by a horse-drawn carriage to retreat to their lodging accommodations. Unlike the fairytale, at the end of their fantasy evening, they would remain together through the night.

Another one of the ranch's couples also crossed a threshold in their relationship. After the completion of their house, Rains Down and Ferdy had blissfully moved into their new accommodations. Rains Down's dream of being the lady of her hacienda had come true. But more importantly, her other dream of having a generous and kind husband she would not have to fear had also come true. All from the church were invited over to see her new abode. Of course, it was customary to help with the furnishing of it. After being informed that everyone wanted to present her with a housewarming gift, she insisted that it be something that they had made themselves or something they had possessed for years. She did not want to fill her new home with cold trading-post goods of no memories or meaningful tales.

Sadly, another Paradise Valley's twosome was not finding life so blissful. At mid-summer, after a trying day in town with Briggs at her heels, Nkechi had returned to the ranch exhausted. She was not in a favorable way. Her belief was that God would not allow her to bring another into the world with her believing that so much evil and anger surrounded her. There would only be the smallest mount of soil over the earth in the cemetery to mark what was to be their new beginnings. A wreath of lilies graced the staff's doorway to Nkechi and Sammy's grief.

As Susan sat with her children at Christmas, she took inventory of the year as she recalled the most amazing thing that she had seen all year. It was a contraption called a *motorbike*. Someone had put only two wheels and a motor on a flimsy frame and thought that it would become something big. Susan felt quite certain that people would not find it as comfortable as a pleasurable carriage ride, and that the motorbike would be a thing of the past in the near future.

It had been a good year...it had been a bad year.

A good year brought Susan happy and healthy children. Her husband was a rich man to have gotten the family that he had longed for. Earth Raven and Painted Pony were jubilant together, and while she was delighted over their union, she also missed Painted Pony's presence at the ranch since the couple were most often in Washington. Painted Pony had always looked up to Susan and she missed being her confidante. Rains Down and Ferdy were also blissfully happy, but Sammy and Nkechi were in ruins. And while family was of the utmost importance to her, Susan was still haunted that they were no more closer to regaining possession of Paha Sapa than in years gone by—as the government was still refusing to open the case for review.

Early in that year had also brought the harshest winter in ten decades, killing off one-fourth of the Paradise Valley Ranch cattle herd. Still, they were fortunate in that it did not take all of the cattle, as some ranchers in the area could profess to. Susan believed that they would have enough financially; however, she could not withstand many more monetary setbacks in the near future.

1887 had been a bitter-sweet year for Earth Raven as well. Even though he was perfectly gratified in his personal life with Painted Pony, before the year's end he would experience heartache and mistrust from the government once again. That was when he had learned of Chief Sitting Bull's trek from Canada, which brought him to surrender at Fort Buford with a trailing population of nearly 200 of his people. Earth Raven was angered to discover that Chief Sitting Bull had been remanded to a prison, rather than being pardoned as he was indubitably assured in order for his surrender. The simulate lawyer's belief in the judicial system was increasingly faltering.

Earth Raven's bitterness continued in the form of the Dawes Severalty Act, which was written to allow tribal land to be converted into separate tracts for individual Native ownership. This in turn allowed that land to be leased to Whites. That document was an attempt by the government to integrate the Natives into the White way of life by become landowners, but only resulted in the defrauding of Natives from their land–once again. The division of tribal land would drive a wedge between the many tribes, due to further reducing the overall size of their respective reservations.

A camouflaged desirable portion of that year was in the form of Natives being offered citizenship. In order for Natives to own these individual land tracts, the government would have to offer them American citizenship. Earth Raven would finally become a whole participant of the Constitution which would entitle his people to fight Paha Sapa's theft under their constitutional rights. Nevertheless, Earth Raven would soon discover that citizenship was just a myth to separate his people from their land. That would also be proven with the hindrance of Earth Raven becoming a legal lawyer, as the powers that be consistently found excuses to deny his application to take the bar exam.

Chapter 38

The year of 1888 began joyously when Susan made an announcement that she would be expecting their third child in autumn. In February, Star celebrated his third birthday with a pony of his own, which was a great honor for such a small boy. By April, Susan would hear of a woman in Washington that had started a Child Society foundation the year before for the benefit of children in need. Susan sent a letter of encouragement and twenty-five dollars back on Earth Raven's next trip to Washington in order to help her cause.

Earth Raven was thankful for a world of those generous people, as in Susan, yet he was becoming increasingly disillusioned in his belief that the greater world did not understand or care about the issues of his people. This was evident each time the petition for aid to the Natives was not being acknowledged. Nor was anything being done to prevent prejudiced people from denying Natives goods and loans to build houses and businesses to become the "civilized" people that the government was demanding them to become. As emotionally exhausted as Earth Raven was with these ceaseless issues, he would not let his spirits be extinguished. He decidedly returned to Washington for a few more months of informational promotions before returning with his wife to the ranch for an overdue vacation.

During that summer, Susan and Snake Catcher snuggled together late one evening after putting their sons to bed. Just before Susan was about to drift off, Killer and Coyote began barking while positioned in the downstairs foyer. Snake Catcher sprung out of bed, demanding his wife to stay put, and he ran out the door before Susan even had time to retrieve her wrap. Earth Raven demanded the same of his wife as he bounded outside. Instantaneously, Buck, Larry, Slim and Sammy rushed out to see that the storage shed was ablaze. Cook ran toward the house to check on the others. With the westerly winds higher than usual that night, all were concerned that the flames would spread to the other structures in the area. The ranchhands tirelessly fetched buckets of water to douse the fire while Master Briggs covertly entered the staff quarters. By then, Ferdy and Rains Down had rushed toward the source of dissension. After checking in on her sons, Susan trotted down the stairs and out the door where she and her unborn child were forced to remain on the porch by Cook.

Unbeknownst to the others, Briggs had Nkechi trapped in the staff quarters and would attempt to take from Sammy what he presumed Sammy had taken from him years ago; the hopes of a family and future with the woman he loved. Cook scolded Susan to stay on the porch as she headed inside toward the kitchen to retrieve baking soda to help extinguish the flames. Nkechi let out a bloodcurdling scream before Sammy headed toward the spine-chilling sound. Snake Catcher would be nearly twenty paces behind him. When Sammy found Nkechi lying on the floor, the light from his eyes had diminished. The moment that Briggs had been plotting for so many years had finally come.

Briggs assaulted Sammy by knocking him unconscious with the back of a chair as he entered the room, but before he could finish the job he'd came there for, Snake Catcher would interrupt him. The warrior had his knife drawn while springing toward the enormous man. Briggs got off one shot before the force of the gun thrust him backward and out of the window due to his unsteady footing; his gun spiraling off in the dark air. As Snake Catcher quickly moved out of the way of the bullet, he twisted his knee to the point of bringing him a sizable limp. Briggs had gotten a head start on him and he waddled toward the kitchen of the main house with Snake Catcher soon to follow.

Master Briggs would pay a hefty price for his unconscionable revenge that day, as it would be Cook who had retribution in her eyes. When she had spotted him from the rear window, she pulled out a kitchen knife from the cutlery and held it out for Briggs to receive, deeply embedding the blade slightly below the third rib on his left side. As Snake Catcher ran in to find Briggs slumped over onto the floor, he quickly stated, "We don't speak of this. You were not here." Cook, somewhat in shock, nodded in agreement, grabbed the baking soda, and left through the house dashing out the front door where she found no one. Susan had not adhered to Cook's demands, and was now tending to Nkechi and Sammy in the staff quarters; meanwhile, the others were putting out the last embers of the fire.

As Earth Raven entered the house to check on Painted Pony, he saw a glimpse of Snake Catcher's shadowy figure in the kitchen. Snake Catcher had pulled out the knife from Briggs, assuming the position of the killer. When Earth Raven entered and assessed the setting, he naturally assumed that they would be calling for the Sheriff. Soon, the others gathered around and as a matter of habit, each of them performed their duties for the disposal of the body. Earth Raven was astonished at the specifics of what everyone's duty was and the speed at which it was executed, as he stated, "You will have to report this death. It is the law."

Susan was quick to respond, "We've had experience with this is the past. You should know better than most what the law cannot do for us; you were here when they tried to railroad my husband."

"But the system worked and he was freed."

Susan retorted, "And how many times do you think they will let him be found not guilty?"

"But I still believe in the law."

Snake Catcher added, "What has the law done for us? Has it fed our people when they were hungry? Has it kept their word; do we have Paha Sapa in our possession? Is this the same system that would not let you into their club of lawyers?"

"I still believe in it" was all that Earth Raven said on the subject. Buck and Larry would pull the wagon to the rear of the house, taking four of them to lift Briggs, before taking his body to be buried down at the north end of the river where the earth was soft–accompanying the Crow entombed there four years earlier.

Susan had bandaged Sammy's head, but she could not help Nkechi that day. The air had been kept from her for too long. She was still among the living, yet Nkechi was lost to them deep inside of herself. She did not speak, nor recognize anyone she had been close to–including her husband. Susan was quick to suggest constructing a story surrounding Nkechi's disability because of explanations they would be forced to make about where Briggs made off to, and they did not know how many people knew of his plans to haunt the ranch that night. The one that they decided on was that she had fallen off the wagon and injured the back of her head.

After several days, Susan knew that it was too soon for Sammy to believe, yet she pleaded with him to fill his life with something other than hate. She suggested that he focus on something that he could be passionate about so he could keep Nkechi's love alive inside of him.

Buck and Lily were seeing more of each other those days, especially after what had happened to Nkechi. Buck did not want life to pass him by without knowing the acquaintance of a wife. Buck, being a bachelor for so long and not paying any mind about saving for his future, asked Lily if they could quietly agree to be promised to each other. Buck would promise to save more of his money for their future and to spend less on drinking and card playing in the saloon. Lily had always been smitten with Buck and would be agreeable to nearly any relationship he had to offer.

Many in the community had called to mind that Slim ought to be ready to find someone new for himself. Painted Pony was now married with a life of her own and no longer giving him excuses to be alone. Susan was the first to jump on the "Slim-single-no-more" band wagon. She made the introduction of Mrs. Gains's youngest daughter. Buck would solicit one of Lily's friends who worked at the saloon for the company of his friend. Painted Pony would lure the attention of her friend's widowed mother to meet the man who had been so wonderful to her during her entire life. And when the matchmaking hostess at the eatery caught wind of the now-available Slim, she too, was willing to make a match for him–herself. Slim hesitatingly agreed to the carnival of follies, and decided to see one of their choices per week until he felt comfortable with choosing only one woman. They all agreed with that plan, except they had not discussed the particulars of who would be going first. They all assumed that their selection was the most viable candidate. Slim would agree to meet his date at the eatery as to not put pressure on either of them to remain in the night's appointment if they were not suited for one another.

When Slim's big night of his first date in years had arrived, he was told that all of the details had been arranged for him and that she would be waiting for him to arrive for supper. As he stepped into the eatery, there was the most caterwauling cackling of hens he had ever heard in his entire life, coming from each woman who tossed her bonnet into the ring for him—except for one, who was grinning at Slim from across the room. It would appear that Slim had in front of him a smorgasbord of ladies-in-waiting-to-be-married-off. It was at that moment that he realized that it was her who he chose to spend his evening with. Lily's friend Sofia was used to the cackling of other men's wives at the saloon for their husbands to retreat from the premises. She found it all so amusing, seeing Slim perplexed by the scene and ill-equipped to handle them. Sofia was also very adept at competition, as she had to be with the other dancers for the attention of the most generous tippers.

Slim and Sofia slipped out the front door without one person noticing them fleeing away. They were all too busy deciding who was going to be in Slim's favor that evening to discover he had made his choice. Slim and Sofia would stroll the length of the town getting better acquainted. They would stop in at the trading post to acquire a meager snack to compensate for their nonexistent supper that evening. Neither of them offered a complaint on the subject, as they were too absorbed with each other to notice any twinges of hunger. Slim and Sofia wrapped up their date an hour later, with Slim walking her back to her boarding house over the eatery. By then, the gathered women had vacated so they could safely take some more moments together. Slim asked Sofia to accompany him to an evening with the household for supper the next Sunday, edging out any possibility for a date with any of the other petitioners that week. She eagerly accepted his invitation.

As the days passed, Sammy kept to himself, was very quiet, and did not socialize at the eatery as he once had. Within weeks of Nkechi's ordeal, he had lost much of his bulk. Sammy would sit with Nkechi for hours tenderly tending to her needs, but she had not been right since the night of the fire with an absence of speech. Cook had no feelings of remorse as she had silently simmered from Nkechi losing her unborn child by the likes of that devil; there was no room for guilt or feelings of degradation in her heart.

At this juncture, the puma's deadly trek across the county was growing more and more alarming. "Obese," he must have been, whispered the members of Sundance. A manhunt from other ranchers scouted the area, with some of them killed during their hours of slumber. The creature took down five men and wounded seven more before the day came that it was taken out. The news was all over the county–they had captured and killed the puma! Many were elated and relieved. When the beast was spread out for all to see, horror filled the hearts of three. "This is not the one who injured our child," stated two of the witnesses. The Sheriff was eager to withhold that information from the public, as he would have to answer to those demanding its capture.

By late summer, Susan would have a joyous spirit in her again as she began redecorating Rains Down's former room into a new nursery for her third child. That autumn was full of colors and pungent scents when, in September, Snake Catcher and Susan's first daughter was born. *Autumn Sky Flower* was as lovely as her name. Sky, as she would be called by her mother, was much anticipated by none more than Susan, as professed at the child-naming ceremony. She would finally get the opportunity to dress one of her children in something other than what would eventually be stuffed with frogs, caterpillars and such.

That was the year Snake Catcher would teach his wife how a dreamcatcher was made in order to fill his daughter's head with many good-natured dreams while chasing off the bad ones. He spoke of the meaning and how it would keep her safe from any nightmares she might have had, enabling her to slumber in tranquility. Susan became adept at making them and even placed some at the trading post on commission.

That winter, Buck and Lily would gather the household to witness them being united as husband and wife. Lily was not wanting a large ceremony, as she was just happy to be married to the man of her dreams. Buck was not wanting the attention of a large service, as he was somewhat shy at the center of a more populated grouping. They both wanted the savings of a small nuptial bonding in order to commit it toward the anticipation of their first child.

Lily was welcome to live her days at the ranch as one of the household. She took over the responsibilities for caring for

Star, Chase and Sky; this allowed Susan to tend to some duties that had been neglected since Nkechi had fallen ill. Susan also devoted more time to her letter-writing campaign for the return of Paha Sapa.

In December of 1888, Susan sat on the porch as she often had after a full year of memories. She thought of where they were in life and what had happened in the world around them. That year was no different in her gathering of memories, but much different in the world. The railroad organization had expanded to Casper in the Wyoming Territory, a town located just southwest of Sundance. The building of the additional track began in June of that year. With the railroad reaching Paha Sapa again, that time by way of Deadwood City, the town was feeling its growing pains once more; many other men had come to the town looking for their riches in the form of golden nuggets, but they found steady work in carpentry by building the town instead. The town of Deadwood City now inventoried a lucrative lumber mill, a gold stamp mill, a liquor dealer, a shingles store, an indoor railway station and a dentist–to name a few. A nationally known banker, Wells, set up a business there and offered to buy Susan's interest in her small banking-business. She was gracious in her refusal as she knew it would be several years before the locals would trust an outsider from the East. Deadwood was now several avenues wide with crossing streets to connect them as Susan remembered of Chicago in earlier days. The streets were also leveled and paved with a dried tar substance, which made it smoother to ride one's wagon through without being pushed out of the mud by the local young lads extorting them for tips.

Sundance was not left behind during the area's building expansion of that era, and it had a few more competitive shops to chose from. The expansion would include a separate bank, a full-time doctor on duty in town, and a general store with a capacious selection of building materials.

There had been news all the way from London that year that on the impoverished side of that great metropolis, murders were taking place by an unknown assailant they had dubbed "Jack." All of the victims seemed to be women of the same equivalence to saloon girls.

In Washington D.C., the Washington Monument, which memorialized President George Washington, had been built, and it opened to the public in October. Earth Raven brought the news back to the ranch and had described it as the tallest building or structure he'd ever seen; one of grand stature being made out of marble, granite and sandstone.

As Susan completed her survey of the year, Snake Catcher and the children joined her out on the porch. They gathered together and huddled as one grouping under a buffalo pelt.

Snake Catcher began telling his children the symbolization of a tepee's position to the environment around it. From under their pelt cover, he pointed out each direction. "The eastern side of a tepee represents source of light, the southern is death and spirit path, while the western side represents darkness and thunderbirds, leaving the northern direction being the path of our forefathers."

Susan smiled at him for his contribution to their children's education, even somewhat premature, as they did not yet understand what a tepee was.

Chapter 39

After losing Nkechi's liveliness last spring and their unborn child the year before, Sammy had filled his days with developing a study group for Blacks in the area who could not read or write. Sammy's dialect had greatly improved with all of his free time, and from the promises that he had made Nkechi every night before putting her to bed.

In early spring of 1889, Star was ready to join his father on hunting and spear-fishing expeditions. Susan had made Snake Catcher promise that he would not allow Star to handle the sharp weapons the first time out, only to watch the experience of his father. Snake Catcher would once again smirk at his wife's squeamishness of sharp objects; that would be mirrored when they returned with an assortment of wildlife. She had hoped that with procuring any wild game, a puma might be in their satchel, as the recapitulated terror that had once flooded the valley with scandalous news had returned with the puma's rumored resurrection.

In late summer, Earth Raven returned from Washington with Painted Pony after several months away. The couple discovered that Slim had proposed to Sofia and that they were planning to joyfully live together in the staff quarters. Painted Pony was surprised to learn that she was actually jealous of her father's attentions toward someone new; but as they all gathered for supper the first evening home, she went on to explain that perhaps it was just all of the emotions floating within her body from expecting her first child. Susan was so elated about Painted

Pony's news that she insisted she and Earth Raven remain at the ranch until the baby was born. That way, Painted Pony would not be bounced around in another carriage or rocked within another train on their return to Washington.

Cook was just as ecstatic, pushing Earth Raven out of her pathway while she excitedly stated, "Out of the way, out of the way–let Painted Pony sit. Your job here is done."

They all found much amusement over Cook's actions and much congratulations for the expectant couple. Earth Raven agreed that Painted Pony should not travel; however, he had to return to Washington to complete some business. He planned to be back at the ranch before the first snowfall. Painted Pony appeared saddened to be without her husband for such a stretch, yet felt comfort in knowing that she would not endure the long and arduous trip with a baby growing inside of her.

One Sunday during the summer, Susan had bestowed the same honor onto Sofia as she had with Lily in church. This time, she would relinquish Sky to her as a token of trust and acceptance into the fold of the ranch. Slim was so appreciative of Susan's generosity that he had chopped three extra cords of wood for her that autumn.

Sofia'd had a good life at the saloon and was actually in possession of a great deal of money for a dancer. She wasn't accepting Slim's proposal because she wanted to escape anything; she was saying yes to Slim because her search for love was over. Still, Sofia quit her job at Willy's Saloon and lived above the eatery until the time they were to be wed. Slim assuredly volunteered a heap more for errands that took him into town. When seeing them together, the women that had put themselves up as marriage material for him, knew now, that *his* search was over.

Nearing wintertime that year, all of the household members gathered around to hear the news from Earth Raven that Congress had divided the Dakota Territory, to the east and within Deadwood City, into two different states and had established boundaries for each of them. North and South Dakota had become the thirty-ninth and fortieth states to the union, respectively. The frustrations of the ranch members were rising with the continuing distribution of what was once Lakota land. The city of Casper had been incorporated as a town in

April of that year, adding to the colonization of the territories surrounding them. There was a wind of change in the air, and the emotions of the townspeople were mixed with the continuing progression of the country coming their way. This was the time when Susan decided to sell her banking business in Deadwood City, South Dakota.

Before the end of 1889, just after Susan's summation of that year's events, Snake Catcher would tell his children about the quadripartite divisions of their world. He explained that the four sections were what completed the Lakota people as a whole whether it be the four colors of red, blue, yellow and green; or the four superior forces of the earth, sun, sky and rock; along with the four elements of the sky being the sun, sky, stars and moon; and then the four sections of time being night, day, month and year. The last would be the four divisions of their gods of superior, associate, subordinate and spirits; bringing them to the four directions in a circle that would come to symbolize totality for them for all time.

Chapter 40

As 1890 began, Susan would again find time to take up her morning routine of sipping her tea and drawing on her sketch pad while in the presence of Paha Sapa. Contemplating the hills, she recalled how each year that had passed seemed to be the best year for Paha Sapa's foliage colors. Susan gently swirled the bassinet next to her which housed Sky's slumbering body. She would smile before adding a ringlet of dew to Paha Sapa's cavities in her depiction each time her daughter would gurgle.

The sunny yet chilly day that Star Catcher turned five, Cook made a six-pointed star pinata for the kids filled with exotic fruits, rich chocolates and colorful candies from the trading post in town. The star represented more than just portions of his name. The history behind it symbolized hitting the devil, forcing his release of all the good things that he had taken hold of. Since that had been a Mexican tradition from Cook's culture for generations, she very much enjoyed the process, the smiles and the laughter which it generated. Susan was thrilled at Star's participation and with the amusement he had engaging the decorative spinning cultural treasure chest high above him. After puncturing it, Star quickly removed his blindfold in time to watch the fortunes swirling to the ground as the other children rapidly gathered.

Soon Earth Raven paced the upper level's hallway for hours anticipating the arrival of his first child. Susan and Cook were Painted Pony's medical staff when *Earth Pony* was born in March. The child-naming ceremony was accompanied by the happy parents bestowing the same honor onto Susan and Snake Catcher for the care of their child as the older couple had onto them years earlier. The idea that it was not a Native tradition to bestow one's children onto another did not discourage them from embracing their new tradition.

As springtime neared, Snake Catcher bundled Star and his hunting equipment before setting out to some favorite hunting grounds. He was eagerly anticipating the first deer sighting of the season. The two would spear-fish as with last year and bond over the fastening of arrowheads to the poles. And like in the year before, Snake Catcher would teach his son the importance of a softly placed prayer of thanks for the sacrifice that the prey would make for them before their deadly deed was performed. That first night, the bugs were biting and out in full force bringing Snake Catcher to sleep lightly.

In the extreme early hours of their second day out, Snake Catcher woke to the sounds of an intruder lurking nearby. While lying motionless, he assessed the camp's occupants. A blackened figure was slinking back and forth, and nearing toward them with each step it placed on the ground. Snake Catcher made inventory of his weapons and of his son's location. They were both within reach of him.

Snake Catcher slowly stretched his arm out to grasp a hold of a cooking pot and brought the vessel slowly to his other hand before returning the first hand to secure his spear. After he purposefully flung the clanging pot a fair distance from the camp, he sprang to his feet with the spear while judging the best manner in which to attack their intruder.

The sounds of the deterrent startled the golden black-striped puma enough to temporarily waver his attention away from the goings-on inside of the campsite. It had also woke Star and brought him to his feet. While the creature skulked about trying to determine whether the pot was worthy of his attention, Snake Catcher attempted to secure the safety of his son; however, the puma had other plans about that and leapt nearly eighteen feet toward the duo. Snake Catcher would position himself just in time to collect his footing and then drive the spear straight into the torso of the puma, letting gravity take most of the credit for the depths to which the spear had funneled into him. The wooden staff of the spear had stood erect from the ground, and it got caught within the rocks arranged around the campfire when the puma vaulted over them. Rich firey scarlet-tinted blood ejected from the wound, spraying the south perimeter of the camp. The deadly creature that had killed, maimed and tortured so many would twitch his paws toward them while giving his last breath before expiring. As Snake Catcher tried catching his breath from such a narrow miss, Star would be the one who whooped the loudest over the triumph.

They both agreed that this was one trophy they would not let go unnoticed, and Snake Catcher and Star unanimously decided to cut their hunting excursion to a shortened version. The lifeless body of the puma swung from the side of Snake Catcher's mule on their trek back to the ranch. None was happier than Susan, giddy at her husband's proficiency, yet the mother also felt maddened that her son was in such imminent danger.

The details of the event had not taken but a few whispers to find its way around town, and it was less than a week before the news reached Deadwood City. The Sundance Sheriff strung the monster's carcass up in the center of town with a sign that read: "This is what happens to those who bring disorder into our town." Some were offended, some were squeamish, but most were amused and grateful to Snake Catcher. Later that week after the news had simmered, the inexperienced warrior laid in his bed one night thinking of how greatly proud he was of his father. Of the four cardinal virtues in life, Snake Catcher had undoubtably taught his son about bravery that day.

Earth Raven and Painted Pony spent a few months at the ranch that spring after the birth of Earth Pony in March. Painted Pony was healthy and could withstand the labors of childbirth, and young enough to appreciate the speediness at which her slender figure had returned.

The farewells were sad, but Earth Raven and Painted Pony were now anxious to return to their Washington acquaintances to sport their newest addition. That time, Earth Raven's Holyman friend would accompany them on a goodwill tour.

The trail did not take them far from the ranch before they would be abruptly stopped by Albert, a former husband want-to-be of Painted Pony's past. As a pal of his stood by, Albert called for restitution for Earth Raven ungentlemanly stealing Painted Pony away from him.

"I demand satisfaction," Albert blistered, halting them with his horse in their way. "Get down off of that carriage, you coward," he challenged Earth Raven.

Painted Pony pleaded with Earth Raven to remain in the coach and continue their ride into Deadwood to catch their train, as the baby began to wail sensing her profound anxiety.

Albert threw his riding crop at Earth Raven, coercing him to step down off of the carriage and submit to a duel. When that did not draw Earth Raven out of the carriage, Albert assaulted Painted Pony's virtue by claiming he was husbandly to her before Earth Raven had been.

Earth Raven sprang from his seated position and leapt off of the carriage to pull Albert down from his horse. Albert's pal then jumped off of his horse and pushed them apart before recommending, "There is a better way to handle this–the gentlemanly way. You must draw a pistol and settle this like civilized men." As the pal pulled Albert over to a clearing off the path, he retrieved a set of dueling pistols from a saddlebag. Clearly, the event was orchestrated in advance with the ready existence of the pistols.

However distasteful the Holyman would find the whole ordeal, he would be credited as Earth Raven's second, a position of confirming a fair match between the duelers. The pistols were presented and examined by each of the opposing men, even though Earth Raven had never so much as held a pistol much less fired one. As Albert's second began to load the weapons and fill their chambers with powder, the air around them smelled sweet with the aroma of freshly ground gunpowder. Painted Pony was now down off of the carriage and pacing with her crying child in her arms, furious over the unyielding enormous egos of the men.

After the pistols were in place and their backs were toward one another, they took their paces regimentally and deliberately. After the countdown, Albert was the first to quickly turn and fire his weapon piercing Earth Raven's shirtsleeve and catching a sliver of his arm. As Earth Raven stood aiming his weapon at his contender, Albert despairingly sunk to his knees pleading for his life. It was then that Earth Raven knew he had won the war against his enemies. It was then that he knew life would no longer be oppressed for him and his family. He had the power to change his future with one well-placed bullet. As the anger welled up inside of him, he discharged his weapon in the precise place in which he had aimed–into the ground just left of Albert. Earth Raven also knew that sparing the life of his enemy would be a good lesson to teach his son that day. As the coward's second stood out and applauded Earth Raven's generosity, Albert was thoroughly humiliated.

Painted Pony was greatly relieved, and intensely urged Earth Raven to climb aboard the carriage once again. As part of her plea, Painted Pony vaguely suggested that she would not be garmentless in front of him for a good long time if he did not return to the coach. He accommodated his wife with a meager smile on his face; however, she was not amused. During the remainder of that day, there was a certain sureness about Earth Raven, and as they sat back on their train to safety, he would quietly plan how he would gain the next available seat of a councilman in the next available district, city or state.

One night of sparkling stars overhead soon thereafter, Snake Catcher and Susan gathered their children for another Lakota story. Many members of the household joined the audience procession, as they knew Snake Catcher's stories were always insightful. He began by telling their children that a wonderful Lakota woman would come back to them and heal the wounds of the land someday soon. He also said that the mixed blood running through their veins was proof that harmony was possible between the two worlds. The children listened with extreme concentration as Snake Catcher paraphrased his story:

"A vision was made upon a buffalo calf pelted all in white. Long ago thousands of years now, White Buffalo Calf Woman, who transformed from a white buffalo into a young beautiful Native woman, approached two warriors hunting in Paha Sapa. The one of evil thoughts was abolished by a dark cloud overhead. The other was sent to his village with news of her existence and of her impending appearance, within four days, bringing with her a sacred bundle to include a sacred peace pipe. On that day, a cloud appeared bringing White Buffalo Calf Woman in the form of a white buffalo before altering her into the young woman. This woman brought along the promised sacred bundle plus seven other gifts. These gifts were in the form of rituals and traditions to be carried out through to eternity. Among them was a purification ceremony, a child-naming ceremony, a healing ceremony, an adoption ceremony, a marriage ceremony, a vision quest, and a sundance ceremony. For four days, she taught our forefathers songs and the meaning of these gifts. She then told our people to perform the seven ceremonies in order to secure the eternal duty of custodians over this sacred land to ensure its survival for our children. Before leaving, she informed them that her return would be marked by the birth of a white buffalo calf. At the time of this birth, she would return to claim the sacred bundle, then purify the world bringing harmony, spirituality and balance back into our lives once again."

Snake Catcher ended the story with: "No matter how the White man blocks the trails into our sacred land of Paha Sapa, the fight to reclaim it will never be blocked while the spirit of White Buffalo Calf Woman is in our hearts."

On July 10, 1890, the Wyoming Territory was admitted into the Union as the forty-fourth state. Many townspeople in Sundance were joyous, but Susan wondered what that would do to the rights of women to vote she and others had worked tirelessly to accomplish. The territory had the right to vote for women, but would the state recognize it since the other states in the union did not have the women's vote? In addition to those concerns, she would once again put pen to paper, this time to request funds to help those women with children who were widowed and in need now being in the state of Wyoming, and entitled to such funds. She would also solicit help from Earth Raven's contacts in Washington to aid them in that endeavor.

Amazingly, later that summer when Susan's prize heifer had produced a snowy-white calf, Snake Catcher could not recall his wife having a more radiant smile. Her enthusiasm was astounding. "I know it's not a buffalo with dreams of White Buffalo Calf Woman being resurrected, but can you see the message of the vision here? Can you believe this has happened in the wake of so many tumultuous times for us?" Susan rhetorically asked of her husband. "It is a sign, I can feel it. There are good things coming our way, and we are going to see Paha Sapa as ours once more."

The devotion and kind words from his wife invigorated

Snake Catcher's spirit. The day would bring just the two of them to their favorite picnic and swimming location.

In August, Chase had a delightful birthday party with the same type of pinata that his brother had. It swung from the porch rafters for all to partake in. Sky was still too young to pierce the surface of the starred papier-mâché, but that was not for lack of trying while wanting to keep up with her big brothers. Susan had hoped for a more feminine kindred soul in a daughter than what she had witnessed thus far.

As autumn was upon them, word of a Lakota religious leader emerged. Earth Raven and Snake Catcher made much conversation about a man, Wovoka, who was also claiming to be their new Messiah. He professed to possess the ability to heal the riff between the Lakota and Blue Coats for all time to come. They did not know quite what to make of this man who was raised by a White man and believed in the White God, but clearly was that of a full-bred Lakota.

As the end of the year was nearing, Susan sat on the porch to recall the events of the past twelve months. She smiled at the sight of the white calf and gave thoughts of the Wyoming Territory becoming a state. She recalled how Deadwood City had completed its municipal tribute–their pride: the new block-wide City Hall building, a structure made of brick and mortar, and the first of its kind in that area. It housed a fire station and was several stories tall. Its construction was partly due to the completion of the railroad into Deadwood two years earlier, which brought many new innovated articles of technology into the city as well as the engineers who designed them.

When word of Chief Sitting Bull's murder came to them in December, Earth Raven and Snake Catcher formed much discussion about what needed to be done to head off the onslaught of war and find peace for the Lakota people. They had decided that Snake Catcher would be the one to make the trip into their future for all Lakota people. As the morning of December 20th arrived, Snake Catcher held his last debate with Susan about his participation in Wovoka's Ghost Dance movement, as Susan was clearly against his participation.

Snake Catcher had added, "Hail Maker would have found much honor in a journey such as this when sent by his people. You would have denied him his day?"

"I loved him like a brother, but he was not my husband.

If you are caught outside of these borders, you could possibly be jailed for the remainder of your life."

"I am Lakota. We are ready for peace. You of all people know how we have suffered for it. It is not about loss to one, but honor to many. I would sacrifice more than freedom to complete this honor for my grandchildren's grandchildren." Proudly, Snake Catcher pulled his fist from his heart, then waved it away. "I have no worries, the choice has been made."

As she stood before him, Susan was inconsolable. Still, Snake Catcher remained determined about leaving for Wounded Knee, which was located in the southeastern part of South Dakota some 160 miles away. He went on to explain, "Wovoka knows the way to peace for us. He has blended the White Christian ways with our Native beliefs to find something suitable for us all. I must go to support the crusade with him." Snake Catcher mounted his horse while saying, "It is time for peace."

Susan's last words to her husband that day were: "Please come back to me. If I can no longer have you, I will live my life in darkness."

Snake Catcher held his wife's head from his horse for only a moment before turning and riding off. Susan would stand there for the longest time, waiting for the strength to take herself back into the house to explain to the children about their father's quest.

Snake Catcher's notoriously conquering reputation of a warrior took him in to meet with Wovoka without the hindrance of an appointment. Their discussions were long and many pipes were passed. One evening turned into a full day, and the day turned into a week. Wovoka would tell of how dead Natives would rise again to revel in a world free of their victors in the prophecies that he had made with the abolishment of all Whites to leave that land to the Natives once more. This feat was not to be taken by force, but to be seized by way of dance, song and bullet-repellent shirts. By the afternoon of his eighth day away from the ranch, Snake Catcher was silently feeling skeptical and wary of the method of Wovoka's message. One would have to have much faith in the ramblings of this man to continue on his path with him. Snake Catcher confidentially made his plan to return to the Paradise Valley Ranch the following day.

Early the next morning, the participants of the camp were informed by the Blue Coats that they were not allowed to leave, and that all weapons were to be surrendered at once.

However difficult and oppressive it was for the warriors to be obedient, all seemed to have complied, but the Blue Coats were not convinced of the Lakota's word of honor. While they negotiated a search for any other weapons in the camp, a flicker of impatient annoyance emanated from the Blue Coats. An impaired Lakota man among them did not understand to relinquish his gun as previously requested. After he realized what he was to do, the Lakota began to surrender his weapon by handing it to an officer. When the officer took possession of the gun, he jerked it toward himself in his impatience of the man's incomprehension, ultimately firing it into himself. A whisper of distrust and disbelief willowed over the Natives which resulted in a barrage of blazing shrapnel swarming about. As the holocaust of the camp began, Snake Catcher instinctively grabbed an expectant woman standing next to him while guiding her to the ground before shielding her from the gunfire. After many minutes had passed and the familiar eerie plague of silence loomed over them, the woman cradled her stomach housing her unborn child and scurried away from the ravaged camp before the Blue Coats could see past the clouds of jettisoned gunpowder. After the clouds had cleared, the retreating footsteps of the Blue Coats were all that could be heard.

The unharmed woman was seen sometime later, by those few who had escaped the siege, crying over the dead bodies of her friends and family.

By the next day, the Blue Coats had returned to the slaughter grounds to assess the conditions. As they stood within the ruins of the Lakota people, they chose not to bother with shrouding them from the wildlife. They gathered what few living they found and took them from there.

Wovoka was not amongst the dead.

Shortly thereafter, word of the skirmish between the Lakota and Blue Coats at Wounded Knee on December 29, 1890 had gotten back to the Wyoming ranch by way of the telegraph lines. After hearing about the slaughter there from a telegraph message delivered by Buck, Susan's reaction was one of a horrific blood-curdling scream. Painted Pony and Earth Raven tried to comfort her as her children looked on. Star Catcher at five, Chasing Running Fire at four, and Autumn Sky Flower at two stood nearby looking at the confusing act of the adults not knowing what was expected of them. Shakily, Susan then held her children profoundly close, which also alarmed them.

A week had gone by without word of the ordeal from Snake Catcher or any possible other survivors known to them. Susan was still hopeful that her husband would return. The wife sat on the porch as she did every night waiting for him, or the unwelcome word of his confirmed death.

After nearly two weeks without word from Snake Catcher, Susan was on the verge of accepting that her husband would not be returning, then in the distance there was a flicker that appeared bouncing off the reflection of the moon beaming as daylight. Killer and Coyote were the first to his side. As Susan saw Snake Catcher walking on foot toward the house, she sprung up and ran to the alarm bell ringing it violently, then rushed to his withering body. She helped Snake Catcher to the house as the others rocketed out to assist. Snake Catcher had the deep-embedded eyes of an anguished warrior once more.

Buck and Larry supported Snake Catcher as they navigated him up to the apothecary room with him. There, Susan dug out a bullet lodged in the lower portion of the right side of his back. It was lodged deeply below the surface of the skin this time.

Susan sat in constant vigil beside her husband as he did for her years earlier after a gunshot wound threatened Susan's life. In a waking moment, he told her of his mission and how he made it back to her on sheer willpower alone, only to see her once again.

A clear starry night three days later, Snake Catcher affirmed to Susan, "Now I no longer have regrets about not dying for my people during THE DAY OF DISHONOR. There are many *snakes in Paha Sapa*, as well as on the plains of our remaining land. White Buffalo Calf Woman will return someday to renourish our people and cleanse the world." Then came a crackle in his voice as Snake Catcher whispered to Susan, "My only regret comes in the form of leaving you, my wife, my destiny, my ally in the fight for both of the heritages of our grandchildren's grandchildren."

Susan could not seem to let go of her husband's hand that night, even when she commissioned Buck and Larry to move him from the apothecary room into their bedroom and onto their bed.

The next morning, Susan woke her children early. She dressed them in their Sunday best and ushered them in to see their father for the last time while he lay peacefully in bed. He was dressed in the traditional clothes of his people that Earth Raven had brought to him the first time he visited the ranch, the same clothes he wore the day of his wedding to Susan. Each of Snake Catcher's children kissed their father on the cheek before Susan escorted them into the parlor. Buck, Ferdy, Larry and Earth Raven would place Snake Catcher into a wooden box while Slim dug in a nice resting place located next to the proud Lakota's brother's blood buried there six years earlier.

Chapter 41

Eighteen-ninety had moved into history and 1891 was now upon them. During the transition of one year fading while another came into focus, it took Susan three months after her husband's burial to have the resolve that Snake Catcher had taken his final journey and was lost to her forever. It was then when she finally found the strength to commission and erect a tombstone for her beloved husband.

Susan filled her days with raising her children with enough love for two parents. She taught them about their Native ancestry and to respect the four cardinal Lakota virtues in life. For the sake of Snake Catcher's memory, Susan pushed past her fear of knives and continued the art of teaching both of her sons what her husband had begun. Susan also wanted them to learn, that although some Whites were unscrupulous, they should wear both sides of their heritage proudly.

Painted Pony and Earth Raven, with Earth Pony in tow, reluctantly departed the ranch and set forth to Washington on Susan's insistence. She knew Earth Raven would be able to accomplish more good in Washington then with just holding the hand of an anguished and bittered widow.

In Earth Raven's speeches, one could feel the leviathan depths of the infinite grief that he was feeling from the loss of his lifelong friend. Earth Raven had summarized the activities at Wounded Knee as a holocaust of his people with the inhumane ethnic cleansing of Lakota men, women and their acquiescent children. Earth Raven had learned that approximately 350 Natives were killed as a result of the violence on that day, including his best friend who had died a few weeks later. Earth

Raven would decidedly fight even harder than in the past to regain some sort of dignity for his lineage.

During the half dozen or so months after that horrific day at Wounded Knee, some had speculated that there was no misunderstanding at all, and it was simply all about Natives controlling the leases on millions of acres of land. That perhaps if they could be exterminated, there would be less obstruction and less difficulty in the taking of their remaining land. Some have also speculated that perhaps it was just plain old-fashioned revenge and retribution executed from Custer's longtime buddies–none other than the members of his 7th cavalry that was there and orchestrated the massacre that day at Wounded Knee.

At the end of that year, Susan could not summon the courage to sit on the porch and reminisce about the year gone by as she always had. Her world was filled with too much grief to recall any notable changes except for those just below the surface of her heart.

1892 brought a child for Buck and Lily. That baby girl became the focus of Buck's attention. He had a new appreciation for Slim's unwavering battle to keep his daughter safe, now knowing the challenges of raising a daughter. *Gracie* stole this weathered man's heart from her very first breath. She was baptized and given Sofia and Slim as her Godparents.

Cook longed for a grandchild from her only son; yet Rains Down was content to live her life childless, a desire from being subjected to the purgatory that her father bestowed onto her during her childhood. She refused to absorb the antiquated notions of others who would demean her with a label of being less than a whole woman for being unsuccessful in bearing children. Ferdy was immensely grateful just to have Rains Down as his wife and, of course, a mother who wanted all of the good fortunes that life had to offer for her son. Nevertheless, along with the hacienda, Ferdy was graciously accommodating enough to also build Rains Down a veterinarian hospice next to their home, as she would begin a sanctuary for unwanted and ailing animals with the medical knowledge solicited from Susan. She was delighted that Rains Down wanted to learn the knowledge of medicine, and appreciated being able to pass along all of the medical material that she had accumulated.

With the supplemental income he earned from breaking horses, Larry had found his way to owning a small printing press shop that circulated a periodical within the Sundance area. He'd acquired a partner in the owner of the trading post, as Mr. Smith was in the market for owning another establishment. They hired a pressman and writer, and Mr. Smith entered into the investment as the managing partner. Larry would oversee the circulation of the publication. It was not the saloon that Larry had longed for, but Susan convinced him to take a chance with the alternative business, that way his money might work toward affording a more sizeable venture some day, such as a saloon.

The lessons of law were unavoidable when Earth Raven had secured himself a position writing briefs and researching precedents for a prominent Washington prosecuting attorney. He was greatly looking forward to the experience and responsibility that would better serve his cause for the future of his people, regaining Paha Sapa, and for the preparation when he was no longer banned from taking the bar exam.

Painted Pony had set up a house for herself, husband and child on the northeast side in Georgetown, and she began home-schooling Earth Pony. She would also keep a beautiful stallion named *Popcorn* at the town's eastside stables, where she would make time to ride him four to five times per week. Painted Pony had chosen his name because of the way he feistily popped his head up just before prancing off. She would also find time to donate her organizational skills of planning to worthy causes around town–the children's causes were her favorite.

In November of 1893 during the first snowfall of the season, Slim succumbed to the ravishings of *the cancer*. Painted Pony was notified of her father's passing just before she and Earth Raven were to travel home for the holidays, resulting in Slim being buried on Thanksgiving Day. All of the adults gathered at the ranch cemetery to pay their last respects to their good friend and kin. Sofia respectfully surrendered the place of honor to Painted Pony as the only one to be seated during the burial site ceremony. Along with being Godparents to Susan's children, the burying of her father there would be yet another reminder to Painted Pony that she was bonded to the Paradise Valley Ranch to eternity. During the day of Slim's burial, all of the children would play close to the house, as they did not understand the seriousness of what the adults were enduring. Star Catcher at eight, Chasing Running Fire at seven, and Autumn Sky Flower at five were playing games on the porch. Earth Pony at three, was dancing around the trio trying to keep up with their frolicking–the innocense of the children's laughter filling the air.

The marking of time brought marriages, births, deaths, weekly walks with a fist full of flowers to the ranch gravesite, and the celebrations of life's unostentatious accomplishments to Sundance. During this time interval in 1894, Nkechi was buried in the Paradise Valley Ranch cemetery next to the undeveloped child whose death had preceded her own several years earlier. Sammy was saddened, yet grateful that Nkechi was finally at peace. He had grieved for her many years ago, and celebrated her life with a successful dedication to his tutoring of illiterate Black folks.

Killer met her maker in 1896 after a bear took a swipe at her while she was protecting Coyote, who had gotten a paw caught in-between two rocks down by the riverbank about a mile off the ranch property. The attack severed Killer's carotid artery for a nearly immediate passing. Coyote escaped unharmed but Susan was brokenhearted and despondent for weeks after the unspeakable ordeal. Killer was her unconditional treasure and put the richness of a smile on Susan's face everyday since the moment she was born. She was the first of Susan's treasures and would forever be etched in her memory with the timelessness of her image that hung on the photograph wall in the lounge.

With eight years passing while she raised her children alone, Susan found some comfort in passing along the Lakota stories to those who would listen by the year 1898. It was her way of keeping Snake Catcher's legendary storytelling alive. She wanted the stories to be the legacy that Snake Catcher had left to, not only his children, but to all Lakota children.

When October arrived that year, so did *Hail Catcher*, Earth Raven and Painted Pony's second son. This was the golden child who was favored with the names of Earth Raven's greatest mentors in life. Rewarding Hail Maker for having the courage to befriend a White man, even after all they had endured from them, in order to learn the White words; and Snake Catcher for inviting him into their group to listen to the White words being emitted by them. Had it not been for the fearlessness of these men, Earth Raven would not have been where life had taken him.

Hail Catcher was the chosen one who was assured the teachings of their traditions so he could fulfill the adventures of honoring his people, as did his namesakes, with the entrusted guardianship of that knowledge to become their holiest of the living–a Lakota Dreamkeeper. Hail Catcher was the one who would be groomed with the stories, history, songs and dances of the Lakota people to perfect, narrate and recount the events to the future generations.

When Susan heard the euphoric news, she prepared for the passing of the torch with the writings of what she knew about of all Lakota customs, legends and tales into a journal for Hail Catcher. This record keeping was a safeguard in case her recollection would not be as sharp when he reached the age of maturity. All who knew the wisdom of their words were willing to relinquish their chronicles of time onto him when his day of honor would finally be reached. Earth Raven knew what a dangerous future Hail Catcher would have because of the insidious venom that the White man had for the Lakota illuminating their traditions and language even in secret–as they were legally forbidden to do in the White or any population.

Everyone at the Paradise Valley Ranch had heard the news that a motorized riding contraption called an automobile had been made several years earlier; however, they had not seen one in Sundance as yet. Since it was now being mass-produced in the United States, it was readily available to the public for purchase. Susan's thoughts echoed those she had of the motorized bike she had seen years earlier, wondering how long this fad would last. The others didn't quite know what to think about it, but Painted Pony was very excited to have finally ridden in one with her family in Washington. The vehicle transported them from their home to the train station on the way for a visit to the ranch to introduce Hail Catcher to everyone.

On December 31, 1899, Susan would quietly bring in the new century with her children by her side. She privately gave tribute to her husband as if he were only away for an extended hunting expedition, not giving mindfulness to his departure being nearly nine years back.

Susan had declined an invitation from Larry and Mr. Smith to attend the grand opening of their saloon. It had been built several months earlier after the partners sold the printing press shop to a young couple new to Sundance. Larry promised to offer all of the town's favorite ragtime tunes at the saloon, but that was still not enough to sway Susan to leave the closeness she felt to her husband at the ranch with her children's company.

Chapter 42

For Earth Raven and Painted Pony, it was now the time of motorcars plentifully buzzing about the streets of Washington, as well as, of the thrill at riding the Ferris wheel during a nearby carnival. The year 1902 also brought two more children for the couple when twins were born on a crisp September day. They were the first of the Paradise Valley Ranch community to be born in a hospital–there in Washington. Earth Raven was the talk of the ward when he chose to be in the delivery room, upon Painted Pony's insistence, coaching his wife and being involved with the birth of his next two baby boys.

Cook passed in the year of 1906, and up into the week before her death, she was as feisty as the day she swatted the Blue Coats away from Painted Pony. Before her transition, she would unveil the answer to a baffling mystery that had haunted Earth Raven for years. Living mostly in Washington now but during a visit to the ranch, he had overheard Cook with the Preacher at confession on her deathbed. She was asking God for forgiveness in perpetrating the death of Briggs. Earth Raven felt a twinge of his friend's resurrection as that was the precise moment that he realized Snake Catcher hadn't performed the gruesome obliteration the day of the storage-shed fire. Snake Catcher had covered for Cook out of compassion for his friend while most of the remaining population of the ranch was tending to the fire. Something about that night had always perplexed Earth Raven; there was something that did not jive with him. However, it wasn't until that very moment that he knew the answer to a question that had nagged him...*why would Snake Catcher have used a kitchen knife to kill Briggs when he had access to his own knife?* Earth Raven was ashamed to admit the true answer had never occurred to him...*Snake Catcher hadn't.*

Snake Catcher's firstborn was twenty-one now and had a wife of his own. Her name was *Quiet Storm* and she was part Ojibwa from the northeast region of the United States. They had met when she was eighteen while her family had made a trip out to Cheyenne to see an ailing relative. Star Catcher was there attending a study group for school.

Quiet Storm's Native family was displaced in the downsizing of their reservation back in '96. Her family had sacrificed their attachment for their ten-year-old daughter and thought better of her future by sending her away to live with the White relations of her father. Although this part of the family was kind and provided an education for her, Quiet Storm did not feel genealogically connected to them as she had with her Native side.

Star and Quiet Storm's love was forbidden as the two tribes had never been amicable with one another. Perhaps that was what sparked the initial ember between them that began their attraction, or possibly it was that they both knew the semblance of being a half-breed; nonetheless, they were captivated with each other.

The smitten couple were expecting their first child, being Snake Catcher and Susan's first grandchild. The beginnings of the future generations that they had spoke of years back, before Star was even born, was now in Susan's present. The profoundness of that brought a soft solo-tear to her cheek. That was matched when Quiet Storm had told Susan the amazing story of how their unborn baby would only squirm when Star placed his hand on her stomach. Susan did not want to spoil or upstage Quiet Storm's story, so she only smiled while not explaining how Snake Catcher had the same effect on their firstborn son over twenty-one years earlier.

Star had decided on a career following in his mother and grandfather's footsteps of being an educator. Susan was feeling bittersweet–saddened and profoundly proud at the same time. She had hoped her husband's firstborn of any gender would be more inclined to follow after their father's legacy–being a warrior for human rights; yet she couldn't help being secretly selfish and giddy that one of her children chose to be like her and perform another noble service.

That year also brought the Act for the Preservation of American Antiquities, which made it a criminal act to excavate historic items of antiquity, along with human remains, within federal land–including Paha Sapa. This was, however, if the persons were anyone other than someone associated with the federal government. That type of abusive exploitation brought Earth Raven to scowlingly comment, "The bones of our dead in their final resting places and the offerings for their final journey are being dug up by miners or whomever and being called artifacts. The offensiveness of labeling our sacred sites as heirlooms for the government to profit from is as ludicrous as them deeming us outlaws by possessing an item from a dead kin, which cannot be owned by anyone other than those who claim it as federal property. I would not wish to become federal *property* someday. Why are they not being returned to our people on the reservations for proper reburial, instead of being displayed for all to see? That is humiliating."

Earth Raven's gloomily morbid mood was short-lived that week. He was soon celebrating the living with the birth of their fifth child. This was the first baby girl that Earth Raven and Painted Pony received to carry on the looks of her mother's shy girlish-angelic face.

Many Native schools opened their doors other than the Carlisle, including one in Cantonment, Oklahoma. They would seem to have a better reputation in keeping the Native children amongst the living. These schools were also producing some very bright thinkers, some of them would come to idolize Earth Raven and hail him as a hero for his accomplishments in keeping the Native issues at the surface of political conversations in the country.

By 1915, the world's doors were beginning to open for those of ethnic backgrounds. Earth Raven had begun a vigorous campaign for a seat in the House of Representatives, and although he ran a close race and lost the seat, he had won the respect and notoriety he was seeking. However, he was not to forget how difficult it would be to win as a Native and also with his political platform in returning a seized land to his people that most of these people were not willing to forfeit. Most people had found his campaign and compassion compelling, yet when it came to being asked for the commitment of a vote, they were frozen to help. This was especially hard for Earth Raven, knowing that reservation land had shrunk to one half of their pre-allotment size.

Technology flourished during the past several years. Earth Raven was doing well financially, and within two years after the refrigerator was on the market, he purchased their first one for his family of seven. Susan was still clinging to the past with Buck's invention of the iced box; nonetheless, that was also evident by the fact that no electricity had reached the Paradise Valley Ranch.

Painted Pony was relieved to learn that the Carlisle School closed its doors in the year of 1918, not to contribute to the deaths of any more Native children striving for a better life through education.

Through the days, weeks and months, and within the first twenty years of the new century, the current and former members of the Paradise Valley Ranch were all getting on with their lives and fighting for their beliefs. After many years of Earth Raven continuously lobbying for support in convincing lawyers to file suit, that year was when the Natives would finally be granted governmental approval for the right to proceed in filing a claim against itself for the return of Paha Sapa–a day that the Lakota nation never gave up hope of witnessing. In their celebration, Earth Raven was smiling while holding up a newspaper with the news; however, the celebration was short-lived when the Lakota people were informed that the claim filed on their behalf could only be done for monetary compensation and not that of the hill's return as they were previously promised.

It was Earth Raven's patience that had been tested beyond human capacity, and the respectful boundaries of the law that once limited him to fair-play were perhaps the reasons he was brought to a deception. Regardless, both his patience and those boundaries were wearing thin now, or perhaps it was just the trickster of the raven that had always been deep within him that made it possible for him to step into the testing room of the bar exam with the ancestral art of making a paler face and of shorter hair. Even though he would not be granted a license *or* a seat, he was a changed man for it.

A glorious day was upon them in 1924 when the Natives in the country were told that they would become United States citizens–again. Congress passed the Indian Citizenship Act, guaranteeing them citizenship *for real* this time. However, many were still intimidated and strong-armed into giving up their voting rights, and others were *persuaded* to vote with comparison to those of lighter skin when they approached their polling place.

Many Natives in the country were being admitted into the bar exams in other states; however, it was only those whose indigene blood was mixed with White. Earth Raven knew of the Native Vice President, elected in 1928, who practiced as a lawyer years earlier, but this man was of half English blood. Finally, the gatekeeper had no more excuses for disallowing him in, and Earth Raven eventually took the test officially in 1929, entering through the doors of the Virginia state bar exam facility under his own name and using the face of what the spirits had granted him. On his first attempt, he passed with a score to match that of a "genius." There was a lack of reasons to wonder why he had such a high score, being given over forty years to study for the exam.

Five years later in 1934, the Indian Reorganization Act reversed the 1887 Dawes Act, abolishing the allotment policies to the delight of many Natives. The next year showed the beginning signs of governmental support when a Native arts and craft board was procured by the United States Department of Indian Affairs to promote the certification of authentic Native vendibles.

Chapter 43

When the first day of spring arrived in the year 1940 at the Paradise Valley Ranch, Susan Paradise sat on her porch sipping her favorite tea while looking out over Paha Sapa as she had done during the past days, weeks, months, years and decades of her life. She was feeling her elderly age of eighty-four, patiently awaiting the day when she would reunite with her husband. She had seldom wandered far from her home since Snake Catcher had died back in January of '91. He was buried there, so that was the place she wanted to be; and even though she had many offers to move east with some of her children and friends, she had fought with her life to save that ranch from extinction and was not going to abandon it for the comforts of the era.

The modern marvels of technology were upon them, and her family could not see a woman of her age living in the wilderness anymore. They could not understand what kept her living in the past in such a rustic place with only the minimal of comforts. The benefits of electricity, running water, appliances and a telephone were only included in the house in recent years, and that was only at the insistence of her family, who came to visit infrequently due to the lack of these necessities.

Prior to those visits when Chase's house, that was built on the north side of the property in 1929, was at full occupancy, the children of their children would be told that they were going on an adventurous camping trip to see their great-grandmother. Susan's family was also at a quandary as to why she would remain at the ranch when she was wealthy enough to live anywhere ever since Chase convinced her to send money east to be invested in the stock market. Being an entrepreneur, he was one of the few who saw that the market was in dire straights before pulling out all of their money in '28 to invest in real estate. Chasing Running Fire had listened to his mother when she had told him that land was most important and how they had fought for it. She explained that she had not seen the importance of land, that it was her father's dream, yet she was glad to have continued his quest because it was going to be her children's someday.

The ranch cemetery was expanded with the passing of many of her relations and former staff from the old days. The fence surrounding the site was moved back in '26 to accommodate the augmenting list of burials, with a prominent spot remaining next to Snake Catcher in the center of the graveyard. Buck and Lily were now resting there, while their daughter Gracie had moved to Texas where her Godmother Sofia was last known to live. Sofia had left the ranch a few years after Slim died, saying that she did not feel capable of staying with the daily reminders of him. Susan could not understand that since it was the daily reminders of her husband which kept her there; nonetheless, she did not fault Sofia for grieving in her own way. Rains Down and Ferdy were also there; Susan had converted their house into a veterinary teaching hospital, and with the hospice and animal sanctuary that Rains Down had begun many years ago, the facility was flourishing with activity. Sammy had gone back to Georgia to find whatever of his family that he could. The last letter that Susan had received from him was back in '17. Larry, while never marrying, had moved into Sundance in a room over the saloon before his death, and was buried in the town's cemetery before Susan could be asked about her wishes. Coyote was now next to Killer with a dozen or so faithful treasures succeeding them.

Another of Susan's saddest days was when her daughter had passed three years earlier from breast cancer, a disease Susan could not help her survive as it had been with her own mother dying from tuberculosis. Susan whispered to her husband's tombstone the day of Sky's burial that no one should be allowed to outlive their child, it was too hard to bear. Sky had a beautiful soul for helping people during her life through midwifery, and she would be deeply missed by all who had crossed paths with her. The anticipated family reunion would be the first without Susan's daughter being by her side. Susan had made much debate in getting Sky's husband to agree to allow her burial at the ranch. She made the argument that the ranch was the one constant in all of their lives, and all who would travel the earth would eventually come back to that place.

Except Susan, all from the days of the past had departed in one form or another. It was Chase who would return from living in New York to run the ranch for Susan, just prior to the crash of '29. He built a grand house and filled it with his wife and six children. They had included a wing for Susan, but she was comfortable with the rituals of living life in her own house. None of their following staff ever found the ranch to be their home, and all of them had family that they eventually went back to live near. Never were the days as communal as when Susan had a life surrounding her time with Snake Catcher.

Many were expected at the ranch on that start of the reunion day–the first day of spring. Back in 1915, Susan had decided that her family was just too spread out to visit them, so she began what was to become a tradition every five years. She organized for everyone to visit the ranch for a five-year family reunion with that year celebrating the sixth such event. That was a way to track their accomplishments in life and to reconnect the community that she had once built years earlier. Earth Raven and Painted Pony were expected to arrive with most of their family of five children, including some of the children's families. Earth Raven had been retired from his law practice for many years by then, but still gave counsel on many Native matters when asked.

As Susan sat on the porch watching all of these people arrive in their motorized transportation and swarm around her, she was fascinated to realize that out of all of her children's children, only two had married and had children with a White person. There was even an Asian woman, who was married to Sky's son. It made her smile that there was such a wondrous variety of people and that so many different nationalities could co-exist in a family. She wished the world could see the amicable unity in such pairings as in the example that spanned in front of her.

In the early afternoon, after the midday meal during the first day of the family reunion, and after the traditional reunion photograph had been taken with her three-year-old great-granddaughter sitting on her lap, Susan would be asked for a story. While she rocked on the porch with many of these people gathering around her, she mustered the strength to tell a Lakota story directed at her great-grandchildren about their brave warrior great-grandfather, Snake Catcher. Hail Catcher, who was the chosen one charged with the continuation of the stories, granted her the privilege of narrating a story as told from a first-hand account of this courageous man. It was now Susan's ten-year-old great-granddaughter by Chase's firstborn son who she spent most of her time tutoring about the ways of the world as she did for Painted Pony those many years ago.

As Susan sat wearing the dress from the Native women in Earth Raven's tribe that he had given her during their first meeting with each other, she finished her tale with: "He was a man who could not be tamed. Snake Catcher was a hunter and a warrior for human rights. He was very much my husband. Some believe that we may never get Paha Sapa back, but at least we are trying by fighting and not sitting by silently. Twenty years ago, the Lakota filed a court claim for land taken from them. They were not told until after the case had been filed that the claim could only be filed seeking monetary compensation for the irreversible eminent domain infamy, instead of the return of their land–contrary to the wishes of our Lakota people. There are many lessons we have learned but none more important than this: never lose sight of who you are; fight for the right for the continuance of our cultural survival that your forefathers shed their blood to preserve; and never give up on what you believe in. There would lie the *real* crime."

It was something to behold the depths of the love that Susan felt for Snake Catcher and Paha Sapa; one could see it while she told the story. That was why it was so perplexing to most that Star began a debate with his mother later that day about the ritual of fighting for land and their rights, the fight that had become her life. He had felt bitter trying to live up to the image of a man who would become a legend, while missing this man as a father who he had just begun to idolize when he left. Also, he wanted something more for his mother in the remaining days of her life than just to live in the past.

Star had not realized he was speaking until he began with: "I don't know why you insist on living in the past while telling these meaningless stories. I have watched you for years living in a world not of your own. We are your family; and he is dead because he chose to leave his family. We are here and we want you to come live with us and let us take care of you."

Chase, being offended, blurted, "*We* take care of her."

Susan responded courteously to her firstborn, "Star, all of the world's people in need are my own. I was an advocate of helping all of God's people long before you were born. I know you have missed out on much in life with not having a father and I know I have been preoccupied with the fight for our causes; these things have not gone unnoticed by me. We were only trying to make the world a better place for you."

"A better place would have been with a father that was there, and a mother who was here in the present instead of living in the past with him."

As others gathered around to listen to the dispute, Susan added, "You are a teacher. You have an analytical mind, not one of tolerance for those who are in need of being supported. I have known this since the day you chose a path not of your father's. I understood your choice and embraced it knowing that was who you were. Your father was not that man; he was a man who did not leave his people behind because he found a new life for himself. Family was most important to him, as all he ever wanted was a family."

"If that were true, then why did he leave to fight in yet another war?"

"You of all people, being an educator, should know that it was not a war in which he died–it was a mission for peace."

Frustratedly, Star asked, "Why did he leave his family at all if all he wanted was a family? Was it family or peace that he wanted the most?"

Susan answered, "He wanted to make the world better for his people."

"Then he chose his people over his family, over us."

"No, he chose you. You were why he was fighting for peace, so that you would not have to fight so hard during your lifetime. His people were *you*."

The conversation was left with Star's profound understanding of his father's quest for his children. That made him miss him all the more.

Later that night while all of Susan's family and lifelong friends were gathered together for the family reunion and as she knew that all of these loving people were all around her came a shadowy whisper from her husband to be reunited with him. As she sat there in the peacefulness of her bedroom, the last words of Susan Paradise's life were of that for her beloved Snake Catcher in a prayer to him. "Even today when I awake, I can still feel your bounty here next to me. In my emptiness, I can feel your breath upon me and the safeguard of your shadow blanketing overhead. My fortune comes in the form of joining you soon, my husband, my destiny, my ally in the fight for both of the heritages of our grandchildren's grandchildren. We may not have accomplished our goal as yet, but we have fought the good fight and planted the seeds of a legacy for our children to preserve."

Chapter 44

Through the years, Susan's and Snake Catcher's descendants got on with their lives and very few had the resources to make it their mission in life to continue the fight for the rights of their people. For those who had continued their fight, their next struggle took them to 1942. The 1920 case filed by the Natives was dismissed in '42 when the United States Court of Claims Commission concluded that since the Natives refused to consider a monetary settlement for just compensation for their land in the violation of their constitutional rights, and were only interested in the return of the land with its resources, the court had decided it to be of a moral issue and of one they could not deliberate. While calling it a theft through eminent domain, the Natives had never been interested in anything other than its return.

It was during that year that more devastating news was brought to this family; Earth Raven had died from a heart attack during his sleep. His penance for leaving his wife of fifty-five years and the mother of his five children would be to spend the next three years laboriously preparing a euphoric utopia in the spiritual world for his beloved Painted Pony.

Chapter 45

The year was 1991 when Savannah Elise Peters turned fourteen. Elise, as she was called by her parents, had been raised not knowing much about her ancestry. It had never occurred to the teenager to ask about it, until the time when she and her two older brothers visited their grandmother in Rapid City, South Dakota that summer.

Being the only girl and wanting to be accepted into their club of mischievousness, the petite five-foot Elise normally followed her brothers into whatever trouble they could seem to find for themselves. While their grandmother had taken a short trip to the market, they were to unpack from their trip and get settled in; nevertheless, they decided to take advantage of their time alone to roam the large two-story 1955 house to discover what had changed from their last visit the summer before. In their travels, they happened upon a short cord clipped to a bracket attached to the ceiling on the second level. They had never seen it there before. The cord was attached to a hidden ceiling staircase that unwrapped itself as they pulled it to the floor. The boys coerced Elise into being the first to travel up into the assumed tomb of death where gigantic poisonous spiders would certainly pounce on them in protecting their territory. Wanting to prove herself worthy of inclusion in their adventures, she fearlessly agreed even though her mostly Native skin was turning somewhat ashy from fear. As Elise stepped lightly with each ladder rung that was then behind her, she brought herself to enter into the dark web-decorated room.

To her profound amazement, Elise's face lit up as she looked around the neglected oversized attic enticing her brothers up to join her. Once all were in the room, they were transformed into another era as the siblings secretly scavengered around the sizable space, finding a wonderland of archaic articles from the past that mostly appeared to be from around one hundred years ago. While only a female would probably notice, what was odd to Elise was that not all of the items were dusty, some appeared to be placed up there quite recently.

Among a small Steinway piano and a cabinet housing musical arrangements, and behind the velvet sofa and a side desk with a floral incandescent lamp placed on it, there were several framed photographs vertically stacked in the corner of the attic room. Her brothers were more interested in some forgotten treasures rattling inside a star-shaped pinata than what Elise was drawn to there. Although the romance of the vintage women's clothing including a silk embroidered purse fascinated her, Elise felt an attraction to the photographs as if they were summoning her to them. As she flipped through the framed images, the faces of a past era in time seemed to be speaking directly to her while asking for the beholder to come closer and examine their lives. Her heart sang as she came across one of a young woman with a bewitching smile and a sparkle in her eyes that would illuminate a coliseum–a face that was clearly in love. Elise's exploration unearthed many other photographs of a time that appeared pleasant and carefree. While her brothers became bored and left her alone with these bridges to the past, Elise was enchanted by the communal atmosphere of weddings, baptisms and festivals that she had never known. *Her* family consisted of a mother, two older brothers, and an absentee father who had divorced their mother six years earlier. Her mother's mother was the only grandparent Elise had ever known, someone who had always brought her and her brothers to visit during the summers, especially feeling a loneliness since her husband had died twenty years earlier. Elise did not know what a life was like with aunts, uncles or cousins as the riches she had imagined of those in the photographs. She had an uncle and cousin, yet knew nothing much about them. Elise's mother would find any excuse as to not visit with them. The only constant in her life that she could count on was moving every two years, mostly within South Dakota, and visiting her grandmother for a few weeks every summer.

Elise wanted so desperately to know the stories surrounding the lives of those who were staring back at her in the prints.

After apologizing for the intrusion of snooping, Elise petitioned her grandmother, Elizabeth, to tell of what she knew beginning with how she acquired the articles in the attic, which brought the siblings' secret discovery to an end.

Elizabeth was hesitant at first; however, with the boys investigating the list of which teams were playing in the finals that year with the help of a report on her Sony widescreen television, she went on to swear Elise to secrecy from her mother, Margarete, before disclosing any information. "You have to be doubly sure that your mother knows nothing of what you have found."

"I promise," said Elise with intrigue.

Elizabeth wondered out loud, "Do you think the boys would tell her of what they found?"

"No. They knew they weren't suppose to be up there, and they don't know what we are discussing, so they wouldn't have any reason to," speculated Elise.

Elizabeth went on to explain, "My mother stored them up there. You see, there's a cattle ranch in Sundance, Wyoming, that was built by a White man long ago. This White man befriended one of our own—a Lakota. After the White man died, he left the ranch to his daughter. When she passed in 1940, her will stipulated that the ranch and the property's guardianship was to be passed on to the firstborn of the firstborn of the firstborn of Susan Elizabeth Paradise. When the next of those firstborns had reached the age of twenty, they legally became qualified to be the guardian over the land, provided that they would live on the land and tend to the cattle, and the previous guardian would then step down. My mother was the firstborn to a man called Star who was Susan's firstborn from a Lakota man. His brother, Chase, was running the ranch in 1940 but relinquished the property immediately when my mother, January Dew, was thirty-four, which was in the year that the will was read."

Elise seemed shocked, except for being part Lakota, she had never known any of this information before. "So she was my great-great...?"

To help Elise with the relations, she answered, "Yes, this woman was your great-great-great-grandmother."

After a moment of absorbing the enormousness of the news, Elise commented, "You have her middle name."

"Yes, and we come from a long line of strong women."

"I wish I had gotten something from her."

"You did, dear. The name Elise is another English form of Elizabeth. In addition to her strength, you have her initials, SEP."

Elise continued, "I didn't see that–that's great! And January Dew is a pretty name that your mother had. Is there a story behind how she got it?"

Elizabeth unfolded the story that was told to her by her mother. "Mother was born in January, and said she had come to receive her name because her grandmother Susan had always liked to watch the dew rise from the hills nearby; something that her son had watched her do every morning for years."

Elise daydreamed, "It must have been so beautiful there to have done that every single day of your life."

"Yes, it was. I spent most of my childhood there."

"How old were you when you were there?"

"I was three when my family began working the land with my father. It was open to any of our kin to live on the property provided that they too would work the land and help tend to the cattle. My mother's uncle, Chase, and his family were living on the property when we took it over, but he confessed that the only reason he became a rancher was to help his elderly mother. He was ready to move on; by then, his children had been raised and he had nothing detaining him."

Inquisitively, Elise asked, "What did he do after that?"

"He had made quite a bit of money in the market before the crash of '29 and wanted to return to that activity; we moved into his former house on the north side of the property. My older brother was the firstborn, however, he was not willing to work the land at age twenty and wandered the country for a while. By then, we children were raised and out of the house, and my mother and father wanted to retire so they left the ranching to other relations before moving into a smaller house, only to find that there was no room for the attic articles. Since I was married to your grandfather and living in this big house, that was how I came to acquire them, and they have been up there for over thirty years. Mother didn't want to leave those things at the ranch with the other family members who were working the land for fear that the younger generation would not be as protective of them as my parents had been."

"What happened to Chase and his family?"

"He moved to New York and was a broker on Wall Street,

and his children are in various places with families of their own."

Elise went on to ask, "Have you ever seen them again?"

"Yes. I have seen the rest of them at the family reunions that were held at the ranch up until around the mid-1950s, and also at the reunions that have since been relocated to a more accommodating and urban location for the family. We had our last one just a year ago in the spring."

"It must be a big family to have a reunion."

"Yes, you have a whole herd of family that has never been introduced to you, but most of them know about you and your brothers. You are the seventh generation that we have traced from Susan's grandparents who were from Chicago."

Elise's eyes were widened with the news. "How did I not know about all of these people and that I had such a large family?"

"What I am about to tell you will risk your coming here to visit, as your mother has forbade me to speak of them. I have told her that I would not lie to you if you ever came to me with questions and she understands that. But in order for the summer visits to continue, the three of you children would need to avoid any contact with these people who wronged your mother. I have even had to relocate some items that may spark questions from you to the attic each summer before you arrive because of your mother's insistence to secrecy."

"I won't tell her, I promise. Why doesn't she like them, and who are these people that wronged her?"

"I have always thought that you had a right to know, that is why I will risk telling you. They are your family. Your mother became estranged from them before you were born. She was to be married to a man who these people adored. He was the most revered man among their circle, but then she broke it off with him to take up with your father who they felt was not worthy of her. I am sure that you love your father, but you are now old enough to know of his ways and those other women. I am not here to tell you bad things about him, just what I know of the issues they had."

Elise acknowledged knowing of the other women in her father's life, yet was still baffled before asking, "So they didn't like him. Why would that make her not want to see them ever again, especially now that she and my father are divorced?"

"Because they all refused to wish her well on her

wedding day to him, and did not attend to see how beautiful she was that day. Your grandfather, Uncle Jacob and I were the only ones who were there from her side of the family. She was headstrong and would not forgive them."

"Oh," Elise said as she understood her mother's anguish. "How many family members are out there?"

"Many, hundreds–I'm not sure exactly. At last count I believe you have seventy-one cousins of one form or another within your generation."

Elise was quick to respond, "Wow, really? Who are they? Where are all of them?"

"They are scattered around the country now. Perhaps someday we can do a family tree and track them for you. However, for now, we have to keep this information to ourselves," Elizabeth said with a fair amount of fear in her voice.

Elise agreed before asking, "Does cousin Russell know these people? Is he keeping it a secret? Is that why we haven't been allow to visit him, because he would probably spill mom's secret?"

"Yes, I'm afraid so, dear."

After a moment of absorbing that information, Elise went on to ask, "Who is running the cattle ranch now?"

"My brother's firstborn son is running the ranch, but his daughter will be entitled to guardianship in a few years when she turns twenty," answered Elizabeth. "She is your cousin, three years older than you."

Elise asked, "What does a guardian do?"

"They make sure that the ranch produces cattle for the surrounding markets. It is not a big ranch, but it still makes the family money; most of which is put into foundations for the children's educations and charitable organizations. That is the way Susan set up the will with a lawyer friend of hers."

"So I guess since I am not a firstborn to a firstborn, I will never be able to be a guardian."

Elizabeth interjected, "Not necessarily. There was another somewhat cryptic feature to the will that Susan had outlined."

"Ooo, what was that?" Elise asked with intrigue.

"Most everyone in the family knows the writings to the outline. Susan had included a clause within her will stating that the land must be passed down to each of those firstborns until one person of blood could name the one thing that Susan had wished to be produced on the land."

"To produce what?"

"No one knows, that's the cryptic part."

"Then how do they know if they've produced it?"

"Well, I guess someone at the law firm knows from her instructions, but they are the only one. And they have passed the will down from partner to partner with the cryptic information inside. Over the past dozen years or so, the firm has made it more difficult to make a guess, since many people were calling them every day making their guesses. We've even posted the rejected words and phrases on a flyer that we circulated at the family reunions. I don't know of anyone who has even tried identifying it within the past few years because the list of guesses gets shorter and shorter. Anyway, regardless if they chose to produce whatever this is, they just have to know her well enough to name it and the land is all theirs."

As Elise sat listening to her grandmother, she fantasized about the day she would get to meet these people who had descended from this mysterious woman, Susan. However, Elise's thoughts also included that she did not fancy the fact that some of them had disrespected her mother.

Unbeknownst to her grandmother, Elise would return to the attic the next day to gaze again upon the citizenry of the past. There, she would also find a package of books and sketch pads behind a large serving-tray and stacked dishes. In addition, she would uncover another piece of her ancestry, as it was then when she confirmed that the man who was Susan's husband was the one who ultimately gave herself life–Snake Catcher. Among the sketches, she also found others who could not be matched to those in any of the photographs.

The books were also a captivating surprise to Elise as she saw among them a few prayer books and one coverless journal of lessons that had poems inscribed in it. Around the outer sides of the pages was a stain from a pale reddish substance sprinkled indiscriminately, and on the first page was a faded sketch of a White man and a young woman. She would recognize the woman to be Susan but she did not know the man; Susan was married to a Lakota man, not White, which was also confirmed in her sketches where labeled, "My Husband." That prompted her to wonder, "So why would she be sketched standing next to this other older man?" Elise again flipped through the photographs for answers. A likeness of that man was found in someone named Jacob–the same name as her uncle.

From further sleuthing, Elise came across a print of Jacob, Susan and another Native man, but not the one she had labeled her husband. Elise was at her wit's end and was thoroughly confused. One riddle would open an enigma to which a conundrum was offered. The more the answers to her questions were unfolding, the more mysteries Elise would encounter, bringing her to the answers she sought, and so on.

That summer would end in record time as Elise was not ready to leave her haven of discovery. She did, however, remove one picture from its frame and slipped it into her backpack before leaving. It was labeled–"The Sixth."

As Elise turned the corner on another year, she would be more proficient at scouring the reference books in her city's library for any information about her family. She would become equally proficient at hiding her exploration from her mother. Elise would go on to discover that Elizabeth's granduncle's name "Chase," was short for "Chasing Running Fire." This name was written on the back of some of the photographs that she found in the attic, and apparently someone who was in the image she had secretly freed from there during her last visit. With calculating the ages of everyone in that photograph, she would learn that her grandmother would have been around three years old. There, in the center of the photograph, graced a small child sitting on the lap of an elderly woman in a rocking chair on the porch in front of an old ranch house. She could tell from the angelic smile on the elderly woman's face that it was the same person in the bewitching photograph labeled "Susan E. Paradise."

One by one, Elise would learn the identities to each person in the photograph attending the function of "The Sixth" which exhibited nearly fifty signatures on the reverse. She had begun her own family tree, branch by laboriously tedious branch.

Through the months then years, Elizabeth would be grilled by her granddaughter for more information about the people of the past, until the day she passed away when Elise was only eighteen. That was a devastation for Elise. Elizabeth had become Elise's best friend and confidante in something that she felt extremely passionate about. After Elise said good-bye to her and picked up the pieces of her life without her grandmother in it, she was in a quandary regarding whom she would turn to for that magnitude of support in her quest for knowing her blood-relations. She would become even more conflicted and disillusioned about them when none of these folk attended the funeral of her beloved grandmother.

The time of the funeral was also when Margarete had discovered Elise knew of the family, as Elizabeth had bequeathed the contents of the attic, with the photographs, to Elise along with a sizable trust for the express purpose of attending college. Margarete fiercely threatened to notify the current owner of the ranch, claiming that the prints were the property of the ranch, and could not be given to her daughter; however, she then determined that Elise knew much more than what a few photographs could have told her.

Margarete realized that there was no stopping Elise, yet still she did not offer much information about the family relations, not only because she felt abandoned by them for shunning her, but also because she had lost track of most of them. The more Margarete would speak of them in an attempt to deter Elise from finding these people, the more Elise would have questions surrounding her doing the right thing by wanting to know the people who treated her mother so horribly. Margarete did, however, have the power to swear Elise's Uncle Jacob and cousin Russell to secrecy. With the information of knowing her mother could silence anyone, Elise assumed the guardians of the ranch had also been silenced. Margarete assured her daughter that she was not being malicious; she only wanted the best for Elise and to protect her, and she felt that would mean staying away from them. Elise placed the contents of Elizabeth's former attic into a storage unit, with the exception of a few prints, mainly to safeguard them from her mother, then she began to plan her future.

Elise thought to herself, "Now that I know who they are, how will I ever find out *where* they are? And more importantly, where the family reunion will be held?" She would often bring herself to wonder, "Even if I do find them, what would I say to them? Would they even care that I am their kin, seeing how there are a million of them? Would they want to get to know me, knowing that I am a product of a man that they hated so much they let one of their own be forgotten?" Elise struggled with her insecurities through the months ahead while she prepared to begin college and choose a major.

From her interest in her heritage, Elise decided on a

political science degree with an emphasis on Native studies in order to quench the desire to know more about her Native blood. She was pleased that she could also get credits in college toward her degree while learning about this. Elise's first year in college at the University of Wyoming in Laramie brought her much information on the technical historic side of Native studies, such as treaties and acts. She adored the sign above the threshold entering into her history classroom which read, "How do you know where you are going if you do not know where you have been?" Elise knew she needed to discover where her people from the past had been. With the photographs, the prayer books and one coverless journal, Elise set forth to find her future.

Further research that semester would take Elise to a photographer who had purchased the rights to the negatives of the attic photographs. The photographer hadn't reviewed many of the treasures that he acquired several years earlier but was fascinated with the gems that Elise had brought to him for advisory. Especially with the photographs that had not been labeled on the back, as he was anxious to learn the identity of these people. The photographer pulled what information he had from other photographs of that era and of the town of Sundance. They were both amazed to discover that, within his collection, there were many shots of the town's festivals and some of the beginning years of the town. Among these findings were some prints of the church parishioners with Susan and Snake Catcher standing next to someone they thought to be a Mrs. Gaines. One in particular mesmerized Elise–it was labeled as featuring a child by the name of Hail Catcher, who she had learned had been a famous Dreamkeeper for the Lakota people.

With the information she received from the photographer, Elise was eventually directed to the Native hall of records for Native antiquities. There, she found Hail Catcher's journals which were left behind for all to bask in. There, on display, she would also find journals written for Hail Catcher by Susan during the time of his childhood, along with treasures from other Lakota people.

Elise would find some of the answers to questions that had haunted her for years. She would also find the answers to questions she had not known to ask: what relationship Susan and Snake Catcher had with this famous man–Hail Catcher. Although she suspected that they were not kin, she knew she was connected to him for all time due to the friendship of two courageous men from the past. As the story unfolded from the photographs and journals, Elise became aware of much more than just the family that she had longed for. She was inadvertently building evidence of historic governmental misuse of power and the mistreatment of her people. Unbeknownst to her, Elise would be planted with the seed of preserving the Lakota way of life which were the beginnings to build a career around the very same legacy her great-great-great-grandmother had begun.

During the break between her first and second year in college, Elise stumbled across a woman in Deadwood City who would know of an elderly man who called himself a historian. Soon she discovered that this man was not particular about documenting many of his findings. To Elise, he was more of a modern-day crier who *gossiped* the news around town.

After introductions were made, Elise explained that she was writing a term paper on the past characters of the area and asked if he knew any of the people in the few photographs that she had brought with her.

He was quick to name most of them short of viewing the signatures on the reverse. "You see this one here? It is of Susan Paradise who scandalously married an Indian man. Many thought it to be a marriage of convenience; of course, that was before she bore three of his children. He died in 1891 from a gunshot wound, but she went on to live to be eighty-something. The ranch house that they owned is in Sundance across the boarder in Wyoming, and it was known as the Paradise Valley Ranch. Don't know if it's still standing, but there is some sort of animal hospital out there. My nephew's neighbor took his prize heifer there with something wrong with its tooth and they fixed it right up."

Elise smiled at his rendition of the world that they lived in there, then asked, "Do you know who this man is?"

"I don't recall his name, but he was a lawyer friend to the Indian man that was Susan's husband. The reason I know that is because her husband was accused of killing a big-time rancher in the area," the old man said as he reached for some papers. "Here is an article in a Deadwood City periodical about him being tried for murder in Sundance, but the case was dismissed," the said as he presented Elise with a news clipping which was columned alongside of a photograph of three people

standing on courthouse steps. It was labeled with very prominent names: Susan Paradise, Snake Catcher and Earth Raven. He
added as he pointed to the photograph, "Here it is, Earth Raven."

"Do you think that they were related?"

"No, no. They were from the same tribe, but not related
as far as I know." He would also tell her of the story surrounding Snake Catcher catching a deadly puma, as outlined in the
Deadwood City summer periodical of 1890. He could not wait to
tell Elise of the rumors that he'd heard from his grandfather
about cattle rustling, stampedes and strange disappearances at
the ranch.

During the next semester in the beginning of her second year,
Elise would take her findings to her college professor. He was
much impressed with her capabilities as an investigator. Elise
was also impressed with herself and proud that she had caught
the eye of a man with whom she had grown infatuated. Perhaps
it was the intellect of a professor that she found alluring, or
maybe it was the father figure in this older man that she had
been missing. Or perhaps it was only because she was so
enamored by her romantic visions of the past that his being a
Native man had made him attractive to her. In all of her
explorations, Elise had never found time to fall in love. She
would enter into a relationship of a forbidden affair with this
professor, who was not the White man that she had seen in her
father; rather, the professor was a Native blend of her mother's
heritage.

Nonetheless, she would learn an impactful and painful
reality lesson in life from him. Just before her nineteenth
birthday that year, Elise found herself pregnant and alone. Nine
months later, after completing her second year in college, she
would give birth to her daughter, *Cassandra Margarete*, with
only her mother by her side.

Elise would be forced to put her education on hold while
she tended to her new family. Cassie was a joy to Elise, yet she
yearned to return to what had her focus for so many years.
Skipping one year only, Elise returned to begin her junior year
while her mother moved to Cheyenne, just outside of Laramie,
to care for Cassie during the day. With the financial security that
she had been bequeathed by her grandmother, Elise would be
able to move closer and closer to these people she had wondered
about for so long. Now she had one more reason to know her

family—a family of her own.

However sad, that arrangement would be short-lived, as Margarete died from an automobile accident just after Elise's second semester in her third year had begun. This put Elise's education on hold yet again, this time to orchestrate her mother's funeral. She had hoped her father would attend the funeral since Elise hadn't seen him in years, but that was not to be.

Elise was drained from all of the turmoil in her life. Her brothers had gone on with their lives and were married with children and mortgages of their own; they were of no help during the funeral arrangements. As Elise grew into a woman, she discovered that the world was not always kind to her gender. That was magnified with being a Native in a land that had done everything to exile her people. Elise had always had the shelter of her mother, who would not let prejudice touch her children. Now she was without even that.

Elise would need a break to find her focus again and to find someone she could trust to care for Cassie. It would take her over six months to find a Native support system called "Taking It Out In Trade" that would trade one specialty for another. Elise would offer informational research and typing reports for daycare services for her daughter. There was a menu of services offered and another menu for services sought. It worked on a point system that the directors of the program had designed; they determined how many points a skill was worth. No money ever changed hands, which was perfect for Elise.

After procuring her daughter's safety for when she had to be away, Elise continued her education and the search for her future—that took her through to 1999. Even though Elise had lost nearly two years of time while pursuing her four-year educational plan, she was back on the path to graduate in a year-and-a-half. That was when a profound breakthrough happened for her. She would solicit the help from a local genealogist to find the descendants of those in the photographs by searching for their birth records. It was somewhat harder, discovering that Native babies were not documented as well as White babies were, during the 1800s.

The genealogist began with locating Elise's grandmother's birth records. He tried to locate January Dew's, but none were registered. He then located the birth records of January Dew's firstborn, Elizabeth's brother who was out helping to run the ranch the last Elise knew from the information that she had received back in 1991 from her grandmother.

Finally, Elise's search would bring her to locate the names of all of Chase's children from an article that had been written about him in *The New York Times* about being a Wall Street broker at an older age. From there, she requested birth records on all six of his children. Only the last child had been registered with the records registry, Rains Pony in 1921; however, they thought it odd they could not find her death records. Then from there, Elise would only find one son born to her in 1943. He had one son who had been born in 1962, but there was no record of marriage or children after that male child. Elise then received a call from her genealogist, telling her that he had acquired a telephone number for the thirty-seven-year-old as well as a place of employment. He had the surname of *Running Fire*, and the full name of *August Running Fire*.

Chapter 46

Elise was at a crossroad. She would have to now decide if she was brave enough to contact August. While playing with Cassie in her jamboree class, Elise would find soul-searching to be her next assignment. With her mother dying the year before, her absentee father living up to his reputation, her grandmother gone, no husband, nor a father for her daughter, and her brothers off living their lives, Elise held onto her two year old daughter feeling very lonely in the world.

That May, she had decided to *accidentally* meet with August at his workplace just to see how friendly and respectful he would be to her–or not be. He was living in Denver, Colorado and working as a pharmacist.

After securing Cassie with the service support-system, Elise flew standby to the Denver airport. Once there, she made inquiries about directions before taking a bus to his workplace. As she took her first step toward the drug store, Elise's eyes instinctively ran along the outside of the window at all of the specials being advertized. She then stopped and stood in amazement for a moment while blocking traffic into the store. She could not believe that the answers to so many questions was hanging within her sight being held by a single piece of tape onto the window. What had caught her eye was a flyer that read: "The Eighteenth Quinquennial Paradise Valley Ranch Family Reunion, being held at the Cherry Creek State Park in Denver." Everything that she had worked toward was within arms reach.

Elise felt somewhat ashamed that she had just taken the flyer without asking, yet excited to have information that could possibly change her life. She left without asking for August, traveled back to the airport, and read the information on the paper over and over before her plane touched back down in Cheyenne.

Elise was ending that semester in June, being her last full semester, before she planned to graduate in the fall later that year; the fall graduation was due to her absences from school. She decided that she would just show up at the 2000 family reunion at the end of July. By that time, the reunion event was just two weeks away, and had been scheduled for a week beginning on a Sunday at the Cherry Creek State Park southeast of Denver. Elise did not know how she was going to pay for such an expense because the previous trip to Denver was all that she could afford for years to come. All she knew was that she wanted it more than just about anything. Her funds were dwindling since it had taken her five-and-a-half years to complete a four-year college program, and she also had to pay for Cassie's care. Elise decided to solicit typing work from wherever she could. That would earn her two plane tickets and a one-night stay in Denver.

After arriving at the Cherry Creek State Park, Elise was not sure that she had happened upon the right function, as there were hundreds of people there; many of whom were all laughing together or hugging hello. Many outdoor activities were commencing simultaneously around their picnic area, and some on the water. Through the sparkling twinkling of sunlight off silverware-covered tables, Elise could see red and white checkered tablecloths lined with a variety of picnic paraphernalia. Toward the beach, many children were flying kites on that breezy, yet warm sunny day. Dogs were leaping while catching flying disks sailing through the air. Small sailboats and canoes lined the shoreline with both skilled and amateur captains giving invitations to climb aboard their vessels. In the distance, a small trampoline amused some children of all ages.

While holding her two-and-a-half year-old child, Elise's knees began to buckle from the weight of her own anxiety. As Elise was making the commitment to turn and run away from there as fast as she could to save her self-respect, her daughter cried out for her binky-blanket that had fallen to the ground. An elderly woman and a teenage boy walked over to them, and while the teen picked up the blanket for Elise, the chatty woman offered, "Hello and welcome. My name is Rains Pony, which is Sukawaka Magazu in Lakota, but most people just call me Rain. I am the last child of Chasing Running Fire and was born in 1921." After welcoming Elise, she leaned over and whispered jokingly, "I was several years younger than my siblings and probably a mistake, but you will not hear me complaining about that."

Elise smiled, but did not offer any of her personal information to the woman. As Elise stood there, it was as if her feet were planted in cement; she felt that she could not be rude and just walk away from them after their shower of politeness, so she endured her nervousness and listened to the woman.

Rain went on to continue the one-sided conversation as she guided Elise and Cassie closer to a picnic table, "I am Susan's granddaughter but was named after two of her friends, Painted Pony and Rains Down. Painted Pony's kin are around her somewhere. The other had no kin that I am aware of. I thought I knew all of the children from my father's side of the family, but you are not familiar to me. You will have to forgive me; perhaps it is the age catching up to me. Who are you dear, and who is this precious child you are holding?"

Elise quickly stated, "I don't think we are in the right place, so we should go."

As the woman looked down at Cassie, she noticed the flyer that Elise had sticking out of the side pocket of her purse. "Of course you're in the right place, you have one of the flyers," stated the elderly woman.

Elise was steady yet nervous about possibly having her daughter witness the harshness so early in life. She feared that she would be banished just as her mother had been over twenty years earlier. Elise had not expected to have her identity discovered so soon before getting a better feel for these people. She did not want to see the face of this charming woman go to anger in just one quick revelation of hearing her name. Elise prepared for their exile as she offered, "This is my daughter Cassie, and I am Elise...Savanna Elise Peters."

The woman stood back and appeared confused for a moment, but then while holding her hand to her heart, she gasped. "Oh my superior God" was all that the astonished woman could add as others began forming a circle around them. The teenage boy ran up to another woman and whispered to her.

Elise knew that she would get some opposition to her

crashing their event, but she was not prepared for the woman's strong reaction to their presence. She was prepared for snarls, being the daughter of the woman they banished from their world, but this began to frighten her. Elise held her daughter closer as she was startled by not being able to depart with so many unfamiliar faces huddling around them. "Who is she?" whispers came from the gathering crowd.

After the elderly woman confirmed her name, then came a thousand whispers passing the news: "It's Savanna, it's Savanna, it's Savanna." That was when a distinguished gentleman stepped forward to ask, "*Where* have you been?! We have been looking for you for so long, and then here you are."

Another stepped forward to say, "We had tracked you to Casper, but then lost you and your brothers after the school said you had moved, and again to Santa Fe, but with the same results."

Someone added, "We were recently told by a man in Deadwood that you had been there researching a paper for school, but he didn't know which school or where you were from. He said you had an old photograph and were asking about the people in it."

In her astonishment, all Elise could manage to say was: "What?"

As each of them asked their question regarding her whereabouts while growing up, another would offer information about what they had discovered about her and her brothers while they were being moved around by their mother. Elise was not given the opportunity to answer their questions before the next would step forward. All the while, each of them smiled and patted her arm or touched her hand as if receiving her into their fold. Even the teenagers knew to be respectful, nothing like what she nor her brothers had ever been taught about being respectful while growing up.

A wave of emotions came over Elise as she then knew the answers to so many haunting questions from the past. *Acceptance* was one scenario that she was remiss in formulating for the day of their introduction. As she became overwhelmed with sentiments of these people, Rain shooed them to make a path for Elise to sit at their table while offering her some water.

Elise and Cassie sat with everyone still staring at them. One by one from the line that had formed, they would reach out to touch her as if to confirm that she really existed or that she had returned from a long journey, all the while saying, "Welcome, Savanna and Cassie." She tried correcting them with "Elise," but they did not respond in kind to the correction. Elise was not used to anyone calling her Savanna, as no one ever had except for her teachers on the first day of school or the woman down at the DMV office. She could not understand why no one would accept her explanation that most people called her Elise.

That was until Rain had explained, "It's no use, dear, they won't call you that. We have searched for your brothers and you for so long while asking people if they knew you by your first names, and then when making our prayers we have always called you Savanna, so anything else to us would not be you."

That was when Elise came to her revelation before stating, "Come to think of it, all of us kids go by our middle names." Elise could see the look on Rain's face, knowing that was how Margarete had kept them hidden.

Elise nervously smiled as another woman trotted up to the table and offered, "You must join our table at supper."

Elise was quick to answer, "No, we can't. We have to be going. We did not bring anything to offer and I was not planning on staying."

Just as quickly, Rain responded matter-of-factly, "Nonsense," and waved her hand away. "You cannot go without feeding that small face of your child."

Elise finally took a breath to clear her emotions as she looked down at Cassie and asked, "Are you hungry, sweetie?"

Her daughter nodded. Elise looked back up at Rain and smiled over thinking, "No one could be this nice, much less a hundred of them. Maybe someone here needs a kidney."

There were so many questions from them that filled the air about her life and about her mother. They were saddened to learn that Margarete had passed before they could make amends with her. Elise also told them of Elizabeth's passing, but they already knew about it.

Rain's adult grandniece, Simone, asked, "Where is your husband? Did he come with you?"

"No. I mean, I'm not married. Cassie's father is not in our lives."

A sadness came over the over-sensitive Simone as a tear came to her face. She sat down next to Elise before saying, "That is so sad. You must be a very strong woman to have decided to raise your daughter alone, especially now with both your grandmother and mother gone."

"I did not have a choice; it was not my wish to be alone. That is what happens in life. Besides, I'm far from being alone; I have Cassie and she is a handful sometimes."

Simone added, "You are very brave. I would be lost without my family around me. Sometimes I wish I wasn't so co-dependent."

Rain wittingly responded, "As do we, dear." The adults that were standing around sipping their beverages laughed at her quick-wit critique of Simone. Then Rain turned and said to Elise, "Besides, you are no longer alone. You found *us*."

The teenage boy who had helped her with Cassie's binky returned and jokingly whispered loudly to Elise, "Run, run for your lives! Save yourselves! Save yourselves before you get stuck in *this* family!"

Many of the adults around the area laughed and Rain swatted the teen before chasing him off. Elise could see a sense of humor that was missing from her life, a quality she had only seen a glimpse of in her grandmother. Her mother had been bitter and alone for so long that she did not have a carefree way about her. Elise sweetly smiled but could not find the voice to comment.

Simone went about her duties of the day as she picked up a megaphone to announce to the hundreds of people gathered that they were about to begin the benediction. Most everyone, with feet on dry land, maneuvered into seats as they began to bow in prayer. Simone had instinctively handed the megaphone and responsibilities to Rain as if she had been the master of ceremonies of the events through the years. Rain raised the megaphone, and after she gave the blessing for their food that day, she would go on to add, "Thank you to the spirits for answering our many prayers for bringing Savanna and Cassie and her brothers with their families back to us, for now our search for them is over. We now have all of our children safely home. Amen."

As the crowd mimicked, "Amen," indiscriminate sniffles were heard in the silence before the shuffling of plates and conversation filled the air.

As the day wore on, Elise watched the hundreds of people around her. She watched them converse in Lakota and listened to their legendary stories as well as their modern ones of everyday life as a Native. She could not believe the enormous communal spirit within them. They were a well-oiled machine of love and appreciation for one another. Never had she dreamed there were people out there who would make her feel as though she belonged. She smiled to herself thinking that this setting alone would be enough to fill a dissertation had she had the finances to go on to get her doctorate. Turns out her family was a normal group of people and not the ogres that her mother had made them out to be. There were mothers squawking at their children to get out of the water and to their teenagers to get off their cell phones. There were fathers teaching their children how to fish and men bragging of how they scored the big account no one in their office could manage to get. All around her was a world within a world, a tightly knit community. Something else had definitively occurred to Elise–she found a profound recognition of what appeared in her own mirror in the faces smiling back at her.

Elise would eventually find the courage to inquire from Rain of what had happened the day of her mother's wedding, and why they all treated her so badly. She would come to find out that it was the doings of one person who gave them biased information about Elise's father that they had gone on to believe. Rain confessed, "We all regretted the choice we had made on that day, but your mother would not forgive us. This is why it is now mandatory for this family to go directly to the accused and ask for their version of a dispute. We will no longer lose our children. We had pleaded with Elizabeth through the years to give us some information of where you were but Elizabeth did not want to jeopardize her visitations with you and we understood that. Your mother became very good at disappearing, and Elizabeth did not want her daughter to hide from her mother, too."

Elise asked, "Why did none of you attend my grandmother's funeral?"

Rain answered, "Elizabeth lived alone and the only connection that we had with her and about her life was from her. We did not know of the funeral because it was not told to us, nor was there ever an announcement in the newspaper, assumingly because Margarete was in hiding from all of us."

Elise nodded at her explanation as she whispered, mainly to herself, "I wish I had known this world when growing up, and that my mother had taught me some of the things that I have learned here today."

Rain was not critical of Margarete's choice to leave her culture; her only response was: "Sometimes our children wander far from the path. We can only guide them so far and then it is their turn to guide themselves."

The awkwardness of the intense subject matter was broken as a fresh shy face of a girl appeared around her mother. The girl smiled at Elise and Cassie. Rain said, "Come here, child" to the girl, then continued, "This is Penny, Earth Raven and Painted Pony's kin. They were friends of Susan and Snake Catcher's."

Elise smiled at the girl as others around Elise's age came up to the table and introduced themselves. As they sat, they asked Elise what she did to support herself and her daughter, and where they were living.

"Well, right now I am living in Laramie just outside of Cheyenne, going to school at the University of Wyoming."

"Wow, that's great" came from Justine who was the great-great-granddaughter to Autumn Sky Flower. "What is your major?"

She smiled and said, "Political Science with an emphasis on Native Studies."

They all smiled and someone asked if that was how Elise knew in what manner to acquire all of the information that she had about them.

Elise answered, playfully smiling, "It was helpful."

Rain asked, "And you are doing all of this on your own? AND raising a child? But you do get support from Cassie's father, right?"

Elise was unprepared to answer such a personal question, so she went on to answer the others first. "My grandmother left me the money to go to college when she died, but it is mostly gone now. I had to take some time off of school after Cassie was born and again after my mom died to plan her funeral. I trade typing services for Cassie's daycare and I do research for local businesses for extra money, but that is all that we receive."

"When will you graduate?" Justine asked, sensing a need to change the awkward topic.

"With the year-and-a-half I had to take off, I'll be done by the end of the year in the fall. I only need six more credits and this is my last semester. That's when the real work begins, looking for a job."

They all agreed. The group of young adults spoke a while

longer before Elise announced she had to leave.

Simone, in spite of all of her fickleness, had organized a support system for Elise and Cassie of those who lived near the Cheyenne area. They all were eager to sign up to help with daycare for Cassie or housecleaning while Elise studied or whatever she would need. Even the teens offered to wash cars to raise money for her until she found a job. As they all chatted that afternoon, Elise felt a connection that went beyond blood. She felt that they were reaching out to her when she was most lost while holding onto her last hopes of completing school. Elise had come there with accusatory questions, and was leaving with salvation.

As they encumbered her with hospitality, her family members insisted that at least some of them were invited to her graduation. Elise did not feel that she could refuse them after they had been so nice and accepting of her and her daughter; however, she had to tell them that she did not know if the money would be available to go back to Cheyenne and *walk* in June when the students officially got their diplomas if she had gotten a job outside the state.

Many offers were made to provide Elise with a ride home in order to allow her to refund her plane ticket, and one offer came from someone who was not staying the week that the rest of them had planned. Elise accepted this kind offer.

In June of the next year as she stood in line waiting for her turn, Elise began assessing the path which had brought her to that place. While cell phones were chirping around her and many people were having a one-person party on their phones, Elise realized that she had learn more about political science on the day of the reunion than she had in her stint in college. That was profound for her, especially standing there on that day of all days. When it was her turn to walk, Elise was paying more attention to not tripping in her graduation gown than she was to the thundering roar from the crowd as her name was being called. When she arrived at the podium to accept her diploma, others around her laughed, and looked at her for an explanation as to the deafening sounds. Elise rolled her eyes, laughed and then leaned into the microphone smiling while only offering, "That's my family."

August and Justine had surprised Elise with the rental of a local teen center for holding her graduation celebration. Not all, but many of the family members with the money and the means had made it out to see her graduate. As the night went on, Elise sat and tried to decide on what to do with her future. Even though Elise had won a position in Pierre, South Dakota, researching at a law office specializing in discrimination, and even though she had quenched her desire to know about her blood, she still did not know what to do with all of the information that she worked so hard to acquire.

Elise's only regret about finding the photographs in her grandmother's attic would come in the form of not knowing the personalities of the people who surrounded Susan in her time. Not a whisper of a moment later did August ask, "So when are you going to go for your PhD and add another doctor to this family?"

Elise was quick to retort, "Oh, I just don't think that I have it in me to do that all over again. I don't know how you stayed in school for so long to become a pharmacist."

August added, "Well, with as much as you've been through, if any of us have the strength–you do."

Elise would go home that night with another dose of family unity. And that evening was special in another way for Elise as well. During the graduation celebrations, she had met a nice man to share her life with. With the help of a modern-day matchmaker secretly sought out from the elders in her new family, Elise had been paired with a decedent of Earth Raven and Painted Pony. *Robert* was their great-great-great-grandson from their youngest child and someone nice for Elise's daughter to call "Daddy." Everyone else called him "Rocky" because of his fighting spirit in being an activist for Native rights. He would give Elise the opportunity to seek her PhD.

Chapter 47

By the time Elise was twenty-six, she was her own woman, which would have made her pioneer great-great-great-grandmother very proud because of her work with bringing awareness to the Lakota's fight for land rights. Elise would reach out to those in the Lakota Nation which was her focus of concern in her thesis.

In her five-foot petite frame, Elise stood staring out her window while reflecting on the first half of her thesis describing the atrocities from 1868 to the 1950s. From there, Elise paced the room while she read aloud her final draft of the latter portion of her dissertation, describing each decade between 1960 to the current day of their struggles:

"The forthcoming attempts to recount the political ramifications of what the Lakota have endured. In my lifetime, I have witnessed oppression, discrimination, and poverty. As I place my feet on the path to my future, I follow the trail of my ancestral footsteps in this year of 2005. In spirit, I am in full Native dress as I embark on a future that was predetermined by my forefathers and my very brave foremother who was a pioneer in her time. Susan Paradise was a woman who was decades before her time in helping those in need. I can only wish I were like her. I am making aware to others that I am not a warrior nor a hunter; I am simply an advocate for the Lakotas who are living in poverty in this country from the events that unfolded in our history. I am neither a beggar nor an alarmist; I am simply preserving the legacy left by my great-great-great-grandfather, Snake Catcher, a Lakota warrior for human rights.

"As the Natives reached the 1960s, Congress had terminated their governmental aid to free approximately sixty-four tribes in the United States of services. This forced the majority of them to be relocated to urban areas, since no funds remained to house or feed them in the wildernesses of the reservations. During that time, a Native Youth organization was founded and had been considered by some to be a militant group. This was despite the fact that many White youths had similar clubs equal in wearing uniforms, earning decorations, raising funds by selling manufactured good, and reciting ritual oaths of charitable influence.

"The 1970s brought much uprising to the foreground of national issues in the country by way of demonstrations, sit-ins and informational literature–for the Natives as well. While they were legally and peacefully protesting the treatment of Natives in this country, sixty-four members of a Native organization were found murdered within the area of the Pine Ridge reservation in South Dakota. No one was brought to trial, yet the federal authorities found the time and resources necessary to convict a Native man of the murders of two federal officers during that time of dissension–to which he claims to be wrongfully accused. By the end of that decade, areas of self-governance for the Natives were defined and granted. With gradual assistance from governmental aid, the Natives issued some programs mainly for children's services but none for the elderly or the impoverished.

"My Lakota descendants had taken their fight for the return of their land, including Paha Sapa, as outlined in the FORT LARAMIE TREATY OF 1868, to the United Nations located in Geneva in the year of 1974. It failed to produce a favorable outcome. In 1978, the Natives in the country regained the legal right to speak the Native tongue of Lakota, practice their tribal rituals, and perform shamanic customs of the past when the American Indian Religious Freedom Act was imposed. This was a right that was to be granted under the First Amendment when they were allowed their United States citizenship back in 1924 under the Indian Citizenship Act, but never were—where the government shall produce no law forcing a constructed religion upon the people nor forbidding the right to freely be in practice of one. We were *then* allowed to practice our religion—a religion that includes Paha Sapa, which we are without.

"While 1980 proved to be a turning point for many Americans enabling them to afford home mortgages and new automobiles, it brought the Natives another monumental defeat. The United States Claims Commission awarded a financial sum of $105 million to eight Lakota Nations, equivalent to Paha Sapa's value in the year 1877, plus interest, instead of returning the land to the rightful owners; who contend to the present day, the hills are not for sale and never were. The consensus of those who brought forth the decision was that the government, however greedy, exercised their legal right to eminent domain to seize the land but did not give just compensation as outlined in the Fifth Amendment to the Constitution.

"The 1980 settlement decision by the Supreme Court offered $105 million, even though their research indicated the land to be estimated at about $4 billion. Additionally, in 1978, other experts estimated Paha Sapa to be worth $800 billion due to the uranium discovered in 1951. Some say that the $1 billion already extracted has been used to finance the Homestake Mine Company and the Hearst Newspaper along with their own mining empire. Some interpreted the 1980 settlement to be for compensation for violating

the treaties, not for just compensation for purchasing the land. These violations included the
stealing of gold which resulted from allowing
trespassing prospectors to mine, and the disallowing of hunting rights for the Lakota people, along
with the stoppage of the treaty-binding rations
due to the Lakota not selling Paha Sapa when it
was demanded of them by President Grant.

"The Lakota people have refused to accept
the money settlement, stating that sacred land
cannot be bought nor sold. Shannon County,
South Dakota, home of the Oglala Lakota on the
Pine Ridge Reservation is one of, if not the,
poorest counties in the United States. Even if the
Lakota were interested in the award and split the
current $570 million between the various plaintiffs, it would still not improve the conditions in
the impoverished nation; however, it is argued
that $800 billion might.

"Senator Bill Bradley from New Jersey was
the driving force behind two political objectives
in the 1980s to return over 1.25 million acres of
land federally owned, not privately owned, in
Paha Sapa back to the Lakota people. These
efforts were defeated by the South Dakota congressional delegation. Senator Tom Daschle, being
one of those delegates, also granted immunity to
the Homestake Mining Company by attaching a
rider to a defense bill that allowed them to leave
the depleted mine without purifying the pollutants or reconstructing the landscape of the seemingly bottomless cavities they had created. This
was, before their closing in 2001, an illegal gold
mining operation from 129 years ago, birthed in
1876 according to their own website, while the
Black Hills Act wasn't imposed until 1877; founded and manufactured before governmental eminent domain without any legal repercussions.

"There are very few who believe the
federal government would ever forfeit this land
with all of its rich natural resources and do the
right thing in returning Paha Sapa to the Lakota

people. It has also been speculated that the people of this country are not nor would ever benefit from any capital extracted from land in Federal possession. The $105 million portion of the $570 million being held in trust for the Lakota people did not come from the government nor the gold mined–it came from the taxpayers. It has been widely suggested for the fairness to all the taxpaying people to collectively claim eminent domain on this land and give it back to the Natives instead of paying the millions out of their pockets; money the Lakotas do not want anyway. Further debate would ask: Would it not be *for the good* of all the hard-working patriotic taxpaying people in this glorious country to hold onto more of their hard-earned money than to suffer financially because of a few greedy politicians?

"With that to be further debated for years to come, in 1989, the Native remains that were being looted from Paha Sapa to be put on display at our national museums were ordered returned to them when the National Museum of the American Indian Act was introduced. Our forefathers would *finally* come home to rest.

"Even with the numerous tales of the horrific events surrounding stealing from the Lakota people, the story of theft did not stop with Paha Sapa and the shrinking reservations. In 1996, after the government had leased out millions of acres of Native land held in their trust due to the breakup of that land into tracts during the Dawes Act of 1887 to lumber, gas and oil companies, the Bureau of Indian Affairs found that nearly sixteen percent of the over $440 million in trust was unaccounted for. By 1999, Robert Rubin and Bruce Babbitt had been cited by a federal Judge for official accounting deceit of trusts belonging to approximately 500,000 Natives.

"These events were only some of the turmoil that has plagued my ancestors and have forced us into poverty and despair from the now ignominious *Snakes in Paha Sapa*."

Elise's husband was now sitting on the floor watching his wife pace the room. He was in awe of her delivery and had a tear to show for his applause. She smiled at Rocky's appreciation before asking, "Do you want to hear more?" As he nodded, she admitted, "I don't know how to add the rest because it comes more from my heart and rumor than from facts." After she shuffled some papers, Elise continued.

"As of this year, the Lakota's fight for their land had unarguably been the longest court case disagreement in United States history, and is about to become longer. There have been rumors as to the Lakota nation taking their appeal to the World Court in *The Hague, Netherlands*, being the United Nations' principal judicial assembly. No matter how the government spins the larceny with all of their constitutional amendments, it was a hostile takeover–one that a corporate raider would be proud to claim responsibility for. If the Natives weren't of the Constitution, with not being allowed to become United States citizens at the time, then how can they take land by eminent domain under a Constitution they were not part of or entitled to? Would that not be considered taking land by aggression? If so, would that not be grounds to grant them the right to reclaim land through the World Court since it was taken illegally and hostilely while the government would no longer be able to claim it through eminent domain?"

Rocky nodded and then said, "I think you should leave it as it is without the benefit of that last piece of information. Everyone knows it had been the longest dispute in history and no one need know of our intentions. I think a surprise attack would be warranted at this point in history."

Chapter 48

Elise was twenty-eight when she stood on the porch of the newly renovated rustic ranch house in Paradise Valley on the bright sunny day of Cassie's eighth birthday. Cassie was nearby, riding a beautiful palomino that her stepfather had gotten her for a birthday present.

The house that Elise stood in front of was not for living in. She had wanted to restore it to its natural condition from the first moment she saw it–as it was when Susan had lived there without electricity or phones or any of the modern conveniences. With the restoration, Elise returned all of the items that were taken from the house, including the photographs on the walls, before opening the home to all who wanted to see how Susan had lived her life. Even Susan's vintage clothes were placed back into her bedroom, all except one outfit. After years of wondering what had happened to the beautiful Native dress that Susan was wearing the last day of her life as told by the photograph labeled "The Sixth," Elise came to realize that this was what Susan wanted to be seen in when Snake Catcher saw her once again.

Elise and Rocky built a modest house for their needs on the northeastern end of the property, with a glorious view of what Susan had begun each day with–Paha Sapa.

Elise stood watching the grounds crew set up chairs around forty conference-size tables on the newly landscaped lawns of the ranch. She had embarked on a fresh beginning with her family as she was charged with the planning of "The Nineteenth Quinquennial Paradise Valley Ranch Family Reunion of 2005" after receiving guardianship over the estate, making attendance mandatory that year. And since cattle production was up, the ranch foundation could afford travel expenses for everyone.

There was a will-custodian from Earth Raven's original law firm who was responsible for the security of the will's components. The firm now employed Earth Raven's great-great-grandson as an associate, a man who was an uncle to Rocky. This uncle was the one who had ceremoniously turned over all of Susan and Snake Catcher's land leases, deeds, and foundation money to Elise nearly two years ago.

Even with her busy life of PTA meetings, teleconferencing, speaking engagements and charity functions, Elise had found time to govern the ranch and all of its many foundations.

With Rain's passing that year, it was the next elder who was charged with making the grace on that year's supper that afternoon. After he had completed his message, Elise stepped forward and claimed the microphone to begin her speech in front of the hundreds of kin. She self-assuredly began:

"As I stand before you today, I am in the presence of my future. As I look among these faces of my people knowing that we are embarking on a new beginning, I cannot help but to feel unity. As I look beyond to the hills of my people, I cannot help but to have hope for our spiritual future. As I look at the souls deep within us, I cannot help but to recognize the charity we give to all Lakota people.

"In order to obtain this land, I did not have to produce anything at all. All that I had to do was name what it was in Susan's will that she attached all of her desires for unity, hopes for the future, and charity for all on. For doing so, the ranch, the property, the cattle, the veterinary hospice, the foundations, the estate, and the legacy of what she had begun would all be mine to do with it as I choose. I can now sell it all for the profits, I can donate it all to a worthy charity, or I can run it myself. There are no limits to my avenues. However, my mission here was clear. I know that many of you are wondering what it is that I will be doing here. I know that many of you have wondered what it was that our beloved

Susan had wanted produced at the ranch that equated unity, hope and charity, and it is that in which I am offering to you today. Not only did I name it–I produced it. My mission here was clear.

"If you will all look toward the stables, Rocky will show you what it is that Susan's *unity*, *hope* and *charity* has produced."

As Rocky pulled down a tarp concealing the product, silence loomed over the crowd at first, then one could only hear gasps and indiscriminate sniffles from those gathered there that day. There, standing alone to be viewed and worshiped by all, was a female buffalo calf pelted all in white.

Hehayaoihake (The End)